Donna Douglas

Nightingales on Call

arrow books

Published by Arrow Books 2014

2 4 6 8 10 9 7 5 3

First published in Great Britain in 2014 by
Arrow Books
Random House, 20 Vauxhall Bridge Road,
London SW1V 2SA

www.randomhouse.co.uk

Addresses for companies within The Random House Group Limited can be found at: www.randomhouse.co.uk/offices.htm

The Random House Group Limited Reg. No. 954009

A CIP catalogue record for this book is available from the British Library

ISBN 9780099585152

The Random House Group Limited supports the Forest Stewardship Council® (FSC®), the leading international forest-certification organisation. Our books carrying the FSC label are printed on FSC®-certified paper. FSC is the only forest-certification scheme supported by the leading environmental organisations, including Greenpeace. Our paper procurement policy can be found at www.randomhouse.co.uk/environment

MIX
Paper from
responsible sources
FSC® C016897

Typeset in Palatino 10.75/13.5 pt by Palimpsest Book Production Limited, Falkirk, Stirlingshire

Printed and bound by
CPI Group (UK) Ltd, Croydon, CR0 4YY

Acknowledgements

As ever, I would like to thank my agent Caroline Sheldon for all her support and encouragement. I'd also like to thank everyone at Arrow, especially my editor Jenny Geras, the very organised Katherine Murphy, and Andrew Sauerwine's hard-working sales team.

Thanks must also go to everyone who has helped me with my research. This includes the patient archivists at the Royal College of Nursing, the Bethnal Green Local History Library, and the British Library. I'm also grateful to my new friends in the York League of Nurses, who invited me for tea and gave me so much new material to work with!

Last, but certainly not least, I would like to thank my husband Ken for holding the fort at home when I was locked away finishing the book. And as ever, thanks to my daughter Harriet for reading each chapter as I wrote it, and offering lots of good advice. I couldn't have done this without you both.

To Daphne Anderson

with love from Julia (and me)

Chapter One

'Your duties will begin at five o'clock sharp. You will lay the fires, draw the curtains and make sure the boiler is lit. You will then wake me at precisely half past five with a cup of tea and my breakfast. I like two boiled eggs and buttered toast. Lightly boiled, mind. I can't abide eggs like rubber.'

The Home Sister glared at Jess as if she doubted she could ever be equal to such a task. Jess smiled back, her tongue rammed in her cheek to stop herself answering back. She didn't want to lose this job before she'd managed to get it.

'At six o'clock you must wake the students,' Sister Sutton went on. 'Once they have gone, you will clean the bathrooms, sweep, dust and polish all the halls and stairs, and clean the students' sitting room. The nurses are supposed to keep it tidy, but they tend to be rather careless.' Her nose wrinkled with distaste. 'I will carry out my inspection at midday, so I expect everything to be in order by then.' She stared at Jess, her eyes as tiny and dark as raisins in her doughy face. 'You have been in service, you say?'

Jess nodded. 'Since I was thirteen.' Although none of the houses where she had been employed as a maid of all work were anywhere near as big as the student nurses' home. With its grand entrance, sweeping staircase and long passages, it was like one of the great manor houses she had read about in her favourite Jane Austen novels.

Except there were no works of art on the drab, brown-painted walls, and the floors were covered in polished lino and not Turkish rugs. But the ornate plasterwork on the high ceilings still whispered of the house's elegant past.

As the Home Sister continued to list the maid's duties, Jess gazed up at the twisting plaster vine leaves and carved bunches of grapes and wondered how she would ever be able to reach up there with a duster.

'Are you listening to me, girl?' Sister Sutton's sharp voice interrupted her thoughts. 'I hope you're not daydreaming? I have no time for daydreamers.'

'No, Miss. Sorry, Miss.'

'Please address me as Sister.'

'Yes, Miss – I mean, Sister.'

Jess bobbed her head. She wasn't easily intimidated, but Sister Sutton was as imposing as the house she presided over. She wasn't much taller than Jess, but at least three times as wide, her grey uniform stretched over her solid bulk. Wisps of wiry silver hair escaped from beneath her starched white bonnet, tied in a bow amid her quivering chins. A Jack Russell terrier pranced around her feet, yapping up at Jess. The din filled the echoing passageway where they stood, but Sister Sutton seemed oblivious to it.

'It says in your references that you're a hard worker and quick to learn.' The Home Sister looked doubtful as she consulted the letter in her hand.

'I am, Miss – Sister.'

'Your previous employer seemed very satisfied with you. So why did you want to leave?'

'I want a live-in job, Sister.'

'Really?' Sister Sutton's brows rose. 'Most young girls seem to want to live out these days.'

Most young girls don't come from where I do, Jess thought. 'I would prefer to live in,' was all she said.

The terrier scrabbled at her leg, its claws digging through her stockings. Jess bent to stroke it but it lunged forward, snapping at her outstretched fingers. She snatched her hand back sharply.

'I wouldn't do that if I were you. Sparky is very fussy about people,' Sister Sutton said.

Jess eyed the dog. He stared straight back at her with hostile black eyes, as if he knew exactly who she was and where she had come from.

The front door opened and two students came in, chattering together. As soon as they spotted Sister Sutton they froze and fell instantly silent. They tried to slink towards the stairs, but the Home Sister wheeled round to confront them.

'You two! Where do you think you're going?' she demanded.

The girls exchanged nervous glances. They weren't much older than Jess, one pretty and blue-eyed with dark curls, the other brown-haired and sharp-featured.

'Please, Sister, it's two o'clock,' the dark-haired girl whispered. She had a lilting Irish accent that was as sweet as her round face.

'I can tell the time perfectly well, thank you very much. Why aren't you on your wards?'

'We've been sent off duty until five, Sister,' the other student explained. Her voice was clear and crisp, each syllable perfectly pronounced, like one of the lady announcers Jess had heard on the wireless.

'I see. Why couldn't you have said that, O'Hara?' Sister Sutton swung her bulk around to face the Irish girl again.

'I – I – sorry, Sister,' she mumbled.

'I should think so, too. And look at the state of you.

3

Crumpled apron, grubby collar – and is that a pin I see sticking out of your cap?' She drew in a sharp breath. 'Tidy yourself up immediately or I shall cancel your half-day off.'

'Yes, Sister.'

Jess stared at the Irish girl as she fumbled with her cap. Jess couldn't see why Sister Sutton was making so much fuss. The girl looked immaculate to her, in her blue-and-white striped dress and spotless apron. But she couldn't imagine how hot that heavy fabric and those woollen stockings must feel on such a warm April afternoon.

Jess caught the brown-haired girl's eye and gave her a sympathetic smile. The girl tossed her head, stuck her turned-up nose in the air and stalked straight past her towards the stairs, the Irish girl hurrying behind with her head down.

Charming, Jess thought. She pulled a face at the girl's retreating back, then quickly stopped when she realised the Home Sister was watching.

'Are you sure you're capable of this kind of work?' she said. 'You don't look as if you could lift a broom.'

Jess knew what Sister Sutton was thinking. At seventeen years old, she was still as slight as a child.

'I'm stronger than I look,' she shot back, squaring her shoulders. 'Just give me a chance, and you'll soon see what I can do.'

Sister Sutton pursed her mouth. 'You're certainly good at speaking up for yourself, I can see that.'

Jess pressed her lips together. Trust her to let her temper get the better of her! And she'd tried to be so careful not to put a foot wrong.

But then Sister Sutton heaved a sigh that shook all her chins and said, 'Very well, you may have a trial. One month and then I shall decide whether you're up to the job or not.'

Jess untwisted her cramped fingers from the folds of her skirt. She had been keeping them crossed since she arrived on the doorstep of the nurses' home. 'Thank you,' she said.

'Thank you, *Sister*,' Sister Sutton corrected her. 'You must refer to me and the other nursing sisters correctly at all times. You must also remember not to speak to anyone unless they speak to you first, and to stand up whenever a sister enters the room. And you must keep your distance from the other girls here. They are student nurses at the Nightingale Hospital, and as such they are your social superiors. They must be treated with due deference.'

Jess thought about the sharp-featured girl, tossing her head so haughtily and walking past Jess as if she didn't exist. But after four years in service, she was used to being treated like part of the furniture.

And if that was what it took to escape from her home, then she would willingly become invisible.

'Now,' Sister Sutton went on, 'I will show you to your room.' She bustled off down the passageway, a bunch of keys jingling from her belt. Reaching the door at the farthest end of the passage, she took the keys in her hand and held them close to her face, squinting at each in turn until she selected the right one.

'Here we are,' she said, unlocking the door and throwing it open. 'The room's small, but perfectly adequate for your needs.'

Jess stepped inside. Sister Sutton was right, it *was* small. Scarcely bigger than a cupboard, with just enough room for a narrow bed and a chest of drawers. But to Jess, it seemed like a palace. There was even a small shelf above the bed where she could keep her books.

She stepped inside, breathing in the clean smell of furniture polish and fresh linen. Spring sunshine flooded the room, making everything bright and cheerful.

Jess went over to the window and gazed out over the garden. It couldn't be more different from the grim tenement she lived in now. Living here would be like waking up in Victoria Park, surrounded by grass and trees and flowers every day.

'It's beautiful,' she breathed.

Sister Sutton huffed. 'Well, I don't know about that,' she said. 'But as I said, it's perfectly adequate for a maid's needs.'

Jess looked around her again. Whatever the Home Sister might think, to her it was perfect. Almost too perfect. Jess Jago didn't usually get that kind of luck.

Perhaps 1937 was going to be the year everything changed for her, she thought.

Jess delayed going home for as long as possible, turning her steps towards Columbia Road Market instead. In the middle of a Monday afternoon it was a lively mass of people and colourful stalls. The cries of the street vendors mingled with the banter of the stallholders as they plied their wares, everything from second-hand clothes, fruit and veg, pungent cat meat and trays of Indian toffee. The pot mender pushed his clanking bicycle up and down the street, laden down with the tools of his trade. The air was rich with the smell of freshly baked bread and the sharp tang of pickled fish from the Jewish grocers.

Jess lingered at the second-hand bookstall, imagining what she would buy once she had a few spare pennies to her name. The titles all seemed to call to her, each one promising great adventure, the chance to escape from her own life for a while. She could be transported back to the

6

court of King Arthur or into the heat of the Arabian desert, just by turning the pages. Jess wasn't sure she could have endured the last few years without being able to shut herself away in a quiet corner and live in someone else's imagined world.

A copy of *Great Expectations* caught her eye. It had seen better days, its cover stained and worn, the spine tattered. But it had been her mother's favourite, the story of a boy taken from his humble home and raised to wealth by a mysterious benefactor. Jess still remembered the tears running down her mother's cheeks as Sarah Jago had read it out loud to her.

'One day that will happen to you, Jess,' she would whisper. 'One day you'll have the chance to get away from this place. And when that day comes I want you to go and never look back.'

'Only if you come with me,' Jess would always reply. 'I'm not going anywhere without you.'

Her mother would look around at the damp, crumbling walls with her saddest smile on her face. 'It's too late for me, my love,' she would sigh.

And she was right. That dingy terrace house had been Sarah Jago's prison until the day she died.

The stallholder was leaning against the wall, smoking. He was a young man, no more than twenty years old, his dark hair slicked back off his face with brilliantine.

'The penny romances are over there,' he said carelessly, pointing with his cigarette to a heap of books spread out on a sheet on the pavement.

'I prefer Dickens.'

Out of the corner of her eye Jess caught the young man's look of surprise.

'Oh, yeah? And what have you read?' he asked with a smirk.

Jess paused for a moment, ticking them off on her fingers. 'Oliver Twist, David Copperfield, Nicholas Nickleby . . .'

He looked impressed. 'Is that a fact?'

'And how much Dickens have you read?' Jess fired back.

The young man grinned. 'I'm more of a Racing Post man myself.'

'And you run a bookstall?' She couldn't imagine being surrounded by books all day long and not wanting to read them.

'It's my dad's. I'm just helping out till something else comes along.' He took a long drag on his cigarette. His slicked-back hair emphasised the narrowness of his face. With that and the shiny patches on his suit, Jess got the impression of a young man trying too hard to be someone he wasn't.

He looked down at the pile of dog-eared books. 'Not much call for Dickens round here,' he sighed. 'Dunno why my dad bought them, to be honest. Reckon he must have got a job lot cheap.' He regarded her with interest. 'You know, I would have had you down as more of a romantic.'

Jess knew when she was being flirted with. She kept her eyes fixed on the gold lettering down the spine of the book. 'I haven't got time for all that nonsense.'

'Go on! I thought every young girl liked a bit of love in her life.'

She ignored him. 'So how much do you want for this?' she asked, holding up the book.

'A tanner?' he said hopefully.

Jess laughed. 'You just said you couldn't get rid of them. Besides, it's falling to bits!'

'Yes, but it's what's inside that counts, ain't it?' He winked at her.

Before Jess could reply, an angry voice startled them both.

'Oi, you! Sling your hook.'

Jess glanced around and realised the shout was directed at her. A costermonger from a nearby fruit and veg stall was bearing down on her, red-faced. Jess regarded him calmly.

'You talking to me, Mister?' she asked.

'Yes, I am. We don't want your sort round here.'

'Do you mind? She's a customer,' the young man put in.

'Customer?' The costermonger's mouth curled. 'Don't make me laugh. She's one of them Jago kids, from the hatcheries. They'd nick the teeth out your head if they thought they could get away with it.' He turned on Jess, jabbing his finger inches away from her face. 'I caught one of your lot pinching apples off my stall this morning. Little sod thought I couldn't see him.'

Jess squared up to her accuser. 'I wasn't going to pinch anything,' she said.

'No, 'cos you ain't going to get the chance.' The coster moved to grab her arm, but the young man stepped in.

'Leave her alone,' he said. 'She's got a right to look at the books, same as everyone else.'

The coster let out a snort of laughter. 'Oh, I see. That's the way the wind's blowing, is it? Well, you wouldn't be the first to be taken in by a pretty face. More fool you.' He turned his sneering attention back to Jess. 'She probably can't even read. She's just waiting till your back's turned so she can nick summat to pawn.'

'And you'd know all about that, wouldn't you?' Jess snapped back. 'I'll bet your missus is down the pop shop often enough.'

Her barb must have hit its mark because the coster's face contorted with rage. 'Cheeky little cow! I'll give you a clip round the ear—'

'You just try it.' Jess didn't flinch. She could see him weighing up his chances. But she knew for all their bluster, there weren't many people in Bethnal Green who would take on the Jagos.

'You ain't worth the bother,' he muttered.

'What was that all about?' the young man asked as the coster stomped back to his stall.

'Ain't got a clue.' Jess tried to hand the book back to him, but he waved it aside.

'Keep it,' he said.

'But I couldn't—'

'I told you, we don't have much call for that sort of thing around here.'

Jess hesitated, aware of the coster watching her from across the street. Other eyes were turned on her too. She could tell what they were thinking. Typical Jagos, always wanting something for nothing.

She made up her mind and pushed the book back into the young man's hands. 'Thanks, but I don't take anything I haven't paid for,' she said firmly.

As she walked away, her head held high, she heard the young man sigh.

'Blimey, I'm going to tell my dad we can't even *give* bloody Dickens away now.'

In spite of her simmering anger, his comment made Jess smile all the way home.

Chapter Two

Black Monday, the locals on the hatcheries called the day the rent was due. As she walked by, Jess could already see the line of women outside Solomon's pawnbrokers with their belongings, waiting to see 'Uncle' for a few bob. Her cousin Betty was among them, a bundle under her arm.

Jess crossed the road to her. 'Not Uncle Johnny's suit again?' she laughed.

'It's all we've got left,' Betty sighed. She was eighteen, a year older than Jess, with the same dark colouring. But she was a head taller and had blossomed into a much more womanly shape. Jess always felt like a child next to her. 'Dad won't miss it till the end of the week.'

'Let's hope he doesn't have to go to any funerals before then!'

'Or up before the magistrate,' Betty said. 'That's more likely, knowing my dad.'

Jess grimaced. 'And mine.'

Betty gave her a sympathetic look. 'He'll be out soon enough, ducks.'

Worse luck, Jess thought. She knew she was supposed to feel sad her dad was behind bars, but the truth was she hadn't been sorry when the judge sentenced him to jail for stealing the lead off the roof of a church hall.

She would never have been able to escape if he was still at home, at any rate. He would have given her the buckle end of his belt for even thinking about it.

You haven't got away yet, a small voice inside her head reminded her.

Jess chatted to Betty for a minute or two longer, then said goodbye to her cousin and plunged further into the hatcheries, the place she called home.

The hatcheries sat between Shoreditch and Bethnal Green, and no one with any sense went near it. No one was sure how the dark warren of stinking alleys, narrow back-to-back houses and cobbled yards had got its name. But the locals called it 'Sweaters' Hell' because of all the people toiling in the overcrowded terraces and makeshift workshops, making clothes pegs and boxes, stitching clothes and leather, or curing and drying fish. The corporation had been trying to clear the place for years, but the locals clung fiercely to their closed-in little world. It might have been damp and overcrowded and seething with vermin, but it was also safe from the prying eyes of the outside world. And especially the local constabulary. Not many outsiders ever ventured into the hatcheries.

In the warmth of the afternoon, the stench of dung, fish and sulphur from the nearby match factory hung in the air. Flies buzzed against Jess' face as she picked her way down a narrow alley, the cobbles slippery with rotting rubbish, pushing her way past the washing which sagged on lines strung from side to side like drab, grey flags, already grubby with soot from the factory chimneys.

Women gossiping in their yards sent her wary looks as she passed. It was easy to tell she was a Jago, with her blue-black hair, sharp features and dark eyes. Even in the hatcheries, people gave her family a wide berth.

There was a row going on in their house as usual. Jess could hear a baby howling and women's voices screaming curses at each other, even before she reached the back door.

She stifled a sigh. With four brothers, their wives and ten kids packed together in a tiny house, there was always a fight brewing.

Her twelve-year-old stepbrother Cyril sat on the back step, whittling a stick into a sharp point with his penknife, unmoved by the racket raging behind him.

'What's going on in there?' Jess asked, jerking her head towards the door.

Cyril lifted his skinny shoulders in a shrug. 'I dunno, do I?' He carried on striking at the point of the stick with his knife, not meeting her eye. He might not have been blood family, but he was as sly as any Jago with his narrow, foxy face and sinister birthmark like an inky thumbprint on one cheekbone.

'Better find out for myself then, hadn't I?'

Jess braced herself and lifted the latch on the back door. The tiny scullery was a mess as usual, with washing up in the sink and a pot of cold stew congealing on the stove. Baby Sal sat howling alone on the stone floor, her screams barely heard above the quarrel going on in the next room. When she saw Jess she stopped crying and held out her fat little arms to be picked up.

'Mama,' she mewed. Tears traced pink tracks down her grubby face.

'We'll find her, shall we?' Jess hitched the child on to her hip, grimacing at the acrid dampness that seeped through her nappy. With her free hand, Jess pushed aside the curtain that separated the scullery from the kitchen.

Her stepmother Gladys stood in the middle of the room, all screaming rage as usual, her arms waving and fingers jabbing. Uncle Johnny's wife Hannah stood toe to toe with her, hands planted on her hips as they spat curses into each other's face.

'I told you, you silly mare, I ain't got it!' Gladys was screeching. 'Why would I want your bloody jewellery? I've got enough of my own, thank you very much.'

Aunt Hannah snorted. 'You're having a laugh, ain't you? You and that light-fingered son of yours are always helping yourselves!'

'Oh, and your lot are bloody saints, I suppose?'

'We don't nick from our own, that's for sure.'

'No one would nick something like that! Nasty old paste brooch, like something you'd hang off a Christmas tree. I wouldn't be seen dead in it!' Gladys declared with a proud toss of her head.

'Then give it back!'

'I told you I ain't had it, you silly cow!'

'I swear to God, Gladys Jago, if I find out you've had your hands on my property, I'll rip every one of them dyed hairs out of your head!'

As soon as she saw her mother, Baby Sal started howling and wriggling in Jess' arms. Gladys instantly forgot her argument with her sister-in-law and turned on Jess.

'What are you doing home? Why ain't you at work?' she demanded.

'I got a new job.' Jess shifted Baby Sal's writhing weight. 'This one wants changing. She stinks to high heaven.'

'You change her, then.' Gladys gave her a hostile glare. 'I'm busy.'

'Busy helping yourself to other people's stuff!' Aunt Hannah put in. The next moment they were arguing again. Jess dumped Baby Sal on the rug between them and went into the back room, which she shared with the five other girls in the family. A large bed almost filled the room, the faded counterpane thrown haphazardly over an assortment of pillows. Jess automatically straightened it, wondering which of her cousins had left it in such a mess.

At least it wouldn't be her problem for much longer. Soon she would have a room of her own and she could have it as tidy as she liked.

She was plumping up the last of the pillows when Gladys appeared in the doorway. She was done up to the nines as usual. She told everyone she was thirty, but the thick powder settling into the lines on her face told a different story. Her hair was bleached till it looked like the straw in Dicky Fothergill's donkey yard. She reeked of cigarettes and cheap scent.

Gladys Grimshaw had been a barmaid at the Three Beggars when Stan Jago married her four years earlier, less than two months after Jess' own mother had passed away. And by then she was already three months pregnant.

'What's all this about a new job?' she demanded.

'I've got a job at the hospital. As a maid,' Jess hauled her suitcase from under the bed.

'That's the first I've heard about it.'

'I'm telling you now.'

'Don't you give me any of your cheek! I'm in charge while your dad's locked up. I say what goes in this family.' Gladys's scarlet-painted mouth pursed. 'Anyway, what do you want another job for? You've already got a perfectly good maid's position.'

Her gaze fell on the suitcase and Jess could see the truth slowly dawning in her stepmother's dull eyes. 'You ain't got a live-in job, I hope?'

'That's all they were offering.' Jess shrugged. She opened the drawer and started gathering her belongings together. Thankfully she didn't have much, just a few clothes and her beloved books.

'I knew it! You sly little bitch. Wait until your dad's gone, then sneak off and leave us . . .' Gladys planted herself squarely between Jess and her suitcase. 'You can't

15

go! I ain't allowing it. I need you here at home. How am I supposed to manage the kids on my own?'

'You could start by spending less time at the pub.' Gladys had wasted no time in going back to her old haunts once her husband was locked up. She didn't go short of male company either, by all accounts.

Not that Jess really cared what she did. Life was easier when her stepmother was out with her men friends.

The slap was sharp and sudden, catching her off guard. Jess flinched, angry with herself for not evading it. After four years, she could usually tell when Gladys was about to strike.

'Don't you dare take that tone with me!' Angry colour clashed with the bright spots of rouge in Gladys' cheeks. 'After everything I've done for you, too. I've taken you on as my own . . . not many women would do that. Treated you as my own flesh and blood, I have.'

In spite of her stinging face, Jess fought to stop herself from laughing out loud. She had never known a moment's kindness from her stepmother. Jess' own mother was barely laid to rest before the newly installed Gladys had insisted her stepdaughter should leave school and get a job to start paying her way.

'Anyway, you ain't going,' she said flatly. 'I'm in charge of this family while your dad's banged up, and what I say goes.'

'You can't stop me,' Jess said.

'Can't I, now? We'll see about that, won't we? You're not twenty-one yet. You can't just do as you please, whatever you might think. You've got to listen to your mother.'

'You ain't my mother!'

'I'm the only mother you've got!' Gladys shot back at her. 'You can pull a face, miss, but your sainted mother's dead and gone. And good riddance too by all accounts.

16

You're just like her, ain't you? *She* thought she was better than the rest of us too.'

'She was better than you,' Jess muttered.

'What's that? You answering me back again? What have I told you about talking back to me, you lippy little bitch?'

Gladys lunged at her again, but this time Jess was ready for her and sidestepped out of her reach.

'Go on, then,' she taunted. 'But if you touch me again I'll tell Aunt Hannah what really happened to her brooch.'

Gladys stood still, her hand raised in mid-air. 'I dunno what you're talking about.'

'I found the pawn ticket. In that biscuit tin under the bed where you hide everything.' Jess lifted her chin. 'I wonder what Aunt Hannah would say about that? I don't expect she'd be too pleased. Nor would Uncle Johnny, come to that.'

Gladys paled under her make up. For all her bluster, she knew she had broken the unspoken Jago rule that the family never nicked from their own.

Jess slammed her suitcase lid closed, and fastened the buckle. 'I'll be off then,' she said.

She half expected her stepmother to make a move to stop her, but she shifted aside to let Jess get to the door.

'You needn't think you're coming back,' Gladys called after her. 'I'm warning you, my girl. If you set foot out of this house you're not welcome here again. This is not your home any more!'

Thank God for that, Jess thought as she walked away, her stepmother's curses ringing in her ears.

Chapter Three

'Burn it,' said Sister Parry.

Dora looked at the teddy bear that dangled from the ward sister's outstretched hand, then back at the little girl in the cot. Her howls of despair cut straight through to Dora's heart.

'But, Sister, she's so upset—'

'She'll calm down,' Sister Parry said dismissively, not even glancing in the child's direction. 'They always do, once they realise they're not getting any attention.' She thrust the teddy at Dora. 'Her parents were told the rules. No toys from outside on the ward. Heaven only knows what germs this thing might be carrying.' She shuddered. 'It needs to be destroyed before it infects the other children.'

Dora looked down at the teddy. It had been loved to death, with bald patches, only one eye left and an ear hanging off by a thread. She could imagine the little girl hugging it close to her every night, comforting herself to sleep.

And now she was all alone. Wasn't it bad enough for the poor little mite, being abandoned in a strange place, full of bright lights, unfamiliar smells and stern-looking women in uniform, without having her only comfort taken away from her too?

She glanced back at the child. Barely three years old, she was too young to understand, but her huge, wet eyes were fixed on Dora as if she were her last hope.

'But Sister—'

Sister Parry stiffened. 'Are you arguing with me, Nurse Doyle?'

'No, Sister,' Dora said. 'But she's so young, and this toy is all she has. Surely it wouldn't hurt for one night . . . ?'

'Wouldn't hurt? Wouldn't *hurt*?' Sister Parry's nostrils flared. 'You are a third-year student, Doyle. Surely by now you must have a basic idea of how disease spreads?'

'Yes, but—'

'All it takes is a few germs and the whole ward will be infected. We have some very poorly children here, Nurse Doyle. Are you happy to let them die so that one child can keep her plaything? Or perhaps you know better than I do?' she said. 'Perhaps you feel you're better qualified to run this ward than I am?'

Their eyes met. 'No, Sister,' mumbled Dora.

'I thought not.' Sister Parry snatched the teddy bear out of her hands and handed it to Lucy Lane who, as ever, was lurking just behind her shoulder, waiting to be useful. 'Here,' she said. 'Perhaps you wouldn't mind taking this to the stoke hole for me, Nurse Lane. Unless you too wish to question my authority?'

'Not at all, Sister.'

Dora caught Lucy's quick smirk as she sauntered off, teddy in hand. She didn't even glance towards the bed where the screaming child still held out her arms beseech- ingly. Knowing Lane, she would have put a match to the toy before the poor child's eyes if she thought it would win her more favour with Sister Parry.

'I'm glad to see someone understands about following orders.' Dora cringed under Sister Parry's scathing look. 'You should be careful you don't end up with a black mark on your hospital report,' she warned. 'You're six months away from qualifying, you don't want to be branded a

19

troublemaker, do you? I can't imagine any hospital wanting to employ a nurse who argued over every simple instruction.'

'No, Sister.' Dora stifled a sigh. She already had too many black marks against her name, and she'd only been on the ward a few days.

'Now, go and start the dressing round. Unless you want to argue with me about *that*, too?'

Dora went to prepare the dressings trolley, but couldn't shut out the sound of the little girl howling from the other end of the ward. How Sister Parry could ignore it she had no idea. Dora couldn't bear to hear a child crying without wanting to go and comfort them, but Sister seemed deaf to such distress.

And to think Dora had been looking forward to coming to this ward. She had wanted to nurse children ever since she started training. But now she was here, she was finding it a very different place from the one she'd imagined.

She didn't get on with Sister Parry at all. The ward sister looked like a favourite auntie, with her plump, rounded figure and pink cheeks. But inside she was as hard as nails. Dora had known they weren't going to get on from the first day, when she saw Sister order a probationer to tie a child's hands behind his back to stop him scratching his chicken-pox spots. And she had been proved right.

Now she wasn't sure she could face the Children's ward for much longer if it meant continuing to work for Sister Parry.

Dora finished setting up the trolley and pushed it out into the ward. It was a long, high-ceilinged room, with tall windows that flooded the ward with April sunshine. On one side were twenty metal-framed beds, and on the other were the same number of cots for the babies. In the centre of the ward stood a long table, and beside it Sister's desk.

But it was the silence here that struck Dora, and had since that first day. Every bed was occupied, and yet apart from the sobs of the little girl at the end, none of the children made a sound.

She paused, listening. It wasn't right. Even poorly kids should be making a bit of noise.

'All right, Nurse?'

She started as Nick Riley brushed past her, pushing the linen bin in front of him. They had been courting for more than six months, but the sight of his dark curls and tall, powerful frame in his brown porter's coat still made Dora catch her breath.

'Yes, thank you, Mr Riley,' she replied politely, treating him with distant courtesy as she knew she must on the ward. But their eyes locked, telling a very different story. Nick could smile without moving his lips. The warmth in his intense blue gaze made Dora blush.

Even after all these months she could still hardly believe he loved her as much as she loved him.

'Can I see you tonight?' he whispered. 'I need to talk to you.'

Dora glanced around to make sure Sister wasn't watching. If she were caught talking to a man, it would be another black mark against her name.

'I finish at five,' she hissed back.

'Meet you at six? The usual place?'

Before she could reply, Lucy interrupted them.

'Sister said I must help you with the dressings.' There was a sour expression on her sharp-featured face.

'I can manage, thanks.'

'Sister doesn't seem to think you can, otherwise she wouldn't have sent me, would she?' Lucy turned to Nick. 'What are you doing here?'

'Linen collection.'

'Well, you'd better get on with it, hadn't you? I don't know why you're standing around here, wasting time.'

'I'm on my way, Nurse.' He leaned his weight against the trolley, pushing it forward towards the double doors of the ward. Dora watched him go. At the doors, he turned and winked at her.

She started to smile back, but quickly composed herself when she saw Lucy staring at her.

'I hope you weren't flirting with him, Doyle?'

'Of course not.' Dora prayed Lucy wouldn't see her blushing face and guess the truth. She knew she would be dismissed instantly if Matron ever found out about her and Nick. And knowing Lucy Lane, she would be only too eager to report anything she discovered.

Dora changed the subject. 'We'd better get on with these dressings, then.'

'Yes, we should. Do buck up, Doyle, for heaven's sake. The sooner we get started, the sooner we can get this over with.'

Lucy seized control of the trolley and strutted off towards the first bed, leaving Dora trailing behind her.

Typical Lane, always had to be in charge, Dora thought. In the three years they had been training, Lucy had never missed a chance to try and make her feel small. But Dora was an East End girl, and far too tough to allow herself to be bullied by a petty snob like Lucy Lane. After three years of constant sniping, they had at least learned to tolerate each other. But being stuck together on the same ward for fourteen hours a day was testing Dora's patience to its limits.

With Lucy taking charge, they moved briskly down the ward from one bed to the next. If she'd been working on her own, Dora would have taken the time to chat to the children as she changed their dressings but Lucy worked quickly, barely sparing a glance at the faces of her patients as she worked.

When Dora did stop for a moment to admire a drawing one of the boys had done, Lucy stood at the foot of the bed, drumming her hands on the rail.

'Oh, do let's get on, Doyle,' she sighed. 'We haven't all day. I'm due to finish at five, and I want to get off duty on time, even if you don't.'

'Keep your hair on, I'm coming.' Dora put the drawing carefully back in the boy's locker and followed Lucy to the next bed.

She felt Lucy twitching as they prepared the dressings for the next patient, desperate to say something.

'Don't you want to know why I have to finish on time?' she burst out finally.

'Not particularly,' Dora shrugged.

Lucy ignored her. 'My parents are having a soirée,' she announced. 'There will be all kinds of very important people there.'

Of course there will, Dora thought. Lucy's father was Sir Bernard Lane, a millionaire who'd made his fortune manufacturing lightbulbs. Lucy never let anyone forget how rich and well connected he was.

As they reached the end of the ward, the little girl was still crying behind the bars of her cot. Her howls had subsided to a pathetic whimper that cut through Dora even more than her screams of protest.

'I do wish that wretched child would shut up,' Lucy snapped, pressing her fingers to her temples. 'All that whining is giving me a headache.'

'Have a heart,' Dora said. 'She's in a strange place, and she's had her only comfort taken away from her.'

'For heaven's sake, it was only a stupid teddy bear!' Lucy retorted. 'Besides, it was practically falling apart. Sister

Parry was quite right, it was probably crawling with all kinds of germs.'

Sister Parry was quite right, Dora mimicked behind her back. No wonder Sister liked Lucy so much. They were as heartless as each other.

'You take the trolley back to the sluice. I'm going to comfort her,' Dora said.

Lucy stared at her, appalled. 'You heard what Sister Parry said. We're to leave her be until she stops crying.'

'She hasn't stopped yet, has she?'

'But Sister—'

'Sister's on her break, she won't know anything about it.' Dora handed the trolley over to her. 'It's all right, you don't have to break any rules. Just keep an eye out and warn me in case she comes back.'

Lucy hurried off, her turned-up nose in the air, the picture of disdain.

Dora tiptoed to the cot and peered over the bars. The little girl was curled on her side, whimpering and sucking hard on her thumb to comfort herself. Something else Sister Parry would not approve of, Dora thought.

'All right, love?' Dora gently lowered the bars of the cot. The little girl looked up at her, red-rimmed eyes wary. Dora didn't blame her. In the few hours she'd been on the ward, all she'd known was unkindness from the nurses in their uniforms. 'It's all right, don't be scared. I expect it's not very nice for you, is it, being away from your mum and dad?'

'Mum?' The little girl pulled her thumb from her mouth, her wide eyes filling with hope. 'Want Mum!'

'Sorry, love, she's not here.' Dora saw the little girl's mouth begin to tremble. 'You'll see her soon, though,' she said desperately. 'Oh, no, please don't start crying again—'

But it was too late. The child stared at her, eyes

brimming with fresh tears. Then, as Dora froze in horror, her mouth began to widen into a gaping hole of despair. Dora braced herself a second before a howl filled the air.

'What do you think you're doing, Doyle?' Dora jumped back just as Sister Parry came bustling over, Lucy Lane at her heels.

'I—'

'Did I ask you to attend to this child?'

'No, Sister, but she was still very upset . . .'

'And you've made her feel so much better, haven't you?' Sister Parry sighed and consulted her watch. 'It's five o'clock. Lane, you may go off duty. Doyle, you can stay behind and scrub those mackintoshes in the sluice before you go. Perhaps that will teach you to follow orders when they're given to you. And you can be sure I will be mentioning this in my ward report,' she added darkly.

It was nearly six before Dora finished all her duties. Her hands were raw with scrubbing when she hurried back to the nurses' home. Her friends Millie Benedict and Katie O'Hara were in the bedroom, studying. They looked up as she rushed in, already tearing off her starched collar.

'I'm going to throttle Lane if I get my hands on her,' she muttered under her breath.

Millie smiled sympathetically. 'What's she done this time?'

'Dropped me in it with Sister Parry.' Dora explained what had happened as she pulled off her shoes and stockings. 'I wouldn't be surprised if Lane went to fetch her,' she added. 'That's just the sort of spiteful thing she'd do.'

'Surely not?' Millie looked shocked. 'We're all in the same set, we're supposed to stick together.'

'She's never liked me, though, has she?' Dora said. 'Remember how she tried to turn everyone against me? She said I shouldn't be allowed to train because I wasn't educated enough. Just because I didn't go to a posh finishing school, I've never been good enough for her.'

'No one's good enough for Lane,' Katie O'Hara said, not looking up from her book. 'I should know, I've shared a room with her for three years.'

'I don't know how you've managed it,' Dora said, throwing open the wardrobe and grabbing the first dress she found. 'I would have smothered her in her sleep by now.'

'Believe me, I've been tempted. She's always making fun of me, telling me I'm a country bumpkin, just because I come from a little village in Ireland.' Katie pulled a face. 'And she says I'm fat . . .'

Millie and Dora glanced at each other. The truth was, Katie was a little on the plump side.

'You seem in rather a hurry,' Millie smiled up at Dora. 'Are you meeting someone?'

Dora opened her mouth, then closed it again. She'd shared a room with Millie for nearly three years and she was her closest friend at the Nightingale. But she daren't even tell her that she was courting Nick Riley.

And she certainly didn't say anything in front of Katie O'Hara, who was the biggest gossip in their set.

'No one special,' she lied, her fingers fumbling over the fastenings of her dress. She didn't dare look up at Millie in case her face gave her away.

She changed the subject quickly, turning back to Katie. 'At least you won't have to share a room with Lane for much longer,' she said. 'Once we pass our Finals, we'll be moving to the proper nurses' home.'

'*If* I pass them,' Katie put in gloomily. There was a brief silence as they all considered their prospects. There were still six months to go before the State Final Examinations, and as the weeks went by Dora felt less and less prepared for them. She had started to have nightmares about exam papers.

'I was actually hoping to share a room with my sister when she starts here in a couple of weeks,' Katie went on. 'I wondered if Sister Sutton would let me swap with someone for the last few months I'm here. Effie's bound to be shy when she first arrives, and it would be nice for us to be together. I know my mother is worried about her.'

'You'll have to catch Sister Sutton in a good mood,' Millie said.

'Is Sister Sutton ever in a good mood?' Dora wondered. She grabbed a hairbrush and began to drag it through her thick red curls.

'That's true' Katie said. 'It wouldn't hurt to ask, anyway.' She grinned. 'Perhaps Lane could move into your room? You have a spare bed since Dawson left.'

Dora pointed her hairbrush at Katie. 'Don't you dare put that idea in Sister Sutton's head. The next six months are going to be hard enough without Lane making it worse. I don't think I could stand to listen to her for hours on end, going on and on about how rich her father is, and all the dresses and jewels he's bought her, and all the soirées she's been to.'

'Not to mention all the times her photo has been in the society columns,' Katie added.

'And how she's so clever she could have gone to university, but she decided to give us poor unfortunates in the nursing profession the benefit of her presence instead . . .'

Dora was suddenly aware the others had gone very quiet. She felt a cold creep of dread up her spine and turned round. Just as she'd feared, Lucy was standing in the doorway.

Millie found her voice first. 'Won't you join us, Lane?' she said, her impeccable manners immediately to the fore.

'No, thank you,' Lucy refused stiffly. She turned to Katie. 'I only wanted to remind you I have a sleeping out pass this evening.'

Her room mate nodded. Across the table, Dora could see Katie's cheeks growing redder with the effort of holding in her emotions.

Lucy glared at Dora then turned on her heel and walked out, letting the bedroom door swing shut behind her.

'Oh, dear,' Katie giggled.

'Poor girl,' Millie sighed. 'That can't have been nice for her to hear.'

'She deserves it,' Katie said. 'She's been horrible enough to everyone else in the past. It's time she had a taste of her own medicine.'

Dora was silent. Whether Lucy deserved it or not, Dora didn't think it would make her own life on the ward any easier.

Chapter Four

Lucy sensed the tension in the air the moment she arrived at her parents' house in Eaton Place.

There was the usual flurry of activity that went with preparing for a party, with staff going back and forth, setting out tables, polishing glasses and arranging flowers. But Jameson the butler seemed ill at ease as he helped her off with her coat.

'Where is my mother?' Lucy asked, looking around the marble-tiled hall.

'Her ladyship has retired to her room, Miss Lucy.'

A second later a scream from upstairs ripped through the silence of the hall. Lucy drew in a deep breath, feeling the familiar tightness in her ribs.

'Is my father with her?' she asked.

'I believe so.' Jameson's expression didn't waver. Like her, he had seen this drama played out too many times.

Lucy paused for a moment, gathering her thoughts. 'Are the preparations for the party all under way?' she asked calmly.

'Everything is in order, Miss Lucy.'

A crash on the ceiling overhead shook the chandelier. Jameson barely flinched.

'Very well,' Lucy said. 'In that case, I will go up to my room and get ready.'

'Will you be requiring Higgins to help you, miss?'

Lucy shook her head. 'I can manage by myself, thank you, Jameson.'

As she walked up the grand staircase to the first floor, she could hear the argument gathering force, like an approaching storm.

'Where were you?' Lucy heard her mother's voice, loud and demanding.

'I told you, I spent the night at my club.' Her father sounded weary.

'I don't believe you. You were with *her*, weren't you?'

'Who?'

'I don't know her name, do I? How can I keep track of your mistresses when there are so many?'

Lucy heard her father's sigh. 'Now you're being ridiculous.'

'Ridiculous, am I? I don't think so. There must be another woman. How else do you explain all those nights you spend at your club? You spend more time with her than you do with me.'

'Clarissa, please. We've been through all this before—'

There was a choked sob from the other side of the door, then her mother's voice screamed out, 'No! Don't you dare touch me!'

Lucy tiptoed past and let herself into her own room. It was her sanctuary, a beautiful retreat decorated in delicate shades of apricot and lilac, with a silk coverlet on the bed. The muffled sounds of quarrelling still seeped through the walls, snagging her attention. Her father was shouting now, his booming voice matching her mother's screams.

Lucy sat down at her dressing table and clamped her hands over her ears. She stared at her reflection, forcing herself to focus on her own face, the hazel of her eyes and the smooth swathe of chestnut-brown hair that framed them. It dawned on her that she had grown up doing this, comforting herself by gazing at herself while her parents raged and argued and ripped each other apart next door.

'Clarissa, Please!' she heard her father shouting. 'How am I supposed to find time for a mistress when I'm working every hour God sends?'

'So you say!' Her mother's voice was shrill and mocking. 'Do you think the factory runs itself?'

'No, but I think you have people to run it for you. You don't need to spend every waking hour there.'

'You have no idea, do you? You don't have a clue what running a business like mine involves. All you're interested in is how much money you can spend. If you only knew what I go through . . .'

'What *you* go through? What about me?'

Lucy went to her wardrobe and threw open the doors. She was faced with a sea of silks, satins and furs, each in its lavender-scented cover, each a couture garment that she and her mother had chosen together. Lucy's mother adored shopping. It was one of the few things that gave her any pleasure.

Shutting out the raised voices, Lucy concentrated on selecting a gown. Not red, she decided. Not blue either. Green? She reached in and pulled out a delicate bias-cut silk in a soft mint colour, trimmed with bronze beading.

She held it up against herself and examined her reflection in the cheval mirror, trying to imagine what her mother would say about it. Clarissa Lane took as much pride in her daughter's appearance as she did in her own.

Appearances are everything. Those words had been drilled into Lucy from an early age.

'I'm not naïve, Bernard, whatever else you may think of me!' her mother screeched.

'No, but you're clearly drunk.'

'Is it any wonder, when you treat me so cruelly?'

Her father laughed harshly. 'You think all this is *cruel*?'

'You neglect me,' her mother sobbed. 'You only pay me

any attention when you need me to entertain your dull friends.'

'They're hardly friends, Clarissa. These people are important to the business.'

'That's all you think about, isn't it? Your wretched business. Sometimes I feel like a glorified employee.'

'Oh, believe me, if you were an employee I would expect a great deal more from you, for the amount you're paid!'

Lucy sat down at the dressing table and turned her attention to her hair, humming to herself as she pinned it up and admired the elongated arch of her neck.

'That's typical of you, isn't it? You may think you're a gentleman because you've made a fortune, but underneath it all you're nothing more than a glorified tradesman. You can't buy class and breeding, you know!'

'So you're always telling me.'

Or perhaps she should leave it down and let it fall in waves around her face? A looser style softened her sharp features. Inherited from her father, as Clarissa never failed to point out.

'Sometimes I think you only married me because you needed someone to introduce you to polite society!'

'And you only married me because you knew I was a better bet than one of those chinless aristocrats your father wanted you to marry!' Lucy's father was angry now, his raised voice reverberating through the wall. 'So stop pretending we didn't both do well out of this marriage. If it weren't for me you'd still be stuck in some crumbling old castle, freezing to death because no one could afford to light a fire. If this is a cage, Clarissa, then it's a bloody gilded one!'

Lucy jumped as a door slammed, making the walls tremble. A moment later her father stomped down the stairs.

Lucy tensed, waiting. Then, when she knew she couldn't put it off any longer, she went to her mother's room.

Clarissa Lane lay on her bed, curled up on the silk cover. Lucy glanced at the empty glass on the nightstand, her heart sinking. How could her mother do this, tonight of all nights? Surely she must know how important it was for Father to make a good impression? There were at least two members of the Cabinet dining with them this evening, who could perhaps help her father achieve the peerage he longed for.

'Mother?' she said softly.

Clarissa looked up. 'Oh, it's you. I thought it was your father.'

As Lucy bent to kiss her mother's cheek, she caught the smell of gin mingled with the heady scent of her perfume. 'I've come to show you my dress for the party.'

Her mother sat up to cast a critical eye over Lucy. The early-evening sunlight streaming through the curtains caught the jutting bones of the older woman's sharply angled face, casting harsh shadows over it. Clarissa Lane had once been considered a beauty, but now her fashionable slenderness made her seem drained and gaunt.

'Those shoes are quite wrong,' she said flatly. 'And you're wearing far too much colour in your cheeks. You look like a shop girl.'

'I'll take it off.' Lucy fumbled in her bag for a handkerchief. 'What are you wearing this evening?'

'I will not be attending your father's party.'

'But you must!' Lucy froze, handkerchief pressed to her cheek. 'Father is relying on you.'

Her mother snorted. 'All the more reason why I shouldn't go. Perhaps if I'm not always dancing to his tune he'll start to be a little more attentive towards me.' Her mouth tightened. 'He spent last night at his club – again.'

'He probably had a meeting that went on until late and didn't want to disturb you.'

'That's the third time this week he hasn't come home.'

'Father is a very busy man.'

'I might have known you would rush to his defence. You always have been a daddy's girl.' Clarissa's lip curled. 'You're like a besotted little spaniel, running along after its master, waiting for a pat on the head. As if he takes any more notice of you than he does of me!'

Before Lucy could reply there was a soft knock at the door, and Higgins, her mother's maid, entered.

'Please, your ladyship, I've come to help you dress.'

'That won't be necessary,' Clarissa dismissed her.

'But—'

'It's all right, Higgins. I will help my mother dress,' Lucy said, as the girl looked confused.

'Yes, Miss.' Higgins glanced at Clarissa, sprawled on the bed, and back at Lucy. The flicker of sympathy in her eyes made Lucy's skin burn with humiliation.

When Higgins had gone, Lucy went over to the wardrobe. 'Come along, Mother, let's choose you something to wear,' she said bracingly. 'We always used to have such fun choosing your clothes together, didn't we?'

It was one of Lucy's happiest memories from when she was growing up: being allowed to go through all the glorious silks and velvets in her mother's wardrobe, helping her to dress up for one glamorous social occasion or another. The little girl would take it all so seriously, selecting shoes and going through Clarissa's jewel case looking for just the right necklace and earrings to complement her outfit. And then she would sit on the bed for hours, watching in fascination as the maid twisted and pinned her mother's hair into the latest fashion.

'I told you, I'm not going.'

'But you've got to go, Mother. You're the hostess. And Father is relying on you.'

Clarissa lifted her bony shoulders in a shrug. 'Why should I care about that? Your father rarely concerns himself with my needs.'

Lucy gazed around her at the vast silk-draped bedroom, its luxurious trappings a testament to her mother's extravagant love of shopping and the finer things in life.

'That isn't true, Mother. Father has given us everything,' Lucy said quietly.

Her mother laughed harshly. 'He really can't do any wrong in your eyes, can he?' she mocked. 'You truly believe he's some kind of hero. But let me tell you something – he was nothing before he met me. Oh, yes, he had a business, a few ideas. But it was my father's title that gained him entry to all the best houses, helped him meet the right people. I opened all those doors for him. If it hadn't been for me, he would still be using the tradesmen's entrance!' Righteous anger flared in Clarissa's eyes.

'I know, Mother,' Lucy said patiently. She had grown up hearing the same refrain. 'But surely that's all the more reason why you should be at this party?' she coaxed. 'All these important people will be here to see you as well as Father, don't you think? And how will he know how to conduct himself if you're not there to guide him?'

'He doesn't deserve my help,' Clarissa sniffed. But she was already sitting on the edge of the bed as she said it, eyes drifting towards her wardrobe.

Lucy felt weak with relief. She understood there was no arguing with her mother when she was in one of her moods, that it was best to allow her to rant and rave, even though Lucy knew the truth. Bernard Lane might have come from humble beginnings, but he was now one of the richest and most powerful men in the country. The people coming to his home this evening were there because they needed his wealth and patronage as much as he needed theirs.

But even so, it was best to let her mother believe what she wanted. Powerful or not, the last thing Lucy's father needed was a drunken wife making him into a laughing stock.

The party was rather fun, once her mother had decided to behave. Lucy couldn't help marvelling at how quickly Lady Clarissa managed to transform herself into the perfect hostess, soignée and beautiful in her Fortuny gown, charming everyone in sight.

But as Lucy had expected, it was her father who attracted most of the attention. She watched him admiringly as he worked his way around the room, shaking hands and chatting with everyone. Sir Bernard Lane was a slightly built man and not particularly handsome, with his sharp-featured face, keen hazel eyes and neatly trimmed beard. But he had a charisma and energy about him that more than made up for his lack of looks. He had a way of fixing a person with his intense gaze that made them feel, for a few minutes at least, as if they were the only one in the room worth speaking to.

'Quite a host, isn't he?'

The deep American voice came from behind her. Lucy turned around. Standing at her shoulder was a tall, fair-haired young man.

'Yes, he is,' she replied, smiling with pride.

'I guess he needs all the friends he can get right now.'

Lucy stared at the American. 'What do you mean?'

'A little bird tells me his plans for European expansion aren't going too well.' The young man glanced around. 'I guess that's what this party is all about. To muster some support for his cause.'

Lucy gazed across the room at her father, who was laughing appreciatively at the French Ambassador's joke.

She looked back at the young man by her side. He looked like a film star, broad-shouldered and muscular, with a firm, square chin and twinkling blue eyes. He was attractive and he obviously knew it, judging from his confident grin.

'If he's hoping to impress someone, he'd better make sure they stay well away from his wife,' the young man said with a smirk. 'Have you seen her? I don't know how much she's had to drink, but she can barely stand!'

Lucy bristled, and any shred of attraction she'd felt towards him instantly disappeared. 'That's my mother you're talking about,' she bit out.

He laughed. 'Oh, hell, and my editor told me I was supposed to be making friends!' He grinned at her, unabashed. 'I guess it's too late for that, huh? Or maybe we can start again? I'm Leo. Leo Alderson.'

Lucy stared with disdain at the hand he held out to her. 'You're right,' she said. 'It is too late.'

'Oh, come on! How was I to know you were family?'

Before she could reply Gordon Bird approached them. He was Lucy's godfather, and her father's oldest friend. Gordon had worked at Sir Bernard's side for so long, her father often joked the company should have been called Lane and Bird's Lightbulbs.

'Lucy,' said Gordon, 'I've been looking for you everywhere. Can you spare me a moment, please?' He turned to the American. 'I hope you'll excuse us, Mr Alderson?'

'Sure. It was nice meeting you, Miss Lane. Maybe we can get off on the right foot next time.'

I hope there won't be a next time, Lucy thought, as Gordon bore her away to the other side of the room.

Once they were alone, she said, 'What is it, Uncle Gordon?'

'Nothing, my dear. You just looked as if you might need rescuing from our colonial cousin, that's all.' Gordon smiled at her. He was the same age as her father but seemed much older. His lugubrious face always reminded Lucy of an undertaker's, but that solemn countenance hid a warm and generous nature.

'You were right. What an odious man.' Lucy glared across the room at Leo Alderson. He had already turned his back on her as he chatted with the wife of a Cabinet minister. 'Who is he?'

'A journalist. London correspondent of the *New York Herald*, I believe. He's been here less than a month and is already making rather a nuisance of himself.' Gordon sighed. 'I can't think how he came to be invited. Although, knowing Mr Alderson, he probably waltzed straight in without an invitation.' He looked hard at Lucy. 'What did he say to you? Did he ask you anything?'

'He was talking about some problem with the European expansion, but I had no idea what he meant.'

'Was he now?' There was something about her godfather's thoughtful expression that made Lucy wary.

'What did he mean, Uncle Gordon?' she asked. 'Is there a problem with Father's business?'

Gordon shook his head. 'Not at all, my dear. Things are just taking a little longer to get off the ground than we'd planned. But it will happen eventually. At any rate, it's nothing for you to worry about. And nothing for our Mr Alderson to concern himself with either. But all the same, it might be better if you didn't speak to him again. He's rather a charmer by all accounts, and I should hate him to set you in his sights.'

Lucy looked back at Leo, who was still talking to the

minister's wife. As if he know he was being watched, he turned and raised his glass to her in mocking salute. Lucy turned away sharply.

'I don't think he's charming at all,' she declared.

Fortunately Leo Alderson left shortly afterwards, so Lucy could relax and enjoy the rest of the party.

As soon as the last guest had left, Clarissa's mask slipped and she lapsed back into her mood of sullen resentfulness.

'I'm going to bed,' she announced. 'This evening has utterly exhausted me.' She looked around. 'Where is your father, Lucy?'

'In his study, I think.'

Clarissa gave a martyred sigh. 'So nice of him to wait and say goodnight,' she said. 'But that's your father, I suppose. He can spend all evening making small talk with strangers, but can't bring himself to spare a kind word for his own wife.'

Lucy waited until her mother had gone upstairs to bed then went to her father's study to bid him goodnight. But just as she lifted her hand to knock on the door, she heard voices coming from within.

'This can't go on, Bernard,' she heard Gordon Bird saying. 'You have to do something about it.'

'Gordon, you worry too much.' Her father's tone was warm and confident. 'I promise you, everything will be all right. We just need to have a little patience. These things take time.'

'But we don't have time!' Gordon sounded exasperated. 'The bank—'

'The bank will be perfectly happy by the time it's sorted out,' her father finished for him. 'Dear me, Gordon, we've been in far more difficult situations than this and come out the other side. Have some faith, man!'

Lucy heard her godfather sigh. 'I hope you're right, Bernard. But it seems a rather risky strategy to me.'

'And since when have I ever shied away from taking a risk?' her father said. 'Being willing to take a risk is what's made this business so successful. That and sheer damn luck!'

'I just hope our luck isn't about to run out.'

'Gordon, please,' her father sighed. 'This has been such a wonderful evening. Don't spoil it.'

Lucy heard footsteps approaching the door, and ducked back into the shadow of the stairwell. Gordon emerged from her father's office, left the door open behind him and went off down the hall. Lucy heard him bidding Jameson goodnight as the butler helped him into his coat, and then he was gone.

She peered through the open door into her father's office. Sir Bernard was sitting at his desk, alone in the pool of light cast by a lamp, his gaze fixed and distant.

He seemed so deep in thought Lucy didn't want to disturb him. But as she tried to tiptoe away, the floorboard creaked under her foot.

'Hello?' her father called out sharply. 'Who's there?'

Lucy put her head around the door. 'It's only me, Father,' she said. 'I'm sorry, I didn't mean to disturb you.'

'You're not disturbing me at all, my dear.' His smile was back in place, lighting up his face. 'Did you have a pleasant evening?'

'Yes, thank you, Father.'

'I wanted to thank you too – for helping to calm your mother down.'

'That's all right, Father. I knew how important this evening was for you.'

'Yes, it was – very important.'

Lucy looked at him then, and Leo Alderson's words came back to her.

Your father needs all the friends he can get.

She pushed the troubling thought from her mind. Leo Alderson knew nothing about it. Her father was an invincible force. He didn't need help from anyone.

Chapter Five

'Well, you can't say I don't know how to treat a girl,' Nick said with a wry smile.

They were sitting side by side on the canal bank, watching the sun sink behind the factory buildings.

Dora snuggled against him. 'I don't mind where I am as long as I'm with you.'

'All the same, I'm sick of having to keep it a secret between us.' Nick frowned, snapping a blade of grass between his fingers. 'I can't even hold your hand when we walk down the street.'

'I know,' Dora sighed. 'But we can't take any risks. Not while you're still married. It would only take someone to see us together and tell Matron, and that would be it for me.' She saw his darkening expression, and reached for his hand. 'Cheer up, it's only two years until you can get your divorce. We've already waited six months. You don't really mind, do you?'

Nick didn't reply. Dora studied his profile as he kept his gaze fixed on the distant bank. He had something on his mind, she could tell. He'd been in a strange mood ever since he'd arrived to meet her.

No one would call Nick Riley handsome, but there was a harsh kind of beauty about the raw planes of his face. He had the flattened nose of a boxer, but his eyes were thickly lashed and the colour of indigo ink. They had known each other for years, but even after all this time, she still couldn't always tell what was going on behind that guarded expression of his.

She wondered if tonight's unsettled mood had anything to do with his brother. Nick went back to Griffin Street to check on him nearly every day after his shift at the hospital finished.

'How was Danny?' she asked.

'All right.'

'Your mum's looking after him all right, then?'

Nick's mouth twisted. 'I dunno about that. My mother can hardly look after herself, let alone Danny.'

Dora studied his brooding face, trying to work out what he was thinking. She understood how deeply Nick worried about his younger brother, even though he tried not to show it. Danny was a young man physically but still had the mind of a child. Nick had cared for him ever since their brutal father walked out on them, but when he got married he'd had to leave Danny behind to the tender mercies of their drunken mother June.

'You know he can come and live with us, after we're married?' Dora said, trying to soothe him. He didn't reply. 'I know it won't be for a while, but—'

'I saw Ruby.' Nick cut her off.

'Oh, yes?' Dora winced at the sharp spike of jealousy that lanced through her. Nick and Ruby might be separated, but she was still his wife in the eyes of the law.

She looked away, plucking at a leaf while she tried to compose herself. Of course he was bound to see Ruby from time to time. She and her family lived upstairs from the Rileys in Griffin Street. Dora knew Nick no longer had feelings for his wife, not after the way she'd betrayed him. But the thought of them seeing each other still made her uncomfortable.

43

'What did Ruby have to say for herself, then?' she asked, as lightly as she could manage.

'She says she's met someone.'

Dora sent Nick a quick glance. Was that why he was in such an odd mood? 'Who is he?'

'His name's Eric. Got a proper office job in Poplar – insurance, I think she said. Ruby reckons he's keen to marry her.' Nick smiled thinly. 'I think she was trying to make me jealous.'

'And did she?'

He looked up at her, a frown knotting his brows. 'Of course not. How could you ask that?'

Dora tried to smile. 'Take no notice of me, I'm just being daft.' But inside she still felt uneasy. Nick Riley was everything to her. She wanted to believe she was everything to him, too. But Ruby had taken him away from her once, and Dora was sure she could do it again if she set her mind to it.

Ruby had had her pick of boyfriends while they were growing up next door to each other in Griffin Street, but she'd set her sights on the one boy Dora loved.

By the time Dora realised how she felt about Nick, he and Ruby were already courting. When Nick tried to end it with her, Ruby announced she was pregnant. Shortly after their hasty wedding, she apparently suffered a miscarriage. Nick was heartbroken at the loss of his baby, until Ruby confessed to Dora that she had lied about being pregnant to make him marry her. When Nick found out later on how he'd been deceived, and that Dora had known about it, she had thought he'd never forgive her.

The secrets and lies had almost torn them apart. All they wanted now was to be able to marry like any other young couple. But Ruby went on casting a shadow over their lives.

'Anyway, it's good news for us if she does want to get wed,' Nick went on.

'How do you work that out? We've still got to wait two years before you can divorce?'

'Not necessarily.'

Dora stared at him. 'What are you saying?'

'I'm saying Ruby is willing to be named in the divorce papers, on the grounds of her adultery.'

'Never!' Dora could barely speak for shock. No self-respecting girl would ever allow her name to be read out in court, letting everyone know she'd broken her marriage vows.

'I told you she was keen to marry this bloke, didn't I?' Nick smiled at her. 'If this all goes through, I could be free in six months. Just think, we could be married by Christmas. What do you say to that?'

Dora was silent. The truth was, she didn't know what to say. Of course she wanted to marry Nick, it was all she had ever wanted. But not if the cost was someone else's good name.

'We can't.' She shook her head. 'It wouldn't be fair on Ruby . . .'

'Do you think she was fair when she lied and told me she was pregnant, to make me marry her?' Nick snapped. 'She didn't give you or me a second thought then, did she? She's the reason we're all in this mess, so she should be the one to get us out.'

'I know,' Dora agreed. 'But all the same it doesn't seem right . . .'

'It was Ruby's idea,' Nick reminded her. 'She's the one who's pushing for it, not me. Says she's willing to put her name on the papers and take the consequences.'

'That sounds like Ruby.' Her friend was so impulsive, she rarely thought about the results of her actions. That was why she'd lied to Nick about being pregnant in the first place.

'Dora?' Nick was frowning at her, hurt in his blue eyes. 'I thought you'd be pleased?'

'I am,' Dora said. 'Of course I am. You know I want to marry you, more than anything. But—'

'What?' Nick prompted her.

'Surely it's only fair if we were the ones named in court, not Ruby?'

He shook his head. 'Not a chance! I'm not having your name dragged through the mud,' he said firmly. 'You just said yourself, if Matron found out about us you'd be sacked. How do you reckon she'd feel about one of her students being named in a divorce case?'

'Yes, but it wouldn't really matter,' Dora reasoned. 'I'll have to give up nursing anyway, once we're married.'

'But that won't be until after you finish your training. You've worked so hard to get this far, Dora, and you've only got six months to go. I don't want you to give that up for my sake.'

'But it still doesn't seem right,' she reasoned. 'After all, you left her for me—'

'Now you listen to me.' Nick grasped her arms, turning her to face him. 'You're not to blame for any of this. You and I would have been married a long time ago if it hadn't been for Ruby's lies. And besides,' he added, 'we haven't committed adultery, have we?'

Dora felt the blush rising in her face. That was true. Much to her frustration, Nick was absolutely determined to wait until their wedding.

'We could change all that?' she said softly.

His dark brows lifted. 'Dora Doyle! What are you suggesting?'

'You know.' She looked up into his eyes and felt a delicious tingle of anticipation building up inside her.

She let her gaze linger on the curve of his lips as she

always did, enjoying the thrill of expectation moments before his mouth came down on hers. She had dreamed of kissing Nick so many times in the past, but nothing she imagined could ever be as wonderful as this feeling. Warmth spread through her body, turning her insides to liquid, and she pressed herself against him, compelled by a sudden, desperate need, as if she would melt into him completely if she could.

But it was more than a physical need. Being in Nick's arms and kissing him reassured her, made her feel safe. While she was there she could block out the feeling that this was all too good to be true, that one day something would happen to take him away from her again.

And then, suddenly, a noise in the undergrowth behind them made Dora pull away from him.

'Did you hear that?'

'What?'

'That noise. Down there, in the bushes.'

'No.' He started to pull her back towards him, but she heard it once more. A crackle in the dry grass, like a footstep.

'There it is again. There's someone watching us!'

'A Peeping Tom, you mean? There'd better not be!' Nick jumped to his feet and headed towards the scrubby undergrowth close to the bank. 'Oi! Who's there?' His voice echoed across the stillness of the canal. He peered closer, pushing the bushes aside for a better look. 'I can't see anyone . . .'

'Must have been my imagination, then,' Dora said. She scrambled to her feet. 'We'd best get back anyway.'

'Are you sure?' Nick stood close to her, so she could feel the warmth of his body. 'I was just about to let you have your wicked way with me.'

'No, you weren't,' she smiled back. 'You've got too much self control.'

'I dunno about that. One of these days you might push me too far.'

'We'd best go then, before I lose my honour!'

Hand in hand, they started to walk up the bank, but something stopped Dora in her tracks.

'Are you all right?' Nick asked. 'You've gone a bit pale.'

'I dunno. I feel ever so funny.' She stared back at the water and gave a shudder. 'As if someone's just walked over my grave.'

'Maybe we should stay here after all?' Nick gave a wry smile, his eyes alight with desire.

Dora looked back at him, daring him. 'Maybe we should.'

Nick groaned. 'You're a wicked woman, Dora Doyle. First thing tomorrow morning I'm going down that solicitor's office to make an appointment,' he said. 'The sooner we're man and wife, the better!'

'How is that new maid of yours turning out, Agatha?'

Sister Sutton peered at her stitching as she considered the question. It was a sunny Thursday afternoon, and she was sitting in the garden of the students' home with her old friends, Sister Tutor Florence Parker and Assistant Matron Veronica Hanley.

The three of them had been meeting on a Thursday to sew a patchwork quilt together for years, although very little sewing ever seemed to get done as they sipped tea, ate biscuits and chatted.

'She seems very satisfactory,' she said at last.

Florence Parker peered over her spectacles. 'Satisfactory, eh?' she said. 'That's high praise indeed from you, Agatha.'

Agatha Sutton frowned at her. Was Florence being sarcastic? It was always so difficult to tell. The sharpest comments seemed softened by that gentle Scottish lilt.

'The girl is keen enough,' she said. 'But they're all keen to start with, aren't they? Only time will tell.'

But she had to admit, Jess Jago had made a very promising start in the three weeks since she started at the home. She worked hard, was quick to learn, and didn't try to cut corners hoping no one would notice. Agatha had even tried to catch her out a couple of times by deliberately leaving dust behind the curtains but each time it was swept clean when she went to check. Jess liked to do a good, thorough job, and Sister Sutton approved of that.

'I'm pleased to hear it,' Miss Hanley commented, her eyes still fixed on the two patches of cotton she was stitching together. 'You never know, perhaps this girl of yours could be promoted to assist you in running the home one day?'

Agatha dropped her sewing into her lap. 'Assist me?' she said faintly. 'What on earth do you mean, Veronica?'

'Well, we're none of us getting any younger, are we? The time might come when you'll be grateful to leave some of the heavier work to someone else.'

In spite of the warm spring afternoon, Agatha Sutton suddenly felt cold all over. 'Are you saying I can't manage?' she said. 'Are you implying that running the students' home is too much for me?'

A flush spread over Miss Hanley's plain, mannish features. 'No, no, of course not,' she said hastily.

'I'm pleased to hear it. Because I'll have you know, I've run this home for the past twenty years, and I could run it for another twenty if I chose to!'

Agatha Sutton picked up her sewing again, but her hands were shaking so much she could hardly manage her needle. She knew Florence and Veronica were exchanging glances, but she didn't dare look at them.

Thankfully, Florence changed the subject. 'I daresay

you'll be very busy once the new set of students arrives,' she said. 'I wonder what this lot will be like?'

'As silly and muddle-headed as the last lot and the one before that, I shouldn't wonder,' Agatha muttered, still vexed.

'Really, Agatha!' Florence chuckled. 'That's the flower of the nursing profession you're talking about.'

'I'm sure they will be, once we've finished with them,' she agreed. 'But they're nothing more than little girls when they arrive. Over-excited children who have hardly been away from their mothers before and haven't the first idea how to fend for themselves.'

'Then they're lucky to have you to look after them, Agatha.'

She looked up again, still not sure whether Florence was teasing her or not. Her blue eyes seemed suspiciously twinkly behind those pebble glasses.

'I do my best,' Agatha replied primly. 'Most of them come round in the end, but there are always those who seem to defy all my efforts to bring them to order. The Irish girls are the worst. They always give me a great deal of trouble.'

'I wonder how you'll get on with the new O'Hara girl, in that case?' Veronica mused.

'Another one?' Florence Parker's brows rose. 'Good heavens, how many O'Hara sisters are there?'

'This is the fifth, I believe,' said Veronica. 'The oldest two returned to Ireland after their training, one is now a staff nurse here on Male Orthopaedic, and the other is a senior student.'

'Oh yes – young Katie.' Florence sighed, shaking her head. Agatha knew exactly what she meant.

'Oh, that girl! I can't think how many times I've caught her breaking rules. She hardly seems to heed anything I say.'

'Perhaps this youngest sister will take after the older girls?' Veronica said. 'They have all been exceptional nurses. I know Sister Blake wouldn't be without Staff Nurse O'Hara on Male Orthopaedics.'

'Katie isn't that bad,' said Florence. 'I'll admit she can be a bit silly at times, but she has a good heart. And she's finally starting to buckle down to her work.'

'Just as well, with her State Finals only a few months away,' Veronica huffed.

'Katie has asked if she and her sister might share a room for the last few months while she is a student,' Agatha said.

'Did she indeed?' Veronica Hanley looked disapproving. 'I hope you told her not to be so impertinent? We can't have students dictating who they share rooms with.'

Agatha shot her friend a glance. Actually, she had used those very words to Katie O'Hara only a few days before. But she was still smarting over Veronica's remark about her needing help to run the students' home.

'As a matter of fact, I believe it might be a good idea,' she replied. 'Being responsible for her sister might make the girl more mature.'

'Or it might cause twice the trouble!' Veronica said.

'Perhaps, but that is my decision,' Agatha said. 'After all, I am still in charge of the students' home, am I not?'

'Of course.'

Agatha Sutton had the brief satisfaction of seeing her friend's face tighten as she fought to keep her feelings to herself. It was only when Florence leant over and whispered, 'I hope you know what you're doing, my dear,' that it dawned on her that she would have to follow through with her decision.

Katie O'Hara would be delighted.

Chapter Six

The boy looked warily at the bathtub and then back at Dora. 'I ain't getting in that thing,' he declared

'Oh, yes, you are.'

'I don't need a bath. I already 'ad one.'

Dora folded her arms and frowned at the boy. She could smell the dirt and stale sweat on his clothes from the other side of the room. And she had no idea whether that matted mop of hair of his was fair or brown.

'When was that? King George's Coronation?'

Archie Duggins glared back at her. He was ten years old and had been admitted to the ward with pleurisy. He was doing his best to put on a confident front, but under the bravado Dora could see the fear in his grubby face.

But that didn't stop him resisting their attempts to clean him up.

'Come on, let's get you bathed and into your pyjamas,' Dora coaxed. 'The sooner we get you into bed, the sooner we can start getting you better. You'd like that, wouldn't you?'

Archie warily eyed the steam rising from the bathtub. 'I s'pose so,' he mumbled.

'Good boy. Now let's get those clothes off you.'

She made a move towards him but he jerked away out of reach. Poorly or not, he was still as slippery as an eel. 'I will not! Not with you watching.'

'Oh, for heaven's sake!' Lucy sighed from the doorway. 'We've seen it all before.'

'Not mine, you ain't!'

Dora struggled not to smile. 'How about if we look the other way while you get in?' she suggested.

Archie considered it. 'All right,' he agreed at last. 'But you've got to stand over there in the corner and promise not to look?'

'Now you listen here—' Lucy started to say, but Dora shook her head.

'Let's just humour him, shall we?'

Lucy's expression was truculent as she stood with Dora in the corner. 'I'm far too busy to play these games,' she muttered, looking at her watch.

'If you can think of another way to get him into that bath, then please—' The sound of skittering footsteps behind them made Dora swing round. Archie was running for the door.

'Oi! Get back here!' Dora threw herself at him, grabbing him around the legs just as he got the door open. Pain shot through her shoulder as she hit the hard tiled floor, but she clung on grimly, Archie struggling in her arms.

'Let me go!' He kicked out at her, catching her in the shins.

'Not likely!' She looked at Lucy, still standing in the corner. 'You could lend a hand,' she hissed.

'I'm not touching *that*,' Lucy shuddered.

'Then at least stand by the door and make sure he doesn't escape again.' Dora struggled to her feet, still holding on to Archie. 'Look here, young man, you ain't leaving this room until you've had a wash. So you might as well just let us get on with it, all right?'

Archie shot her a baleful look, but he must have realised she meant business because he stopped wriggling. 'All right,' he grunted.

The boy's clothes were scarcely more than layers of

dirty rags. Underneath them, his malnourished little body was grey with dirt and covered in livid sores. Even Dora had to hold her breath as she helped him into the bath. Lucy hung back, not even trying to hide her disgust.

'How did he ever get into such a filthy state?' she muttered.

Archie shot her a look. 'I can hear you, y'know!'

'I'm surprised, the state of your ears,' Dora said, setting about him with a flannel. 'And you can stop using language like that, young man,' she added, as Archie mumbled a curse under his breath. 'Unless you want me to wash your mouth out with this?' She brandished the carbolic soap.

'I don't know why these people have so many children, if they can't look after them,' Lucy went on. 'It's utterly revolting, the way they breed like sewer rats.'

'Who are you calling a sewer rat?' Archie said.

'Take no notice, love,' Dora whispered as she scrubbed the dirt out of his hair. She knew the unkind comment was aimed as much at her as it was at Archie.

He was a lot quicker hopping out of the bath than he was getting in. Dora wrapped his shivering, skinny body in a warm towel.

'There, doesn't that feel better?' she asked. Archie didn't reply. He stood there, submitting to her ministrations in offended silence.

'Well, that's nice, isn't it?' Lucy snapped at him. 'Aren't you going to say thank you?'

Archie stuck his tongue out at her. Dora smiled to herself as she reached over to the radiator for the pyjamas Sister Parry had found for him. Sister kept a stock of donated nightclothes in the linen cupboard and handed them out to children whose own clothes were too dirty or unfit to be worn.

'If you ask me, your mate's the one who needs to have

her mouth washed out with soap!' Archie said, when Lucy went off to find a pro to clean the bathroom.

I can't argue with you there, Dora thought, but all she commented was, 'She's not from round here. She doesn't understand people like us.'

Archie regarded her with sharp-eyed interest. 'Are you from round here then?'

Dora nodded. 'Griffin Street, the other side of the park. How about you?'

'Wicker's Yard.'

'You might know my mum's cousin Ivy then? She lives near there. Got a son about your age – Freddie Jackson?'

His face brightened. 'He's in my class at school.'

After that Dora seemed to win his trust. Archie explained that his mother was a widow with six children, and he was the eldest.

'That sounds like my family,' she said. 'Except I'm not the eldest. I've got an older brother, Peter. He works as a porter here.'

By the time she'd got him into his pyjamas, Archie was looking a lot brighter. Until they came out of the bathroom and found Sister Parry waiting for them, arms folded. Lucy was with her. She reminded Dora of Sister Sutton's terrier Sparky, the way she stuck so closely to her mistress' heels.

'There you are, Nurse. What on earth took you so long?'

Dora shot a glance at Lucy. 'Sorry, Sister.'

She tensed, waiting for the inevitable telling off.

'Well, I must say, he's looking a lot better than he was when he came in.' Sister Parry made a grab for Archie and examined behind his ears, holding him fast as he tried to squirm away. 'Oh, do keep still!' she barked. 'I hope we're not going to have any trouble with you, young man?'

She turned to Lucy. 'Put this patient to bed, and make

sure he's comfortable,' she ordered. 'Mr Hobbs will be up to see him shortly. Nurse Lane?' Her voice sharpened. 'Are you listening to me?'

But Lucy wasn't listening. Her horrified gaze was fixed on Dora. 'Please, Sister . . . I think Doyle's caught something . . .'

Dora looked down, and let out a scream. Her snowy apron bib was covered in reddish-brown dots. And they were crawling in a steady line up towards her chin.

'Lice! Just what we need.' Sister Parry tutted impatiently. 'You'll have to go to the Porters' Lodge and ask Mr Hopkins to fumigate your clothes.' She turned to Lucy. 'Go and get Doyle a fresh uniform to put on. Really, Nurse, you should have been more careful.'

'I was completely mortified,' Dora told Millie later as they sat in their room, trying to study. 'Can you imagine, having to wash yourself down with disinfectant in the Porters' Lodge? Not to mention having to listen to Mr Hopkins lecturing me because he's got better things to do with his time than fumigate nurses' uniforms.'

'I shouldn't worry about it if I were you,' Millie soothed her. 'It happens to everyone sooner or later. The perils of being a nurse in the East End, I'm afraid.'

'Lane didn't make it any better,' Dora said. 'I swear she was laughing at me behind Sister's back.'

'Oh, take no notice of her,' Millie said. 'You know what a cat she is. Anyway, at least you know now how to deal with a case of pediculosis of clothing, which is one of the questions in this book.' She consulted her nursing manual. 'Now, describe the preparation of a surgical fomentation.'

'That's easy,' Dora replied. 'A surgical fomentation is to be placed over a wound, so it must be prepared with every aseptic precaution. The fomentation is boiled in a steriliser for five minutes, then wrung dry and handed in the wringer to the dresser. Boracic lint should be used, or other antiseptics may be added to the boiling water.'

'Such as?'

'Carbolic acid one in eighty, perchloride of mercury one in two thousand, lysol half a drachm to the pint, or eusol equal quantities.' Dora pulled a face at her. 'You see? You can't catch me out. Now it's my turn.' She flicked over the pages of her book. 'What is the difference in sputum between the early and late stages of phthisis?'

'Well, I know in the later stages it becomes nummular,' Millie said. 'But in the early stages . . . is it tinged with blood?'

'It can be,' Dora quoted. 'But it's generally greenish-yellow.'

'I get confused with so many different samples.' Millie put down her book. 'Sometimes I wonder why I'm bothering, since I'm getting married straight after the exams anyway. What's the point of storing up all this information if I'm never going to be able to use it?'

Dora caught a wistful expression on her face. 'You do want to get married, don't you?' she asked.

'Oh, yes,' Millie said. 'I adore Sebastian, and I can't wait to marry him. But sometimes I wish I'd been allowed to find out what life was like as a proper Staff Nurse. You know, just for a few months.'

Poor Millie, Dora thought. Most girls would have envied her privileged position. Millie, or Lady Amelia Benedict to give her her full title, was the daughter of an earl. She had grown up living with her widowed father and her grandmother in a castle in the heart of the Kent countryside. But Millie had turned her back on her privileged debutante's life to train as a nurse, much to her grandmother the Dowager Countess' horror.

57

'Couldn't you put the wedding off for a few months?' Dora suggested.

Millie laughed. 'Grandmother would have apoplexy! She's been desperate for this day to come for so long, I don't think she could stand to wait any longer.' She shook her head. 'Poor Granny! All her friend's granddaughters are safely married off, and some have already had their first child. I'm a terrible embarrassment to her as it is. And she's also terrified that Papa will die before I manage to produce a suitable heir for the estate. And then we'll all have to squash into the Dower House, which will be utterly horrifying for her.'

Dora stared at her in wonder. Millie was so matter-of-fact about it, but her future had been set in stone from the moment she was born. If she didn't marry and produce a son, her father's estate would pass to the next male in line, an obscure cousin in Northumberland.

Fortunately for everyone, Millie had fallen in love with Lord Sebastian Rushton, the youngest son of a duke, just in time. But Dora wondered what the reaction of her friend's family would have been if Millie had decided to stay single and continue with her nursing.

She and Dora were so different it was a marvel that they had become such firm friends. But after three years of sharing a room, laughing and crying together and helping each other through all kinds of sorrows, Dora couldn't imagine life without her now.

They had grown so close that Millie had even asked her to be a bridesmaid at the wedding. Although how an East End girl from the back streets of Bethnal Green would manage at a posh society do, Dora had no idea.

'Anyway, we must press on,' Millie said briskly, picking up her book. 'We still have to get you through this exam, don't we? I expect to see you in the blue dress of a staff nurse by Christmas.'

It was on the tip of Dora's tongue to say that she could be married herself by then. Ever since Nick told her there might be a chance of him getting his divorce more quickly, she had been desperate to share her exciting news. But she'd kept silent. She couldn't trust anyone with such a secret. And besides, she could still hardly believe it was true. She wouldn't allow herself to put any faith in it until she saw the divorce papers in Nick's hand.

Millie was in the middle of a complicated question about Fowler's position when there was a knock on the door and Jess the maid staggered in under the weight of an armful of bedding. The top of her dark head was barely visible over the pile of blankets and pillows.

'What's this?' Millie asked, putting down her book.

'Sister Sutton told me to bring it up.'

Dora looked at Millie. 'We must be getting a room mate at last.'

'Gosh, how exciting!' Millie's eyes shone. 'Do you think it's one of the new students?'

Dora stood up as Jess lurched across the room towards her. 'Here, let me help you with that.'

'Thank you, Miss.'

'You can leave the bedding, if you like. We'll make up the bed, won't we, Benedict?'

'Of course,' Millie said, standing up.

'Oh, no, I couldn't.' Jess looked from one to the other, her face full of concern. 'Sister Sutton might not like it.'

'I'm sure we can make a bed to Sister Sutton's satisfaction by now.' Dora smiled at the frightened girl.

'Even me,' Millie added cheerfully. 'Well, most of the time anyway.'

'Oh, for heaven's sake, Doyle. Mind your own business and let the maid do her job!' said a sharp voice from the doorway.

Dora looked up. Lucy Lane stood there, a deep scowl on her face.

'Why don't *you* mind your own business?' Dora snapped back.

Lucy's scowl deepened. 'It is my business,' she said. 'Didn't Sister Sutton tell you? I'm going to be sharing this room from now on!'

Chapter Seven

Jess gave the skirting board a final polish, then straightened up and massaged her aching back while she admired
her handiwork. It was after two and she had been up since
before dawn, turning mattresses, making up beds, cleaning
out cupboards and making sure everything was in order
for when the new students arrived later that day.

Now she had turned her attention to the seniors' rooms.
The students were supposed to keep their own accommodation tidy, but the rooms were rarely cleaned to Sister
Sutton's satisfaction, and Jess felt so sorry for the poor,
exhausted girls coming home to stripped beds and a
tongue lashing from the Home Sister that she had taken
to cleaning them herself.

She threw open the small skylight window and shook
her duster out. It seemed strange to see the third bed
in the attic room made up at last. She wondered how the
two girls were getting on with their new room mate.
The ginger-haired one hadn't looked too happy about it,
and Jess didn't blame her. She could never forget how that
sharp-faced girl Lucy Lane had snubbed her so rudely on
the day she'd come for her interview.

After nearly a month Jess had started to get to know
the individual students. Not personally – Sister Sutton
would never allow that – but she had built up a picture
of them from seeing them in the passageways and cleaning
up after them. Dusting photographs told her the Irish girl
on the first floor had lots of sisters, and a sweetheart who

was a policeman. Tidying piles of *Picturegoer* and bottles of hydrogen peroxide under a bed told her the blonde on the second floor loved Clark Gable and secretly bleached her hair. And all the belongings strewn on the chest of drawers in this room told her the fair-haired, nicely spoken girl was very scatty indeed.

Jess smiled to herself as she put the girl's jewellery carefully back into its box. She didn't mind too much about tidying up after her. At least the fair-haired girl and her ginger friend were always pleasant to Jess, and greeted her whenever they passed. Not like some of the girls, who walked right past her as if she was no more worth their attention than the grandfather clock in the hall.

She reached under the bed to check for dust, and her hand touched something heavy. A book.

Jess pulled it out and dusted off the green cloth cover with her hand. *A Complete System of Nursing* by E. Millicent Ashdown, read the gold letters on the spine.

She flicked through it. There were hundreds of pages of text, interspersed with pictures of people in various splints and bandages.

Did the nurses really have to learn all this? wondered Jess. No wonder they always looked so tired.

She sank down on the fair-haired girl's bed, and started to read. There were a lot of long words in the book, most of which Jess couldn't untangle, but it was utterly fascinating, like looking through a window into a strange new world.

But this was real, not fictional. This was all about the human body, and how it worked. Jess flicked through the pages faster and faster, taking it all in, soaking up the information like a sponge. And all the while her mind was working, thinking what a privilege it must be to be able to go to lectures and learn so much every day.

She jumped at the sound of heavy footsteps creaking

up the stairs. She barely had time to slip the book under the pillow and scramble to her feet when the door opened and Sister Sutton stood there, Sparky at her feet.

'Good gracious, girl, what are you doing here?' She eyed Jess. 'Isn't it supposed to be your half-day today?'

'Yes, but I wanted to make sure everything was done,' Jess replied, stepping slightly to one side so Sister Sutton couldn't see the corner of the book sticking out from under the pillow. 'I know we'll be busy when the new students arrive, so I don't mind staying.'

'That won't be necessary, child.' Sister Sutton folded her fat hands in front of her and looked around. 'Are you sure you've done everything? Polished the banisters? Tidied the linen cupboard?' She thought for a moment. 'Did you clean the bathrooms properly? I hope you haven't been slapdash.'

'You can inspect them if you like,' Jess said.

Sister Sutton stiffened, her chins wobbling. 'I most certainly will, you can be sure of that. I don't need you to tell me my job, girl.'

She bustled off down the stairs, Sparky trotting after her, his nose in the air. Jess followed meekly behind.

She waited tensely as Sister Sutton walked around, running her finger along the tops of the doors and the windowsills.

'As you can see, I managed to scrub those marks off the taps,' offered Jess, breaking the silence. 'It took a bit of elbow grease, but I did it.'

Sister Sutton sniffed. 'I suppose you've done a passable job,' she conceded, then added, 'although you might have used a little more elbow grease on those tiles.'

'Yes, Sister.' Jess tried not to smile. How typical! She could have been up all night scrubbing those tiles and Sister Sutton would still have found fault.

But Jess had learned not to take offence. It was just the Home Sister's way.

'Now get off with you,' Sister Sutton said. 'And see you return by five,' she added. 'I daresay there will be plenty to do when the new girls arrive.'

'Yes, Sister.'

'And Jess?'

She turned. 'Yes, Sister?'

'Are you aware your month's trial is up at the end of this week?'

'Yes, Sister.' Jess swallowed hard. She had been aware of little else for several days.

Sister Sutton paused. 'I can see no reason why we shouldn't make the arrangement permanent,' she said. 'If that is acceptable to you?'

Jess fought to stop herself from smiling with relief. 'Yes, Sister,' she said. 'It is.'

'Very well. Then I will see you at five o'clock sharp.'

Her mother was right, Effie O'Hara thought. The East End of London was very different from Killarney.

As she stepped off the bus in Wapping, the sights, sounds and smells of the city rushed in to fill her senses. The air was alive with the sound of shouting, street vendors selling their wares and the scream of seagulls wheeling overhead around the nearby docks. Distant factory chimneys belched smoke into the grimy sky. Even the sun that had been so clear and brilliant over the fields and lanes as she left Ireland cast no more than a dismal grey light over the damp city streets.

And all those people . . . Effie had never seen so many, not even on the busiest market day in Killarney. The drab tide pushed and nudged past her as she stood on the corner, her bags at her feet.

Effie felt her optimism fading. It was only the thought of facing her mother that stopped her getting straight back on the bus and catching the next boat home.

She squared her shoulders. This won't do, Euphemia O'Hara, she told herself. You wanted life, and here it is. Besides, once she reached the Nightingale Hospital, she would have her sisters to look after her.

All she had to do was find her way there.

But it seemed so different from when she'd come for her interview two months earlier. Then her mother had been with her, and her sister Bridget had met them from the station and brought them in a taxi, and Effie hadn't had to worry about anything.

'You lost, Miss?'

A voice behind her made her start. She swung round. A boy stood behind her. He was about twelve years old, with untidy tufts of mud-brown hair sticking out from under his shabby cap.

'I'm looking for the Florence Nightingale Hospital.' She tried not to stare at the birthmark on the boy's cheek. Her mother was always telling her off for gawping.

'I know it. I'm going that way myself, as it happens. I could show you the way?'

Effie hesitated. He was just a child, not the kind of stranger her mother and sisters had warned her about.

'Thank you,' she said. 'That would be very kind.'

'Right you are, then.' He picked up her heavy bag with ease and started briskly down the road. Effie bobbed along behind, doing her best to keep up with him.

He talked as fast as he walked, chattering to her over his shoulder. His cockney accent was so strong Effie could barely understand him. She was too out of breath to keep up a conversation anyway.

'This way, Miss.' The boy dodged around a corner and

ducked into a narrow alleyway. Grim, blackened walls running with damp rose on either side of them, leaving only a thin strip of dull daylight high above to show the way. 'Now you don't want to be coming this way by yourself. It's not safe,' he warned. 'But you're all right with me. I know my way around, see.'

Something scuttled past in the gloom, inches from her foot. Effie let out a shriek and quickened her pace, her shoes skidding on the slimy cobbles.

They emerged into a busy market, a narrow street lined with stalls and teeming with people. It was a welcome burst of noise and activity after the deadened silence of the alleyway. Effie had never seen anything so lively and colourful. On one side people picked up and argued over second-hand clothes spread out on canvas sheets across the pavement. On the other were stalls selling fruit and veg and all kinds of seafood. The sharp, salty smell mingled with the aroma of fried onions.

It was all so overwhelming, Effie found it hard to keep her eyes fixed on the boy's cap as it bobbed along ahead of her, cutting easily through the crowd which swiftly closed behind like waves in the wake of a ship, pushing her further and further back.

'Oh, please wait!' she called out, but her voice was lost in the din. The boy glanced back over his shoulder, searching for her. Effie waved to him and he nodded, but a moment later he was gone.

Effie craned her neck, looking this way and that, but he had disappeared.

She chewed her lip. How could she be so stupid? Her mother was always telling her off for being a dreamer, and now she had managed to get herself totally lost.

She searched for the boy for a few minutes, but it was no use. She sat down on the doorstep of a shop and tried to think. The best thing to do was to stay put and wait for him to find her, she decided. Wandering around, they could miss each other for hours in a crowded place like this.

Jess hadn't meant to visit the bookstall again, but once she reached the market she couldn't help herself.

The stallholder's son was there, dawdling against the wall, smoking as usual. He smiled and dropped his cigarette on to the cobbles when he saw her.

'Hello again,' he greeted her cheerily. 'Read any good books lately?'

'I might have.'

He reached under the stall and brought out the copy of *Great Expectations*. 'You know this is still here, waiting for you.'

'No one's bought it yet, then?'

He shook his head. 'I'm keeping it especially for you.'

She tightened her lips to stop herself from smiling. 'And I told you, I don't take anything I ain't paid for.'

'Suit yourself. Are you always this contrary, Jess Jago?'

She stiffened. 'How do you know my name?'

'I might have been asking around about you.'

Jess glanced over her shoulder at the other stallholders. 'I'm sure everyone's been falling over themselves to tell you what my family's like?'

He shrugged. 'They have, but I don't take any notice. I prefer to make up my own mind about people.' He sent her a long, considering look. 'My name's Sam, by the way. Sam Cordwainer.'

'I wasn't aware I'd asked.'

'No, but I thought I'd tell you anyway. So you know what to call me when I take you out.'

Jess was so surprised she couldn't help laughing. 'You think a lot of yourself, don't you?'

'I think a lot of you.' He cocked his head. 'So what do you say? Can I take you out one night?'

Jess picked up a book and flicked through it for something to do. 'Can't,' she said. 'I'm busy.'

'But we haven't set a date yet!'

'Whenever it is, I'll still be busy.'

Sam grinned. 'Playing hard to get, are you?'

'If that's what you want to think.' She closed the book and handed it back to him. 'Anyway, I can't stand round here talking to you all day long. I've got more important things to do with my time.'

'If you say so. But you'll be back,' he predicted.

'Of course I will.' She smiled sweetly at him. 'This is the only second-hand bookstall in Bethnal Green.'

As she walked away, Sam called after her, 'You'll see. You won't be able to resist my charm for ever!'

Of course she didn't have anything to do with her time except wander around the market, trying to stay out of Sam's line of sight. As she wandered among the stalls Jess kept sneaking looks over at him. He was standing behind his display of books, that soppy grin of his all over his face, charming the customers. She noticed how he perked up whenever a woman went by, how his gaze followed them. They didn't seem to be falling for his daft patter any more than Jess had.

She bought an apple turnover from the baker's, and started back across the market. It had started to rain again, sending cold drips down the back of her collar. She abandoned her plan to go to the park and decided to hurry back to her room instead. With any luck she could finish another chapter of her book before it was time to return to duty.

She was heading down Bethnal Green Road when she heard a commotion coming from outside the pie and mash shop on the corner.

'But I'm waiting for someone!' a girl's voice said.

'Then you'll have to wait somewhere else. You've been sat on my doorstep this past half hour.'

As Jess drew closer, she saw the proprietor of the pie shop, a giant of a woman, towering over a young girl who sat at her feet. The girl wasn't much older than Jess. She was wrapped in a heavy raincoat, a beret perched on top of her dripping dark curls. There was something oddly familiar about her.

'But I can't leave,' she explained in a gentle Irish voice. 'Otherwise the boy won't know where to find me.'

The woman frowned. 'What boy?'

'The one who kindly offered me directions to the Nightingale Hospital. I'm going to be a nurse there, you see. But we got separated in the crowd.'

'Did you now?' The woman folded her arms across her chest. 'And I suppose you let him carry your bags for you, too?'

'How did you know that?'

The woman gave a shout of laughter. 'Blimey, love, how green are you?' she roared. 'You didn't lose him – he lost you. Good and proper, by the sound of it.'

'But I don't understand. Why would he—' The girl hesitated for a moment. 'You mean he stole my bag?'

The woman nodded. 'Sorry, ducks, but I reckon that's the last you'll see of him or your bag. Was there much in it?'

'Everything I have.' The girl's voice was choked. 'Oh, God, and I've only been in London two hours. My sisters are going to kill me!'

Sisters! Jess suddenly realised why this girl seemed so familiar. She turned and walked back to where the Irish girl was still sitting stubbornly on the step, hugging her knees.

'Excuse me, your name wouldn't be O'Hara by any chance, would it?' asked Jess.

The girl looked up, her blue eyes swimming with tears. 'How did you know?'

'I work at the hospital. I recognised you from a photograph your sister has.' Jess searched her memory, mentally scanning the list she had seen pinned up in the hall. 'You must be – Euphemia?'

'Effie.' The girl's face brightened and she wiped her face on her sleeve. She scrambled to her feet and held out her hand. She was as tall and leggy as a colt, and towered over Jess. 'I'm pleased to meet you . . . ?'

'Jess.' She felt awkward as she shook the other girl's hand. 'I can show you the way to the Nightingale, if you like?'

'Yes, please.'

'Thank gawd for that!' The shopkeeper rolled her eyes heavenwards. 'I thought she was going to be stuck on my doorstep till Kingdom Come!'

'But what about my bag?' Effie said.

'There's not much we can do about that for now.' Jess shrugged. 'But let's get you to the Nightingale, shall we?'

Effie cheered up on the way to the hospital. She bounced along beside Jess, chattering all the while. 'I can't wait to see my sisters,' she said, her sadness seemingly forgotten. 'Katie's written me so many letters, telling me all about the larks she gets up to. It sounds so much more fun than our village in Ireland.' She turned to Jess. 'Are you a nurse too?'

Jess lowered her gaze. 'No, I'm a maid in the students' home.'

She stiffened, waiting for Effie to turn snooty. But she just smiled and said, 'So we'll be seeing a lot of each other, then? That's grand. I was worried I wouldn't have any friends, but now I've met you.'

And I daresay you won't want to know me in a week

or two, Jess thought. 'I expect you'll make lots of new friends in your set.'

'I hope so,' Effie replied. 'I really want to have some fun.'

Jess thought about the grey, exhausted faces that greeted her in the hall every evening, and the weary feet that could barely drag themselves up the stairs. 'I think you'll be expected to work hard, too.'

'Ah, I'm sure it won't be that difficult,' Effie dismissed.

They approached the gates to the Nightingale, and Jess felt a touch of pride as Effie admired the grand Georgian building. 'It looks so much bigger than when I came for my interview,' she said. 'Although I suppose then I was too nervous to notice anything!'

Jess directed her to the Porters' Lodge to sign in.

'And where are your bags?' Mr Hopkins asked, looking around. 'Or will your things be coming later?'

Effie's lip trembled. 'They were stolen!' she blurted out. 'My clothes, my shoes, my watch – everything is gone!'

'Come on,' Jess said quickly, seeing the startled expression on the Head Porter's face. 'Let's get you to the nurses' home.'

But Effie had suddenly remembered her predicament again, and this time she couldn't be consoled.

'I don't know how I'm going to tell my sisters,' she said. 'I expect they'll say it's my fault for being foolish.'

'You were trusting, not foolish,' Jess soothed her.

'Well, I wish I'd never trusted that boy, that's for sure. But he seemed so friendly!'

'You'll have to tell the police,' Jess said.

'That's a good idea.' Effie nodded. 'Katie's boyfriend is a policeman, he'll know what to do. And it shouldn't be too hard to find the culprit. Not with that birthmark of his . . .'

Jess stiffened. 'Birthmark?' she heard herself say faintly.

Effie nodded. 'Just here, on his cheek.' She pointed to the spot. 'Almost like a fingerprint, I'd say. Ah, now, I remember this courtyard.' She stopped and looked around. 'It's hard to believe, isn't it, that there are all these buildings behind the one at the front? It's like a . . . what do you call it? You know, out at sea.'

'An iceberg,' Jess said faintly, her thoughts elsewhere.

'That's it. An iceberg.' Effie stood beside the plane tree in the centre of the courtyard, gawping around at the buildings that surrounded them. 'I'm never going to find my way around this place. I swear to God, it's bigger than my whole village.'

'You'll get used to it.' Jess took her sleeve, tugging her towards the archway that led to the nurses' accommodation. 'Right, now all you have to do is go through there and down to the end of the path, and you'll see the students' home straight ahead of you. You can't miss it. I expect Sister Sutton will be looking out for you.'

Effie stared at her, blue eyes round with dismay. 'Aren't you coming with me?'

Jess shook her head. 'I've just remembered, there's someone I need to see.'

Chapter Eight

It didn't take her long to find the culprit.

Typical Cyril, he didn't even have the sense to hide. Jess found him in the back yard of their tenement, going through Effie's suitcase, his face alight with greed.

He looked up sharply when she let herself in the back gate. 'Oh, it's you.' He turned away and carried on going through the suitcase.

'What's that you got?'

'It's mine.' He hunched his narrow shoulders over it, like a starving dog guarding a bone.

'And since when have you been wearing these?' Jess reached past him and snatched up a pair of flannel knickers. 'You thieving little sod! You can't keep your hands to yourself, can you?'

She elbowed him to one side and started putting the things back in the case. Cyril stared at her. 'What are you doing?'

'Taking this back where it belongs.'

'No, you ain't!' He sprang at her, but Jess dodged and cuffed him round the ear. He made another grab for her, but she tripped him and he went sprawling headlong on the cobbles. He landed heavily on his knees with a yelp of pain.

'Oi, what's all the racket?' Gladys appeared at the back door, cigarette in hand. 'Oh, it's you. I thought I said you weren't welcome round here any more?'

'Don't worry, I ain't stopping. I just came to get this.' Jess fastened the catch on the suitcase.

'It's mine!' Cyril whined, still clutching his knee. 'I – I won it in a bet!' He turned to his mother. 'I was going to sell it, Mum, to make some money. I came by it fair and square, honest!'

'Honest? Don't make me laugh!' Jess retorted.

Gladys looked from one to the other, dragging on her cigarette, her rouged cheeks sucked in as if she would draw the very life out of it.

'You leave that suitcase where it is,' she said finally. 'If my son said he didn't nick it, then that's good enough for me. You're nothing but a troublemaker, Jess Jago. We don't want you round here no more!'

'All right then, if that's what you want.' Jess folded her arms across her chest. 'But I'm warning you, the girl it belongs to is talking to the rozzers this very minute. She got a good look at you, don't forget,' she said to Cyril. 'Shouldn't take them too long to find a kid with a birthmark like yours round here, should it? I expect they'll give you three months' hard labour, at least.'

Cyril's gaze flew to his mother, full of alarm. 'Mum?'

Jess looked at her stepmother. Gladys' mouth thinned, her eyes calculating. 'Take the suitcase,' she snapped.

'But, Mum—'

'You heard me!' Gladys turned on Cyril. 'Do you think I need any more trouble? My old man's already in jail, I don't need you behind bars too.' She took another drag on her cigarette and aimed a stream of smoke into the air. 'And as for you,' she wheeled towards Jess, 'you can sling your hook, before I set the dog on you!'

Her stepmother's harsh voice followed her as she dragged the case through the gate out into the alleyway. 'You've forgotten where your loyalties lie, Jess Jago. You think those posh girls are bothered about you? You're only fit to skivvy after them. You'll never be friends, you're not one of them. You'll see, they won't want to know you in the end.'

Meanwhile, Effie was in her new room, listening to her sister Katie telling her over and over again how stupid she had been. As if she didn't know.

'I can't believe it!' She paced around Effie as she sat miserably on the bed, eyes downcast. 'I told you, didn't I? I warned you. Don't talk to strangers, I said. And what's the first thing you did? You gave all your worldly possessions away to one!'

'I thought he was helping me.'

'Helping himself, you mean!' Katie gave a derisive snort. 'Honest to God, Effie, how could you be so daft?'

'I know! You don't have to go on about it!' Tears stung the back of her eyes, but she was determined not to cry any more. She hardly ever cried at home. But somehow since she'd arrived in London she hadn't been able to stop. So much for a big, exciting adventure!

Surely today couldn't get any worse? She had already had a bruising encounter with the Home Sister. Effie had thought Katie was exaggerating when she complained about Sister Sutton in her letters home. Effie had expected her to be like their mother, cuddly and comforting. She'd thought she might be offered tea and cake and at least a bit of sympathy after her horrible ordeal. But instead the vicious old woman had shouted at her to dry her eyes, told her she didn't have time for Irish girls and their nonsense, then ushered her to a room with instructions that she should settle in, change into her uniform and report for supper at eight o'clock. And to top it all, her stupid dog had tried to bite Effie when she tried to pet it.

And now Katie was being awful to her, too. Back at home they'd always been best friends, much to the despair of their mother and stuffy older sisters. But Effie had hardly recognised Katie when she'd walked into their room in her prim starched uniform. London and the Nightingale had changed her. She was nearly as bossy as their big sister Bridget, and that was saying something.

The exhaustion of her long journey overcame Effie then, and she buried her face in hands. She heard Katie sigh, and then felt her arm come around her shoulders.

'I'm sorry for getting so cross with you,' she said. 'I'm just worried about you, that's all. I don't know what Mammy is going to say about this either.'

Effie looked up sharply. 'You can't tell her!'

'She'll find out in the end.'

Effie let out a despairing sigh. Katie was right; their mother might be hundreds and hundreds of miles away but she had a sixth sense where her daughters were concerned. Especially Effie.

'She'll make me come home, I know she will.' Mammy O'Hara hadn't wanted her to leave Killarney in the first place. Effie was her baby, the last to leave the nest. Mammy had cried every day since Effie received her acceptance letter from Matron.

'All right, we won't tell her yet,' Katie promised. 'But you have to be more careful, Effie.'

'I – I haven't got anything left to be careful with!' The realisation hit her again. She had nothing to her name, no shoes, no clothes, none of the pretty dresses or the keepsakes she'd brought from home. They'd all gone. 'Oh, Katie, what am I going to do?'

'Shhh, it's all right. I can lend you some clothes.'

Effie eyed her sister warily. Katie was at least a head shorter than her, and a great deal plumper. Effie couldn't imagine ever wearing one of her sister's dresses. 'I'll look like a fool!' she blurted out.

'Well, you are a fool.' Katie stood up. 'Now cheer up. Let's get you into your uniform before Sister Sutton starts chasing you.'

Effie was glad of Katie's help then as she pulled it on. The dress felt thick and cumbersome, its calico lining scratching against her skin. And the starched collar and cuffs she had to attach were as hard as cardboard.

'It's so heavy,' she complained. 'I'll be sweating like a pig if I have to wear this all day.'

'You'll get used to it. But you'll need to be a bit quicker with those cuffs,' Katie observed as she watched her sister fiddling with the studs. 'You have to take them off when you're doing any cleaning, or washing a patient. But you need to put them on again when you serve meals, or when the doctor is doing his rounds.'

'Honestly, what difference does it make if a doctor sees me with my sleeves rolled up?' Effie laughed, but Katie sent her a dark look.

'Don't you let the ward sisters hear you talking like that,' she warned. 'And it's best to take a clean apron with you whenever you go on a ward,' she went on. 'You're bound to need it, and the sisters are never pleased if you have to go off and fetch one.'

Effie pulled a face. All Katie seemed to talk about was Sister this and Sister that. She was already fed up with hearing about them all. Surely no one could be that bad?

She scrutinised her reflection in the mirror, not liking what she saw. The uniform couldn't have been less alluring if it tried. Her dark hair was all hidden away underneath a monstrous starched cap, and the blue-striped dress covered every other inch of her, from the high collar down to just above her ankles. 'Honest to God, Katie, the nuns at Saint Bernadette's get away with more than this!' she complained. 'Surely it would look better if I just took it up a little—'

She started to hitch the skirt up towards her knees, but Katie stopped her. 'Don't,' she warned. 'Sister Sutton will notice, believe me. She regularly measures our hems to make sure they're no more than ten inches from the ground.'

Effie sighed. 'How am I ever going to get a handsome doctor to fall in love with me while I'm looking like this?'

'Don't let any of the sisters hear you talking like that, either!' her sister laughed. 'You're there to care for the patients, Nurse O'Hara, not pursue your romantic interests,' she mimicked a stern voice. 'Besides, no doctor is going to look at you anyway when your apron's covered in vomit and you've got a sputum mug in each hand!'

As Effie glowered at her reflection, Katie explained what she could expect to be doing for the next few months. She would spend three months in Preliminary Training, or PTS, with the Sister Tutor, where she would learn all kinds of boring things like cleaning and cooking. From the way Katie described it, it sounded worse than being at home.

Then, if she passed her test at the end of PTS, she would finally be allocated to a ward. Over the next three years she would work on each ward in the hospital for three months each so she could learn all the skills she needed, and then she would take her State Final exams.

'But for the first year, you'll mainly be cleaning and doing bedpans and all the filthy jobs no one else wants,' Katie told her. 'That's why the probationers are called dirty pros.'

Effie was hardly listening. She could hear voices and laughter outside in the corridor, and the scuffle of footsteps going from room to room. The other new girls were all settling in, getting to know each other. Effie longed to join them, but instead she was stuck listening to her sister's dreary lecture.

She'd thought it would be fun to share a room with Katie, but now she really wasn't so sure.

She looked up hopefully at the sound of a knock on the door. Perhaps it was one of her set coming to introduce herself?

Katie opened the door. 'Yes? What do you want?' Her voice was cool and distant. Effie jumped up from the bed and hurried over. If it was one of the other girls, she didn't want her sister to put them off.

She grinned in delight to see a familiar figure standing in the doorway. 'Jess!'

Katie stared at her. 'Do you know her?'

'Oh, yes, we're friends. She found me when I was lost.'

'That's not all I've found,' the other girl said. 'I think this belongs to you?'

Effie gave a cry of surprise as her case was hauled into view. 'My suitcase! Oh, that's grand.' She nudged past Katie into the hall and bent to run her hands over the battered leather. She had never been so pleased to see anything in her life. 'Where did you find it?'

'It was . . . in the park. I was just passing the boating lake, and I saw something sticking out of the bushes.'

'Really? Imagine that.' Effie flung the case open and rifled through it. 'And look, everything's still here. My money, my watch . . . nothing's been taken.' She frowned. 'I wonder why someone would steal my suitcase and then just leave it behind?'

'It's very odd, I must say.'

Effie looked up at her sister. Katie was fixing Jess with one of her suspicious looks, the kind she used to give Effie when she accused her of helping herself to her belongings. Jess was staring back, her face expressionless.

'Anyway, I've got my things back now, and that's what matters.' Effie fastened up the case and straightened up.

'I'm glad,' Jess said.

As she turned to go, Effie remembered her manners. 'Wait,' she said. 'You must let me give you something for your trouble—'

She looked around for her purse, but Jess shook her head.

'I don't want anything.'

'But you deserve a reward—'

'I said, I don't want anything!'

Effie started at the sound of Jess' raised voice. Had she offended the girl in some way? she wondered. She wasn't used to dealing with London people, perhaps they didn't like being offered money.

'Well, thank you anyway,' she said. 'I'm sure I'll—'

But she didn't get a chance to finish her sentence before Katie shut the door in Jess' face.

Effie stared at her. 'Why did you have to be so rude to her?'

'I don't trust her. I wouldn't be surprised if she'd stolen it herself.'

'Don't be daft!' Effie laughed. 'I told you, it was a young lad who took it.'

'They might have been working together.'

'In that case, why would she bring it back? And why wouldn't she have taken anything out of it? And—'

'I don't know, do I?' Katie snapped. 'I don't have all the answers, Effie. I just think it's a bit strange, that's all.'

'You're too suspicious,' Effie said.

'And you're too trusting,' Katie shot back.

Effie smiled. She had her suitcase back, and she'd made a new friend. Perhaps London was going to be fun after all.

Chapter Nine

The boy's name was Ernest Pennington, and he had suspected rheumatic fever. He was to be specialed, which meant he had a private room and his own personal nurse assigned to him from the ward. But even that wasn't good enough for his mother.

'Is this it, then? Is this what we're paying for?' Rosa Pennington looked about her, mouth turned down.

What did you expect, a suite at the Ritz? Dora gritted her teeth to stop the comment escaping as she set about making Ernest comfortable. He was a podgy, unattractive child, a cap of pale hair framing his fat, solemn face. He lay in bed looking mournfully about him while his mother found fault with everything.

'Are you sure this locker's clean? And is this water fresh?' She peered dubiously into the jug. She was tall and thin, with cords of tension standing out in her long neck. Her dark hair was scraped back, showing off sharp cheekbones. She looked too old to be the mother of a ten-year-old boy.

'I filled the jug myself, just before you arrived.' Dora forced herself to smile sweetly. Rosa Pennington was just being a protective mother, she decided.

Dora moved to the boy's side. 'How are you feeling now, Ernest?' She touched his forehead. His skin was clammy, slick with acid-smelling perspiration.

'He doesn't like to speak to strangers,' Mrs Pennington put in.

'I'm sure he'll get used to me.' Dora smiled down at him. 'We're going to be great friends, aren't we?'

Mrs Pennington shot her a doubtful look. 'You must remember, Nurse, Ernest is not like other children. He is special.'

'Every child is special on this ward, Mrs Pennington.'

'You don't understand, do you?' Rosa Pennington insisted. 'Ernest *is* special. You must have read about him in the newspapers?'

'I can't say I have,' Dora admitted.

Rosa Pennington gave a little 'tsk' of annoyance. 'My son,' she explained with exaggerated patience, 'is one of the country's top violinists. A musical genius. He has been called a young Paganini.'

And who's he when he's at home? Dora wanted to ask. But she had already offended Mrs Pennington enough with her ignorance.

'We care for all the children here the same, whoever they are or wherever they come from,' she said.

Mrs Pennington pursed her lips. 'I'm not paying a fortune for my son to be treated like any other child,' she said. 'I told you, Ernest has a unique ability. And he must not be allowed to mix with the other children,' she added. 'Who knows what nasty things he might pick up?'

Dora bristled. 'We are very careful about hygiene on this ward, Mrs Pennington. Besides, your son will be confined to bed for some time.'

'You see that he is.' Mrs Pennington cast one last, critical look about her, then hooked her handbag over her arm, ready to leave.

'Mother?' The whisper from the bed made them both turn round. Ernest was watching them, his eyes solemn under his pale fringe. 'You . . . you're not leaving me?'

'I must go, Ernest. Your father and I have an important

meeting this afternoon. We have been invited to play with the Concertgebouw Orchestra in Holland.' She glanced at Dora, who did her best to look impressed.

'But, Mother, I'm afraid—'

'Don't make such a silly fuss, Ernest. You know how important this is to your father.' Mrs Pennington didn't look at him as she pulled on her gloves.

Ernest fixed his gaze on the turned-down bed sheet. 'Yes, Mother.'

'That's my brave boy.' Mrs Pennington leaned over to peck his forehead. 'Besides, you'll be quite all right with Nurse – with this person.' She waved her hand vaguely in Dora's direction.

Another quick, disparaging glance around her and she was gone. Dora listened to the clack of her heels disappearing down the corridor, then turned to Ernest.

'She's right, love. We'll take good care of you.' She smiled. 'Anything you need, or anything you're worried about, you just call for one of us, all right?'

Ernest lifted his head to look at her, grey eyes sullen in his podgy face. 'Please don't be over-familiar with me,' he said, his timid manner gone, replaced by his mother's frosty hauteur. 'You may unpack my suitcase and then leave.'

Being chosen as the special nurse in charge of a private patient was a real honour among the students, and usually the subject of much debate and speculation. But for once Dora didn't mind that Sister Parry chose her favourite Lucy to special Ernest. As far as Dora was concerned, Lucy was welcome to him.

Although Dora wasn't so pleased when Sister told her she had to assist Lucy with her duties.

'I daresay she'll have me carrying bedpans back and forth like a dirty pro,' she sighed to Daphne Anderson, another senior. 'She and Ernest will probably get on like a house on fire. They both enjoy ordering people about!'

Things hadn't got any better between the two girls in the week they'd been sharing a room. If anything, they were even worse. Lucy had taken over more than her share of space, squeezing Dora's few belongings aside to make room for all her dresses, hats and shoes, not to mention her jewellery collection. She made a real effort to be friendly to Millie but barely spared a word for Dora, who was beginning to feel like the outsider in her own room.

Lucy stood outside the kitchen door, listening to Dora complaining. She felt like bursting in and telling her that she wasn't exactly delighted at the idea of Dora assisting her either. This was Lucy's first assignment as a special, and she was determined to do everything right and show Sister Parry she was worthy of the responsibility. The last thing she needed was Dora making mistakes and messing everything up for her.

But Dora didn't think of that, did she? She could never be wrong about anything. It made Lucy sick to see her sometimes, swanning around the ward, laughing and joking with the children, cuddling and playing with them even when she was behind with her worklist. She didn't seem to care that Sister Parry despaired of her.

She even managed to quieten the babies with colic, when their screaming drove Lucy to hide in the sluice. Only yesterday morning Staff Nurse Ryan had said that Dora had a magic touch.

It frustrated Lucy that she didn't have a magic touch, too. She was easily the cleverest student in their set, and was always being mentioned favourably in ward reports for her neatness and efficiency. But when it came to working with children, she was lost. She could make their beds and sponge them when they got too hot and treat their shaven heads for ringworm, but she didn't know how to make them smile or how to dry their tears.

Not that she really cared, she told herself. She didn't like children, they unnerved her. They seemed to sense it, too, which was why they were always so fretful around her. She couldn't wait to be assigned to another ward, preferably one without Dora Doyle on it.

The consultant, Mr Hobbs, came to see Ernest later that morning. Lucy felt very important as she stood at Sister Parry's shoulder, listening to the great man in his pinstripe suit.

Mr Hobbs confirmed the diagnosis of acute rheumatic fever and prescribed complete bed rest, a liquid diet, and an intensive course of salicylates for the first forty-eight hours: 'One dose of thirty grams, followed by twenty grams every three hours until the temperature has subsided,' he said, scribbling it down on Ernest's notes.

After he'd gone, Lucy administered the first dose watched by Sister Parry, then carefully wrapped Ernest's swollen knees in warmed wool and erected a frame over his legs to keep the blankets off his painful joints.

By the time she'd finished it was one o'clock, and Sister sent her off duty for the afternoon.

'I will instruct Staff Nurse Ryan to take over until you return.'

'Please, Sister, I thought Doyle was supposed to assist me?' Lucy said.

Sister Parry's face took on a pinched look. 'Assist you, yes,' she said. 'But I'm afraid Doyle may not be up to specialing on her own. Not until she has learned to take orders, at any rate. Now get along with you, and I'll explain to Staff Nurse Ryan.'

'Yes, Sister.' Lucy couldn't keep the smile off her face

as she sauntered from the ward. She passed Doyle, who was showing one of the new pros how to change a baby's nappy. Lucy almost wished she could have told her what Sister Parry had said, just to see the look on her face.

It was another bright, sunny May day, and Lucy was planning how to spend her afternoon off when Sister Sutton pounced on her in the doorway of the nurses' home.

'There you are, Lane. Thank heavens.'

'Did you want me, Sister?'

'Not I, Nurse. But your mother has telephoned six times since nine o'clock this morning.' Sister looked put out. 'I tried to explain that I didn't know when you were off duty, but nevertheless she continues to telephone.'

As if to prove her point, the hall telephone jangled, shattering the peace.

'I daresay that will be her again.' Sister Sutton shook her head, chins quivering. 'Perhaps you could indicate to her, Lane, that I am not your secretary?'

'Yes, Sister. I'm sorry, Sister.'

Lucy waited until Sister Sutton had bustled off, then answered the telephone. 'Hello?'

'Lucy?' Her mother's voice sounded shaky on the other end of the line.

'Mother?'

'Oh, thank God it's you! I've been trying to get in touch with you all morning.'

'I know, Mother.' Lucy stifled a sigh. Her mother's voice was slurred, a sure sign she had been drinking again. 'What is it you wanted?'

'You must come home immediately. It – it's your father.' She burst into tears. Lucy tensed, gripping the receiver, fearing the worst.

'What is it?' she whispered, her throat suddenly dry. 'What's happened to him? Mother?'

'Oh, Lucy!' her mother sobbed. 'He – he's disappeared!'

Dora enjoyed helping with the babies. Staff Nurse Ryan was supposed to be in charge of their care, but when she had to go off and special Ernest Pennington, she allowed Dora to take over supervising the feeding and changing.

Most of them were on the ward because they were underfed and not thriving. A couple, like little Bobby Turner, were suffering from more serious illnesses. Poor Bobby was in the late stages of infantile syphilis. He screamed constantly, his little limbs swollen, his skin turned coppery-brown by the rash that slowly ate away at him. Everyone knew his fate was sealed, but they went on feeding and cuddling him, trying to fill his last days with all the love his mother hadn't given him.

'He's looking a little better today, don't you think, Nurse?' one of the pros, Clara Jessop, said as she changed his nappy. 'I'm sure the rash is going down.'

Dora smiled at her. Sister Parry would have been matter-of-fact about it, told her bluntly that the child was dying and there was nothing anyone could do. But looking at the soft-hearted girl's face, Dora couldn't bring herself to say the words.

'We must just hope for the best,' was all she could manage.

A cry of alarm from the far end of the ward made them jump. Dora looked up. 'What the—'

She hurried away to find another of the pros, Joanna Rudd, on her feet, a screaming baby in her arms. As Dora approached, a familiar sour milky smell stopped her in her tracks. Sure enough, Joanna's apron was soaked.

'Let me guess,' she said. 'You've been feeding Teddy Potts?'

'That horrid creature!' Rudd exclaimed. 'I'd just finished giving him the bottle and he suddenly – did this – all over me!'

'Give him to me before you drop him.' Dora took the baby out of her arms. 'How much did you feed him?'

'He took the whole bottle, the greedy little wretch.'

'No wonder he was sick, in that case. He has pyloric stenosis,' Dora explained. 'He has to be fed a little and often, otherwise – that happens.'

'How was I to know?' Rudd muttered.

'You would if you'd read his notes,' Dora said sternly. 'You must always read the patient's notes for yourself, even if you've been told what to do by a senior. You are as responsible as anyone else for a patient's care and wellbeing, don't forget that.'

She looked at Rudd's soaked apron and tried not to laugh. 'Luckily in this case you came off worse than the baby,' she said. 'You'd better go and change before Sister catches you.'

Rudd stomped off, and Dora glanced back to where Clara was also trying not to smile.

'Poor Rudd,' she said.

'Perhaps that will teach her to stop and think.' Dora looked at her watch. Nick was due to collect the laundry soon. If she was lucky Sister might remember it was time for Dora to go off for tea and she could manage to speak to him outside.

Yesterday she'd watched him go off, dressed in his best suit, to the solicitor's office up west. She hadn't heard a word from him since and was anxious to find out what had happened.

But one look at his grim, unsmiling face when he arrived on the ward and Dora felt her stomach sink. She sent him a questioning look but he just gave the slightest shake of his head before disappearing into the sluice.

Dora quickly checked the coast was clear before slipping in after him.

'I can't be too long,' she whispered. 'Sister is with a patient behind the screens, but she could appear at any moment . . .' She stared into Nick's face. 'It isn't good news, is it?' He shook his head. 'Why? Don't tell me Ruby's changed her mind?' That would be just like her friend, raising their hopes only to dash them again.

'Oh, no, she still wants a divorce. This new man of hers is mad keen to wed, she reckons.'

'Then what's stopping us?'

'Divorces cost money.'

'How much money?'

'Fifty pounds.'

Dora gulped at the figure. It was far more than she'd expected. 'Well, we knew it wouldn't be cheap, didn't we? We talked about how we'd manage. We wouldn't need a lot to live on. I could try and find some shift work, we could pay it off in instalments—'

Nick shook his head. 'It ain't going to work like that. The solicitor wants it all up front.' He looked grim. 'It ain't like buying a new couch, Dor. You can't do it on HP.'

She reeled. 'But who has that sort of money?'

He shrugged. 'Rich people. Why do you think the likes of us never get divorced?'

Dora gripped the cold hard edge of the steel sink for support. She'd been so sure she and Nick would be together soon, but now her dream had been snatched away again.

'I'm sorry, Dora.' Nick's voice was gruff. 'It's a kick in the teeth, ain't it?'

'Well, it ain't the best news I've heard all day, that's for sure.'

'And the worst of it is I had that much saved up, until Ruby got her hands on it.'

For as long as Dora had known him, Nick had been saving his money for the chance to go to America. He'd had big plans to make it as a champion boxer over there, and had also hoped that the doctors in America might have the treatment that would make his brother Danny better.

But marriage to Ruby had put paid to his dreams. She had got into trouble running up debts all over town, and Nick had had to pay them off. It had taken every penny he had ever saved.

Dora looked at his downcast expression. 'Don't get too fed up about it,' she said bracingly. 'We saved the money before, we can do it again. And once I've passed my State Finals, I'll be earning a bit more.'

His expression darkened. 'It's not fair you should have to help pay for my mistake.'

She put out her hand to cover his. 'It's our future I'm saving for, Nick Riley.'

'I suppose you're right.' He gave a reluctant smile. 'Tell you what, I'll go and see Jimmy my old trainer. He should be able to fix me up with a few fights.'

Dora frowned. 'Are you sure that's a good idea? You haven't been in the ring for months. Not since you fractured your pelvis—'

She suppressed a shudder at the memory. Nick had almost been killed last October, and it still terrified her to think how close she had come to losing him. His injuries had healed well, but she wasn't sure how he would fare in the ring.

'We'll find out, won't we?' He shrugged his broad shoulders. 'What else can I do?'

'I don't want you hurt.'

He grinned. 'You know me, love. I haven't met the bloke yet who can lay a glove on me!'

Chapter Ten

'What do you mean, he's disappeared?' Lucy demanded once she was face to face with her mother.

'I told you, he's vanished into thin air.' Lady Clarissa curled up in a leather-covered wing armchair, as small and fragile-looking as a child. 'I telephoned his office but he hasn't been seen for three days.' She lifted a glass shakily to her lips.

'Have you tried his club?' Lucy asked.

Her mother shot her a filthy look. 'Do you think I'm stupid? Of course, that was the first place I tried. They haven't seen him in nearly a week.' She turned her tear-ravaged face towards the window. 'This is it, isn't it? He's finally left us.'

'Oh, for heaven's sake, Mother!' Lucy dismissed impatiently. 'Father wouldn't do such a thing.'

'I know you refuse to believe the worst of your father, but it's true. I'm sure of it,' her mother insisted. 'A wife always knows these things.' She sighed dramatically.

Lucy ignored her as she stood at the window and tried to force herself to think. Below her, people in Eaton Place were going about their business in the afternoon sunshine, unaware that her world had been thrown into turmoil.

And to think, a few hours ago she had been so free from care, pleased with herself because Sister had given her a special job to do. And now . . .

'I'm going to ruin him,' her mother declared, self-pity turning to anger. 'I shall destroy Bernard's good name.

He's not going to get away with humiliating me like this.'

A thought struck Lucy then. 'Are his clothes missing?'

Her mother shrugged. 'How should I know?'

'Didn't you think to look? Surely if he was intending to leave he would have taken his belongings with him?'

'I suppose you're right,' her mother agreed. She took another sip of her drink and stared towards the window, not moving.

Lucy sighed. 'I'll go and look, shall I?'

'Would you, darling? I don't think I could bear to.'

Her father's room was uncompromisingly masculine and unadorned. The musky scent of his cologne lingered on the air. He had it specially blended in Paris so it was as unique as he was.

Lucy took a deep breath and threw open the wardrobe doors. All her father's suits, tailored in Savile Row, were there, along with a neat row of his handmade Italian leather shoes. On his dresser was a walnut inlaid box containing his cufflinks and collar studs.

Lucy allowed herself to breathe out. In a way, she had been hoping that he had packed his bags and taken everything. At least then she might know he was safe.

The alternative was too awful to contemplate.

She hurried back downstairs and met Jameson, crossing the hall carrying a crystal glass on a silver tray.

'What's that?' Lucy asked.

'Her ladyship asked for more gin, Miss Lucy.'

'Take it away and bring us some tea instead.'

'But—'

'Take it away, Jameson. Please?'

Their eyes met and held for a moment.

'Very good, Miss Lucy.'

Her mother was still curled in the armchair, a cheek

resting on her hand, like an artist's model in repose. She sprang to life when Lucy walked in.

'Well?' she said.

Lucy shook her head. 'Everything is still there. Nothing has been taken.'

Her mother's mood instantly changed. She sprang from her armchair, her hand pressed to her mouth. 'Oh God, something has happened to him!' Her voice quavered. 'He must have had an accident.'

'Surely someone would have informed us if he had?' Lucy said, but her mother wasn't listening.

'That must be it,' she whispered. 'He's had an accident. He could be lying injured somewhere . . .'

'Stop it, Mother. Thinking like that isn't going to do any good.'

'Or perhaps he's dead? Perhaps he fell in the river and was washed away by the tide. You hear of such things happening, don't you? It could be weeks before they find him—'

'Mother, please!' Lucy snapped. Clarissa shut up at once, surprised into silence.

'Really, Lucy,' she said, when she'd found her voice again. 'I was only—'

They were interrupted by a knock on the door. Jameson entered, bringing the tea tray.

He cleared his throat. 'Mr Bird is here to see you, your ladyship,' he announced.

'Gordon?' Clarissa sat up.

'Thank God!' Lucy cried. Uncle Gordon would know what to do. He of all people would know where her father was. There was bound to be a simple explanation, a business trip that her mother had forgotten about or something similar.

But then her godfather walked in, and Lucy saw his

lugubrious expression and realised he was as worried as they were.

'Clarissa, my dear. I've been away from the office for a few days and my secretary has just told me you are looking for Bernard. Is it true? He is missing?'

'Oh, Gordon!' Her mother fell into his arms, sobbing.

'It's true, Uncle Gordon.' Lucy took charge. 'Mother says she hasn't seen him for three days. And he hasn't been to his club for nearly a week. But none of his belongings have been taken, so we don't know if he's really gone or . . .' She stopped talking, not trusting herself to speak.

Gordon nodded, his face grim. He didn't seem surprised, Lucy noticed.

She watched him carefully as she busied herself pouring tea for them. Gordon pacified her mother and settled her back into her seat and sat himself down in the wing chair opposite.

Her father's chair. It seemed odd to see someone else sitting there, Lucy thought as she placed the cup and saucer on a table beside him.

Lucy perched on the tapestry-covered couch. 'Where is he, Uncle Gordon?' she asked quietly.

Her godfather turned sad, heavy-lidded eyes towards hers. 'I wish I knew, child,' he sighed. But once again, Lucy had the feeling he knew more than he was willing to say.

Lucy tried to compose herself as she sipped her tea, but her hand was shaking so much she could barely hold the cup.

She put the cup down. 'Is it something to do with the problem with the bank?'

Gordon's eyes met hers. 'How did you know about that?'

'I heard you and Father arguing about it, on the night of the party. You seemed very worried.'

'What's this?' her mother demanded, interrupting them. 'What are you talking about? What bank?'

But Lucy had already guessed. 'Is my father's business in trouble, Uncle Gordon?'

'Trouble? Of course it isn't in trouble!' Clarissa gave a shrill laugh. 'What is she talking about, Gordon . . . Gordon?'

Lucy kept her eyes fixed on her godfather's face. 'How bad is it?' she whispered.

'Very bad, I'm afraid.' His expression was grave. 'Your father has been making plans to expand the business into Europe by taking over several factories in Germany and France, which has meant borrowing rather a lot of money. More than the banks were willing to lend.' He put down his cup. 'Bernard has had to mortgage everything to make this deal happen, but it isn't the first time he's taken such a risk. He was confident it would come good in the end, just as it always has before.'

'But this time it didn't?' Lucy guessed.

Gordon shook his head. 'I'm afraid not. Three days ago we discovered that the factories in Germany had been taken over by the government there. Your father now owes a fortune on something he no longer owns.'

Lucy stared at him, stunned. 'But that can't be true,' she whispered. 'Father would never have made a mistake like that. He's far too astute . . .'

'There you go again, thinking your precious father is infallible!' Her mother's voice sounded harsh. 'You're as bad as he is, thinking he can do no wrong. But he has, hasn't he? That's so typical of Bernard, taking ridiculous risks. Now look where it's landed him. The stupid man has lost his business!'

Not just his business, Lucy thought. She turned back to Gordon Bird. 'How much?' she asked quietly.

Her godfather looked at her. He understood the question but from the expression on his face he didn't want to answer her, any more than she wanted to hear the answer.

'You said Father mortgaged everything on this deal,' she said, struggling to keep her voice even. 'What do you mean by everything?'

Gordon looked away, unable to meet her eyes. 'Everything he has,' he said. 'Including his personal fortune.'

'What?' Clarissa was looking from one to the other, frowning, trying to understand. 'What are you saying?'

Lucy fought to keep her voice even, even though she could feel her world beginning to crack around her. 'Uncle Gordon means we're going to lose the house and everything in it, Mother.'

'No!' Her mother's scream of anguish ripped through the air. 'No, I won't believe it! I can't believe it! The stupid, stupid man, how could he have done this to me?'

Lucy picked up the bell and summoned the butler.

'I think my mother would like some brandy, Jameson,' she said, surprising herself with her own calm. What did it matter if Mother drank herself senseless now? Nothing mattered any more.

She waited until Jameson had gone, then turned back to her godfather. 'Is there nothing we can do?'

Gordon paused for a moment, considering. 'I think the best course of action would be to stay quiet for now,' he said. 'The bank has faith in your father. That's why they were prepared to accept such a risky investment . . . because they believed he would make it pay off in the end. Even now they have found out about the German government taking over the factories there, they will still be expecting your father to pull off a miracle, as he has in the past. That's why they haven't moved in to foreclose yet.'

'Except there won't be a miracle this time,' Lucy said.

'We don't know that,' Gordon replied. 'We have no idea where your father is. He could be in Europe at this very moment, doing a deal that will save everything.' He tried to smile comfortingly at her. 'That's the kind of man he is.'

Or he might just have run away from the mess he's created, Lucy thought. Perhaps that was the kind of man he was, too?

But she understood that her godfather was trying to make her feel better, and so smiled in appreciation. 'And the best thing we can do is to keep quiet about his disappearance?'

Gordon nodded. 'It's vital the bank doesn't find out he's vanished. Otherwise they'll realise something is seriously wrong and act to wind up the loan, with disastrous consequences for you.'

'So what will we tell people?'

'We can say he's gone abroad, that he's in America drumming up new business. That will keep the bank happy for now. Believe me, they won't want to look foolish when it transpires they have lent so much money on a failed project. They won't ask too many difficult questions at the moment.'

'And hopefully, by the time they do, my father will be back home and everything will be sorted out,' Lucy said. It was all she could cling to, the idea that he would be able to make everything right, just as he always had.

Gordon gave her a narrow smile. 'Let's hope so, my dear,' he said. 'For everyone's sake.'

Chapter Eleven

Nick saw the gloved fist coming at his face seconds before it slammed into him. He tried to dodge the punch but his feet moved sluggishly, as if trapped in thick mud. He felt the sickening crunch of his jaw as the fist drove into it, the spasm of his neck muscles as his head jerked sideways from the force of the blow.

Stay on your feet . . . stay on your feet . . .

He staggered but somehow stayed upright, the roar of the crowd muffled by the ringing in his ears. He wasn't sure if they were yelling encouragement or outrage. The metallic taste of blood filled his mouth and pain blossomed in his head as the world blurred before his eyes.

Stay on your feet . . . stay on your feet . . .

It shouldn't have been this hard. He'd faced Jackie Masters in the ring four times, and each time had knocked him out before the end of round three. But now it was round six, and Nick was struggling.

Through a mist of pain he saw his opponent bobbing in front of him, fists raised, ready to strike again. Another hook like the last one, and Nick knew he'd be down. As Jackie took his swing, Nick's reflexes took over. He swerved, curving his body away from the blow, then came in with a swift uppercut to his opponent's exposed chin. He saw Jackie's eyes widen briefly in shock as he reeled backwards then hit the canvas like a felled tree. Nick felt his own knees buckling but willed himself to stay upright. He gulped in air, feeling the warm drip of blood off his chin as the referee counted his opponent out.

'Eight . . . nine . . . ten!'

The yells of the crowd seemed to be coming from a long way away. Nick barely knew what was happening as he felt his hand jerked into the air in salute. All he could think about was getting out of the ring before he collapsed.

Jimmy, his trainer, was furious as he sponged Nick's shattered jaw in the dingy back room.

'What did I tell you?' he said. 'I told you not to fight. I said this would happen. "Don't get in the ring again, Nick," I said. "It's too dangerous." But did you listen?'

'I won, didn't I?' He forced the words out, his lips already stiff with congealed blood.

'It was a lucky punch. Another minute and he would have had you on the ropes.' Jimmy's face was creased with anxiety as he pressed the sponge against Nick's face. 'You're not as quick as you once were – not since the accident. You can't get yourself out of trouble like you used to. And you don't have to look at me like that,' he went on. 'You might scare other people with that stare of yours, Nick Riley, but you don't scare me. I've known you since you were a nipper, don't forget. I'm not frightened to tell you the truth.'

'More's the pity,' Nick grunted. Jimmy was the only one brave enough to face up to him. He was like a father to Nick, far more so than his own useless father had ever been. Nick respected his trainer. Also, even though Jimmy hadn't been in the ring for thirty years, he still had the sinewy strength of someone who knew how to deliver a killer punch.

Nick was only angry with Jimmy because he was right. Nick's fractured pelvis might have healed, but it had slowed him down. He might still pack a punch like a freight train, but he couldn't dodge or weave away from blows liked he used to.

'I'm serious, Nick. I don't want to see you in the ring again,' Jimmy said.

'I ain't got a choice. I need the money.'

'Nothing's worth getting clobbered for, night after night.'

Nick thought of Dora. The idea of never being married to her was too dreadful for him to contemplate. 'That's where you're wrong,' he said.

Jimmy shook his head. 'Then I hope the next bloke you fight manages to knock some sense into you.'

After Jimmy had patched him up, Nick went to find Terry Willis, the promoter who'd arranged the fight. He was in the bar as usual, talking to a dark, thickset man Nick had never seen before.

'Nicky boy!' Nick caught a waft of whisky on Terry's breath as the promoter turned to face him. 'Were your ears burning? We were just talking about you. What are you drinking?'

'I'm not. I've come for my money.'

Terry turned to him, his smile slack in his narrow, foxy face. 'Have you now? I'm not so sure I should pay you, after that performance.'

'I won, didn't I?'

'By the skin of your teeth.' He shook his head. 'It's not what I've come to expect from you, Nick. Not what the crowd expects, either.' He sighed. 'Bit of a disappointment, to be honest—'

Nick's hand flashed out, grabbing Terry's lapels. 'I won,' he growled. 'And now I want my money.'

Terry grinned nervously. 'No need to get uppity, son,' he squeaked. 'I was only having a laugh. Of course you can have your money.'

Nick released him, and Terry took a moment to straighten

his pinstripe suit before he reached into his pocket and pulled out a wad of notes.

'I see what you mean, Terry. He's got a short fuse, all right!' the stranger said. 'I reckon he's just what I'm looking for.'

Nick turned around to face the man who had spoken. He looked as if he'd been battered himself a few times, judging from his flattened nose and cauliflower ears.

'And who are you when you're at home?'

'Let me introduce you to Lew Smith,' Terry said. 'He's in the fight game, like myself.'

'Hardly!' The other man grinned, showing off a mouthful of gold teeth. 'I provide a different kind of – entertainment.'

Nick narrowed his eyes. There was something about Lew Smith he didn't care for. 'Yeah? And what's that then?'

'Ever done any bare-knuckle fighting?'

Nick nodded. 'A bit.' He'd been a street fighter when he was a kid, to earn money for his family. Luckily, Jimmy had found him and encouraged him into the ring instead. And Nick was grateful for it. Bare-knuckle boxing was brutal.

'Lew runs the boxing booth at his family's travelling fair,' Terry explained. 'He's always looking for likely lads to fight all comers. Ain't that right, Lew?'

The man nodded. 'It's easy money for a fighter,' he said. 'Most of the fellows who step up are amateurs, wanting to try their luck and impress the girls. A couple of taps and they're usually down. But, of course, you have to put on a decent show for the crowds, make 'em think the local lads stand a chance. That way they might come back for another go, see?' He put down his drink. 'So how would you like to earn some decent money? I reckon it would suit you down to the ground. And you wouldn't have to get battered every night for it either.' He cocked his head. 'What do you say?'

Nick hesitated. Once upon a time he'd hoped to go to

America and fight Max Baer, the world champion. He would have been insulted at the very idea of taking on strangers in a bare-knuckle boxing booth. And God only knew what Jimmy would say about it.

But then he thought about Dora. He wanted her more than he'd ever wanted any boxing title.

'I'm interested,' he said.

Jess looked around to make sure no one was watching then aimed a vicious kick at the vacuum cleaner.

Stupid, cumbersome thing! The supervisor at the main nurses' home was very taken with it, insisted it was a marvellous labour-saving device that would make their lives much easier, but Jess couldn't see how. By the time she'd hauled its heavy iron bulk up three flights of stairs, she was bathed in sweat and more exhausted than if she'd used a broom.

And then there was the noise . . . It bellowed like an angry bull, which generally brought Sister Sutton or one of the students running out to complain. As if Jess enjoyed it any more than they did! She went back to her room at the end of every day with ringing ears and aching temples.

And then there were some days, like today, when the wretched thing just wouldn't start. It squatted in the middle of the students' sitting room, silent and malevolent.

Jess flopped down on one of the settees and tucked a tendril of damp hair back under her cap. She wasn't even supposed to be cleaning in here, but Sister Sutton had insisted.

'But I cleaned the sitting room yesterday,' Jess had protested.

'You obviously didn't make a very good job of it, or it wouldn't need doing again,' Sister Sutton snapped back.

'You told me I had to clean the bathrooms this morning first thing.'

'No, I didn't,' Sister Sutton said.

'Yes, you did. You said . . .'

'Good gracious, girl, I think I should know what I said or didn't say, don't you?' Sister Sutton glared at her. 'Now please don't argue with me, or I shall start to think you're a troublemaker.'

So now Jess had to waste her time cleaning a room that was already spotless. She stood up with a sigh and started plumping the cushions to make it look as if she'd been busy. As she did, she noticed a book wedged down the side of the settee.

She pulled it out. It was another textbook, *Anatomy and Physiology for Nurses* by Evelyn Pearce. Jess couldn't resist flicking it open. She had been reading the students' textbooks whenever she found them in their rooms, snatching a few minutes here and there to stop and devour a chapter. And the more she read, the more she started to understand all the long words and Latin names. And the more she understood, the more fascinated she became. Until she had started reading books like these, she'd had no idea how extraordinary the human body was, or how all the bones and muscles and organs worked in harmony with each other. It was like a complex puzzle, the pieces fitting perfectly together.

How could the girls sigh and roll their eyes and complain about having to study something so wonderful? Jess wondered.

She was so transfixed by her reading she barely caught the flash of brown and white out of the corner of her eye. She looked up sharply to see Sister Sutton standing in the doorway, Sparky dancing around her fat ankles.

Jess dropped the book and jumped to her feet. 'I – I'm sorry, Sister,' she stammered. 'The vacuum cleaner overheated again, so I was waiting for it to settle—'

'What were you reading?' Sister Sutton's brows met in a frown over her beady eyes.

'Just a book I found, Sister. I wasn't doing any harm,' Jess gabbled on. 'I was going to put it back, honest.'

'Never mind that.' Sister Sutton held out her hand. 'Give it to me, please. I sincerely hope it wasn't one of those cheap romance novels? I've warned the girls before about filling their heads with—'

She fell silent as Jess handed her the book. Sister turned it over in her hands and then flicked through the pages as if she suspected a trick.

'What were you doing with this?' she asked finally.

'Reading it, Sister.'

Sister Sutton's frown deepened. 'Tell the truth, girl. You couldn't possibly understand a book like this.'

Jess' skin prickled with indignation. 'Yes, I do. You can ask me a question about it, if you like?'

'Don't be insolent.' The Home Sister looked down at the book, then back at her. 'Why would you want to read this?'

'I find it interesting.' Jess lifted her chin. 'How the human body works and everything.'

'I wish some of the students shared your interest,' Sister Sutton grunted. She tucked the book in her pocket. 'But may I remind you, you are a maid, not a nurse. It is not your place to study.'

'No, Sister.'

'Now get on with your work. I don't expect to find you slacking again.'

As she turned to leave, Jess said, 'Please, Sister, I've done everything you told me to do.'

Sister Sutton swung round. 'Everything?'

'Yes, Sister.'

'Then you'd best go up to the top floor and clean the landings. And take that thing with you.' She nodded at the vacuum cleaner. 'It gives Sparky a headache.'

Chapter Twelve

Effie sat at the back of the stuffy classroom, chin resting in her hands, fighting to keep her eyes open as Sister Parker the Sister Tutor explained how to clean a broom.

'Let me remind you, Nurses, good work is not done with dirty brooms,' she rapped out in her Scottish accent. 'They should be washed once a week by dipping the bristles into boiling water with a little washing soda. The handles must, of course, be scrubbed thoroughly with soap and a brush.'

Effie looked around the classroom. The other girls in her set were all scribbling furiously, their heads down. Effie frowned at her own empty page. How on earth could they find so much to write about washing a broom?

In the two weeks she had been in PTS, she had seen enough of brooms to last a lifetime. Every morning they had to sweep and damp dust the practice room, cleaning out lockers no one ever used and making the bed that no one ever slept in. When they weren't cleaning and making beds, they spent the morning rolling bandages, stitching splints, and learning to wash the glassy-eyed dummy, in the Nightingale's approved way.

And when they weren't in the practice room, they were crammed together on hard wooden benches in the classroom, listening to dreary lectures on nutrition and physiology, or reciting lists of muscles and bones.

Effie gazed longingly towards the window. It was a glorious day outside, and she hadn't had a breath of fresh air for ages. She'd thought once she came to London her life would be one exciting round of parties, dances and trips to the cinema. But so far the most exciting thing to happen to her had been her set's guided tour of the local sanitation works.

The heat of the classroom overcame her and she stifled a yawn with the back of her hand. Almost immediately, Sister Parker's voice rang out, loud and clear across the room.

'I'm sorry. Are we boring you, O'Hara?'

Effie looked up. Sister Parker's sharp gaze was fixed on her. 'Er . . .'

'Perhaps you feel there's nothing more I can teach you?' Sister Parker went on. 'After two weeks, I imagine you already know everything there is to know, is that correct?'

'Um, I – not at all, Sister.' Effie found her voice at last.

'Let's see, shall we? Perhaps you'd like to explain why we should not use a dry duster when we clean?'

'Er—' Effie heard a couple of unkind sniggers coming from the front row of benches as she scrabbled around in her non-existent notes for the answer. The girl next to her, a bespectacled mouse called Prudence Mulhearn, slid her notes a few inches closer. But squint as she might, Effie couldn't make out the other girl's spidery handwriting.

Sister Parker sighed. 'Don't trouble yourself, O'Hara, I can see we're never going to get a sensible answer out of you. Padgett?' She turned to one of the girls in the front row.

'Because a dry duster would only flick the dust from one place to another, Sister,' she replied primly.

'That is correct, thank you.' Sister Parker turned back to Effie. 'You see, O'Hara, you might know more if you bothered to listen. Unless that is too much trouble for you?'

'No, Sister.' Effie lowered her gaze to the top of her desk, heat flooding her face.

'You have a long way to go before you will prove to me that you deserve your place here. And you can start by staying behind and copying out all the notes on this afternoon's lecture. After which, perhaps, you may finally understand what a duster and broom are for. Because I have to say, from watching you in the practice room this morning, you seem to have failed to grasp their function at all.'

It wasn't fair, Effie thought later, as she sat alone on the bench, her hand cramped around her pen. All she'd done was yawn. She didn't even know how Sister Parker had seen her do it – the old biddy must have eyes in the back of her head.

Sister's eyes were fixed on her now. Every time Effie took a moment to glance up from her paper, Sister Parker was standing in front of her, hands folded, unblinking blue gaze watching her from behind her pebble spectacles.

Finally Effie finished copying out the notes, and handed them to Sister Parker to inspect. She could feel perspiration trickling down inside her heavy uniform as she waited for the elderly Sister Tutor's approval. If Sister Parker made her copy out the notes again Effie didn't know what she would do.

But just as she doubted her legs would hold her up any longer, Sister Parker handed her back the sheaf of notes.

'Perhaps that will teach you to pay more attention in future,' she said. 'Really, O'Hara, I know you come from a long and illustrious line of nurses, but I have to say I am most disappointed in you so far. Most disappointed.' She shook her head in sorrow.

'Yes, Sister.'

It was a relief to escape back to the nurses' home,

although not such a relief when she found Katie in their room. Effie groaned inwardly. She'd forgotten it was her sister's evening off.

Katie sat on the bed, brushing out her bushy dark curls. 'Why are you so late?' she asked.

Effie thought about making up an excuse, but she knew there was no point. Like their mother and the rest of Effie's sisters, Katie seemed to have a way of knowing when she was being untruthful. It was most annoying.

'I had to stay behind and copy out some notes,' she said, bracing herself for another lecture.

Katie stopped tidying her hair and lowered her brush. 'You didn't? Oh, Effie, I hope you haven't been getting into trouble?'

'No, I haven't!' Effie flopped down on the bed and pulled off her shoes. 'I just yawned, that's all. I didn't mean to do it,' she added quickly, seeing her sister's face fall. 'It was so hot and stuffy in that classroom, it's a wonder I didn't doze off completely!'

But Katie wasn't listening. 'You know, you shouldn't upset Sister Parker,' she said. 'You have to get through PTS if you want to work on the wards. It's only twelve weeks, Effie,' she pleaded. 'You can manage that long without getting into trouble, surely?'

'Of course I can. You don't need to talk to me as if I'm a child!' Effie flared back at her. 'For heaven's sake, it was just a stupid yawn, that's all. It's not the end of the world.'

'It will be if you don't pass PTS.'

'I'll pass it, don't you worry.' Effie rubbed her cramped toes. 'You look nice,' she said, trying to distract her sister. 'Where are you going tonight?'

'I'm out dancing with Tom.'

Effie brightened. 'Could I come?'

'Certainly not!'

'Oh, go on, Kitty. I haven't been for a night out since I arrived, and I so want to have some fun.'

'You can have fun with the rest of your set.'

Effie rolled her eyes. 'They wouldn't know the meaning of the word! Honest to God, all they ever do is study. They've got their nose in books all the time, and when they haven't they're chanting lists of bones to each other. I've never met such a boring bunch of girls in my whole life.'

'It wouldn't hurt you to settle down and do some studying yourself,' Katie said, through a mouth full of hairpins. 'I don't think you've even looked at those books since you arrived.'

'Not you, too!' Effie stared at her sister in despair. And to think Katie had always been her favourite sister. 'Mammy would be proud of you. You've turned out just like our Bridget.'

But in spite of all her pleas and cajoling, Katie still refused to take Effie out dancing with her. When she'd gone, Effie made a half-hearted attempt to look through one of her books, then gave up and wandered downstairs to find the other girls. If she was going to be bored to death, she might as well do it in company, she decided.

As she'd expected, they were gathered in the sitting room downstairs, studying. Half a dozen pairs of eyes looked up as Effie walked into the room, then immediately dropped back to their books.

Effie waited for someone to speak to her, but no one did. She prowled around the sitting room, searching for something to do. On either side of the empty fireplace were shelves filled with tattered old novels, board games and a pack of cards, but nothing sparked her interest.

Effie took the cards out of their box and counted them, just for something to do. She couldn't imagine any of the girls wanting to play whist with her. She would have more luck asking that glassy-eyed dummy in Sister Tutor's classroom.

'Why don't we put some music on?' Her voice sounded overly bright in the silence of the room. She was halfway across the room to the gramophone when one of the girls, Anna Padgett, looked up.

'Look here, do you have to? We're trying to study.'

'Don't you ever stop?' Effie flicked through the records piled up beside the gramophone.

'Actually, no. There's too much to learn if we ever want to pass PTS. As you might find out if you ever bothered to do any work,' Anna muttered under her breath.

Effie glared at her. Anna Padgett had unofficially declared herself the head of their set, just because she had already done a year's training as a cadet nurse at another hospital. All the other girls looked up to her because of her age and experience, but Effie wasn't impressed.

'I thought you already knew it all?' she retaliated. Padgett certainly behaved as if she did. She was always going on and on about the way they did things at her old hospital.

Anna opened her mouth to speak, but Prudence Mulhearn got there first.

'Why don't you come and join us?' she suggested kindly. She was a tiny little thing, pale-haired and bespectacled. It made Effie laugh when they were paired together to practise their washing or bedmaking. Prudence barely came up to her shoulder. 'You never know, you might find it useful.'

'Oh, leave her be,' Anna dismissed the suggestion. 'If she wants to fall behind and fail PTS, that's her look out.'

Effie had been about to refuse Prudence's offer. But Anna Padgett's spiteful comment piqued her, and she grabbed the book Prudence was holding out.

'Right,' she said. 'What are we studying?'

'Diabetic diets,' Prudence replied, her nose already buried in her notes. 'We're trying to work out the Line Ration scheme, but I simply can't understand it.'

'It's quite simple,' Anna explained. 'The doctor prescribes a certain number of Rations every day. One Ration is one complete Line and consists of one A and one B portion. Any A portion can be added to any B portion, but you mustn't combine two A or two B portions.'

'And the A portions are carbohydrates?' Prudence said

'Exactly. There's a list of them at the back of the book.'

'We should test each other,' one of the other girls, Celia Wilson, suggested. 'One of us could call out a food, and the others have to say whether it's A or B.'

The next moment they were throwing words across the room to each other and calling out the answers. Effie stared at them blankly. How could anyone get so excited about how much carbohydrate there was in a stick of rhubarb?

Of course, Anna Padgett knew all the answers without even having to look at her book.

'I learned it all at St Martha's,' she said dismissively, when one of the other girls admired her knowledge. 'I was on Male Chronics for a while, so we had a lot of patients on special diets.'

'Why did you decide to come here, then?' Effie asked. 'I wonder you didn't carry on at your old hospital. It would have saved you a year's training, surely?'

Anna Padgett sent her a pitying look. 'Because I wanted a certificate from the Nightingale, of course,' she said. 'Everyone knows it's one of the best hospitals in the country. If you've trained here, it sets you apart from all other nurses. Surely you know that?'

'I didn't,' Effie admitted. 'I only came because all my sisters trained here.'

She felt the other girls staring at her.

'Do you really want to be a nurse?' Anna asked.

'Of course.' A blush rose in Effie's face. The truth was, she hadn't really thought about it. She was so keen to escape from Killarney that she would have done anything that meant getting on that boat to England. And following in her sisters' footsteps was the easiest thing to do.

And now she was here, of course she wanted to see it through and become a nurse. But she didn't see why the other girls had to make such hard work of it.

She closed the book and handed it back to Prudence. 'I've had enough of studying,' she said. 'I'm going outside to get some fresh air.'

'That won't help you get through PTS,' she heard Anna mutter as she closed the door behind her.

Effie hurried along the hall towards the front door and barged straight into Jess, who was laden down with a mop and bucket. The bucket fell from her hands, slopping dirty water all over the tiled hall floor.

'Oh, I'm so sorry. Here, let me help—' Effie reached for the mop, but Jess held it away from her.

'Do you want to get me the sack?' she hissed.

'But it was my fault.'

'All the same, Sister Sutton would have a proper fit if she came out and saw you cleaning up after me.'

Effie watched helplessly as Jess wielded the mop, cleaning up the dirty puddle. 'It's my fault for using the front door,' the maid muttered. 'Sister Sutton gave me strict instructions to use the basement steps to the kitchen. But I didn't think it would hurt to take a short cut just this once, especially as she's still at supper . . .'

'And then I knocked you off your feet. I'm sorry,' Effie sighed. 'I can't seem to do right for doing wrong today.'

'I know how you feel,' Jess sympathised. 'I was supposed

to finish an hour ago, but I'm all behind with my work.' She finished mopping up the spilled water and squeezed the mop into the bucket. 'There, all done. Sister Sutton will be none the wiser.'

She looked hot and worn out, Effie thought. Her dark hair was fastened up in a bun, but stray strands had escaped and clung damply to her face.

An idea struck her. 'Have you got the rest of the night off?' she asked.

Jess nodded. 'Thank the lord.'

'Why don't we go out?'

'What? You and me?' Jess couldn't have looked more startled if Effie had suggested they should sprout wings and fly off the roof of the nurses' home.

'Why not? I'm going to go mad if I don't get out of this place soon. And anyway, I haven't thanked you properly for finding my luggage for me.' Effie beamed at her. 'I've got some money. Not much, but I could treat you to a cup of tea in the café on the corner. What do you think?'

Jess' frown deepened. 'I think,' she said, 'that we shouldn't even be talking to each other, let alone going off for cups of tea.'

Effie stared at her blankly. 'Why not?'

'Because . . . because that's not the way they do things here.' Jess darted a look over her shoulder towards the front door, as if she expected Sister Sutton to come barging through it at any second. 'Besides, I'm already going out tonight,' she added.

'Oh.'

Effie's disappointment must have shown on her face, because Jess added more kindly, 'Look, why don't you try and make friends with your own lot? You've got far more in common with them than you have with me.'

Effie glanced towards the sitting room. Laughter rang out from inside. 'Want to bet?' she said sadly.

The image of Effie O'Hara's forlorn face stayed with Jess on the bus ride to Whitechapel.

Poor girl, she seemed so lonely. It was a shame, thought Jess, because Effie was so sweet. She reminded her of an over-enthusiastic puppy, bounding up to everyone, wanting to play and constantly being brushed off.

Jess got off the bus and walked down Commercial Street to the Toynbee Hall Institute. It was an extravagant red-brick building, its gabled roofs and mullioned windows a grand contrast to the dreary shops and warehouses surrounding it. The hall had been built by Victorian philanthropists to offer ordinary people the chance to improve themselves. And every week for the past two years Jess had been taking herself off for night classes to do just that. She was only weeks away from the final credits she needed to achieve her School Certificate.

It hadn't been easy, keeping her studies secret from her stepmother. She knew Gladys would try to stand in her way if she could. All the Jagos were suspicious of learning. Neither Jess' father nor any of her uncles had ever bothered with school, and her cousins all hopped the wag more often than not.

But with Gladys it went much deeper. She was jealous of anything that reminded her of Jess' mother. The day after she moved in, she had sold all Sarah Jago's clothes and belongings to the rag and bone man, and anything she couldn't sell she'd burned in a bonfire in the yard while Jess sat sobbing on the doorstep.

Gladys could have sold her mother's books too, but she threw them on the fire, instead. Jess could still remember her stepmother's expression, twisted with spite, illu-minated in the flickering light from the flames.

'Sarah ain't going to be needing books where she's gone,' she had said.

Between Gladys' malice and Cyril's thieving hands, Jess had had to keep her schoolbooks and her studies secret. But not any more. Now she was living at the nurses' home, she could read and study as much as she pleased. She had even started coming to the Institute for extra classes, just because she could.

The class finished, and Jess followed her classmates into the main hall. The other rooms were turning out, and the hall was filled with people pushing their way towards the doors.

Jess paused beside them to look at the noticeboard. Sometimes important people came to the Institute to speak, and she didn't like to miss anything.

'See anything you fancy?'

She looked round, and was surprised to see Sam the book-seller's son, grinning at her. 'What are you doing here?'

'Same as you, I expect.' He pointed to the book wedged under his arm.

'You're taking night classes?'

'Don't look so shocked!' He grinned. 'I don't want to work on my dad's stall all my life, ta very much!' He patted the book. 'With any luck, this time next year I'm going to be an engineer. How about you?'

'School Cert.' She stared at him defiantly, waiting for him to make some offhand comment. But he didn't.

'Good for you,' he said. 'I'm surprised we haven't run into each other before.'

'I've only just started coming on a Wednesday.'

They stood there, jostled by the surging throng. 'I don't suppose you fancy a cup of tea?' Sam asked.

Jess eyed the clock at the far end of the hall. 'I ought to be getting back.'

Sam looked as if he might try to persuade her, but at that moment someone called out his name. Jess looked over his shoulder towards the gaggle of young men standing on the other side of the hall. 'Shouldn't you be with your mates?'

'I'd rather be with you.'

'I told you, I have to get back.'

One of the young men called out again. Sam glanced over at him, then back at Jess. 'Some other time then? Next week? After the class?'

Jess smiled. 'If I say yes, will you stop asking me?'

'It's a deal.'

'Then I s'pose I'll see you next week, won't I?'

Chapter Thirteen

The first thing Dora saw when she walked through the back door of number twenty-eight Griffin Street was her grandmother Winnie with her ear pressed against a glass at the wall.

'All right, Nanna?' she grinned.

'Shhh! I think June Riley's got a new bloke next door, but I can't make out who it is.'

Dora took off her cardigan and hung it on the back of a kitchen chair. 'You know what they say about eaves-droppers, don't you?' she said. 'They don't hear any good of themselves.'

'I can't hear anything, good or not.' Nanna polished the glass with her sleeve. 'This thing's no bleeding good. I reckon your mum must have got it cheap off the market.'

Dora pressed her lips together to stop herself smiling. 'Or maybe your hearing's going, Nanna?'

'There ain't nothing wrong with my ears, young lady.' Nanna Winnie glared at her. 'To what do we owe the pleasure of this visit, anyway?'

'It's my afternoon off.'

'I wonder you don't want to spend it with that bloke of yours.'

Winnie's toothless mouth was a thin line of disapproval, and Dora knew why. She had given up trying to explain the situation with Nick to her grandmother. Winnie might not have any time for that hussy Ruby Pike, as she called her, but as far as she was concerned Nick was still the girl's husband and Dora shouldn't be having anything to do with him.

'Where's Mum?' Dora changed the subject.

'In the scullery.' Nanna nodded towards the thin curtain that separated the kitchen from the tiny annexe.

Dora left her grandmother pressing her ear against the wall again and pushed through the curtain into the scullery. Her mother was standing at the stove, stirring a bubbling pot.

'Got enough for an extra one?' Dora asked.

Rose Doyle turned to face her, a smile lighting up her tired face. In her early forties she was still beautiful, although the past few years had left more threads of grey in her dark hair and lines around her brown eyes.

'Dora, love!' Rose reached for a tea towel to wipe her hands. 'Of course there's enough for you. You know I always cook enough to feed an army!' She smiled at her daughter. 'This is a lovely surprise, I must say.'

'I dunno if Nanna was too pleased to see me.' Dora grimaced.

'Take no notice of her,' Rose said. 'Her arthritis is playing her up again, I expect.'

'I think she's still got the hump about me and Nick.'

'Well, it's none of her business.'

Dora watched her mother as she turned back to the stove. Nanna might have had plenty to say when she found out about Dora and Nick, but Rose had kept quiet on the subject.

Her silence worried Dora. The Doyles had to live next door to Ruby's family, and even though Ruby was the one who had lied and cheated, Dora knew Lettie Pike would take it out on Rose that her daughter was now courting Nick. Dora hated the thought of her mother suffering any shame because of her.

Rose Doyle had already been through enough in her

life. Dora's father had died when she was eight years old, leaving Rose to bring up five children on her own. She had remarried, but Alf Doyle had abandoned her, leaving her alone and penniless yet again, this time with a baby son to feed too.

'You know it wasn't my fault their marriage broke up, don't you?' said Dora.

'I know that, love.' Rose went back to stirring the contents of the pot.

'And it's not as if Nick and I are doing anything wrong. We ain't even properly courting,' Dora went on, addressing her mother's turned back. 'We daren't, not until this divorce business is all sorted out . . .'

Her mother put down her spoon. 'Why are you telling me this?'

'Because I want you to understand,' Dora pleaded. 'I'm sick and tired of people thinking I'm some kind of tart who goes after married men.'

'Who'd ever think something like that?'

'Lettie Pike. And Nanna thinks so, too. I can tell.'

'Well, I don't,' Rose said firmly. 'You listen to me, Dora Doyle. I know you're a good girl, and so does your nanna. She's only upset because she wants you to be happy with a nice young man, same as I do.'

'I am happy,' Dora said. 'I just wish I could tell everyone, that's all. But I can't talk about Nick. I can't even hold his hand or say his name out loud . . .' She stopped abruptly, knowing she was about to cry. The Doyle women never shed tears if they could help it.

'I know, love. But you will one day.' Rose patted her arm. 'You've just got to be patient, that's all. Things will come right in the end, you'll see.'

'I hope you're right.' Dora sent her a rueful look. 'So you don't think I'm a disgrace, then?'

'You could never disgrace this family, my girl. Not in a thousand years.'

'That's not what Lettie Pike thinks.'

'Lettie Pike knows better than to speak her mind in front of me.'

Dora noticed her mother's white-knuckled hand gripping the spoon. Rose was a woman of great dignity and forbearance, but she turned into a tigress when it came to anyone mistreating her children.

Dora helped her with the cooking, boiling and draining potatoes for the shepherd's pie Rose was making. They chatted as they worked together, and her mother was full of news about the rest of the family. Especially Lily, Dora's sister-in-law, who was due to give birth in the autumn.

'You should see her, she's blooming.' Rose beamed. 'It will be so lovely to have a baby in the house again, especially now Little Alfie's not so little any more.'

'I can't believe he's nearly six.' Dora shook her head as she rifled in the drawer for a fork to mash the potatoes with.

'Nor can I, love. It doesn't seem five minutes since he was a baby in my arms, and now he's off to school. Doing well, too. You should see how he reads.' She sighed. 'I only wish his dad—'

Dora glanced over her shoulder. Rose was staring out of the window, deep in thought. Her mother barely mentioned Alf Doyle's name these days. Dora hadn't been sorry to see her stepfather leave after the abuse she and her sister Josie had suffered at his hands. Her mother hadn't been sorry either, after finding out that Alf had betrayed her with another woman – and a young girl at that. But Dora wondered if her mother missed having a man in her life.

'It sounds as if he's going to take after our Josie,' said

Dora, to distract her mother. 'She's the clever one of the family.'

'As long as he doesn't take after his sister Bea, that'll be a blessing.'

Dora stopped mashing and looked up at her mother. 'Why? What's she been up to?'

As Rose opened her mouth to speak, the back gate crashed open and the yard was filled with the raucous sounds of girls' voices.

'Talk of the devil!' Rose rolled her eyes. 'I s'pose we'd better see what trouble she's in now.'

Josie and Bea fell through the back door, fighting like cats. Little Alfie, who was with his sisters, immediately ran to his nanna and buried his face in her skirt.

'You can't tell me what to do!' Bea screamed, grabbing a handful of Josie's dark hair.

'Yes, I can. I'm the eldest.'

'*I'm* the eldest,' Dora said, planting herself between them. The girls stopped fighting and turned to her.

Bea pushed her dishevelled red curls off her face. 'You can't tell me what to do either,' she said truculently. 'You don't even live here any more.'

'Never mind all that. What's going on?' Rose said. Bea and Josie shot poisonous looks at each other, but neither of them spoke. 'Come on.' Rose folded her arms. 'No one's going to get any tea in this house until this is sorted out, so you might as well speak up.'

'She's been hopping the wag from school,' Josie spoke up first.

'And you couldn't wait to tell on me, could you? Goody two shoes!'

Rose turned to Bea. 'Is this true? Why ain't you been to school?'

'I was ill.'

121

Dora looked at her sister, so defiant and full of herself. They looked alike, with their ginger curls and broad, freckled faces. But Bea was far more brazen than Dora had been at fourteen.

'Not too ill to run around the streets with your mates all day, I'll be bound,' Nanna muttered. 'Go on, what have you been up to?'

'I ain't saying,' Bea muttered sullenly.

'Well, if you don't want to go to school, you can always leave and go to work in the glue factory for ten hours a day, like I had to,' Nanna said. 'Then you'd know where you were well off!'

'I wouldn't mind going out to work,' Bea shot back. 'Then I could please myself what I did.'

'You please yourself anyway!' Josie said.

'Shut up, you!' And then they were fighting again, and it took all Dora's strength to pull them apart.

The atmosphere was tense around the tea table, with Bea and Josie sniping at each other.

'I dunno what's got into Bea,' Rose said, as Dora got ready to leave after tea. 'She's always been a handful, but she's such a madam these days. And secretive, too.'

'That's definitely not like our Bea!' Dora laughed. Her sister was well known for spilling secrets the second she heard them. 'Do you want me to have a word with her?'

Rose shook her head. 'Don't worry yourself about it, love. I expect she'll grow out of it soon enough.'

As Dora let herself out of the back gate she came face to face with Ruby, picking her way up the cobbled alley towards her.

They both froze for a second, eyeing each other like cats, poised for a fight. Then Ruby smiled.

'Hello, stranger. Fancy seeing you here.'

'I was visiting my mum.' Dora's voice felt tight. It was

so strange to think she and Ruby had once been so close. Now Dora could barely think of anything to say to her. 'Have you just finished work?'

'Yes, thank God. I'm back at Gold's Garments. The old man gave me my job back, would you believe?' Ruby adjusted the rakish angle of her feathered hat. As always, she looked like a fashion model, her crimson dress clinging to every curve of her body. 'I'm going home to change, then my Eric's taking me out dancing up west. I told him, I'm just as happy going to the Palais, but he wants to show me off.' She smiled at Dora. 'How are you and Nick getting on?'

Dora stiffened. 'I dunno what you mean.'

'Come off it, Dor! I know you two are courting. Look at you, you blush every time his name's mentioned. And why else would Nick be round here, bothering me for a divorce?' Ruby laughed. 'Don't worry, girl, I ain't going to tell anyone. Your secret's safe with me. I owe you that, I suppose.'

Dora flashed her a look. Ruby looked sincere enough, but Dora had never known a secret to be safe with her for more than five minutes. And just to make it worse, her mum Lettie was a ward maid at the Nightingale. She detested Dora, and would go to any lengths to cause trouble for her. Another reason why Dora and Nick had to be so secretive.

But she couldn't afford to get on the wrong side of Ruby, either. Who knew what damage she could do if she chose? And Dora knew from bitter experience how capricious her friend could be.

'At any rate, the sooner he gets that divorce sorted out, the better it will be for all of us, I reckon.'

'If he can afford it,' Dora said.

'Is that why he's taken this new job of his? I suppose

it pays better than being a hospital porter, doesn't it? Although it's a funny way to make a living if you ask me, getting knocked about!' Ruby giggled.

Dora stared at her. 'What are you talking about? What new job?'

'Don't tell me he hasn't told you? Oh, dear, have I let the cat out of the bag?' A slow smile spread across Ruby's face. 'Nick's going off with a travelling fair as a bare-knuckle boxer. Bit of a comedown for him if you ask me, but I suppose if he needs the money . . .'

'You're lying,' Dora said flatly.

'I'm only telling you what I heard.' Ruby's pretty face was the picture of injured innocence. 'My dad heard it from the landlord of the Rose and Crown. He reckons Nick's packing his job in today.' Her blue eyes glinted with malice. 'Fancy you not knowing that! Looks like your boyfriend's planning to run off without telling you, Dora Doyle.'

Nick was heavy-hearted as he trudged back to his lodgings in Spitalfields.

He'd put off telling Mr Hopkins for as long as he could, but finally knew he couldn't put it off any longer. In less than a week he would be on the road with Lew Smith's travelling fair.

The Head Porter had taken it better than Nick could have hoped.

'I can't say I'm not disappointed, son,' he'd said, reaching up to clap him on the shoulder. 'You're a good worker, one of the best I've had. And as you know, I don't give out compliments lightly.'

'Thank you, Mr Hopkins.' Nick replied, his voice gruff with emotion.

'I mean it, lad. I know we've had our differences in the

past, and I used to wonder if I was right to take a chance on you, given your background. But I'm not afraid to say you've proved me wrong. You're a decent, honest young man and you're not afraid of hard work. I always had high hopes that one day you might take my job, when I retire.' Mr Hopkins shook his head sadly. 'I only hope you're going somewhere that appreciates you. You deserve to do well.'

Nick could only nod, not trusting himself to speak. He hoped Mr Hopkins wouldn't ask him where he was going. He couldn't bear to see the respect disappear from the old man's eyes when Nick told him he was going to travel with the fair as a bare-knuckle boxer. He didn't even want to admit it to himself, he was too ashamed.

He didn't want to admit it to Dora either. But he knew he had to tell her sometime. Although he wasn't sure how she would take the news that he would be away from her over the summer.

It would be worth it, he told himself bracingly, as he walked home in the moonlight. Lew Smith had promised him a decent wedge for his trouble, and that was all that really mattered. With a bit of luck, by the time Nick returned he would be able to afford to march straight down to that solicitor's and get those divorce papers sorted out.

As he turned the corner into Quaker Street he noticed someone was sitting on the kerb outside his building. Nick saw wild red curls illuminated in the silvery light from the streetlamp, and his heart lifted.

'Dora?' She stood up as he started towards her. She was out of uniform, huddled in her old blue coat. 'What are you doing here? It's nearly ten, you'll get in trouble if you're caught . . .' Then he saw her face and realised she knew.

'Is it true?' she asked. 'You're going away?'

'Who told you?'

'Never mind who told me. It's true, then?'

'I was going to tell you—'

'When? Tomorrow? Next week? Or were you just going to take the coward's way out and write me a letter after you'd gone?'

Nick's jaw tightened. 'I've never been a coward in my life. You know that,' he muttered.

'No, but you've been a bloody fool more times than I can count!' Dora looked up at him, with those eyes that seemed to see right into his soul. 'Why, Nick?' she whispered, more sorrowful than angry now. 'Why would you give up your job to go off and fight in a travelling fair?'

He looked away, unable to meet her eye. The disgust in her face made him feel dirty. 'We need the money.'

'And we'll get it. We don't need you traipsing up and down the country in a sideshow!'

'So how do you think we're going to get it otherwise? I can't save it on my wages, I'm no good in the ring any more . . .' He heard his voice crack, betraying the emotion he tried so hard to hide. 'You said yourself we ain't going to save that much in a month of Sundays. What are we going to do?'

'I dunno, do I?' Dora considered it for a moment. 'We could ask Ruby's boyfriend? She says he's got a bob or two. Maybe he could help.'

Nick shook his head. 'No,' he said. 'I ain't going cap in hand to him. I wouldn't give her the satisfaction. I got my pride, Dora.'

'Pride?' Her mouth curled over the word. 'You're planning to join a travelling fair, and you tell me you got pride?' She shook her head, her face full of reproach and disappointment. 'I would never have thought it of you, Nick. I never thought you'd stoop so low. To do something like that for money.'

'I'm doing it for us!' he snapped. 'For you and me, so we can be together.'

Dora looked up at him, her green eyes as cold as the rain that dripped down his collar. 'Oh, no, Nick Riley. You ain't doing this for my sake,' she said. 'I'm telling you now, I don't want you going off and fighting on street corners. If you want to go and get killed in some back alley, then you ain't doing it in my name!'

'I ain't going to get killed.'

'You don't know that, do you? You don't know how vicious some of these fighters can be.'

'I can handle myself, don't you worry.'

'Oh, I know. I grew up with you, remember. I know all about your reputation – and your temper. What if you lose it one night? What if some stranger gets a bit lairy with you and you end up half killing him? You could be locked up.' She stepped away from him, out of his reach. 'I mean it, Nick. I'd rather not marry you.'

'You don't want to marry me?' He reeled back as if she'd struck him.

'Not if it means you lowering yourself like this. You're worth more than that, Nick.'

He stared at her. She looked so prim and proper, standing there in the lamplight. Suddenly she didn't look like his Dora any more, the scruffy girl from Griffin Street. She looked like those other nurses, the ones who stared straight through him when he passed them on the wards or in the passageways, as if he was worth nothing more than the rubbish cart he was pushing.

He was losing her. All his long buried insecurities rose up, choking him. He wanted to explode, to drive his fist into the nearest wall just so he could scream out the pain. She was too good for him, and she'd finally realised it.

'You're worth more, you mean,' he bit out.

'I dunno what you're talking about.'

'I mean perhaps I'm not good enough for you any more. Perhaps that's the real reason you don't want to marry me?'

'Don't talk daft.' The proud toss of her head was like a slap in the face.

'What's daft about it? Why should you want to waste your time with someone like me, when you could find yourself a nice, rich doctor instead?'

'I don't want a doctor!'

'Well, you don't want me, that's for sure!'

'I just want you to use your brains instead of your fists for once!' she flashed back.

'Well, I'm sorry I ain't as clever as you.'

Dora sighed angrily. 'I didn't mean that—'

'I'd do anything for you, Dora. Anything in the world. Even if that meant getting a stranger's blood on my hands or never knowing another moment's peace in my life, I'd do it for you. And if that's lowering myself then I'd be proud to do it!'

'Nick . . .'

'But you don't care that much, do you? All you're interested in is me not making a fool of you. Well, you needn't worry. I ain't going to make a fool of you for much longer!'

He forced himself to walk away from her towards his lodgings.

'Nick! Nick, wait, I didn't mean . . .'

He heard her call out his name but he kept on walking, putting one foot in front of the other, every muscle in his body held rigid, determined not to fall apart until he'd closed the front door on her.

Chapter Fourteen

Effie stared at the mess in her pan. It was supposed to be calf's foot jelly, but it didn't look anything like the one Sister Parker had produced.

She looked around the classroom kitchen in despair. The other girls didn't seem to be having any trouble; Anna Padgett was already straining her mixture through a flannel bag.

Effie looked back into her pan. She could hardly get her spoon in it, let alone strain it.

'Any clue what I should do with this?' she hissed to Prudence Mulhearn, who stood beside her. Prudence looked over into Effie's pan, steam fogging her spectacles.

'Oh, dear.' Her tone was not promising. 'How on earth did it get stuck to the pan like that?'

'I don't know,' Effie sighed. 'I haven't taken my eyes off it for a minute—' She caught Prudence's knowing look. 'All right, maybe for a few seconds. But not long enough for this to happen.'

'Well, you'd better do something about it quick. Sister's on her way.' Prudence glanced over Effie's shoulder. 'Put some boiling water on it, and hope for the best.'

Effie grabbed the kettle and splashed water into her pan. It sent up an evil-smelling, hissing cloud of steam that enveloped Sister Parker as she approached.

Effie heard her long-suffering sigh through the fog. 'What are you doing, O'Hara?'

'I – I don't know, Sister,' Effie admitted helplessly. 'I've made rather a mess of it.'

Sister Tutor flapped her hand to clear away the steam. 'Let me see what you've done.' She peered into the pan. 'Ah. Yes, I can see you were not exaggerating, O'Hara. That is rather a mess.'

'I'm sorry, Sister.'

'These dishes are supposed to entice a patient who is off their food.' She waved the pan under Effie's nose. The acrid smell made her recoil. 'This is hardly appetising, is it?'

'No, Sister,' Effie agreed gloomily.

Sister Tutor put the pan down with a sigh. 'I think this is beyond rescue. You had better find a clean pan and start again.'

'But I can't!' Effie blurted out, then regretted it instantly as the Sister Tutor's icy blue eyes turned towards her.

'I beg your pardon?' she said.

Effie caught Prudence's horrified look from behind the Sister Tutor's shoulder. On the other side of the classroom, one or two of the other girls were shaking their heads. But she had started, and so she had to finish.

'It's nearly five o'clock, Sister,' she mumbled.

'And?'

'I won't be finished by the time the class ends, Sister. And . . . and some of the girls are going to the pictures.'

'I see,' Sister Parker looked as if she was considering the matter. 'And your social life is important, is it?'

What social life? Effie wanted to reply. It had taken a month for her to persuade the other girls to leave their books and venture out.

Sister Parker drew in a deep breath, a sure sign she was building up to one of her lectures. 'May I remind you, O'Hara, that a good nurse doesn't watch the clock? Do you think if a dangerously ill patient needs your care you can just drop everything and go off duty?'

'No, Sister.'

'No, indeed. And you must learn that by staying late and finishing what you are doing.'

'Yes, Sister.'

'And while you're waiting for your jelly to cool, you can set about getting this clean.' Sister thrust the pan at her. 'I want to be able to see my face in it by the time you leave, do you understand?'

'Yes, Sister.'

As Sister Parker moved on, Prudence swung round to face Effie. 'Now you've done it,' she hissed. 'Why did you have to go and answer her back? You'll be cooking and cleaning all night!'

'It won't take very long,' Effie replied, without conviction. 'You will wait for me, won't you?'

Prudence looked doubtful. 'I would, but Padgett says we have to leave by seven. And you know what she's like.'

'But it's not fair!' Effie threw the pan into the sink and turned on the tap. 'This night out was my idea, and now I'm going to be the only one to miss it!'

'I know, I'm sorry.' Prudence sent her a sympathetic glance. 'Look, shall I help cut up your calf's feet for you? That might save you a bit of time.'

It was nearly seven o'clock by the time Effie had turned out an acceptable calf's foot jelly and cleaned the pan to Sister Parker's satisfaction. Effie watched, her fingers crossed in the folds of her apron, as Sister Tutor held it up to the light, peering closely into its depths.

'That seems acceptable,' she said finally. 'Well, O'Hara, I hope this will make you think twice about watching the clock so closely in future?'

I'll think twice about letting you catch me! Effie thought. 'Yes, Sister,' she replied meekly.

She had just finished wiping down the sink in the practice room kitchen when a flash of movement outside the window caught her eye. Out in the garden, something was billowing in the breeze, ghostly white in the fading evening light. Effie yelped, thinking it was a ghost, until she realised it was attached to the ash tree at the far end of the garden. She peered closer, unsure of what she was seeing. It was no phantom, that was for sure. But it did look suspiciously like a pair of . . .

'Bloomers!' she cried out.

Sister Parker looked up sharply from her desk in the corner of the practice room. 'I beg your pardon, Nurse O'Hara?'

Effie looked over her shoulder. 'There's a pair of bloomers hanging from that tree, Sister,' she said.

'Nonsense, child, you must be mistaken . . .' Sister Parker stopped at the window and stared out. She took off her spectacles, polished them on her apron, then put them on and looked again.

'Good gracious!' she said. 'So there are.'

Effie followed her outside, thoroughly enjoying the entertainment. She'd even forgotten about her misery at being kept late.

Sister Parker stood under the tree, looking up into the branches. The bloomers fluttered overhead, tantalisingly out of reach. Effie had never seen such large undergarments in all her life.

'They look like Sister Sutton's,' she commented.

Sister Parker turned on her sharply. 'That's quite enough, Nurse!' she snapped. 'The question is, how did they get up there?'

She gazed around her. Effie gazed around too – and spotted a movement in the bushes. She shaded her eyes, peering closer. Yes, there was definitely someone there, moving about in the shrubbery.

As she went on staring, a dark head suddenly popped up among the bright pink rhododendrons. A young man, not much older than herself. He grinned at Effie, and put his finger to his lips. She squeaked with shock.

'Yes? What is it?' Sister Parker wheeled round to look at her.

'Nothing, Sister.' She composed herself quickly, turning away from the bushes. 'Should I – um – fetch the porter?' she suggested.

'Yes,' Sister Parker said. 'I think that is a very sensible suggestion.'

By the time Effie had watched the porter climbing the tree to retrieve the bloomers, it was long past seven o'clock. She hurried back to the nurses' home, stripping off her apron as she went. She couldn't wait to tell Prudence and the others her story.

She knocked on Prudence's door. There was no answer.

'You've missed them.' Jess appeared at the other end of the landing, her arms full of linen. 'They left about twenty minutes ago.'

Effie stared at the closed door, feeling her eyes sting with tears of frustration. 'I thought they might wait for me.'

'I don't think they were in the mood to wait. They seemed very giddy about something.' Jess paused. 'Are you all right?' she asked.

'I'm just disappointed, that's all.' Effie fumbled for her handkerchief. 'I'd been so looking forward to this night out. Now I'm stuck in here by myself again, while they're all out having fun!'

The unfairness of it overcame her, and she started to cry. Out of the corner of her eye, she saw Jess hesitate for a moment, then put down her armful of laundry.

'Look, I've only got this lot to put away then I'll be

finished for the night,' she said. 'Why don't we go down to the café for a cup of tea? It should be all right as long as Sister doesn't find out.'

Effie looked up at her. 'Can we go to the pictures instead?' she asked.

Jess frowned. 'I dunno about that.'

'Please? I was *so* looking forward to it. And you're not doing anything else, are you?'

'Well no, but . . .' Jess glanced around her, as if she was looking for a way of escape. 'I don't think it would be right,' she said.

'I won't tell anyone if you won't,' Effie offered. 'We'll even go to a different picture house, if you like? Please, Jess?'

Effie saw the look of resignation in the maid's dark eyes, and knew she'd got her way.

'All right,' she sighed. 'But don't you dare tell a soul or Sister Sutton will have my guts for garters.'

The Regal Cinema lived up to its name: it was like a palace. Effie had never seen anywhere so big or so grand. There were carpets everywhere, so soft underfoot it was like walking on air. Even the woman who showed them to their seats looked fancy in her maroon uniform with gold trimmings.

But the best part was when the music started and a man rose like magic from a hole in the stage, playing an illuminated electric organ that flashed different-coloured lights as he played.

Effie couldn't hold back her squeal of delight. 'Will you look at that?' she cried.

Jess sent her a sideways look. 'Don't you have organists in Ireland?'

'Only in church.' And Paddy O'Keefe the church organist

had never come up through the floor. It would have livened up Father Dwyer's endless services a treat if he had.

'We don't have a picture house in Killarney,' Effie explained. 'The only one we have is in the next big town, and that's a poky little place, nothing like this. We all sit on benches, and half the time the projector breaks down halfway through and we don't see the end.' She unscrewed the brown paper bag of humbugs they'd bought to share. 'We never bother going anyway. The last bus is at four, so you either have to go to matinees, or walk six miles there and back along the lanes in the dark.' She offered Jess the bag. 'Humbug?'

'Ta.' Jess took one, just as the organist sank slowly back down under the stage and the heavy gold-trimmed curtains swished back to reveal an enormous screen, bigger than anything Effie had ever seen.

The other girls had gone off to see a Will Hay comedy at the Rialto, but Jess and Effie had chosen *Camille* with Greta Garbo and Robert Taylor. Effie was completely entranced, her gaze riveted to the screen. Even the bag of humbugs lay forgotten on her lap as she lost herself in the tragic story.

Tears were streaming down her face as the lights came up and they made their way out into the darkened street.

'Oh, wasn't it sad?' she sighed. 'I'm so glad Armand came back for her in the end, aren't you?'

'Look at you, crying over a film!' Jess laughed. But in the light of the streetlamps Effie could see that Jess' eyes were glistening too.

'Admit it, you found it just as sad as I did!' she said.

Jess shrugged. 'I suppose so.'

Effie tucked her arm under Jess' as they walked back to the hospital, eating the last of the humbugs. They chatted as they went, and Effie made Jess laugh with the story of the bloomers.

135

'I wonder who put them there?' Jess said.

'Probably one of the medical students. Katie says they're holy terrors.'

'Poor Sister Sutton.'

'Oh, she deserves it. She's awful.'

'She's not that bad once you get used to her,' Jess said, helping herself to another humbug.

Effie also confessed her disaster with the calf's foot jelly.

Jess laughed. 'That Sister Tutor of yours must despair of you!'

'I despair of myself,' Effie sighed. 'I'm sure no one makes as many mistakes as me.'

'Everyone makes mistakes,' Jess said.

'Not as bad as mine.'

'Oh, I don't know. I made a shocking mistake the other day. Almost got myself the sack, I did.'

Effie glanced at Jess. 'What did you do?'

Jess shook her head. 'I dunno if I could even tell you, it was so awful.'

'Go on! You can't say something like that and then not tell me. It's too unfair!'

'Well, all right . . .' Jess shot her a wary look. 'But you've got to promise not to tell another soul?'

Effie nodded. 'Cross my heart,' she swore solemnly.

Jess took a deep breath. 'It all happened when I was working over at the Sisters' home. One of the maids had been taken poorly so Sister Sutton sent me over there to help out.' She paused. 'I had to wake up the Sisters and take them all their breakfast in bed.'

'Lucky them, getting breakfast in bed!' Effie sighed.

'The supervisor told me to go up to Sister Everett on the top floor,' Jess went on. '"Take her a cup of tea and pull the covers off the old bird,"' she said.

'That seems a bit unkind,' Effie said.

'That's what I thought. But when I went into her room and put the tray down she was sleeping soundly, snoring away. I called out to her but she didn't wake up. Then I remembered what the supervisor said. I thought it was something they had to do to wake her up. Y'know, because she was a deep sleeper or something.'

Effie was round-eyed. 'Go on?'

'Well, I yanked at the blankets and pulled them right off. That woke her up, all right. She yelled like the devil. I was so frightened I ran away. But as I was running out of the door, I spotted the cage in the corner.'

Effie's mouth fell open. 'You mean . . .'

'How was I to know she had a parrot?'

They looked at each other, and both burst out laughing.

'That's priceless!' Effie cried. 'You've made me feel a lot better about my wretched calf's foot jelly, that's for sure.' She squeezed Jess' arm. 'I've had such a nice evening. We should do it again.'

She immediately sensed she'd said the wrong thing. Jess' laughter faded and she gently drew her arm from Effie's.

'We can't,' she said. 'I told you, I'm not allowed to mix with the students. Sister Sutton would be furious if she found out.'

'So you've said, but I don't understand why.'

'Because you're a different class from me,' Jess explained coldly. 'You and the other girls are going to be nurses, and I'm always going to be a maid.'

They trudged along the street in silence, the light-hearted mood between them gone. Effie was thoughtful.

Rich or poor, you treated everyone as you found them, so her parents had taught her. She certainly couldn't imagine snubbing someone because of where they were born or how much money they had in the bank. Even old Frank Weedon, who lived in a shack on the edge of the village and didn't have a farthing to his name. Her da and every other man in the village would always stand him a pint in the pub.

Life in London might be exciting, but it could also be very cruel, she decided.

Chapter Fifteen

'You're not reading that again, are you? I'm surprised it ain't worn out by now, you've turned those pages so many times!'

Dora grinned at Archie as she applied a linseed poultice to his sore ribs. He submitted patiently to her ministrations, still clutching the tattered *Comic Cuts* his mum had brought in for him last visiting day.

He looked so different from the grubby child they'd dragged into the bathtub that first morning. Underneath all that dirt he was a handsome little boy with a shock of fair hair and a cheeky grin that split his face from ear to ear.

He was very poorly, but he didn't make a fuss. No matter how much pain he was in, that broad smile was always in place whenever Dora approached.

'I like to make it last,' he said. 'I read the stories slowly, one every day. That way I don't finish it too quick, see?'

He gazed down at the comic with wonder. Dora's heart went out to him. She knew his family didn't have much, and it must have cost his mum dear to bring her son such a gift. But it was money well spent, as it had cheered him up no end.

'So what have you been reading about today?' asked Dora, as she pressed the poultice against his skin. His ribs stuck out like a birdcage from his hollow belly.

'Jackie and Sammy the Terrible Twins.' Archie immediately launched into a complicated story involving the twins' latest bit of mischief. Dora listened as carefully as she could, but barely took it all in.

'Well, I hope it doesn't give you any ideas about getting into trouble here,' she warned when he'd finished.

'Me, Nurse?' He gave her a look of mock innocence. 'Not much chance of that with you lot watching us all the time!' He looked down at his comic again. 'When I've finished reading it, I'm going to cut out some of the pictures . . . the drawings of planes and trains. I love trains, don't you?'

'I can't say as I've ever thought about them, Archie.'

'I have.' He beamed at her. 'I'm going to be a train driver when I grow up.'

'Good for you. There, all done.'

As she pulled up his bedclothes, Archie said, 'What's wrong with that boy?'

'Which boy?'

'That boy down the end. I reckon it must be serious, 'cos he's got a room to himself.' Archie leaned forward, his eyes wide. 'Is he dying?'

'Oh, you mean Ernest?' Dora shook her head. 'No, love, he's just got rheumatic fever. And he's recovering nicely,' she added.

Archie looked disappointed. 'Is that all? I thought it was something really bad.'

Dora smiled. 'Well, rheumatic fever ain't much fun, you know.'

'I s'pose not.' Archie thought about it for a moment. 'So why is he shut away all by himself?'

'Because his mum and dad have paid for him to have his own room.'

'Why?'

'Because . . .' Because they don't think anyone else is good enough to breathe the same air as their little boy, Dora thought. 'Because they think it will be better for him.'

'It's meant to be a treat, then?'

'I suppose so, yes.'

'It doesn't seem like much of a treat to me, being shut away from all the fun,' Archie declared. 'I thought he was being punished. Like when my dad locked me in the coal hole once.'

'I never thought about it like that.' Dora glanced towards the door. She couldn't imagine young Ernest minding too much about it. He seemed to share his mother's opinion that he was too good to mix with other children.

'I feel sorry for him anyway.' Archie thought for a moment. 'Do you reckon he'd like to have a read of my comic?'

'But you haven't finished it yourself!'

'It don't matter. He could read it – as long as he's careful and he promises to give it back?'

'That's very kind of you, Archie,' Dora said. 'Right, that's you sorted. And I don't want you hopping out of bed when my back's turned, all right? You know Sister doesn't like it.'

'All right, Nurse Doily!' Archie grinned.

Dora sighed. 'And don't let her hear you calling me that either!' She didn't mind Archie's nickname for her, but she was sure Sister Parry would say he was being too familiar.

Archie laughed. The sound immediately drew Sister Parry who bustled up, her starched uniform crackling.

'Are you still here, Nurse Doyle? Lane has gone for lunch so I'll need you to watch her patient in room two. I don't want you to leave his side until she returns, do you understand?'

'Yes, Sister.'

'And when she comes back, I'll need you to take the tonsils down to Theatre.'

Dora caught Archie's eye as Sister walked away. 'No rest for the wicked, eh, Doily?' He grinned.

'Looks like it, Archie.'

'If you're going to see that boy, don't forget to give him this.' Archie proffered the comic. 'But make sure he knows it's just a lend, mind.'

Ernest was reading a book, but Dora could tell from the way his eyes skipped over the pages that he wasn't really enjoying it. He looked up sharply when she walked in.

'Where have you been?' he demanded.

Dora pasted a smile on her face. 'I'm sorry, Ernest, did you want something? If you do, you only have to ring the bell, you know.'

'You're not supposed to leave me alone. That's your job,' he reminded her.

'Heavens, Ernest, you were on your own for five minutes! Besides, you're not the only patient I have to look after, you know,' Dora said. 'We do have other children on the ward.'

'Yes, but my mother and father are paying you to look after *me*!' Petulance made his fat cheeks wobble.

Dora took a deep breath. He's just a little boy, she told herself. Being ill was bound to make him bad-tempered.

She turned her attention to the airmail envelope lying on his bedside locker. 'Have you had a letter from your parents this morning? How lovely,' she said. 'Are they still in Europe?'

Ernest stared at the letter. 'My father is playing with the Bavarian State Orchestra now,' he said in a flat voice.

'I expect you miss them, don't you?'

Ernest looked at her, his face sullen. 'I'd like a drink of water,' he said.

'Of course.'

Dora felt a twinge of pity for him as she poured his

drink. With his parents away, Ernest's only visitor had been an elderly housekeeper. His mother sent letters, but they only seemed to leave him even more fretful and demanding than ever.

It was a shame because one of the privileges of being a private patient was that parents were allowed to visit whenever they chose. Unlike the children on the main ward, whose parents could only visit once a month.

He needed cheering up, she decided. And reading that dull book wasn't going to do it.

'I've got something else for you.'

'What is it?' Ernest asked sullenly, not looking at her.

'This.' Dora took the comic out from under the bib of her apron and put it down on the quilt in front of him.

Ernest stared at it for a moment. Then he turned his face away.

'I'm not allowed to read comics,' he declared. 'My mother doesn't like it.'

Your mother isn't here, is she? Dora thought. She's off, gallivanting round Europe. 'I'm sure your mother wouldn't mind, just this once?' she coaxed. 'I expect she'd like you to have something to cheer you up. I'll put it in your locker for now, shall I? You might decide you want to read it later.'

She busied herself, checking his temperature, pulse and respiration, straightening his bedclothes and making sure he was comfortable. All the while Ernest's gaze was fixed longingly on his locker.

'Where did it come from?' he asked finally.

'Archie, one of the other boys on the ward, wanted to lend it to you. But it's his pride and joy, so please be careful with it.'

Ernest looked at her blankly. 'Then why would he lend it to me?'

'He thought you might be lonely and need cheering up, I suppose.'

Ernest frowned, taking this in. But before he could speak, Lucy appeared at the door.

'I'll take over now,' she said. 'Sister says the tonsils are ready to go down to Theatre.'

Thank you for looking after my patient, Doyle. Not at all, Lane, it was my pleasure, Dora thought to herself. It really wouldn't hurt Lucy to smile or be polite once in a while. She wondered how Lane got on with Ernest. They probably snapped at each other all day long.

'I'm on my way.' As Dora headed for the door she looked back to see Ernest's gaze still fixed on the locker. She smiled to herself, wondering how long he would resist before he asked for the comic. Pompous prig he might be, but Ernest Pennington was still a little boy.

Her smile died when she closed the door and found Nick there, waiting with an apprehensive-looking boy in a wheelchair. Dora's brother Peter, who worked alongside Nick as a porter, stood behind him with a little girl in another wheelchair.

'All right, Sis?' he greeted Dora cheerfully.

'Hello, Pete.' She avoided looking at Nick as she picked up the patients' notes and led the way to the lifts. They hadn't spoken to each other since their argument the previous week and Dora sensed he was doing his best to avoid her, just as she was him.

She had been so angry that night. But it was fear more than anything that had made her flare up at him the way she had. She hated the idea of him going off with the travelling fair, standing up in a boxing booth for other people's amusement, like a tethered bear in a circus. Nick was a real boxer, he had talent and he took pride in his training. She couldn't bear to think of him demeaning himself, especially not for her sake. She had meant what she'd said; she would rather never marry him than see him brought so low.

But instead of explaining how she felt, she'd let her temper get the better of her and taken out her anger on him. She knew she'd hurt him, and she was sorry for that.

But it wasn't all her fault, she thought as she watched Nick standing rigidly beside her, his gaze fixed on the doors as if he couldn't bring himself to look at her.

He was the one who'd slammed the door in her face, told her he didn't want to be with her any more. But getting any apology out of Nick Riley would be like getting blood out of a stone, or a smile out of Sister Parry.

They made an awkward group as they went down in the lift together. Peter seemed oblivious as he chatted to the children, singing silly songs and making faces and turning their tears to wobbly smiles.

'You're a natural with them,' Dora remarked.

'I should be, all the time I've spent keeping you and the other kids entertained!' Peter grinned. 'Anyway, I've got to practise for when I've got a nipper of my own.'

He sounded so proud when he said it, Dora was pleased for him. 'You'll make a good dad,' she said.

'I hope so.' His freckled face flushed with pride. 'I know I've made some mistakes in the past, but I've settled down now, I know what's important. And that's my missus and my kid.'

The lift doors opened and Nick barged through them, pushing the wheelchair ahead of him like a battering ram.

Peter made a face at Dora. 'Me and my big mouth,' he said. 'Here I am, going on and on about the blessings of married life, and I forgot that him and Ruby ain't together any longer.'

Dora didn't reply as she walked down the basement

corridor towards Theatre. Peter had no idea about her and Nick. Only her grandmother and mother knew her secret.

'He's been in such a rotten mood since Ruby found herself another fella,' Peter mused. 'I expect that's why he's decided to up sticks and go off with this travelling fair, too. Daft idea if you ask me. Old Hopkins has been trying to talk him out of it ever since he found out, but Nick's dead set on going. Reckons there's nothing for him here any more.'

Dora looked down at the notes to hide her blushing face, and said nothing.

'Personally, I can't wait for him to go, the way he's carrying on at the minute,' her brother went on. 'He's like a bear with a sore head, he really is. The sooner Nick Riley leaves, I reckon the happier we'll all be!'

Chapter Sixteen

'I say, you there!'

Jess didn't hear the voice at first over the drone of the vacuum cleaner. She was too busy trying to finish the landings so she could get away in time for her night class at the Institute.

Then, suddenly, the vacuum cleaner died. Jess turned around to see one of the probationers, Anna Padgett, standing before her with the plug in her hand.

'I'm talking to you,' she said.

I've got a name, Jess thought as she straightened up. Not that this girl ever used it. As far as Anna was concerned, Jess was always 'you there'.

'What did you do that for?' she asked.

'You're making far too much noise,' Anna replied. 'Some of us are trying to work.'

Jess glanced past her at the faces gathered around the doorway to Anna's room. Effie's was among them.

'I can't help that. I've got my own work to do.'

Anna sent Jess a withering look. She was tall and solidly built with a square, pugnacious face. 'Your work isn't nearly as important as ours.'

'You tell that to Sister Sutton. She'll have my guts for garters if she finds a speck of dust in this hall.'

'Well, you'll just have to do it later,' Anna said dismissively. She started to walk away, but Jess stood her ground.

'I don't take orders from you,' she said.

Anna turned slowly, a look of disbelief on her face. 'What did you say?'

'I answer to Sister Sutton,' Jess replied, meeting the girl's shocked gaze. 'You can't order me about.'

Anna's eyes bulged with outrage, and for a moment Jess thought she was going to fly at her with sheer temper. She braced herself, hands balling into fists, ready to defend herself.

'Leave her be, Padgett,' one of the other girls put in from the doorway. 'We'd more or less finished studying anyway.'

But Anna stood rooted to the spot, her eyes fixed on Jess. 'How dare you answer me back?' she hissed. 'I've a good mind to report you to Sister Sutton.'

Jess folded her arms across her chest. 'Go on, then.'

Anna opened her mouth to speak, but Effie got in first.

'I thought we were going out tonight?' she pleaded. 'We'll be late.'

'You're right.' Anna glared at Jess. 'She's not worth wasting my time on.'

She tossed the plug on to the floor and stalked back to her room. As the door closed behind her, Jess caught a glimpse of Effie's face, framed by a cloud of dark hair. 'Sorry,' she mouthed, before Anna ordered her to close the door.

Jess pushed the plug back into the socket again, burning with indignation. It wasn't the first time Anna Padgett had picked on her. She was always pulling her up about something, ordering her about as if Jess were her personal maid. And Anna usually made sure she did it in front of her friends, knowing there was nothing Jess could do about it.

She tried to push it from her mind as she hauled the vacuum cleaner up to the top landing. If she didn't hurry she would miss her bus, and she didn't want to be late. Her School Certificate exams were only a matter of weeks away, and even though her teachers were sure she would pass easily, Jess didn't want to take any chances.

She didn't want to miss seeing Sam either. She smiled as she thought about how he would be waiting for her on the corner so they could walk to the Institute together. And then, after their classes, they would head down to the café for a cup of tea and a bun. She would never call it courting, but it had become a pleasant little ritual for both of them.

But it seemed as if fate didn't want her to make her date this evening as the growl of the vacuum cleaner changed to a protesting whine. Jess switched it off with a sigh of frustration. Now she would have to empty it, and by the time she'd carried it down three flights of stairs to the dustbin and back up, she would have missed her bus for sure.

Unless . . .

She eyed the window. If she tipped the contents out she could scoop them up and put them in the bin on her way out, and no one would be any the wiser. It was a risk, as the window overlooked the front of the building. If Sister Sutton returned from the dining room and saw her . . .

Before she had time to change her mind, Jess threw open the window and tipped the contents of the cleaner out.

Straight away she heard a soft *thwump* below, followed by a squawk of indignation. She froze, her hands on the window frame, ready to close it. Oh, no. It couldn't be. Surely not . . .

She braced herself to look down. Below her a group of girls stood coughing and spluttering, fanning dust from their faces as they gathered around in a tight knot. As the cloud of dust started to clear, Jess saw what – or rather who – they were gathered around.

She clapped her hand over her mouth and ran for the door.

Outside, the girls were brushing Anna Padgett down. But she still looked like a ghost, her clothes and face covered in dust, her brown hair turned ashy grey like a powdered wig. Jess stopped in the doorway and stared, caught between horror and the desperate need to laugh.

'It's not that bad, Padgett, honestly,' one of the girls was saying, covering her mouth as she dusted off her friend's shoulder.

'Not that bad? Look at me!' Anna Padgett roared back.

Jess forced herself to step forward on legs which suddenly felt as if they didn't belong to her.

'Here, let me help,' she said.

Anna whirled round to confront her, face taut with fury. 'You!' she screamed. 'You did this! This is all your fault!'

'I know, and I'm sorry.'

'No, you're not! You did it deliberately.'

'I didn't, I swear.' Jess moved forward. 'Here, let's get you out of those clothes. I can wash them, make them as good as new . . .'

She reached forward, but Anna lashed out at her, knocking her back against the wall. 'Don't you dare touch me!' she cried.

'Steady on, Padgett,' Effie said. 'She said she was sorry.'

'Sorry's not good enough!' Anna's eyes gleamed with spite through the dusty grey of her face. 'You've done it now,' she warned Jess, voice shaking with rage. 'I'll get you sacked for this, you see if I don't!'

Jess' stomach plummeted with fear. 'But I said it was an accident!' she pleaded.

'What is going on?' They all looked round as Sister

Sutton loomed into view. 'I heard squawking from the other side of the courtyard. Would someone please tell me what—' She saw Anna and stopped dead. 'Good gracious, Padgett, what have you done to yourself?'

'It was her, Sister.' Anna pointed at Jess. 'She – she tipped dust over my head!'

Sister Sutton stared at Jess, her jowly face quivering. 'Is this true?'

'It was an accident, Sister.'

'No, it wasn't!' Anna shouted. 'You're a nasty, vicious little . . .'

'Nurse, please!' Sister Sutton held up one hand to silence her. She turned to Jess. 'What exactly happened?'

Jess felt everyone's eyes on her as she explained. 'I didn't think it would do any harm,' she finished. 'I didn't know anyone was going to be walking under the window at that very moment.'

'Liar!' Anna broke in. 'You were lying in wait for me up there, just because I told you off earlier. You should be sacked for what you've done!'

'Nurse Padgett, I will not tell you again!' Sister Sutton scolded. 'May I remind you, I am in charge of discipline in this home, not you. If anyone is going to be sacked, I will do it.'

'But, Sister—'

'Padgett, if you don't desist this minute I will send you to Matron.'

'Yes, Sister.' Anna glared at Jess.

'Now go inside and clean yourself up. You girls can go with her.' She dismissed the other probationers, who were standing gawping at the scene. 'And as for you,' she turned to Jess, 'you'd better come with me.'

As Jess trailed after Sister Sutton back up the steps to the nurses' home, she heard Anna Padgett's gloating voice.

'Now she's for it! I bet that's the last we see of *her*.'

Sister Sutton led the way into her office, off the hall just inside the front door. It was a tiny room, barely large enough for a desk and a set of bookshelves. Jess found herself holding her breath as she watched Sister Sutton squeeze her bulk into the narrow gap between the wall and the desk.

As soon as the Home Sister had eased herself into her chair, Jess started to gabble.

'I'm so sorry, Sister, but I promise you it was an accident.' The words came out of her in a torrent. 'I never meant to do anything to Nurse Padgett, I swear I didn't . . .'

Jess caught Sister Sutton's stern look and fell silent. 'Have you quite finished?' the Home Sister asked.

Jess looked at the floor. 'Yes, Sister,' she whispered.

'In that case, perhaps I might be permitted to speak?'

'Yes, Sister.' She caught sight of Sparky's keen black eyes as he sat down beside the desk. Even he looked reproachful.

'Thank you.' There was an uncomfortable creak as Sister Sutton shifted in her chair. 'The reason I called you into my office was to give you this.'

It took Jess a moment before she dared to look up. When she did, she realised Sister Sutton had pushed a book across the desk towards her. Its brown cloth cover was slightly battered at the edges and the gold lettering down the spine faded with age, but Jess recognised it straight away.

'An anatomy textbook?' She was so surprised she forgot to address Sister Sutton properly, but thankfully she didn't seem to notice. 'But I don't understand—?'

'I thought since you have shown such an interest in reading other people's textbooks, you might like one of your own? It's rather out of date, of course, but I don't think the human body has changed a great deal in the forty odd years since I was a student.'

Jess stared at the book and then back at the Home Sister, still unable to believe what she was hearing. 'You're giving me your book?'

'Lending,' Sister Sutton corrected her. 'And I am trusting you to take good care of it,' she added sternly.

'Oh, I will, Sister.' Jess picked up the book and ran her fingers over the faded lettering. She was so overwhelmed she could hardly speak. 'I'll look after it, don't you worry.'

'I'm sure you will.' Sister Sutton sat back. 'Believe me, I wouldn't have given it to you otherwise. But I'm warning you, you needn't think that makes you special in any way, or makes you equal to the students. You are still the maid, and I expect you to act accordingly.'

'Yes, Sister. Thank you, Sister.'

'Very well, you may go. And see you clear up that mess outside.'

Sister Sutton waved her away, but Jess stood her ground. After what had happened she hardly liked to push her luck, but she knew she had to. 'Sister?' she said.

Sister Sutton looked irritated. 'Yes, child? What is it?'

'What's going to happen to me – about Nurse Padgett?'

The Home Sister sighed, her gaze drifting towards the window. 'I must say I'm surprised at you for emptying that cleaner out of the window. You are usually such a conscientious worker.'

'Yes, Sister. I'm sorry. But it was an accident, what happened with Nurse Padgett. I didn't mean to cover her in dust.'

Sister Sutton sent her a long look. 'I wouldn't blame you if you had,' she said. 'I know Nurse Padgett can be rather high-handed at times. But see you don't do it again,' she went on. 'It simply doesn't do to go covering our students with dust, no matter how trying they might be.'

Her mouth twitched and for a moment Jess could have sworn she was smiling.

'I'll remember that, Sister,' she promised solemnly.

Chapter Seventeen

Anna was still bleating about her run-in with Jess, even after the other girls had helped her get changed and brushed the dust out of her hair.

'She shouldn't be allowed to get away with it,' she kept saying as they made their way to the bus stop. 'If Sister Sutton doesn't do anything about it, I've a good mind to report her to Matron myself.'

'Oh, stop going on about it. It was an accident,' Effie mumbled.

Anna turned on her. 'I hope you're not defending her?' Her eyes narrowed. 'Anyone would think she was a friend of yours.'

Effie glanced around at the other girls. They were all staring at her, their faces hostile. She wanted to speak up, to say that Jess had been more of a friend to her than any of them. But she also desperately wanted to fit in, and this was her chance.

'I just don't want it to spoil everything,' she said. 'After all, there's no real harm done, is there? Can't we forget all about it and enjoy our evening? We've all been so looking forward to it.'

Especially me, she added silently. She had finally managed to coax the rest of her set away from their books again. She might never have managed it if the local theatre hadn't offered the hospital a batch of free tickets to a new variety show.

But even as they took their seats in the stalls, the others

couldn't seem to forget their studies. They chattered between themselves, gossiping about the latest goings-on in the class, and only fell silent as the lights went down. Then, as they queued for their interval ice creams, they compared notes on who had studied the most, who was the best at bandaging and who couldn't get their junket to set in cookery that afternoon.

Bored, Effie's attention began to wander. She looked around the crowd, jostling to buy their ice creams from the usherette, and suddenly she spotted a young man. He had his back to her, but she recognised his sleek dark head immediately.

As if he knew he was being watched, he turned and caught her eyes. A fleeting frown crossed his face then he recognised her and smiled.

'It's him,' Effie said out loud.

Anna, who was in the middle of reciting the different parts of the respiratory system, turned to her with irritation. 'Who?'

'The student who played that prank with Sister Sutton's bloomers. You know, the one I told you about? Look, he's over there.' Effie started to point, then realised the young man was edging his way through the crowd towards them. 'He's coming over!' she yelped.

'Do stop staring at him, O'Hara! Pretend you haven't seen him,' Anna advised, patting her hair.

But Effie couldn't drag her eyes off him until he stood before her. She had only seen him at a distance before, but up close he was very handsome, with a perfect profile, slicked-back dark hair and brown eyes that twinkled with devilment. He reminded her of Robert Taylor in *Camille*.

'Hello again,' he said.

Even his voice was perfect, deep and beautifully spoken. Effie felt her knees weaken.

'Hello,' she managed back.

'I've been meaning to find you and thank you for not giving me away the other day.'

'That's all right. It saved me from another of Sister Parker's lectures, at any rate.'

'All the same, you were a good sport.' He held out his hand. 'I'm Hugo, by the way.'

Effie shook his hand. His fingers were warm and strong as they grasped hers. 'Euphemia,' she squeaked. 'But everyone calls me Effie.'

His mouth curved. Even his smile was perfect. 'Why would they do that? Euphemia is such a delightful name.'

Effie felt her face flooding with colour. 'It's awful!'

'It's charming. As are you.' They were both silent for a moment as Hugo went on holding her hand. Effie felt her palm turning clammy and hoped he wouldn't notice.

The interval bell rang, breaking the spell. Still Hugo seemed reluctant to release her hand. 'There's a spare seat in our box. Won't you join us for the second half?' he said.

'I can't, I'm with my friends . . .' She looked around. Anna and the others had bought their ice creams and were shuffling back to their seats. 'Unless there's room for all of us?' she added hopefully.

Hugo glanced over her shoulder at Anna and the other girls. 'I'm afraid not.'

'Then I'd better not,' Effie sighed. Not that the other girls would even notice she'd gone, she thought. But Anna would probably get cross with her anyway.

'In that case, shall we meet after the show?' Hugo suggested. 'I'll bring my friends, and we could make a party of it. Perhaps we could go to the pub?'

'Oh, yes, please. I'd love that,' Effie accepted eagerly.

'It's a date, then. We'll meet you and your friends outside.'

Anna looked up at Effie as she took her seat, just as the

lights went down again. 'We didn't get you an ice cream,' she said sourly.

'It doesn't matter,' Effie replied, her gaze fixed on the box, waiting for Hugo to appear.

Anna tutted. 'I hope you weren't too forward?' she said. 'You should let the man do the chasing, you know.'

'If I did that, I'd probably be waiting for ever,' Effie sighed. She decided not to break the news to Anna until later that they were meeting Hugo and his friends. She would probably never hear the last of it otherwise.

Throughout the second half of the show, Effie couldn't stop herself sneaking glances up to Hugo, sitting with his friends in the box above them. Once or twice he caught her watching him and Effie looked away quickly, wondering if Anna might be right about her being too forward. But then the third time she found her gaze straying back towards the box, Hugo was already watching her. When she caught his eye he lifted his hand and gave her a little wave. Effie waved back, glad the darkness of the theatre hid her blushing face.

Afterwards, she waited for him outside the theatre, in spite of Anna's protests.

'We'll miss our bus,' she complained. 'And I'm not going to end up in trouble with Matron because of you.'

'Just another five minutes?' Effie pleaded, watching the sea of people surging out of the theatre.

'He's probably not coming anyway,' Anna went on. 'I expect he's forgotten all about you.'

'Here he comes!' Effie caught sight of Hugo's handsome face in the crowd and started waving madly. 'Hugo! Over here!'

'Really!' Anna muttered. 'No man will ever respect you if you behave like that.' But Effie was too pleased and relieved to care as Hugo pushed his way towards them.

'I'm so sorry to keep you waiting,' he said breathlessly. 'I'm afraid my friends are being frightful bores. They want to go straight home. But I would be happy to escort you all to the pub myself?' He looked around the group.

'Well, I suppose so.' It wasn't quite what Effie had hoped for, but she was so desperate to spend time with Hugo she would have agreed to anything. But Anna had other ideas.

'Certainly not!' She looked outraged. 'My mother would never allow me to set foot inside a place like that. It's not respectable for young women. Besides, we have to get back to the nurses' home before ten o'clock.'

She started herding the other girls bossily towards the bus stop, but Effie stood her ground.

'I'll come with you,' she blurted out to Hugo.

Anna looked scandalised. 'You mustn't! You'll be in trouble with Sister Sutton if you're caught coming back late. And you've already got enough black marks against your name,' she pointed out.

'I won't get caught,' Effie shrugged. 'My sister told me there's a way in around the back. No one will know, unless someone tells Sister Sutton?'

Everyone looked at Anna. 'Of course we won't tell. Will we, Padgett?' Prudence Mulhearn put in. Anna pressed her lips together and said nothing.

'Between you and me, I'm rather glad they've gone,' Hugo whispered as they watched the other girls heading off towards the bus stop. 'If you don't mind me saying so, that friend of yours seemed rather tiresome.'

'She likes to do the right thing,' Effie said.

'And you don't?' His dark brows lifted.

'I wouldn't be here if I did, would I?'

Hugo grinned. 'That's the spirit. I knew you were a girl

after my own heart.' He tucked her hand into the crook of his arm. 'Now, let's go and get that drink.'

Effie really didn't know why Anna had made so much fuss. The Docker's Arms was hot, stuffy and crowded, the air thick with cigarette smoke and the stench of unwashed bodies. But it was still more respectable than the local village pub in Killarney. At least the sawdust on the floor was fresh and everyone seemed to be minding their own business.

'I'm terribly sorry about this,' Hugo said as he guided her to a corner table in the saloon bar. 'I didn't realise it would be so crowded. We could find somewhere quieter, if you like?'

'It seems quiet enough to me.' Effie shrugged. 'No one's fighting yet, at any rate. That's what usually happens at Kelly's. You know it's payday when someone ends up going through the window, my da says.'

She wondered if she'd said something wrong when she caught the puzzled look Hugo was giving her. But then he smiled and said, 'What would you like to drink?'

Panicking, she said the first thing that came into her head. 'Lemonade?'

'Are you sure I can't get you something stronger, since we're living dangerously?'

Effie looked blank. 'I don't know any strong drinks, except for beer and whisky. And I don't like either of those.'

Hugo laughed. 'Leave it to me, in that case. I'll find you a strong drink you might like.'

He returned to the table with a beer for himself and a fancy glass filled with a pretty deep pink liquid for her.

'What's that?' Effie peered into it suspiciously.

'It's a port and lemon. Try it, I think you'll like it.'

She took a sip. To her surprise, it tasted rather good.

Sweet, but with a slightly bitter edge to it. 'That's gorgeous.' She quickly drained the glass and set it down on the table.

Hugo's brown eyes widened in surprise. 'Steady on! You don't want to get tipsy, do you?'

Effie looked at the empty glass. 'I don't think there's much chance of getting tipsy on *that*.'

'You think you can hold your drink?' Hugo laughed.

'I know I can,' Effie replied seriously. 'Katie and I once got hold of a bottle of my daddy's poteen, just to see what it was like.'

'And?'

'And Katie was sick as a dog after one glass, but I managed half the bottle. And I could still see straight to go out and feed the chickens,' Effie said proudly.

Hugo put down his glass. 'In that case, I'd better get you another one.'

After three glasses, Effie had forgotten her nerves and was chatting away to him as if they were old friends. He asked lots of questions about her family, and her village in Ireland, and he seemed very amused by what she'd told him. Effie began to wonder if she should try to be more aloof and sophisticated, but she didn't know how to be anything but herself.

She tried to change the subject and asked Hugo about himself. He told her he was in his final year as a medical student at the Nightingale, his father was a doctor, his mother a former nurse, and his younger brother was in his first year at Oxford. The family lived in a leafy suburb of London that Effie had never heard of.

'I'm afraid it's all very boring compared to your riotous life in Killarney,' he sighed.

'Do you like being a doctor?' Effie asked.

'I never really thought about doing anything else.' He

shrugged. 'My father was a doctor, and his father before him. It was sort of expected, I suppose.'

'That's exactly like me,' Effie said. 'My four older sisters are all nurses, so everyone told me I should be one, too.'

'And did you want to be a nurse?'

'I wanted to get away from Killarney, and nursing seemed the best way to do it,' Effie admitted frankly. 'I wanted to come to London because it seemed so exciting. Although I haven't seen much excitement up until now,' she sighed.

Hugo smiled at her over the rim of his glass. 'We'll have to see what we can do about that, won't we?'

Effie was disappointed when the bell rang for last orders. Hugo looked at his watch and said he should walk her back to the hospital.

'But I'm having such a nice time!' she cried.

Hugo smiled. 'So am I, my sweet, but it would be very irresponsible of me to keep you out too late. Besides, I promised to meet my friends for cards, and they'll be rather annoyed with me if I keep them waiting any longer.'

As they stepped outside into the moonlight, he reached for her hand. 'Just in case you stumble in the dark.'

'Oh, no, it's quite all right,' Effie assured him. 'It's not nearly as dark as the country lanes in Killarney. I can see where I'm going in pitch black.'

Hugo sighed. 'My dear girl, you do realise I'm only using it as an excuse to hold your hand?'

'Oh! Sorry.' Effie slipped her hand into his. She really should ask Katie more about this courtship malarkey, she decided. She needed to know what to expect if she was going to have a boyfriend.

They had missed the last bus, and so had to walk back to Bethnal Green. It was nearly midnight by the time they reached the wrought-iron gates of the hospital.

'If you can distract the Night Porter, I'll sneak past,' Effie said. 'Once I get to the nurses' home, my sister says there's a drainpipe that's easy to climb.'

'Don't break your neck, will you?' Hugo said. 'I'd hate to find you on Female Orthopaedic when we do our rounds tomorrow.'

'I'll be fine. I'm used to climbing trees.'

Hugo shook his head. 'You're quite unique, Euphemia,' he said.

Effie peered at his face in the darkness, trying to make out whether he was complimenting her or not. It was hard to tell.

'Right, I'll go and have a word with that porter,' Hugo said. Then he turned back to her and said, 'I don't suppose you'd like to have dinner with me next week?'

Effie suddenly thought about Anna's words of wisdom. *Don't be too forward. Let the man do the chasing.*

'I'd love that,' she said.

Jess was sitting up in bed reading her anatomy textbook when she heard the noise outside. It was almost midnight and she should have turned her lamp off hours ago. But the book was so fascinating she kept turning the pages, even though she was worn out and her eyelids were growing so heavy she could barely make out the diagrams.

She hadn't realised she had fallen asleep until the noise woke her up with a start. She put aside the book that had slid out of her hands on to the quilt, switched off the lamp and scrambled out of bed to peer out of the window.

The noise stopped. But just as Jess was turning away from the window she heard it again. A strange rustling, coming from the bushes.

Jess shaded her eyes with her hand and peered again into the gloom, then jumped back with a scream as a face

163

suddenly appeared below her, pale and ghostly in the moonlight.

Then she realised who it was.

She jerked open the window. 'What are you doing?' she hissed.

'Oh, thank God it's you.' Effie smiled up at her. 'I thought Sister Sutton had heard me.'

'It's a wonder she didn't, the racket you're making.' Jess pressed her hand over her hammering heart.

'Sorry. I'm trying to find the drainpipe to climb up. I don't suppose you know which one it is, do you?' Effie gazed about her vaguely. She looked so comical, standing there with her shoes in her hand.

'I think it's round the back.' As Effie started to tiptoe off, Jess sighed and said, 'But it'll be a lot easier if you just climb in through this window.'

Effie hesitated. 'Are you sure? I don't want to get you into any trouble.'

'You'll get yourself into trouble if you end up with a broken neck!' Jess eased the window wider open, cringing at the squeak it made. 'Pass me your shoes and then climb up.'

It took a while to haul Effie through the window. She landed on Jess' mat in an ungainly tangle of long arms and legs.

Jess switched the lamp on, and Effie squinted up at her surroundings. 'So this is your room.' She looked up at the bookshelves and giggled. 'Look at all those books. Are they all yours?'

'Yes.' Jess saw the grin on Effie's face and bristled. 'Why is it funny that I like to read?'

'I'm sorry, it's not funny. I just find it strange that anyone enjoys reading. I hate it!'

'You don't know what you're missing.'

'You might be right. But I prefer to experience real life, not to read about it in books.'

Jess watched her as she untangled herself and stood up. 'You look as if you've experienced real life tonight,' she commented dryly. 'You reek of cigarette smoke.' She leaned closer and sniffed. 'Have you been drinking?'

'Just a bit!' Effie clamped her fingers over her lips to stifle a giggle. 'Oh, Jess, it was wonderful!' Effie's wide blue eyes were dreamy. 'I think I'm in love.'

'Good for you.' Jess went to the door and opened it a crack. 'Now, we've got to get you back up to your room before Sister Sutton notices.'

'Oh, it'll be grand. She'll be fast asleep by now.'

'She's got ears like a bat. And if she doesn't hear you, Sparky will.' Jess peered out, checking the coast was clear. 'Go on, I think it's safe.'

'Thank you.' Effie's whisper seemed to echo around the darkened hallway. 'I won't forget this, I swear . . .'

'Careful!' Jess saw the shadowy outline of the coatstand a split second before Effie backed into it. It wobbled, then fell in agonising slow motion, landing with a crash that reverberated through the whole building. Jess barely had a moment to spring forward and push Effie into the shadowy recess of the broom cupboard before Sister Sutton's door opened and she stood there outlined in the light from her room, her bulky frame swaddled in a flannel dressing gown. Sparky pranced around her ankles, his four feet leaving the ground as he bounced up and down, yapping with excitement.

'Who's there?' she called out into the gloom.

'It's me, Sister.' Jess found her voice. 'I was just – er – fetching a glass of water, and I knocked the coatstand over.'

'Really! How clumsy of you. And most inconsiderate, too, waking everyone up with your unseemly racket.'

'Yes, Sister. I'm very sorry, Sister.' Out of the corner of her eye Jess caught a flash of movement as Effie slipped out of the broom cupboard and made for the stairs. Luckily, Sister Sutton didn't notice her, but Sparky did. He dashed from his mistress' side, yapping madly.

'Sparky?' Sister Sutton peered into the darkness. 'What is it, boy? Where's that light switch? I can't see a thing.'

'I'll get it, Sister.' Jess got to the light switch before her and made a great show over fumbling with it, praying that Effie would make it up the stairs before she switched it on.

'Hurry up, girl!' Sister Sutton ordered.

Jess counted to five and then switched on the light. She heard Sister Sutton's gasp of outrage and hardly dared look over her shoulder.

'Look at this mess!' When she finally steeled herself to look, she saw no sign of Effie. But the coatstand was on the floor, coats and cloaks and hats everywhere, and Sister Sutton standing in the middle of it, her hands on her wide hips. Sparky, thankfully, had given up on his search and returned to her side. 'You clumsy girl! You must make sure everything is tidied up before the morning, do you understand?'

'Yes, Sister,' Jess said.

'And see you're quiet about it, too!' Summoning Sparky to her heels, Sister Sutton stomped back to her room.

Jess stared up at the ceiling.

You owe me a big favour, Effie O'Hara, she thought.

Chapter Eighteen

'Are you sure about this?' Dora asked.

Millie lifted her eyes to heaven. 'Oh, for goodness' sake! We've been through all this before. Of course I'm sure. I wouldn't have asked you otherwise, would I?'

'But what about your grandmother? Won't she mind?'

'My grandmother has chosen everything else for my wedding, so why shouldn't I be allowed to choose my own bridesmaids?'

Her friend hadn't answered her question, Dora realised. She couldn't imagine what the Dowager Countess of Rettingham would say when she found out her grand-daughter had chosen a cockney girl as one of her attendants, and not one of her posh debutante friends.

Dora looked up at the building in front of her, a beautiful Georgian house overlooking Green Park, with a polished brass plaque beside the front door bearing the words: Madeleine Vachet, Couturier. She had been trying to push her fears about this moment to the back of her mind, but now they were actually here, at their first fitting, they threatened to overwhelm her.

Millie smiled encouragingly at her. 'Please don't worry about my grandmother. In spite of any impression I may have given, she is really very sweet. And I want you and Dawson to be my bridesmaids. We've been through so much together over the last three years, I couldn't think of anyone else I would want with me.' She looked up the busy street. 'Speaking of which, where is Dawson? She said she'd meet us here at two, but it's nearly ten-past now. I hope she hasn't missed her bus?'

'I'm sure she'll be here,' Dora said. She didn't want to say it to Millie, but she wondered if there was another reason why their friend hadn't come.

It was less than a year since Helen Dawson had wed Charlie, the love of her life. He had been gravely ill when she married him, and her friends at the hospital had rallied round to give them a wedding to remember. A week later, Charlie died.

Since then, Helen had done her best to keep up a good front. She had passed her State Final exams and moved into the staff nurses' home. Dora saw her occasionally when she had to take a patient down to Theatre, or they would meet for a cup of tea when they both had time off. Helen always seemed to be her calm, smiling self, and gave the outward appearance of quietly getting on with her life. But every so often Dora would catch a glimpse of the haunted loneliness in her dark eyes.

Perhaps this was all too soon for her? She had seemed delighted when Millie first asked her to be a bridesmaid, but maybe the reality had proved too much. Dora wouldn't have blamed her for backing out.

Millie looked at her watch. 'We'd better go in anyway,' she said, reaching up to pull the bell. 'We're late as it is, and Madame hates to be kept waiting.'

Madame Vachet's *atelier* was at the top of several narrow flights of stairs. A maid in a black uniform opened the door to them and ushered them through the waiting room, with its thick carpets, chandeliers and pale yellow brocade sofas, into the fitting room. This room reminded Dora of a painting she had once seen by a famous French artist. The walls were painted a rich cream, with small gilt chairs set out in rows. Heavy swags of black-and-white-striped silk trimmed the two tall windows. In one corner stood a screen, like the ones they used on the wards, except this one was hung with Chinese embroidery. Even the air smelled expensive, richly perfumed with the scent of musk.

The maid helped them off with their coats, hats and gloves, offered them coffee and informed them Madame Vachet would be with them shortly, then disappeared into the waiting room. Millie picked up one of the magazines and started flicking through it, completely relaxed in these grand surroundings, but Dora perched on the edge of a black velvet-covered couch. From down the passageway she could hear the whirring of sewing machines and the sound of women's voices. Dora smiled to herself. It was just like her days on the machines at Gold's Garments, before she'd started training as a nurse.

Madame Vachet appeared shortly afterwards. She was very slight but utterly terrifying, with almond-shaped eyes, and dark hair drawn back off her face in a bun so tight it pulled the skin of her face taut. She was dressed in a tight black sweater and wide crepe trousers that seemed to swish around her like a skirt when she moved.

She greeted them briskly, kissing them on both cheeks, which startled Dora no end.

'I have your gown ready for you,' she told Millie, ordering her assistants with a flick of her tiny hand.

Millie gave Dora an apprehensive little smile as the assistants whisked her away behind the screens. She had already said that she planned to wear her mother's wedding gown. Lady Charlotte had died when Millie was a baby so she had never known her mother.

'But if I wear her gown it will be almost as if she's there, won't it?' she'd said. 'I just hope I don't let her down and look awful in it!'

She needn't have worried. With her wide blue eyes and

doll-like features, Millie was so pretty she would have made anything look good. But when she stepped out from behind the screen, Dora's breath caught in her throat.

'Well?' Millie bit her lip. 'Will I do, do you think?'

'I'll say! You look – beautiful.'

There was no other word to describe it. The dress was utterly heavenly, a simple shape made up of diaphanous layers of lace and tulle. Scary though she might be, Madame Vachet had done an excellent job of fitting it perfectly to Millie's figure. She looked like an angel, with her halo of golden curls.

'You don't think Seb will take one look at me and run away, then?'

'I think Seb will realise what a lucky man he is.'

The voice made them both look round. Helen stood in the doorway, watching them both. A tear trickled down her cheek.

'Doyle is right. You look beautiful,' she said in a choked voice. 'As every bride should look on her wedding day.'

Millie stared at her, and Dora could see realisation dawning in her eyes.

'Oh, no!' She put her hands up to her face. 'Oh, my dear, I'm so, so sorry. How utterly thoughtless of me. I should never have asked you to come here.'

Millie started to cry. Helen rushed forward and gathered her into her arms.

'Shhh, please don't. This should be a happy time for you, not a reason to be miserable.' She sniffed back her own tears. 'I'm just being a drip, that's all. Take no notice of me.'

'But I've been so insensitive!' Millie wept. 'I should have realised that seeing me in a wedding dress would bring back bad memories for you.'

'Bad memories?' Helen shook her head. 'Oh, no, not at

all. I'm only crying because seeing you has made me remember how wonderful my day was. Everyone was so kind to me, the way you all rallied round to make it so special.'

It *had* been a special day, Dora thought. Helen had planned a private service in the hospital chapel, just her and Charlie as he was so ill. But with Matron's permission the tiny chapel had been filled with well-wishers. Sister Sutton had raided the hospital garden for flowers, Sister Blake had played the piano, and one of the girls had even lent Helen her own wedding dress to wear. All in all, it was one of the best days Dora could remember.

'Are you sure?' Millie looked up at her uncertainly. 'Only I'll understand if you don't want to be there on the day.'

'I wouldn't miss it for the world.' Helen smiled back at her. 'Besides,' she teased Millie, 'someone's got to make sure you get to the church on time and don't trip over your train on the way up the aisle!'

'That's true,' Millie agreed ruefully.

But Helen's face told a different story as she and Dora sat together on the couch, watching Madame Vachet fussing over Millie's alterations on the other side of the room.

'It was brave of you to come,' Dora whispered.

'I very nearly didn't,' Helen admitted with a sigh. 'I walked around the block three times before I managed to get on the bus. But don't tell Benedict, will you?'

Dora shook her head. 'Cross my heart,' she promised.

'I meant what I said,' Helen went on. 'I wouldn't miss this for the world. But I wasn't sure how I'd cope, seeing all these preparations, all this excitement. I didn't want to get upset and cast a shadow over everything.' She gave Dora a watery smile. 'Looks as if I did that anyway, doesn't it?'

'I don't think you've cast a shadow over anything.' Dora nodded towards Millie, who was standing with her arms outstretched, waiting to be pinned into the dress. The sun caught the floaty layers, making her look even more angelic. 'You know Benedict can never stay upset about anything for long. Especially not now. She's so happy and excited about this wedding, even if it wasn't her idea.'

'So she should be,' Helen said. 'I was excited about my wedding day too.'

Dora gazed at her friend's profile. Helen was a beautiful girl, there was no doubt of that. But hers was a solemn kind of beauty, nothing like Millie's frothy prettiness. And she seemed to have grown even more solemn over the past year.

'Do you miss Charlie?' Dora asked.

Helen was silent, and Dora wondered if her friend had heard her. Then she took a deep breath and said, 'Every day. There's hardly a minute goes by when I don't think about him and wish he was here.' As she turned to look at Dora, her dark eyes were wells of sadness. 'When it first happened the pain was so terrible I didn't think I could go on. But gradually it lessened. I suppose it has to, or one would simply die of it. It still hurts, and sometimes I'll hear a song or a voice, or see someone in the crowd who looks like him, and I'll feel that unbearable pain again. But most of the time I find I can think about him without wanting to cry. Which is good, because it means I can enjoy my memories.'

'It's so unfair, that Charlie had to be taken from you so soon.' Dora could feel her own emotion choking her. 'I don't know how I'd cope if—' She stopped talking abruptly. Luckily Helen didn't seem to notice.

'Yes, it is unfair,' she agreed, her smile wistful. 'Of course I wish we could have had longer together. But then I realise how lucky I was that I had any time at all with him. I would rather have been with Charlie for a matter of months than never have known him. I suppose that sounds silly, doesn't it?' she said ruefully. 'That I would rather have gone through all this pain with him than have lived a blissful life without him?'

'It doesn't sound silly to me,' Dora said quietly.

'Anyway, the important thing is we made the most of the time we had together,' Helen went on. 'I don't remember us wasting a single day with cross words or silly arguments. That means I can look back at every day as a special memory and not regret a thing.' She smiled wistfully. 'That's good, isn't it?'

'Yes,' Dora agreed, thinking about Nick. 'It's a very good thing.'

'You two!' Millie called over to them. 'When you've finished gossiping, it's your turn to be fitted for your dresses.'

For the next half an hour, all sadness was forgotten as they lost themselves in a haze of measurements, patterns and dress fabrics. Dora and Helen stood patiently while Madame's assistants fussed around them, sticking in pins and making adjustments to the calico dresses they wore.

'I hope this isn't what we're wearing!' Dora joked. 'It's worse than our uniforms!'

'It's called a toile,' Millie explained. 'Once Madame has the fit just right, she'll make them up in the real fabric. Speaking of which, what do you think of this?' She held up an armful of blush-coloured silk. 'Or should I have this blue? It's rather pretty, don't you think? And it wouldn't clash with your hair,' she added.

'That's very thoughtful of you, but I think you should have whichever colour you like,' Dora said. 'I doubt if anyone will be looking at me anyway. Except your grand-mother,' she groaned.

'Then we should choose something truly shocking to take her mind off you. How about this?' Millie held up a bolt of scarlet satin.

After the fitting, Dora and Helen helped Millie choose her trousseau. The three girls perched on gilt chairs while Madame's models paraded in front of them in the latest fashions. Dora watched Millie taking notes, deciding which to buy, and had to pinch herself to make sure it wasn't a dream. Three years ago, she would never have imagined she would ever be in such opulent surroundings, choosing dresses for an earl's daughter.

They were still discussing the various merits of different gowns when voices from the waiting room distracted them.

'What do you mean, I can't have it?' A woman's voice, loud and imperious, drifted through the half-open door.

'I'm sorry, Madam, but there is a problem with your credit.'

'A problem? What sort of problem?'

Dora looked at the others. Millie pulled a face of mock anguish.

'Your last account has not been settled.'

'That's absurd! Where is Madame Vachet? I insist on speaking to her.'

'Madame is busy with another client at the moment.'

'Then we will wait.'

'Mother, please. Can't we just leave? We'll sort out the problem with the account and then come back for the dress.'

Dora looked up sharply at the sound of the girl's pleading voice. 'Is that Lane?' she hissed.

Millie laughed. 'Honestly, Doyle, I know you don't like her but now you're hearing her wherever you go. She'll be haunting your dreams next!'

174

But the woman's next words wiped the grin off her face.

'No, Lucy, I have come all this way to pick up the clothes I ordered, and I will not be dismissed by this – this person. I insist on speaking to Madame Vachet herself. I'm sure she would not want one of her best customers treated in this way.'

Dora leaned forward. Through the half-open door, she could make out a tall, thin woman in a red silk coat. Beside her, she caught a flash of all too familiar chestnut hair.

'Please, Mother!' Lucy's voice took on a pleading note that Dora had never heard in it before. 'Madame Vachet is busy. Let's just go, shall we? You can telephone later to discuss the matter.'

'I think that may be best, Madam.' The assistant's voice was frosty.

There was a long pause. Then the woman said, 'Very well. But be sure I will not forget this.'

A moment later the door banged shut. Dora stared at Millie and Helen. Astonishment was written all over their faces.

'Well, I never!' Helen said. 'What was that all about, I wonder?'

'Sounds to me like the Lanes haven't been paying their bills,' Dora said.

'That's absurd,' Millie dismissed. 'Everyone knows Sir Bernard is as rich as Croesus. He could probably buy this place ten times over.' She turned her attention back to the models. 'Can we decide on these dresses, please? I don't know about you, but I'm longing for a cup of tea and a bun!'

They had arranged to go to Lyons Corner House for tea after the fitting. But when they stepped outside into the sunshine, Dora said, 'Do you mind if I don't join you? Only I've suddenly remembered there's someone I have to see.'

'Ooh, that sounds mysterious!' Millie smiled. 'Do you have a secret assignation, Doyle?'

'Not exactly.' Dora shifted uncomfortably. 'There's just something I have to say to someone, that's all.'

Chapter Nineteen

Clarissa Lane was still raging as they caught a cab back to Eaton Place.

'I have never been so insulted in my life!' she said. 'How dare they say there is a problem with my credit?'

'I know, Mother,' Lucy sighed.

'I have been one of Madame Vachet's best customers for the last ten years,' her mother continued. 'I helped make her name when she first came to this country. If it hadn't been for me wearing her designs and telling my friends about them, she would still be cutting patterns in a back room in Paris. Honestly, you would think she could be a little more grateful. After all, it's not as if I don't pay my bills regularly.'

Lucy turned her face away to stare at the passers-by from the cab window. 'I don't know why you need a new dress anyway, Mother,' she said quietly. 'You know we agreed we shouldn't be spending more money than is necessary at the moment.'

'Oh, do stop worrying, Lucy!' Her mother was dismissive. 'I told you, your father will be back soon.'

How do you know that? Lucy wanted to ask. 'He's been gone three weeks now,' she said. 'No one has seen or heard from him in all that time.'

Gordon Bird had been putting out discreet enquiries for weeks now, but there had been no news. Her father's bank accounts hadn't been touched, and no one had seen him. It was as if Sir Bernard Lane had simply vanished from the face of the earth.

Lucy suppressed a shudder. So far the bank hadn't got word of his disappearance, which was a relief. But she wasn't sure how long they could go on keeping up the pretence.

'Your father is very good at laying low when he wants to,' her mother said. 'You'll see, he'll come back.'

'And what happens when he does?' Lucy said. 'Even if he comes back, we're still in debt to the bank, far more than we can pay. We stand to lose everything.'

Her mother stared at her as if she was simple. 'He'll sort it all out, of course,' she said. 'And when he does, Madame Vachet needn't think I'll be patronising her establishment again!' she added firmly.

Lucy stared at her mother. There was so much she wanted to say, but she was simply too exhausted to say it. Sometimes she didn't know if Clarissa Lane genuinely didn't understand the gravity of their situation, or if she'd just made up her mind to ignore it.

Helen's words stayed in Dora's mind on the bus journey all the way back through the city and out into the East End.

'I don't remember us wasting a single day with cross words or silly arguments.' It struck a painful chord with Dora. She had just spent the last week ignoring Nick Riley, all because of a cross word. Now he was leaving London today and she didn't know when, or even if, she would ever see him again.

She had been such a fool. She didn't know if she was too late to make it up with him, but she knew she had to try. She couldn't bear the thought that he might leave and never know how much she truly loved him.

She jumped off the bus at the end of Bethnal Green Road and ran all the way to Spitalfields. In Columbia Road the market was closing up for the day and Dora had to push her way through the stallholders' boxes and barrows, tripping over the street kids scuffling among the rubbish for any bruised fruit that had rolled under the stalls.

By the time she reached the tall grey tenement where Nick lodged, her chest was burning for lack of breath. She hammered on the door and then leaned against the wall, fanning her face with her hat to cool herself down.

A middle-aged woman came to the door, wiping her hands on her apron. 'Yes?' She frowned at Dora. 'What can I do for you?'

'I'm looking for Nick Riley.'

'You've missed him, love. He's gone.'

'Gone?' Dora looked around wildly. A bunch of children played with an old bicycle wheel, rattling it like a hoop along the cobbles.

'Left this morning. Told me he was on his way up to Wanstead Flats to meet the fair.'

'Did he say when the fair was leaving?'

'He didn't, but he was in a hurry so I reckon it must have gone by now.'

Dora's heart plunged with disappointment. She was too late.

'Sorry, love,' the woman said. 'Was it important?'

'Yes,' she said in a small voice, barely trusting herself to speak. 'Yes, it was important.'

She returned to the nurses' home, utterly dejected. She thought about taking the bus up to Wanstead Flats, but deep down she knew the woman was right. The fair would already have left by now, and Nick would have gone with it.

She couldn't blame him. Why would he stay when he thought Dora wanted nothing to do with him? Now she had no idea where he was going, or whether she would ever see him again. For all she knew, he might never return.

Why had she been such a fool? She should have overcome her stupid pride and talked to him before it was too late. She'd squandered what little time they'd had left being angry and hurt, instead of spending every minute of the day making those memories that Helen had talked about.

The nurses' home loomed up before her, but Dora couldn't face going inside. She needed to be alone, to gather her thoughts before she faced the others. She skirted the main building and headed instead for the overgrown patch of land behind the house. It was hemmed in by shrubs, hidden under a canopy of straggly trees, and the students often went there for a cigarette to avoid the Home Sister's sharp gaze.

Dora sat down on a tree stump and lit a cigarette with shaking hands. No sooner had she struck the match than she heard the sound of a footstep on the other side of the bushes. Dora tensed, expecting to see them part and another student appear, clutching her own pack of Kensitas, in need of escape.

But there was no one.

'Hello?' Dora called out, her voice loud in the silence. The dappled light shimmered through the overhanging tree branches, but no one came.

The match burned down, and the flame caught her fingers. Dora gave a yelp and dropped it, stamping it out on the grass. As she took out another one, she heard the footsteps again. Someone was lurking on the other side of the undergrowth, circling her.

It wasn't the first time she'd felt as if she was being watched. Ever since that evening by the canal with Nick, she'd had the sense of someone lingering close by, just out of sight. Most of the time she could dismiss it as being just her imagination playing tricks. But sometimes, like now, she had a real sense of someone being close by.

Dora stood up. 'Is someone out there playing silly

buggers?' she called out. 'Because if you are, it ain't very funny—'

She pushed aside the branches and stepped out. The late-afternoon sunlight blinded her briefly after the dappled shade of the undergrowth, and it took her a moment to make out the figure striding towards the nurses' home. It was only as it drew closer that she recognised the shock of curly dark hair . . .

'Nick?'

Her voice came out as barely a whisper but he still heard it, his head lifting towards the sound. He saw her and suddenly he was running towards her.

They fell into each other's arms, clinging together as if their very lives depended on it.

'I thought you'd gone,' Dora whispered. 'I came to find you.'

He pulled away from her, holding her at arms' length. 'Did you?'

'Your landlady told me you'd gone this morning. I thought the fair had left.'

'It did. I got halfway to Waltham Abbey and realised I couldn't leave you. Not the way things were.'

Dora's heart lifted. 'You've changed your mind? You're not going?'

Nick shook his head. 'I've got to go,' he said. 'I've given my word. You understand that, don't you?'

'I know,' she sighed.

'But I'll be back,' he promised. 'And I'll bring the money with me.'

'I don't care about the money!'

'But I do. I want to marry you, Dora Doyle. But I need to know you'll be here waiting for me?'

She smiled up at him. 'I will,' she said. 'Always. You should know that by now.'

Nick's face relaxed. 'I know I should. But sometimes I can't quite believe it.' He pulled her back into his arms, his lips pressed against her hair. 'God, I've missed you so much.'

'Me too. I've been such a fool, I didn't mean to get angry with you, I was so worried, that's all.'

'I know. And then I got angry because I thought you didn't care.'

'What a pair we are, eh? We've wasted so much time.'

'Well, I don't want to waste any more.'

He kissed her. Dora melted against him, her hands going up into the thick springiness of his hair, trying to capture every last sensation of taste and touch as if she might never experience it again. They stumbled backwards, Dora leaning against the wall. They were out of sight of the nurses' home, but Dora was so dizzy with longing she didn't care. Nick's body pressed against her, and her own body kindled in response. She moved her hands down to his belt, tugging his shirt free, and heard him groan against her mouth as her hands found his warm, smooth skin.

'Oh, God, I want you so much,' he whispered hoarsely.

Suddenly Helen's words came back to her, loud and clear: 'I don't regret a single thing.'

Dora moved her head, breaking free of him. Nick looked down at her, his eyes troubled.

'What is it?' He frowned. 'I'm sorry, I didn't mean – you know I would never try anything.'

'I want you to,' she whispered. 'I want us to be together.' She could hardly believe she was saying the words. They seemed to be coming from somewhere deep inside her, from a place she couldn't control. 'One night, before you go away. I want us to have one night together.'

He stepped back, his frown deepening. 'Do you . . . really mean that? You want to?'

She nodded. 'More than anything in the world.'

'But we can't. It wouldn't be right. Supposing you got found out . . .'

Dora put her finger to his lips, feeling the softness of his mouth. 'I don't care.' She was so dizzy with longing she would have run away with him then to the travelling fair and not given it a second thought. 'I just want to be with you. Please, Nick? Don't you want that, too?'

His eyes were glazed with desire. 'More than you can ever imagine.' He kissed her again, more urgently this time, his tongue exploring her mouth, entwining with hers. Dora's body ached in response.

'Where can we go?' she whispered.

He thought for a moment. 'You know that guest house on Roman Road?'

'The Albert?' Dora nodded.

'That's the one. I could book a room there? It's a bit seedy, but – '

'I don't care.'

He trapped her face between his hands. 'Are you sure about this, Dora? I don't want to force you.'

'You're not forcing me. I want this, Nick. I want you.' She smiled at him, trying to reassure him. 'I'll fetch some things and meet you there in half an hour, all right?'

He nodded. 'Half an hour.'

Her legs could barely support her as she hurried up the stairs to her room. But once in the safety of the attic, her nerve started to fail her, and she shivered at the thought of what lay ahead.

It wasn't like her to rush into things, but she had rushed headlong into this without thinking. Now she was assailed by apprehension and doubt. Should she be doing this?

She had often imagined what it would be like to make love to Nick. But in her dreams the first time had been romantic, special, in a beautiful room with sun flooding through the curtains. It had never been in a seedy bed and breakfast on Roman Road.

She wondered if she was doing the right thing. She wanted him desperately, but she was terrified, too. What if she couldn't do it? What if she disappointed him, failed him somehow?

The image of Alf Doyle pushed its way into Dora's mind then. He had abused her, taken away her innocence, raped her in her own bed while her mother slept next door. There had been a time when she thought she would never be able to be with another man. But then she'd fallen in love with Nick, and slowly but surely her desire for him had overcome her revulsion.

Now Dora loved him completely, and wanted him more than she had ever wanted anyone. But would she be able to give herself to him? Or would the spectre of Alf Doyle make her freeze and ruin everything?

And what if Nick knew? What if he could somehow tell that she had been with another man, and turned away from her? She would rather never know what it was like to love him than have him reject her.

She was still troubled by her thoughts when Millie returned.

'It's a shame you couldn't have joined us for tea, you missed a treat,' she said. 'Did you manage to do your errand?'

'Errand?' Dora stared at her blankly.

'The reason you had to rush off?' Millie frowned at her. 'Are you all right, Doyle? You look rather peaky.'

'I'm fine.' Dora shook herself. 'I have to go out, and I won't be back until morning.' She turned away, certain her guilt was written all over her face. 'Could you cover for me?'

'Of course,' Millie said. 'You've covered for me enough times, it's nice to return the favour.' Her gaze fell on Dora's bag. 'Are you sure you're all right? Nothing's happened, has it?'

Dora shook her head. Millie sent her a sideways look, but said nothing. After three years, she understood Dora well enough not to ask any questions.

The Albert boarding house was a seedy, rundown place. Dora did her best not to notice the stench of damp and cats, or the way her feet stuck to the peeling linoleum as she stepped inside the dark hallway. A single bulb flickered weakly overhead.

'Can I help you?' A scrawny woman came out of the doorway at the far end of the passage.

'I—'

But before Dora could speak, the woman said, 'Is your name Dora?'

She nodded. She quickly stuck her left hand in her pocket, conscious of the cheap curtain ring she'd stuck on the third finger. She was sure the woman would spot it in an instant.

'A lad called Nick called round. He left a note for you.'

Dora felt the ground shift under her feet. 'A note?'

'All a bit mysterious, if you ask me. He said you'd arranged to meet here, then handed me this and told me to give it to you.' She rummaged in the pocket of her pinny and pulled out an envelope. 'Course, I told him I wasn't no errand girl, but he gave me a tanner for my trouble.' She nodded at the note Dora held limply in her hand. 'Well, ain't you going to open it?'

Dora stared down at the envelope, with her name

scrawled on it in Nick's handwriting. She didn't want to open it, she was too afraid of what it might say. But conscious of the woman's expectant eyes on her, she finally tore it open.

'Dear Dora, I decided it would be better if I went and caught up with the fair tonight after all. Please don't be angry with me. I want you so much, but you deserve better than this. I'll be back soon. Please look after Danny for me. All my love, Nick.'

'Well?' The woman searched her face. 'Is it bad news?'

Dora looked down at the note in her hand, and smiled. Nick understood her better than she understood herself.

'No,' she said. 'It's not bad news at all.'

Chapter Twenty

'Absolutely not,' said Katie. 'I forbid it, do you hear me?'

Effie hardly listened to her sister as she sifted through her wardrobe, looking for something suitable to wear for her date with Hugo. She had always been the best-dressed girl in Killarney, but now all her dresses seemed too home-spun and old-fashioned for a sophisticated night out.

Meanwhile her sister droned on and on.

'You shouldn't even think about courting,' Katie was saying. 'You have your PTS exams coming up in a few weeks, don't forget. You should be thinking about your studies, not boys!'

'And you've got your Finals coming up in a few months, but I've yet to see you slaving over your books!' Effie reminded her.

'That's different.'

'I don't see how.' Effie pulled out her favourite green dress. 'What about this? Will it do, do you think?'

Katie tutted. 'You're not listening to a word I say, are you?'

'I've listened to nothing else for days!' Ever since Effie mentioned that Hugo had asked her out to dinner, Katie had been going on about it, coming up with reasons why she shouldn't go. It was worse than one of Sister Parker's lectures.

'Can I borrow this?' Effie reached for Katie's lipstick, but her sister snatched it out of her hand.

'Over my dead body! Mammy will kill us both if I let you put on make-up.'

'Please, Katie! I can't go out looking like this. Just a tiny bit, please? Or some rouge . . .'

Katie clutched her cosmetics bag to her chest. 'You're not going out with this boy, Effie. And you're certainly not going out looking like – like a tart!'

'You're impossible!' Effie snatched up her hairbrush and went over to the mirror. 'Why don't you want me to have any fun?'

'I don't mind you having fun,' Katie said. 'I just don't want you going out with medical students. I know what they're like, Effie. They're lazy, they spend their whole time gambling and having parties and getting up to all sorts. Believe me, this man's intentions won't be honourable.'

Effie smiled as she dragged the brush through her hair. 'Now you sound just like Da, going on about young men and their intentions.'

'I don't care. Someone has to keep an eye on you.'

'You're a fine one to keep an eye on anyone! I've still got all those letters you sent me, telling me what you were getting up to in London.'

She saw Katie's cheeks turn pink in the mirror behind her. 'That's different,' she mumbled.

'How is it different?'

'I'm older than you, for a start.'

'You were my age when you first came to London,' Effie reminded her. 'Besides, just because you're older doesn't make you any wiser. I've got a brain in my head. I know what I'm doing.'

'Says the girl who lost her bag five minutes after she got off the bus!' Katie snorted.

Effie narrowed her eyes at her sister. Would Katie ever let her forget that one mistake? 'I know what I'm doing,' she repeated.

'Do you?' Katie shook her head. 'You don't know anything

about this Hugo character. You think you've fallen madly in love with him, don't you?' she sighed. 'And I daresay you fancy he's fallen for you, too. But he's not like the farm hands in the village, Effie. You can't just twist him round your little finger.'

'I don't care,' she declared, putting down the brush. 'I'm going out to dinner with him, and that's that.'

'I'll tell Mammy.'

Effie turned to her, shocked. 'You wouldn't!'

'I'd do anything, if it kept you out of trouble.'

'In that case, I'll tell her what you and your boyfriend get up to!'

'Tom and I are courting,' Katie said primly.

'Yes, but you're not married. You're not even engaged!'

That hit a nerve. Effie knew her sister was desperate for Tom to propose. But after over a year, there was still no sign of a ring.

Katie's mouth firmed. 'It doesn't matter. I know Tom is serious about me.'

'And how do you know Hugo isn't serious about me?'

Her sister laughed. 'Oh, Effie! Medical students are never serious about anything.' She shook her head pityingly. 'You're probably just the latest in a long line of innocent student nurses. And you won't be the last, either.'

Her words hit home, but Effie was determined not to show it. 'You don't know that.'

'I do, Effie. That's why I don't want you to go. I'm not trying to spoil your fun, I promise you. But you're my little sister, and I don't want you to get hurt.' Katie's plump, pretty face creased with concern. 'Please don't go out with him, Effie.'

She had never seen her sister so worried, and for a moment she hesitated. But then she remembered that if she didn't go, it would mean another long, boring night in with her books. And she couldn't face that.

'I'll be careful, Katie, I promise. Sure, it's only one night out,' she reasoned. 'What could go wrong?'

Katie kept Effie talking so long, she was almost late meeting Hugo. She was worried he might have decided she wasn't coming, but to her relief he was lounging against the hospital gates, smoking a cigarette.

Effie panicked and broke into a run. She hurtled past the Porters' Lodge, down the gravel drive and cannoned straight into him.

'Steady on!' He put out his hands to catch her, the cigarette caught between his lips. 'You're a bit keen, aren't you?'

'I'm so sorry I'm late!' she panted. 'I didn't think you'd wait for me.'

'Of course I'd wait.' He took out his cigarette and blew a thin curl of smoke into the air. 'I suppose that Sister Tutor of yours kept you late scrubbing floors and whatnot?'

Effie shook her head. 'It was my sister's fault. She didn't want me to come out with you.'

'Why on earth not?'

Effie felt the heat rising in her face. 'She doesn't think your intentions are honourable. Not just you,' she added hastily, seeing him frown. 'She doesn't have a very high opinion of medical students, I'm afraid.'

'Quite right too,' Hugo said briskly. 'Your sister sounds like a very sensible girl. We're all scoundrels to a man.' He blew another languorous smoke curl into the sky. 'But you still came, in spite of her dire warnings?'

'I wanted to find out for myself,' Effie replied.

'Good girl.' Hugo grinned. 'I like a woman with an independent spirit.' He looked her up and down. 'But your sister was right to be worried. You look so utterly ravishing I'm sure you'd bring out anyone's dishonourable intentions.'

'Do I?' Effie looked down at her dress. She still wasn't sure if it was too old-fashioned.

She was even less sure when they arrived at the restaurant. To her astonishment, Hugo had booked a table at a smart establishment in the West End. Effie had never seen anything like it. The room reminded her of a wedding cake, with chandeliers and white walls decorated with gilt plaster curlicues. Waiters in tailcoats swished between the candlelit tables, and everywhere there was the soft hum of conversation and the clink of china and glasses.

Effie sniffed the air. It even smelled expensive, of good food and wine mingled with French perfume.

She shrank behind Hugo's shoulder as the maitre d' approached them, half expecting him to throw her out for looking so shabby. But the man broke into a smile when he saw Hugo.

'Ah, Mr Morgan, how nice to see you again. Please come this way, your usual table is ready for you.'

Effie followed him, bumping into furniture and diners, apologising to everyone as she passed.

There was a kerfuffle at the table as the waiter tried to pull out her chair for her and spread her napkin in her lap. Effie apologised to him, too, while Hugo watched her across the table with lazy amusement.

'You don't have to keep saying sorry to everyone, you know.'

'Sorry,' Effie replied, then put her hand over her mouth. 'I've never been anywhere as grand as this.' She gazed around her.

Even Katie would be impressed, she decided. Surely Hugo wouldn't have brought her somewhere as posh as this if his intentions weren't honourable?

The waiter fawned over them. Effie was perplexed by the French menu, so Hugo ordered for her.

'I hope you haven't asked for anything too complicated?' she whispered.

Hugo smiled. 'You'll see.'

A moment later the waiter arrived with a silver ice bucket. Effie gawped as he made a great show of popping the cork on the bottle. 'Is that real champagne?'

'Don't you like champagne?'

'I've never tried it.'

'Then you have a treat in store.' Hugo nodded to the waiter to fill their glasses. 'Try it, Euphemia. It's delicious, I promise you. And I defy even you not to end up mildly intoxicated after a glass or two of this.'

He was right, it was delicious. She loved the way the icy bubbles fizzed and danced on her tongue. It was so cold, yet it spread a wonderful warmth through her body, making her feel less nervous. Effie sank two glasses of champagne before she finally began to relax in her surroundings. The drink loosened her tongue, and she was soon chatting easily to Hugo about her sisters.

'I think I know your sister Bridget,' he said. 'Tall, dark-haired woman on Male Orthopaedic? Never smiles, never a hair out of place.'

Effie laughed. 'That sounds like Bridget!'

'The students all call her the Ice Queen. Very beautiful but utterly terrifying.' He took a sip of his champagne. 'No wonder she tried to warn you off me.'

'Oh, no, that was my other sister, Katie. She's a student in her final year. We share a room in the students' home.'

'That sounds like fun?'

'I thought it would be, but she's turned out to be a spoilsport.' Across the table, Hugo stifled a yawn with the back of his hand. Effie was instantly mortified. 'I'm sorry, you don't want to hear about my boring sisters.'

'Not at all, I'm fascinated. But I haven't been to bed all night.'

'Have you been playing cards with your friends again?'

'No, worse luck. I've been studying.'

Effie looked at him, impressed. So Katie was wrong about him, then. He didn't spend all his time gambling and having parties.

'I have to work hard, to keep up the family reputation,' Hugo went on. 'My father is a Nightingale man. That's where he met my mother, when he was a humble student.' He smiled at her over the rim of his glass. 'So you see, your sister's wrong. Not all our intentions are dishonourable.'

Their meal arrived, the dishes covered with elaborate silver domes. Effie stared at her plate in horror as the waiter lifted off the dome with a flourish.

'What is it?' she whispered to Hugo.

'Lobster. Wait until you try it, it's divine.'

Effie pleated her thick linen napkin anxiously between her fingers. 'I don't know how to eat it,' she confessed.

'Here, let me show you. It's quite simple, once you get the hang of it.'

Hugo was right about the lobster, too. It was heavenly, delicate and sweet with a buttery sauce. Effie had never tasted anything like it, and before she knew it she'd cleared her plate.

'My goodness, you were hungry, weren't you?' Hugo commented.

Effie glanced around at the other women. They all seemed as thin as rakes in their expensive silks and furs, picking at their food like birds. It suddenly occurred to her that she should have shown more decorum, instead of ploughing in. How many times had her mammy rapped her knuckles with a ladle for diving in for seconds?

She opened her mouth, but Hugo held up his hand. 'And before you start, don't even think about apologising,' he said. 'There's nothing wrong with a girl having a healthy appetite.'

Hugo ordered more champagne, then a couple of brandies with their coffee. They must have been stronger than her father's poteen, because by the end of the evening Effie was feeling quite giddy. She was having the time of her life.

Until the moment Hugo leaned across the table and said, 'I say, I don't seem to have my wallet.'

Chapter Twenty-One

It was as if the waiter had tipped the ice bucket over her head, shocking her to her senses. Effie sat bolt upright and stared at him across the table.

'You must have it. You paid the taxi driver, remember?'

'I know, but I don't have it now. It might have fallen out on the way here.'

Effie reached for her bag under the table. 'I have some money.'

'That's very sweet of you, but I don't think it will be enough to cover this somehow.'

He picked the bill up off the silver tray and waved it under her nose. Effie caught sight of the figures and let out a squeak of dismay.

'I don't think I've ever had that much money in my life!' she whispered. The brown pay packet that was handed to her every week wouldn't even have covered the price of one glass of champagne. 'What are we going to do?'

He shrugged. 'I suppose we'll just have to make a run for it.'

'We can't!' Effie's mouth fell open in horror.

'What else can we do?'

'I don't know, but there must be some other way.' She cast her eyes around desperately. Was it her imagination or was the maitre d' sending her suspicious looks? 'Surely if you just talked to them, promised to send them a cheque . . .'

Hugo shook his head. 'They'd never agree. No,

Euphemia, I'm afraid we're just going to have to disappear discreetly. Fortunately the place is busy, so we won't be noticed.' He patted her hand across the table. 'It's easy, I promise. All you have to do is get up and walk out calmly, as if you're going for some fresh air. Then, once you're outside, run to the corner and wait for me there.'

'What will you do?'

'I'll think of something.' He smiled at her. 'Don't look so worried, darling, or they'll know something's up. Just get up and walk out calmly.'

As Effie rose, her legs were shaking so much she didn't think she could even stand, let alone walk. Studiously avoiding the maitre d's eye, she forced herself to make for the exit. Her eyes were so firmly fixed on the door, she tripped over a chair leg and stumbled but was too terrified to apologise.

The cool night air hit her and she began to run, clattering along the pavement, her heart hammering in her ears, certain that she must have several waiters on her tail. She dived around the corner and hid herself in the darkened recess of a shop doorway. She braced herself, clenching her jaw to stop her teeth chattering with fear.

Minutes went by. Then, just as Effie had convinced herself that Hugo must have been caught, she saw him sauntering down the street towards her.

She hissed his name and quickly beckoned him over.

'Hello, darling.' He grinned at her. 'I see you've found an excellent hiding place.'

'Never mind that! What happened? Did anyone see you? Did they chase you?' She glanced past him up the street.

'Everything was fine.' He glanced at his watch. 'Now, let's get you back to the hospital, shall we? It's almost eleven and I'm assuming you don't have a late pass?'

He strode to the edge of the pavement and held up his hand, whistling for a taxi. Effie hurried out of the shelter of her doorway towards him.

'What are you doing? We can't take a taxi without any money. And before you say anything, I'm not going to make a run for it again,' she warned him.

'I'm not asking you to, darling.' Hugo reached into his pocket and pulled out his wallet.

Effie stared at it. 'Where – where did you find that?'

'It was in my pocket.' He shrugged.

He whistled again and a taxi came towards them. Effie turned her back to it, facing him.

'We have to go back to the restaurant first,' she said.

'Why?'

'To pay the bill, of course.'

'But I've already paid it.'

She frowned at him uncomprehendingly. And then she saw the gleam in his dark eyes, and slowly it began to make sense. 'You – you tricked me,' she murmured.

'I know! I wanted to see if you'd go through with it.' Hugo gave a shout of delighted laughter. 'Oh, Euphemia, you're such an angel. You should have seen yourself as you were fleeing the restaurant. I'm telling you, you must never consider breaking the law. Because that beautiful face of yours will give you away every time.'

The cab stopped and Hugo opened the door for her. Effie stood rooted to the spot, her heart hammering against her ribs. She didn't know whether to laugh or cry.

'You tricked me,' she whispered again.

'It was a prank, darling, that's all. Just a bit of fun. Now hurry along. If I'm not back at my digs by midnight I shall turn into a pumpkin.' He frowned. 'Euphemia? Are you all right?'

She shook her head. 'I'm not going with you.'

'Euphemia!' he sighed. 'For heaven's sake, be sensible. How on earth are you going to get back to Bethnal Green at this time of night on your own?' Effie said nothing. She stood on the pavement, her hands balling into stubborn fists at her sides. 'Look, I'm sorry, darling. I didn't mean to upset you. It was just a silly joke, that's all. The other students and I play them on each other all the time.'

'Well, I don't like it.'

He frowned. 'I thought you had a sense of humour?'

'I do, but that was just cruel.'

'Then I won't do anything like it again to you, I swear.'

He held up his hand in solemn promise. Effie hesitated. He was still smirking, and she wasn't sure if he was joking. But he was right, she had no idea what bus to catch, or if buses even ran at all at that time of night.

Then she looked at his face, so handsome and full of remorse, and allowed herself to smile. 'I suppose there was no harm done,' she conceded.

'Exactly.' Hugo stepped aside. 'Now please allow me to take you home, otherwise I won't be able to live with myself.'

She forgave him on the way back, but only after he'd apologised over and over, and promised never to play such a horrid trick on her ever again.

'But it was rather funny,' he said. 'You should have seen your face. I thought you were going to faint clean away!'

'So did I.' Effie smiled reluctantly. 'Especially when I tripped over that chair!'

By the time they reached hospital, their argument was forgotten. As they said goodnight outside the gates, Effie was trembling.

'Are you cold, darling?' Hugo asked.

'A little.' She didn't want to tell him it was anticipation

that was making her tremble. He was going to kiss her, she knew it.

'You'd better go inside, in that case.'

'Oh, no, I don't have to go straight away . . .' She stopped herself.

Hugo smiled. 'Oh, I think you do, Euphemia. I don't want your terrifying sisters coming after me, do I? I mean to impress them, you see. Then perhaps they'll allow me to start courting you.'

'I don't care what they say. You can court me whether they like it or not.' She pressed her lips shut. When would she learn not to open her mouth? Every time she did, she managed to say something awful.

Hugo laughed. 'I'm delighted to hear it. But I also have an early lecture first thing tomorrow and I don't think the consultant will be too impressed if I fall asleep. I've done it before and frankly it didn't go down very well.'

He moved closer and Effie closed her eyes, waiting for his lips to descend on hers. But instead he planted the lightest peck on the end of her nose.

'God, you're so sweet, Euphemia.' He shook his head in wonder, and then he was gone.

Sweet? Euphemia watched him sauntering towards the Porters' Lodge, ready to distract the Night Porter while she sidled past. She didn't want to be sweet. She wanted to be sophisticated and irresistible, like Greta Garbo.

Fat chance of that, Euphemia O'Hara, she scolded herself.

The nurses' home was in darkness as she tiptoed towards it, trying not to let her footsteps crunch too much on the gravel. But as she approached it the front door suddenly flew open. Effie froze, helplessly trapped in the light that spilled out from the hallway.

'What is the meaning of this, O'Hara?' Sister Sutton's

voice rang out. She stood in the doorway, her bulky frame silhouetted against the light. 'Do you know what time it is? It's almost midnight,' she went on, without waiting for an answer. 'Nearly two hours after lights out, to be precise. Where have you been until this time, may I ask?'

'Please, Sister, I've—'

'Oh, don't bother to tell me, girl, I'm far too tired to listen to you. I don't take kindly to being kept up at night waiting for students. You can explain to Matron first thing in the morning.'

After that there was no chance of creeping in unnoticed by Katie. She sat up in the darkness as Effie came in.

'There you are!' she said. 'I've been worried about you.'

'Don't you start.' Effie put down her bag. 'I've already had a lecture from Sister Sutton.'

'She caught you, then?'

'Oh, yes, she caught me all right.' Effie sat down on her bed and started pulling off her shoes. 'And she's sending me to Matron in the morning.'

'Good,' Katie said. 'Perhaps *she* can talk some sense into you.'

Effie peered at her sister in the darkness. Katie didn't seem nearly as upset about it as Effie had imagined she would. 'You don't seem very surprised?'

'Why would I be? I was the one who told Sister Sutton.'

'What?' Effie stopped undressing, one shoe still in her hand.

'I reported you.' Katie's voice sounded prim in the darkness. 'You wouldn't listen to me, so I thought you needed to be taught a lesson. I told you I'd do anything to keep you out of trouble.'

'I wouldn't *be* in trouble if it wasn't for you!' Effie aimed her shoe at her sister's shadowy shape. It bounced off her shoulder.

'Ow!' Katie yelped. 'You can't blame me!'

'I do blame you,' Effie said. 'If I'm sent home tomorrow, I'll blame you for that, too!'

Chapter Twenty-Two

'Please, Nurse Doily, has Ernest finished with my comic?'

Dora stopped at the foot of Archie's bed. 'Hasn't he given it back to you yet?' she frowned.

Archie shook his head. 'He's had it a while now. I don't want to trouble him if he hasn't finished with it. But I'd be much obliged if he did give it back soon.'

'I'll look for it straight away, love,' Dora promised.

There was no sign of Lucy when Dora went into Ernest's room. He was lying against the pillows, playing Patience on his bed table. He looked blank when Dora asked him about the comic.

'I finished reading it three days ago,' he said, with a touch of regret in his voice. 'I sent it back to him.'

'Well, Archie says he hasn't got it.'

'But I gave it to Nurse Lane.'

'Perhaps she put it back in your locker?' Dora had just crouched down to take a look when Lucy walked in with her arms full of fresh bedding.

'Oh, good, you can help me make up this bed,' she said. 'I was going to get one of the pros to help me, but you might as well do it as you're here.'

Dora stiffened at her careless order. Why did Lucy always act as if she were the senior?

'Have you seen the comic?' Ernest asked. 'I gave it to you to give to Archie.'

'Oh, that nasty old thing? I took it away and burned it.'

Dora stared at her. 'You did what?'

'I asked Sister Parry about it, and she said I should take it down to the stoke hole.' Lucy put the bedding down and arranged two chairs at the foot of the bed. 'Right, young man, let's have you out of here.'

Dora looked at Ernest. He looked back at her, his face aghast. 'But it belonged to Archie,' she said.

'All the more reason it should be thrown on the fire, in that case.' Lucy shrugged. 'Really, Doyle, you should know better than to let the children borrow each other's things. You know what Sister Parry says about spreading germs. I'm surprised she hasn't told you off about it.'

Dora didn't reply. Deep down, she knew Lucy was right. But as far as she was concerned, the happiness it had brought a lonely boy outweighed any risk involved.

Ernest broke the silence. 'I'm sorry,' he said in a choked voice.

'It's not your fault, love.' Dora glared at Lucy.

'Don't look at me like that,' she defended herself.

'I feel as if it is my fault,' Ernest said. 'Shall I go and talk to Archie? I should apologise to him . . .'

'Certainly not!' Lucy cut in before Dora could reply. 'You're not allowed out of your room. No, Doyle can explain,' she said, with a malicious little smile. 'She's so good with all the children, I'm sure Archie won't mind if she tells him what happened.'

Dora would willingly have scrubbed a thousand bedpans rather than break the horrible news to Archie. He looked up as she approached his bed. The sight of his face, bright with expectation, nearly broke her heart.

'Hello, Nurse Doily,' he greeted her. 'Has he finished with it?'

Dora took a deep breath. 'I'm sorry, Archie,' she said.

His smile dropped. 'What's he done to it? He'd better not have torn any of the pages out.'

'It wasn't Ernest's fault. But I'm afraid your comic got taken away and destroyed.'

Archie's face was blank with shock. 'Destroyed?'

'One of the other nurses took it away. It was an accident,' Dora said. 'I'm so sorry, Archie. I'll see about buying you a new one, I promise.'

"S'all right, Nurse.' Archie's chin wobbled, and for a moment she thought he was going to cry. But then he took a big gulp and wiped his nose on his pyjama sleeve. 'Worse things happen at sea, eh?'

The sight of his little set face, so determined not to give in to his sadness, made Dora want to cry herself.

Archie stayed on her mind all day. Whenever she passed down the ward she could see him sitting in bed, staring down at his hands, his face desolate. She was determined to make it up to him, but had a feeling that even a new comic wouldn't replace the cherished gift.

She was still simmering about it when she joined the rest of her set at the third-year table for supper.

'You look fed-up,' Katie commented, as she passed Dora the plate of bread. 'What's the matter?'

'I'm just a bit upset about something that happened on the ward today.'

Lucy gave a loud sigh from the other end of the table. 'Honestly, Doyle, you're not still going on about that, are you?' She rolled her eyes. 'For heaven's sake, it was only a beastly comic. It's not as if anyone died!'

'I know,' Dora said. 'But a little boy was still heart-broken. Not that it would matter to you!'

'I'm sure that's not true,' Millie jumped in straight away, trying to soothe the situation.

'It is!' Dora said. 'She doesn't care about the children at all. She's got no time for any of them.'

Lucy threw down her fork with a clatter. 'Just because

I don't run around like you, trying to make all the children love me.'

'No, you don't. You're only interested in making Sister Parry love you!'

'So what if I do try hard? We need good ward reports if we're going to be invited to stay on here after State Finals. Being nice to some scruffy little urchin isn't going to get me a staff nurse position after I qualify.'

'That's all you really care about, isn't it? Being the best.'

Lucy shrugged. 'Why should I want to be anything else?'

'Just because you come top in your exams doesn't make you a good nurse,' Dora muttered.

'And just because you break all the rules doesn't make you a good nurse either,' Lucy shot back. She stood up, pushing back her chair.

'Aren't you going to finish your supper?' Katie asked.

'I'm not hungry.'

And then she was gone. An uncomfortable silence fell around the table, broken only by the sound of Katie scraping the contents of Lucy's plate on to her own.

Millie sighed. 'Never mind,' she said. 'it's only another week until our ward allocation finishes. Then you won't have to work with her any more.'

'I'm counting the days,' Dora muttered.

Lucy stomped back to the nurses' home, still seething.

How dare Dora criticise her, just because she tried hard to do her job? Of course she wanted to be the best. Her parents had always drummed into her that trying hard wasn't enough. She had to stand out, to shine. Winning was everything in her world.

But the truth was, she was at a loss on the children's ward. The sight of all those little faces looking up at her so expectantly frightened Lucy more than she wanted to admit. So rather than admit it, she took refuge behind her charts and her medicine trolley, and told herself she was doing a good job.

And as for that wretched comic . . . why did Dora have to keep going on about it? However she might try to cover it up, Lucy did feel guilty about her actions. She didn't deliberately set out to upset a child. Left to her own devices, she might have apologised to Archie, even bought him a comic to replace the one she'd destroyed. But Dora went on about it as if Lucy had committed the worst sin in the world, which only made her more determined to defend herself.

At least it wouldn't be for much longer, she comforted herself. Another week and she would be assigned to a new ward. Hopefully one where she didn't have to watch Dora Doyle charming everyone all day long.

She was so preoccupied with her own thoughts she didn't notice the tall figure waiting under the arch that led to the nurses' home, until he stepped into her path and she almost walked into him.

'Miss Lane?'

She recognised his voice first, that lazy American drawl so deep it seemed to come from his boots. She looked up and found herself staring into the disarmingly handsome face of Leo Alderson.

'Do you remember me?' he said. 'We met at your parents' soirée back in April.'

'How could I forget?' Lucy smiled to cover the nervousness that suddenly raced like fire through her veins. 'What are you doing here, Mr Alderson? Are you sick or injured in some way? Only the Casualty department is over there . . .'

'I don't need a doctor, thank you. I'm here to see you.'

'Me?' Panic fluttered in her chest. 'Whatever for?'

Leo sent her a long, appraising look. 'Is it true your father's disappeared?' he asked.

For a moment Lucy couldn't speak. She was conscious of him watching her, knowing that every second she stayed silent made him more suspicious.

Finally, she found her voice. 'I really don't know what you're talking about,' she squeaked.

'Don't you? I've heard rumours Sir Bernard hasn't been seen around for a while. Which is kind of unusual for a born showman like your father, wouldn't you say?' Leo's brows lifted.

Lucy thought fast. 'If you must know, he's in America.'

'That's what his friend Mr Bird says too.'

Lucy relaxed. 'There you are, then. Mystery solved.'

'Except I've been talking to my contacts in the States and no one's seen Sir Bernard over there either.'

Lucy pulled herself together enough to manage a level of frosty hauteur. 'America is quite a big place, Mr Alderson. Surely even you don't know everyone there?'

'No,' he conceded, 'but I know the kind of people your father might need to speak to.' He paused. 'You want to know what I think?'

'No,' said Lucy, walking away from him.

'OK, here's what I think. I think this German deal has gone wrong and he's fled.'

Lucy gave a forced laugh. 'Why would he do such a thing?'

'Because he can't face the fact that he's failed. The great Sir Bernard Lane, Britain's own King Midas, faces financial ruin. Imagine how ashamed he must feel. I guess if I were him I'd probably want to run away and hide, too.'

'You don't know my father. He would never run away from anything.' Lucy was glad the darkness hid her guilty expression.

'So where is he?'

'I told you, he's gone to America.'

Lucy carried on walking. She could see the nurses' home ahead of her. Another twenty yards and she would be safe.

'I don't know why you're defending him when he's abandoned you and your mother,' Leo called after her.

Lucy froze. Leo's footsteps crunched on the gravel as he approached her, but she couldn't turn around to face him. She was too afraid he would look into her eyes and know he was right.

'If my sources are correct then your father has staked everything on this deal, including his personal fortune.' He was standing close to her now, close enough to touch. 'Your family stands to lose everything. What kind of man would run off and abandon his loved ones to that kind of fate?'

Lucy took a deep, steadying breath. 'Not my father,' she said.

'No?'

She flinched as she felt Leo's hand on her arm. Then she realised he was pressing a card into her hand. 'This is where you can find me,' he said softly. 'Give me a call when you're tired of defending him.'

Chapter Twenty-Three

Effie had forgotten how long Sunday morning Mass could be.

Without her mammy to nag her into going, she hadn't been to church at all since she had arrived in London. There had been so many more exciting things to experience, going to Mass was the last thing on her mind.

But now she knelt down at the back of the church beside her sister Bridget, her hands clasped firmly together, praying with all her might that Our Father might forgive her and see fit to answer her pleas.

Because He was her only hope.

Her ears were still ringing from the reprimand Matron had given her that morning. Effie hadn't imagined it would be that bad as she lined up outside Miss Fox's office with all the other nervous nurses awaiting their turn for a telling off. She knew from her interview that Matron was a lovely woman, softly spoken, with kind grey eyes. She wasn't a dried-up old dragon like her Assistant Matron, Miss Hanley, either. If anyone might remember what it was like to be young and foolish, it was Kathleen Fox.

But the woman who faced Effie across the desk was not the friendly, smiling Matron she remembered. Those grey eyes were like flint beneath the starched canopy of her headdress as she took Effie apart with the precision of a surgeon's scalpel.

'You are in a very privileged position, Nurse O'Hara,' she had said, her naturally soft voice tinged with ice.

'Hundreds of girls apply to train at the Nightingale, and most of them are unsuccessful. You were very fortunate to have been chosen.'

Effie remembered her sister's warning to her to keep her head down, agree with everything her superiors said, apologise even when it wasn't her fault and on no account to answer back. 'I know, Matron,' she whispered.

'If you are aware of that, then why are you so determined to waste such an opportunity?' Matron glanced through the notes in front of her. 'According to Sister Parker, you are a capable girl, but you are lazy and inattentive. Sister Sutton also tells me that you are noisy, disruptive and have no idea about punctuality.' Matron looked up. 'Does that sound like the kind of girl we would want in this hospital?'

Effie felt a lump rising in her throat. She shook her head, not daring to speak.

'I have to tell you, Nurse O'Hara, that your future at the Nightingale is by no means certain,' Matron went on. 'Preliminary Training is nothing more than a trial period. Even if you pass your PTS examination – and I have to tell you, from what Sister Parker reports that doesn't look likely – we may still decide not to accept you for further training. To be a Nightingale nurse is to be acknowledged as the best. Consequently we expect high standards. And you, O'Hara, are falling very far short at the moment.'

Effie stared at her. Until that moment it simply hadn't occurred to her that she might be thrown out.

But now, as she knelt in church, the sunshine through the stained-glass windows scattering jewels of coloured light over the worn stone floor, Effie had to accept the awful truth. She was going home.

The service finished and she followed her sister out into

the sunshine. The air was fresh after the heavy scent of incense inside the church.

'Do you mind if I go for a walk?' Effie asked as Bridget turned to head back to the hospital. She couldn't face returning to another lecture from Katie.

'I suppose not, as long as you don't get yourself lost. Do you want me to come with you?'

'No – thank you. I'd rather be on my own, if you don't mind?'

Bridget frowned at her. 'Are you all right? You've been in an odd mood all morning.'

'I'm fine.' Effie winced at the lie. Now she had dishonesty to add to her list of sins. And she hadn't even been to confession. 'I just need a breath of fresh air, that's all.'

'See you don't get into any trouble,' Bridget warned her.

Effie sighed. It's a bit late for that, she thought.

Victoria Park was bathed in midsummer sunshine. Effie sat on a bench and watched the boats on the lake, trying to lift her spirits. But the happiness and laughter all around her only made her realise how much she would miss it all when she was sent back to Ireland. How would she ever be able to bear the shame of being the only O'Hara sister not to become a Nightingale girl? Her mammy would never let her hear the last of it. She would grow old and die in Killarney under her mother's watchful eye.

And she would never see Hugo again. After last night, she was almost certain she was in love with him. But once she was sent away he would probably forget all about her.

Effie pulled the slim textbook out of her bag and opened it. She had brought it with her, hoping that different surroundings might somehow make it easier to take in. But as she forced herself to read a chapter, all she could think of was how far behind she was. Catching up seemed like a hopeless task.

The words blurred on the page as hot tears of frustration sprang to her eyes.

Effie closed the book with a sigh. It didn't look as if anyone was going to answer her prayer after all.

'Heel! Come back, you daft bugger!'

Jess hauled at the lead, yanking Sparky back to her side. He strained on the end of her arm, yapping in frustration at the duck waddling away, just out of reach of his nose.

She couldn't blame the poor little thing for being over-excited. He spent most of his time with Sister Sutton in her office or her flat. The only time he saw the world was his daily amble around the grounds of the nurses' home. No wonder he was always so bad-tempered.

Which was why she'd convinced Sister Sutton to let her take him for a stroll in the park. It had taken nearly a week to persuade her, and even then the Home Sister had only relented on the understanding that Jess shouldn't let him off the lead or out of her sight.

But it had been worth it. Sparky loved every minute of his walk, paddling on the edge of the lake, snuffling through the grass and sniffing trees.

'Come on, boy, time to go home. Sister will be worrying about you.'

As Jess turned to follow the tree-lined avenue back towards the gate, she spotted Effie sitting on a bench ahead of her. Even from a distance Jess could tell she was upset. Her dark head drooped like a flower on the slender stalk of her neck.

Don't get involved, Jess warned herself, pulling on Sparky's lead to turn back the way they'd come. Whatever's wrong, it's none of your business.

She started to walk away, but she couldn't get the image of the girl's downcast face out of her mind. Before she even knew what she was doing, Jess had turned around again and was walking towards her.

'Effie?'

She looked up with a wobbly smile. 'Hello, Jess. Fancy seeing you here.'

Jess noticed the book in her hands. 'I'm sorry, I didn't realise you were studying. I won't disturb you.'

'No, please, you're not disturbing me. I could do with the company.'

Jess sat down beside her. 'I can't stay long,' she said. 'Sister Sutton will be worried about Sparky.'

Effie didn't reply. Sparky stood on his back legs and propped his paws on her knees, but she ignored him. She stared out across the lake, lost in her own thoughts.

Jess tried again. 'Lovely day, ain't it?'

'If you say so.'

Jess sent her a sidelong look. 'Blimey, you look like you've lost a shilling and found a farthing. What's up with you?'

Effie sighed. 'I'm going home,' she said.

Jess sat forward. 'Back to Ireland? Why?'

'Because I'm not good enough to stay here.'

And then it all came out, like a dam bursting. Effie explained that she had been sent to Matron, who had as good as told her she had no chance of passing her PTS.

'And even if I do, they probably won't let me finish my training here, so I may as well not bother,' the girl said. 'I'll be the only one of my sisters not to be a nurse. It's not fair! I tried so hard.'

Jess said nothing. It wasn't worth pointing out that she'd never seen Effie with a book in her hands. The poor girl was already unhappy enough, without making it worse.

'And I was just starting to enjoy being here, too,' Effie went on. 'I'd made some friends, and I have a boyfriend. I daresay Hugo will forget all about me once I'm back in Killarney.'

Tears started to roll down her cheeks and she fished up her sleeve, looking for her handkerchief. Jess pulled hers out of her pocket and handed it to her.

'Here, it's clean.'

'Thanks.' Effie took it and blew her nose loudly.

'When is your PTS exam?' Jess asked.

'In two weeks.'

'That's plenty of time for you to get some studying in, surely?'

Effie shook her head. 'It's hopeless,' she said, sniffing back her tears. 'I can't seem to lodge any of it in my head. I don't even understand half the words in this book.'

Jess glanced at her textbook. It was the same one Sister Sutton had given her.

'Can't you revise with the other girls?' she asked. 'They'll help you, surely?'

Effie pulled a face. 'They'll only make fun of me. You know what Padgett is like.'

'What about your sister?'

'Katie's too busy studying for her own exams. Besides, I don't want her to know how bad things are. I'll never hear the last of it.'

'You mean you'd rather go back to Ireland than admit you need help?' Jess said.

'I suppose not.' Effie sighed. She picked up the book. 'I just wish I knew someone who understood all this, and could explain it to me.' She opened it and showed Jess one of the pages. 'I mean, look at all these bones and muscles. How am I supposed to remember whether the tibia is bigger than the fibula, or the other way round?'

'The fibula is thin, like a flute. The tibia is thick, like a tuba,' Jess replied without thinking.

Effie frowned at her. 'I beg your pardon?'

'It's an easy way of remembering,' Jess said. 'Flute and tuba begin with the same letters as fibula and tibia, you see? That's how you can tell which way round . . .' She stopped, seeing Effie's expression. 'What? Why are you staring at me like that?'

'How do you know so much about anatomy?'

Jess felt herself blushing. 'I must have heard you nurses talking about it.' She rose to her feet. 'Anyway, I'd best get back. Sister Sutton will think I've kidnapped Sparky.'

She set off, walking away briskly, but Effie followed her. 'Wait, Jess. Tell me the truth. Where did you learn all this?'

Jess slowed down. 'Sister Sutton lent me a book,' she admitted reluctantly.

'And you understood it?'

Jess scowled at her. 'I'm not as stupid as I look.'

'I'm sorry, I didn't mean that.' Effie looked shame-faced. 'I'm just surprised that anyone understands it, that's all.'

'It's not too hard, if you work out ways of remembering things.'

Jess saw the spark of hope kindle in Effie's eyes, and realised with a sinking heart what the girl was thinking before she even opened her mouth. 'Could you teach me?' she asked.

Jess shook her head. 'I don't think that would be a good idea,' she said. 'I'm not a proper teacher.'

'You've already taught me the difference between a tibia and a fibula, and that's something no one else has managed!'

Jess smiled in spite of herself. 'Yes, but I don't think Sister Sutton would like it. Besides, I haven't got time.'

'Please?' Effie begged. 'I'm desperate, Jess, truly I am.

You're my last hope.' She snatched up Jess' hand and clung to it. 'I'm begging you. I'll even pay you . . .'

'I don't want your money.'

'Then I'll just have to appeal to your charitable nature.' Effie squeezed her hand harder. 'Please, Jess? I don't want to go home to Ireland. You're my only chance. Please say you'll help me?'

Jess looked into the girl's face, so full of hope. She wanted to say no, she knew she should, but somehow she couldn't bring herself to say the words.

'I suppose I could do it for a few days,' she said. 'But you'll need to work very hard,' she warned. 'I won't put up with any slacking or excuses.'

'No, miss.' Effie looked solemn.

'I mean it. Any messing about, and I'm giving up.'

'I'll work hard, I swear.' Effie beamed. 'Oh, Jess, you're the answer to my prayers!'

'I dunno about that,' Jess muttered, embarrassed. She looked down at Sparky, who sent her a weary look back.

'You are, you really are.' Effie hopped up and down in delight. 'When can we start?'

Jess took the book from her. 'No time like the present, I suppose,' she said. 'Walk with me, and I'll test you on the way back to the hospital.'

Chapter Twenty-Four

It was always sad when a patient died. But it was even more heartbreaking when it was a baby.

It was one of the juniors, Elliott, who found little Bobby Turner in his cot, just after they came on duty at seven. She was still trembling as Sister Parry delivered her morning report to the nurses gathered around her desk in the middle of the ward.

Everyone was saddened by the news, but no one was surprised. Bobby Turner had never really stood a chance. They'd all done their best for him, with injections of mercury and then Salvarsan. But in spite of their efforts, little Bobby had simply wasted away before their eyes, his joints horribly swollen by the infantile syphilis that had eaten away his frail little body.

'He has been moved to side room four,' Sister Parry said calmly. 'Jennings, I want you to take everything away for washing and sterilising. The cot must be stripped right down and scrubbed before it's used again, do you understand? And Elliott, I want you to help Doyle with last offices.'

'M-Me, Sister?' The junior looked stricken.

'Yes, Elliott. It will be good experience for you to observe it being done.'

Dora watched Elliott as Sister Parry handed out the rest of that morning's worklists. The poor girl's face was grey against the starched white of her cap. Good experience or not, it seemed a harsh thing to do to her, after the shock she'd had.

When Sister Parry had finished her report, the nurses went their separate ways to set about their work. Dora went into side room four where little Bobby lay on the bed, covered by a top sheet. The blinds had been drawn. She stood for a moment, her hands folded as she murmured a quick prayer for the dear little soul to find a peace he had never known in this world.

The door opened and Elliott came in, pushing the trolley laden with soap, flannels, scissors, brushes, cotton wool and water.

'I – I wasn't sure whether to bring a comb,' she said shakily, her gaze fixed on the trolley. 'I've only ever practised setting a trolley like this before, and never for an infant . . .'

Dora glanced over the items on the trolley. 'You've done very well,' she said.

'Th-Thank you, Nurse.'

Dora watched her as she pushed the trolley into the room, her face still averted from the bed. 'Elliott?' she said gently.

The junior looked up at her, and Dora saw tears running down her ashen cheeks. 'I'm sorry, Nurse,' she whispered. 'I know I'm being an absolute fool, but—'

'It's all right,' Dora comforted her. 'It's always a shock, the first time.'

'I wish I hadn't been the one to find him.' The words bubbled out of the girl as if she could hold them back no longer. 'I w-was only doing a favour for the night nurse, because she had a headache and wanted to go off duty early. If only I hadn't offered to help . . .' She drew in a deep, shuddering breath.

'I know.' As Dora patted the girl's shoulder, could feel the tension trembling through her body as she fought to hold back tears.

'It seems such a shame.' Elliott sniffed. 'Do you think he was in much pain? You know, before he—'

Dora shook her head. 'You mustn't let yourself think like that.'

'He had no chance, did he? Born to a mother like that. Do you know, she didn't come in to see him once, not since he was admitted? Just dumped him here and went off, so Staff Nurse Ryan said. I wonder if she'll bother to come to his funeral?'

I doubt it, Dora thought. Bobby's mother was probably back on the docks by now, turning tricks for sailors, her baby long forgotten.

'We'd best get on with this,' she said. 'Are you sure you're up to it?'

Elliott nodded, sniffing back her tears. 'You're right, we need to get on,' she said bracingly. But as she went to soak the flannel, her hand was shaking so much she dropped the soap, splashing water everywhere.

'I'm so sorry, Nurse.' She reached down to clear it up and knocked the scissors off the trolley. They went skittering across the linoleum floor.

Dora sighed. 'I think it's probably better if you leave this to me,' she said kindly. 'It's all right, I can manage on my own.'

Elliott stared back at her, terrified and grateful at the same time. 'But Sister said I had to . . .'

'Sister Parry is dealing with a new admission. She won't know anything about it.' Dora smiled kindly at Elliott. 'Go to the kitchen and compose yourself for a minute or two. You won't be any use to us if you're at sixes and sevens all day.'

'Thank you, Nurse.' Elliott hurried out of the room, tripping headlong over the trolley in her desperate haste to escape.

Dora washed little Bobby, then dressed him in the knitted baby clothes they kept in the linen cupboard for this kind of occasion. She took the flowers she'd brought from the sluice and arranged them in his hands.

She was fastening the ribbons on his bootees when Sister Parry's voice rang out.

'Doyle! What are you doing?'

Dora turned round. Sister's plump shape filled the doorway to the side ward. 'Why isn't Elliott helping you as I asked?'

'I told her I could manage alone, Sister.'

'Oh, you did, did you?' Sister Parry's eyes hardened. 'Tell me, Doyle, have you been promoted to Matron recently?'

'No, Sister.' Dora squared her shoulders, bracing herself for what she knew was to come.

'No, and yet you feel you have the right to overrule my specific instructions.'

Colour burned in her face. 'She was upset, Sister.'

'She's even more upset now, I can assure you. I've sent her to Matron.'

Dora gasped. 'But it wasn't her fault!'

'No, it wasn't,' Sister Parry agreed. 'It was entirely *your* fault, Doyle. But perhaps in future Nurse Elliott will learn not to listen when you start giving orders.' Sister Parry took a step towards Dora, so she could see the angry tightness of her mouth. 'I gave Elliott this task for a reason. I know she was upset, but she needs to learn to rein in her emotions if she is to become a good nurse. She won't have a soft-hearted senior there every time she sees a dead body.'

'There's nothing wrong with having a soft heart, Sister.'

Sister Parry's eyes widened with shock. 'Are you arguing with me, Doyle?'

Every inch of Dora was telling her not to do it. Apologise, the voice inside her head said. Say sorry, hang your head and hope for the best.

But she couldn't. Not this time. Sister Parry had picked on her too often.

She lifted her head and met the ward sister's eye.

'Yes, Sister,' she said. 'I am.'

Dora hadn't been summoned before Matron in ages, and she had forgotten how terrifying it was, stepping into the book-lined office. Matron sat behind her desk, her black-clad figure tall and very straight against the sunshine that flooded in through the window behind her.

'Well, Doyle?' she said softly. 'Sister Parry has told me what happened. Perhaps you would care to explain yourself?'

Shaking with nerves, Dora tried to put her side of the story as clearly as she could. Matron listened intently, her steady grey gaze never leaving Dora's face.

'I see,' she said, when Dora had finished. 'Well, I can tell you only acted to spare a junior's feelings.' But just as Dora was allowing herself to relax, Matron went on, 'Nevertheless, you were wrong to act as you did. For this hospital to function properly, everyone has to know their place. You have to learn to take orders, even if you don't agree with them, and especially if you don't feel like obeying.' She clasped her hands together on the desktop. 'What do you think would happen if everyone followed your example and did what they wanted, rather than what they had been told to do? If a probationer decided that instead of cleaning the bedpans as was necessary, she would go off and arrange some flowers instead? No one would have any authority and nothing would get done. The ward would be in chaos in no time. Don't you agree?'

It wasn't a question, Dora knew that. She might have been foolish enough to argue with a ward sister, but no one argued with Matron. If she said it was raining outside, everyone put up their umbrellas.

'Yes, Matron,' she mumbled.

'You will miss your next day off as punishment,' Matron said, making a note in her ledger. 'I want you to apologise to Sister Parry immediately, and make sure there is no repetition of this. If I have cause to reprimand you over such a matter again, it will be the last time. Do you understand?'

'Yes, Matron.'

Dora trailed back to the ward, already practising her apology in her head. But it wasn't the thought of saying sorry to Sister Parry that she dreaded so much as the smug look she knew would be on Lucy Lane's face when she did it.

But the only expression on Lucy's face was a deep scowl. She whisked past Dora into the kitchen, banging the door behind her.

'What's wrong with her?' Dora whispered to Daphne Anderson, who was stacking up dirty dishes on the trolley, ready for washing up.

'She's just had some bad news,' Daphne replied. 'How did it go with Matron, by the way? Was she truly awful?'

'You know Matron. She can make you feel like a worm just by looking at you. I have to apologise to Sister Parry anyway.' Dora rolled her eyes. 'At least we'll be seeing the back of each other in a few days. I don't know which of us will be more relieved.' She caught Daphne's smirking expression. 'What's so funny?'

'I've got some bad news for you, too,' Daphne said. 'You know Staff Nurse Ryan was sent to the sick bay earlier? Well, it turns out she has suspected Scarlet Fever.'

Dora's stomach dropped. 'And?' she said, although she already knew the answer to that one.

'And Sister Parry can't afford to lose any experienced students. Miss Hanley has just been up to tell her that you, me and Lane are staying on here until our State Finals.' Daphne grinned. 'You'd best hurry up with that apology, Doyle. It looks as if you and Sister are stuck with each other for another three months!'

Chapter Twenty-Five

It was Sister Sutton's day off, and she was preparing for it like a military operation.

Jess had never known the Home Sister have a day off, but a former nurse friend of hers had been taken ill, so she and Sister Parker were going down to the south coast to visit her.

Sister Sutton had been going on about it for days, fussing about catching her train, and how she was going to get to and from the station. Every morning when Jess took her breakfast in, she would find a stack of railway timetables on her bedside table.

And when she wasn't fussing about her journey, she was fretting about leaving Jess in charge.

'The windows will need cleaning, and don't forget to polish the floors.' She bustled around the nurses' home, pointing out all the jobs that needed doing in her absence. She looked very different out of uniform, dressed in an old-fashioned tweed coat in spite of the warmth of the July day. 'And I want you to keep an eye on the students, too. Miss Hanley has kindly offered to take charge of the office while I'm away, but I want you to keep me informed of any misdemeanours.'

'Yes, Sister.'

'And don't forget to clean that brasswork and take the lampshades down for washing.'

'Blimey, how could I forget? You've already told me a dozen times!'

Jess' muttered comment was barely louder than a breath, but Sister Sutton still heard it.

'Yes, and I'll tell you another dozen times if I have to!' she snapped.

It was a relief when Sister Parker arrived to collect her friend. She was a gentle-looking elderly lady, as petite as Sister Sutton was bulky, with white hair and pebble-lensed spectacles. Jess couldn't imagine why all the students were so utterly terrified of her.

'Are you ready, Miss Sutton?' Her Scottish accent was soft and pleasant.

'I think so, Miss Parker.' Sister Sutton adjusted her shapeless hat in the hall mirror. 'I'll just fetch Sparky's lead . . .'

'Surely you can't think you're going to take that dog with us?' Sister Parker shook her head. 'I'm afraid they won't allow him in the convalescent home.'

Sister Sutton's jowly face quivered. 'Why not?'

'I know you dote on your little dog, Miss Sutton, but not everyone likes them. Some people find them rather – unhygienic.'

From the look in her blue eyes, Jess guessed Sister Parker was one of them.

Sister Sutton looked down at the terrier sitting at her feet. 'Very well,' she said. 'Then I won't go either.' She started unbuttoning her coat.

'Oh, but you have to!' Jess blurted out, then felt herself redden as she caught Sister Sutton's eye. 'Your friend will be so disappointed,' she added.

'She's quite right,' Sister Parker agreed. 'Besides, we've bought the train tickets.'

'But I can't leave Sparky by himself.' Sister Sutton looked near to tears at the prospect.

'I'll look after him,' Jess offered.

'You? Look after Sparky?' Sister Sutton looked horrified at the very idea. 'Oh, no, I don't think so.'

'But he's used to me,' Jess reasoned. 'And I've been taking him for walks in the park, haven't I?'

To prove her point, she reached down to pet Sparky, who promptly snapped at her fingers. Treacherous little beast, Jess thought.

'Well, I think it sounds like a very sensible suggestion,' Sister Parker said briskly.

'But what if he gets upset without me?'

'For heaven's sake, it's only a wee dog!'

'I'll take very good care of him,' Jess cut in, as Sister Sutton looked upset. 'It's only for a few hours, and your friend will be ever so disappointed if you don't visit.' And I won't be able to help Effie revise, she added silently.

'I suppose you're right,' Sister Sutton's heavy sigh set her chins wobbling. 'I shall at least give him a biscuit before I leave.'

As she went off, Jess and Sister Parker exchanged long-suffering looks. It was hard to tell which of them was more relieved.

Jess worked hard throughout the morning, racing through her duties – which were a lot easier without Sister Sutton following her around, picking holes in everything she did. Although with Sparky trotting after her, watching her closely, it felt as if he'd become his mistress' eyes and ears.

'Yes, I am getting into the corners,' Jess muttered, as he sat watching her clean the window, his head tilted on one side. Then she laughed. 'Listen to me! I'll be as daft as Sister Sutton soon, talking to you as if you're human.' She pointed her cloth at him. 'Don't you dare go telling her I said that, all right?'

When Jess had finished all her chores, she tidied herself

up and went to Effie's room to help her revise. She was waiting for Jess as usual, her textbooks spread out on the bed.

'I think I've got respiration taped at last!' she announced proudly, her blue eyes shining.

'Let's hear it, then.' Jess sat down cross-legged on the floor to listen. She fondled Sparky's ears absent-mindedly as Effie described the whole respiration process.

When she'd finished, she regarded Jess anxiously. 'Well? Did I miss anything out? Please tell me I didn't?' she begged.

'It was perfect,' Jess said.

Effie smiled with relief. 'I'm so glad! I spent all last night trying to learn it. I don't think I ever want to think about it again after this wretched exam is over.'

Jess didn't like to point out that passing PTS was just the beginning. She'd spent most of the past week keeping Effie calm and telling her she could get through it.

And, to Jess' credit, Effie had applied herself. She had spent every night with her books and not sneaked out or stayed out late once.

And now Sister Parker was taking the day off, Effie had all day to seek Jess' help.

'Is there anything special we need to revise today?' she asked.

Effie thought about it. 'Well, I do need to practise bandaging,' she said. 'That is, if you don't mind sitting there while I truss you up like a turkey?'

'If it helps you.' Jess shrugged.

They could hardly contain their giggles as she sat on the chair while Effie put Jess' arm in a sling and dressed her 'fractured' ribs and skull.

As Effie worked she chattered about the forthcoming examination, and how desperate she was to pass.

'I really don't want to go home to Ireland yet,' she sighed. 'Not when I've fallen madly in love.'

Jess rolled her eyes. At least this time Effie had managed nearly twenty minutes without bringing Hugo's name into the conversation. Usually she could turn the subject around within five.

Effie never stopped talking about her new boyfriend. And the more Jess heard about him, the less she liked the sound of him. Not that she could ever tell Effie that.

She sat patiently now, Sparky curled up at her feet, as Effie told her how Hugo had sneaked into the grounds of the nurses' home and thrown stones up at her window to wake her in the middle of the night, just so he could see her face.

'It was so romantic,' she sighed. 'He said he hadn't been able to stop thinking about me since we met. He wanted to climb up the drainpipe to my room.'

Jess stared at her, scandalised. 'I hope you didn't think about letting him?'

'Of course not,' Effie replied, then added, 'Katie would have gone mad.'

'And I dread to think what Sister Sutton would have done!' Jess said.

'Trust you to be so practical!' Effie wound the bandage around her head and pulled it taut. 'You wait until you're courting, then you'll know how it feels.'

Jess thought about Sam. They weren't courting, exactly. A cup of tea in the local café after their night class every week was hardly the height of romance, but she had started looking forward to it almost as much as she looked forward to the class itself. She wasn't sure what she would do when their exams were over and they didn't have to meet every week. Sam hadn't talked about it, and neither had she.

'There.' Effie pinned the last piece of bandage in place and stepped back to admire her handiwork. 'How does that feel?'

Jess turned to admire herself in the mirror. But as soon as she moved her head, she felt the bandage slowly unravelling itself.

'Is it meant to do that?' Jess asked, as the bandage slipped down over her right eye.

'Not as far as I know,' Effie sighed. 'I can't seem to get it right. It keeps coming apart.'

Jess caught her eye in the mirror. Effie looked so despondent, Jess couldn't help smiling.

'It's not funny!' Effie protested. But then a loop of bandage slithered down around Jess' neck, and she started laughing too.

'What's going on?' They were both laughing so hard they hadn't heard the door opening. Anna Padgett stood in the doorway, with a couple of other girls from Effie's set.

Anna looked from one to the other of them. 'What are you doing?' she asked coldly.

Jess jumped up at once, pulling off the bandages. But Effie was unconcerned. 'Jess is helping me to practise my bandaging.'

'You should have come to us. We could have helped you.'

Jess stared at the floor and willed Effie not to say anything, but of course she did.

'Thanks, but I prefer revising with Jess. She explains things to me, you see.'

Jess risked a glance at Anna. Her face was a picture of astonishment. 'How could someone like her possibly help you revise?' she asked

Once again, Jess silently pleaded with Effie not to speak up.

'Actually, Jess is very clever,' said her friend. 'She knows more about anatomy than I do.'

'That's hardly difficult, in your case!' Anna murmured, and the other girls laughed.

Anna turned to Jess, scarcely able to hide her contempt. 'You do know you're not supposed to be in our rooms, don't you?'

'But I invited her,' Effie put in.

'Even so, I don't think Sister Sutton would like it.'

Jess read the threat in the other girl's cold stare. 'I was just leaving,' she mumbled.

'Wait a minute . . .' Effie started to say, but Jess cut her off.

'She's right,' she said. 'I shouldn't be here.'

'But what about my revision?'

'We'll help you,' Prudence said. 'We're a set. We're meant to stick together, aren't we?'

Jess left them and went back to her room. She felt more foolish than upset. She should have known that her friendship with Effie would be exposed and ridiculed. But the way Anna had looked down her nose at her, and her disbelief when Effie had told her how clever Jess was, still rankled.

'No point in getting upset about it, is there?' she said aloud to Sparky. 'We don't need them anyway. We're better off keeping ourselves to ourselves.'

She sought refuge, as she usually did, in her reading. For once she didn't pick up the anatomy book Sister Sutton had given her, but instead chose *Jane Eyre*. The story of the quiet governess who saw her dreams come true was somehow comforting.

She had barely found her favourite place when there was a soft knock on the door.

'May I come in?'

Jess put down her book at the sound of Effie's voice on the other side of the door. 'If you like.'

The door opened and Effie's dark head appeared around it. 'I just wanted to say sorry,' she said. 'About Padgett, I mean. She had no right to talk to you like that.'

Jess shrugged. 'It doesn't matter.'

'Yes, it does. You've helped me so much, even if I don't get through this exam I'll always be grateful to you.' She hesitated. 'And I wondered if you'd carry on helping me?'

Jess looked up sharply. 'What about Padgett and the rest? I thought you were going to revise with them?'

'I don't want to. They're all so busy showing off what they know, they're no help at all to me. I want to revise with you. If you'll do it?' Effie looked up at Jess from under her lashes. 'Will you?'

Jess smiled reluctantly. 'I suppose so,' she said.

Effie grinned. 'I am glad,' she said. 'Because I really need to get this capelline bandage right before next week.'

Effie had just about mastered dressing Jess' fractured skull when Sister Sutton came home that evening.

Typically, she greeted Sparky before she even noticed Jess.

'Have you missed me, my sweet?' She bent down to gather him into her arms. 'Has he been quite well? You haven't neglected him?'

'He hasn't left my side all day,' Jess replied.

'And you've given him his supper? The chicken I left out for him?'

'He ate every scrap. And a few biscuits, too.'

'Did you, you naughty boy?' Jess held her breath as Sister Sutton examined him. 'Well, he seems all right,' she conceded finally. 'And what about your chores? I take it you've finished them all?'

'Windows cleaned, brasswork polished and lampshades taken down, just as you ordered.'

'I shall inspect them later.' Sister Sutton bent down with difficulty to put Sparky on the floor. 'Now I shall go to my room. I'm rather tired.'

Usually Jess would have been relieved to escape. But there was something about Sister Sutton's grey, exhausted face that made her say, 'Would you like me to make you a cup of tea before you turn in?'

Sister Sutton stared at her for a moment. Then, to Jess' astonishment, her fleshy lips curved in the shadow of a smile. 'That would be very nice,' she said. And just as Jess was reeling from the shock of seeing her smile, she added, 'Perhaps you would like to join me? I must say, I am rather in need of some company.'

It felt very odd, to be in Sister Sutton's sitting room as a guest and not just to clean. Jess perched on the edge of the overstuffed armchair, a cup of tea in her hands, and gazed at the mantelpiece. Sister Sutton had a mania for knick-knacks. Every surface in the room was covered in glass paperweights, china ornaments and Toby jugs. Jess dusted them all every day, and lived in fear of accidentally sending one crashing on to the hearth.

'How is your friend?' she asked, breaking the silence.

Sister Sutton, whose eyelids had been drooping, snapped awake. 'Her health is improving,' she said. 'But unfortunately her fall has left her unable to manage for herself. I don't suppose she will ever be able to go home to her cottage. Such a pity for poor Rosemary.' She shook her head.

'Where will she go?' Jess asked. 'Does she have family to look after her?'

'I'm afraid not. She chose to dedicate her life to her profession, you see. She did not marry, so she has no children to care for her in her old age. It's the same for many of us,' Sister sighed.

'So what will happen to her?'

'Oh, there are charitable institutions who will take her in. She has a place at the home for retired nurses in Bournemouth.'

There was something about the pinched look on her face when she said it. 'You don't seem very keen on the idea?' Jess remarked.

'Oh, my dear, I'm not.' Sister Sutton shuddered. 'I'm sure the ladies there are well looked after, and of course if you have nowhere else to go . . . but I have seen them, and I would rather not end my days in a place like that.'

Jess sipped her tea and wondered how to ask her next question. But it seemed Sister Sutton had read her mind.

'I was fortunate, I suppose, that when I retired from the wards, Matron allowed me to stay on here as Home Sister,' she said. 'The Nightingale has been my home since I was your age, and I would very much like to see out my days here. But who can say what the future may bring?' Her expression was desolate. 'Rosemary's accident has brought home to me how precarious our lives really are. It only takes a fall, or an illness of some kind, and suddenly you are unable to continue your duties and have no choice but to go . . .'

Jess looked into Sister's eyes, which were dark with sadness, and realised how worried she was about such a fate. Her visit to her friend seemed to have lowered her spirits dramatically.

'Go on, don't talk like that. You've got years left in you yet!' said Jess. 'You and Sparky will still be following me round when you're a hundred, telling me I ain't cleaned the grates or set the fires properly.'

Sister Sutton looked up at her, and once again Jess saw her small, sad smile.

'I hope so, my dear,' she said. 'I truly hope so.'

Chapter Twenty-Six

The first Sunday in the month was visiting day on the children's ward, and Sister Parry was in an even worse mood than usual as she gathered the nurses around the table for her morning report.

'Staff Nurse Ryan will be away for some time, so her duties will have to be shared out among the rest of you,' she told them all. 'Anderson, I want you to take over specialing room two. Doyle, you can assist her. Lane, I want you to take over most of Staff Nurse Ryan's duties while she's away. You can begin by assisting me with the medicine round.'

'Yes, Sister.' Dora watched Lucy preening herself as Sister Parry handed out the rest of that morning's jobs. Dora shouldn't have been surprised, of course, that Lane had been given nearly all the senior jobs. She was Sister Parry's pet, after all.

'And of course it's visiting this afternoon,' Sister Parry continued, her lips tightening. 'Although I'm sure we could all do without that disruption, since we're short-staffed.'

'That's so typical of her, to only think about herself,' Dora muttered to Daphne Anderson later, as they made up Ernest's bed.

'She has a point, though,' Daphne said. 'You know what the children are like once visiting time is over. This place is absolute bedlam. Half of them are inconsolable because their parents have gone, the other half scared out of their wits because they arrived in the first place.'

It had come as a shock to Dora at first to see the younger patients reeling in terror at the sight of people who had become strangers to them beside their cots. It broke her heart to see the agony on the parents' faces, too. They had waited so long to see their babies, but their babies no longer knew them.

'As far as the children here are concerned, we're their families now,' Daphne said, smoothing down the drawsheet.

'Except we're not allowed to comfort them if they're lonely or afraid. I can't imagine what kind of mother would ignore a crying child.'

'I'm sure Sister Parry knows best,' Daphne replied primly. 'She does care, you know. In her own way.'

Dora sent her a sidelong look. Daphne was like Lucy, desperate to stay in Sister's good books.

'All I know is, I can't wait to get off this ward,' she murmured. 'I thought I'd love working with kids, but Sister's made it an absolutely misery.'

Damn Staff Nurse Ryan and her scarlet fever, she thought. Being laid up probably wasn't nice for her, but it was even worse for Dora, being stuck on the ward for another three months.

As if they weren't busy enough, a new patient was admitted in the middle of the morning, just as Matron arrived to do her rounds. Sister Parry seemed most displeased at the interruption, and immediately had two pros usher the girl off to a bathroom while she discussed the case with Matron.

'She has been sent over from the orphanage in Stepney,' Dora heard Sister Parry saying. 'A most unusual case, I believe. She was adopted by a couple from the church last year, but her new mother returned her to the orphanage two weeks ago, saying they couldn't cope with her any longer. She hasn't spoken a word or eaten since.'

'I expect the poor child is in shock,' Matron said. 'She doesn't appear particularly wild, I must say. I wonder why her adoptive parents couldn't keep her?'

'I'm sure it's not for me to ask questions like that, Matron,' Sister Parry replied primly.

'Quite.' Matron paused. 'When is the doctor coming in to see her?'

'Mr Hobbs is due in an hour, Matron.'

'Please keep me informed, Sister. I would be interested to know what he makes of this child.'

They continued with their round. Dora watched them going from bed to bed, Matron tall and stately in her black dress and elaborate white headdress, Sister Parry and Lucy flanking her on either side. Dora tried to tell herself she wasn't jealous, but the sight of Lucy simpering in the background irritated her. It wasn't fair. Lucy Lane made it clear she disliked children, and barely tried to disguise her contempt for them. And yet she was the one who was shown off to Matron, while Dora was dismissed to the kitchen like a dirty pro.

She helped the juniors get Emily, the new arrival, into bed later.

'She's so pretty, isn't she?' Elliott said admiringly as they tucked her in. 'Like a little china doll.'

She really was like a doll, Dora thought. Emily lay against the pillows, her golden curls arranged around a waxen face. Her blue eyes were devoid of emotion like a doll's, too.

Like Matron, she wondered what the child had done to drive her adoptive mother to take her back to the orphanage. Lying there, lifeless against the pillows, she didn't look as if she was capable of any kind of wickedness.

Dora didn't have much more time to think about the new arrival as it was soon visiting time. The families started to arrive outside the double doors just before two, their faces pressed to the glass, trying to catch a glimpse of their children. Sister Parry positioned herself close by, her eyes on the clock, waiting for precisely two to strike. When it did, she nodded to the pros to open the doors and usher the visitors in, two at a time. They had to file past Sister, who checked over each visitor carefully and then handed out tickets, two per bed. She also confiscated any sweets they'd brought with them.

'Sweets must be shared among all the children,' she pronounced, if anyone complained. 'Either that, or they don't come in at all.'

Archie's family arrived and were very vocal, arguing amongst themselves and with Sister Parry until they finally settled on which of his brothers and sisters should be allowed to accompany their mother inside to visit him. The others had to be content with making a nuisance of themselves on the other side of the double doors, pulling faces at Archie through the glass.

By contrast, Ernest's only visitor was the elderly house-keeper. She turned up in her black coat and hat as usual, a parcel tucked under her arm, and marched unsmiling into his side room.

Her visit certainly didn't seem to cheer him up. When Dora went in to offer her a cup of tea, she found Ernest asleep while the elderly woman sat in silence at his bedside.

'Well, this is nice, I must say,' she grumbled to Dora. 'And to think I came all the way from Hampstead for this. I might as well have stayed at home.'

'I'm sure you're well paid for your trouble,' Dora replied. Inwardly, she decided that if she had a such a boot-faced visitor, she would probably stay asleep, too.

'It's all right, you can wake up now,' she whispered to Ernest, when visiting time was over and the housekeeper had gone off grumbling to catch her bus. 'The coast is clear.'

Ernest did a good job of feigning wakefulness, yawning and stretching and looking around him. But Dora wasn't fooled for an instant.

'Oh, has Mrs Philpott gone?' he looked around him.

'As if you didn't know!' Dora put her hands on her hips. 'It wasn't very fair of you, you know. The poor old dear came a long way to see you.'

Ernest scowled. 'You said yourself, she gets well paid for it.'

'Ah ha! So you were awake!'

His fat cheeks turned deep red.

'All right, I was pretending,' he admitted. 'But I don't want her to come,' he went on. 'All she ever talks about is whether I'm keeping up with my lessons.'

Dora eyed the parcel on his bedside table. It was a long box, fastened with string. 'At least she's brought you a present.'

Ernest cast a disinterested glance at the box. 'My mother sent it from Germany for me.'

'Aren't you going to open it?'

He shrugged. 'I don't need to. I expect it's a train. Mother always buys me trains. I've told her I don't really like them, but she never listens.'

'Can I have a look?'

'If you like.'

Dora unfastened the string and opened the box. Sure enough, inside was a wooden train, a perfect replica intricately carved and painted. 'Goodness, what a beauty,' she said. 'Don't you want to play with it?'

Ernest lifted his plump shoulders in a careless shrug. 'I told you, I don't particularly care for trains. Besides, it's no fun playing on your own.'

Dora felt a twinge of pity for him. 'All the same, it's a very thoughtful gift,' she said. 'And it's a shame to leave it in its box.'

'I think you should give it to Archie,' he said.

Dora stared at him. 'Why would you want to give away your new toy?'

'Because he lent me his comic, and I lost it. I asked Mrs Philpott to bring me another one to replace it, but she said Mother wouldn't approve of comics. So I thought I'd give him this instead. He likes trains, doesn't he?' Ernest looked up at her, his eyes anxious. 'That would be all right, wouldn't it? I haven't taken it out of its box, so it wouldn't have germs or anything?'

'I'll ask Sister, but I'm sure it will be all right. But are you certain you want to give away such a beautiful toy? What will your mother say?'

'She won't care. She probably won't even notice,' Ernest said. 'Will you give it to him, Nurse? Tell him I'm sorry – about his comic.'

Dora smiled. 'I'll be pleased to,' she said.

Archie was overjoyed with his gift. His hands were shaking as he took it out of its box and stared at it reverently.

'It's smashing,' he whispered, his face shining with delight. 'Can I really borrow it?'

'Ernest says you can keep it.'

Archie's eyes were round when they met hers. 'Really? He said that?'

Dora nodded. 'It's to make up for your lost comic.'

Archie gazed down at the train. 'This is worth a hundred million comics,' he sighed.

'I'm glad you like it.'

Archie was thoughtful for a moment, then he said, 'Nurse Doily? Would it be all right if I nipped in to see

Ernest later – just to thank him for the present? I won't stay long, honest,' he promised.

'Certainly not!' Dora did her best impression of a scandalised Sister Parry. 'You know you're not allowed out of bed. Sister would have a fit if she caught you.'

Archie gave her a cheeky smile. 'Ah, but she'd have to catch me first, wouldn't she?'

'Archie Duggins, if I catch you out of bed I won't be responsible for my actions!'

'Anything you say, Nurse Doily.' He looked innocent. But Dora caught the glint of mischief in his eyes and had a feeling that he would do it anyway.

Chapter Twenty-Seven

'I must say, O'Hara, I am very surprised to see you before me today.'

Matron faced Effie across her desk, solemn-faced. Effie clasped her hands in front of her in an effort to stop them shaking.

'So am I, Matron,' she said.

'But it seems that contrary to Sister Tutor's predictions, you have somehow managed to pass your Preliminary Training examination.' Miss Fox consulted the results sheet, eyebrows raised as if she still couldn't quite believe the words written in front of her. 'I suppose it just goes to show what miracles can happen if you apply yourself, does it not?'

'Yes, Matron.' Effie struggled to contain her excitement. It rose like a bubble inside her, and would have exploded into laughter if she hadn't kept her mouth clamped so tightly closed.

She had passed! She had been in a daze since she read the results pinned up on the wall of the dining room. The other girls had all crowded round the minute the piece of paper had gone up, but Effie had lagged behind. She was already mentally preparing herself for what she would tell her mammy.

But there it was, in black and white. O'Hara, E. – PASS. Even then she had to ask Prudence to read it out to her, in case she had made a mistake.

'Are you listening to me, O'Hara?'

She came to, to see Matron watching her closely, brows rising to meet the edge of her starched bonnet.

'Yes, Matron. Sorry, Matron.' Effie felt herself turning red.

'You're really going to have to learn to stop daydreaming if you're going to train here for the next three years.'

It took a moment to realise what she had said. 'You mean I can stay, Matron?' Effie's face brightened.

'I am inclined to grant you the benefit of the doubt, given your family connection with the Nightingale,' Miss Fox replied. 'Your sisters are excellent nurses, and I hope they will be a good influence on you.'

'Yes, Matron,' Effie promised, although her mind was already elsewhere.

She couldn't wait to tell Hugo. Poor boy, the last couple of weeks had been so boring for him. She'd only been able to see him a couple of times because she was studying so much, and even then she'd wept on his shoulder because she was convinced she was going to fail.

'Oh, do buck up, Euphemia,' he'd told her briskly. 'You're absolutely no fun when you're in this mood.'

At least now she could tell him she was staying. He would be so pleased. And she wouldn't have to do any more wretched exams for ages, so she could afford to relax and have a good time.

'You needn't think this is the end of the matter.' Effie looked up sharply. Katie had often told her that Matron had a gift for mind reading, and she seemed to be showing it now. 'You will be spending the next three years on the wards, under the supervision of the sisters, and you will need to pay careful attention to everything you are told and follow their orders precisely. There will be patients' lives at stake, and any small mistake could have dire consequences. Do you understand, O'Hara?'

'Yes, Matron,' Effie replied, although she was already

looking out of the window, her mind wandering to how she could celebrate.

Matron sighed. 'Very well,' she said. 'You may go. I daresay you and your friends will want to congratulate each other.'

Prudence was standing in the passageway, waiting for her turn to go in and see Matron.

'What did she say?'

'I'm staying on,' Effie replied, still dazed.

'Oh, well done!' Prudence's plain face broke into a smile. 'I hope she lets me stay, too.'

'Oh, she will,' Effie reassured her. 'If she'll let me stay, she'll let anyone!' Then, realising what she'd said, she added, 'I'm sorry, I didn't mean—'

Prudence laughed. 'I'm glad you're staying, O'Hara. The place would be so boring without you!'

After she'd finished talking to Prudence, Effie hurried back across to the nurses' home to find Jess.

She didn't have to look far. Jess was in the hall, polishing the linoleum. She must have been waiting for her, because she looked up sharply the minute Effie walked in.

'Well?' she whispered.

Effie forced her features into a sombre look, and saw Jess' shoulders slump.

'Oh, well, at least you know you did your best,' she said. 'Perhaps you're just not cut out for nursing . . .'

'I've got three years to find out, haven't I?' Effie grinned.

Jess stared at her, the truth dawning. 'You! You had me going there.' She prodded Effie with the end of her mop. 'Have you really passed?'

Effie nodded. 'Thanks to you.'

Jess' cheeks turned pink. 'You're the one who took the exam,' she mumbled.

'Yes, but I wouldn't have had a hope of passing it if you hadn't made me buckle down and learn.'

Jess smiled shyly. 'Well, I'm pleased for you.'

'We'll have to go out and celebrate.'

Jess's smile faded. 'Don't you want to go out with the rest of your set? I'm sure I heard them planning something earlier on.'

'I daresay I'm not invited,' Effie said. Anna Padgett had been very off with her since she'd found out about her friendship with Jess. 'Anyway, I'd rather go out with you. So where do you fancy going? My treat,' she added.

Jess still looked doubtful. 'Are you sure you wouldn't rather go out with the others?'

'I told you, didn't I?' Effie replied. She thought for a moment. 'Tell you what, why don't we get the bus and go to Lyons? I've always wanted to go there. Katie says it's a beautiful place. What time do you finish work?'

'I'm supposed to finish at six but—'

'I don't want to argue about it.' Effie held up her hand. 'I'll meet you here at half-past. And don't be late!' she warned.

In the end it was Effie who was late. Jess was waiting for her, standing outside the nurses' home, dressed up in a pink coat and hat.

'You look grand,' Effie said. 'That coat really suits you.'

Jess blushed and shrugged off the compliment. 'I got it for my auntie's wedding. It was only second-hand, mind. I haven't had much call to wear it since, but I thought as this is a special occasion . . .'

'Quite right, too,' Effie said. 'Shall we go? I'm starving. I hope Lyons is as good as Katie says.'

'I wouldn't know,' Jess said. 'I've never been.'

'Never been to Lyons?'

'Never been past Aldgate.'

Effie stared at her in astonishment. 'You mean to tell

me you've lived in London all your life and you've never been up west?'

Jess looked awkward. 'Never had any call to go. Although I did see the Tower of London once. From a long way away,' she added.

Seeing Jess' sheepish expression, Effie wondered if she'd embarrassed her friend. She always seemed to be putting her foot in it. 'I suppose I'd never seen the sea before I got on the ferry to England,' she admitted.

They had reached the hospital gates when she heard someone calling out her name.

'Euphemia! Wait!'

Effie turned around to see Hugo running down the drive towards her. Before she could react, he grabbed her and lifted her off her feet, swinging her round in the air.

'I've just heard the news. You clever girl!'

Effie laughed with delight. 'Put me down, you fool! You're making a show of me. Whatever will Mr Hopkins say?'

Hugo lowered her back to the ground. 'I must take you out to celebrate. Let's go dancing.'

'I'd love to. When?'

'There's a dance on at the Palais tonight. Why don't we go?'

Effie felt a moment's excitement, then remembered Jess standing beside her. 'I can't,' she said. 'I've already made plans to go out with my friend.'

'I'm sure she won't mind?' Hugo said, not looking at Jess. 'This is a special occasion, after all. It's not every day my girl passes an exam!'

My girl. The words rang in Effie's ears. It was official then. She and Hugo were courting.

He turned to Jess. 'You don't mind, do you?'

''Course not,' Jess mumbled.

'You see?' Hugo said. 'She doesn't mind at all.'

Effie glanced at Jess whose expression was unreadable. 'Are you sure?'

'I said so, didn't I?' There was an edge to her voice. 'Besides, I'd rather stay at home and read a book anyway.'

'We'll go out another night,' Effie promised.

Jess didn't reply. Effie had a feeling of unease as she watched her friend walk away, back up the drive towards the hospital. But then Hugo seized her hand and pulled her into his arms, and she was so happy she told herself she was imagining Jess' frostiness.

But she started to regret abandoning her friend even more when she found out a group of Hugo's medical student friends were going dancing with them. There were some other student nurses, too, senior to Effie. They looked down their noses at her when she and Hugo met them outside the dance hall.

'You've found a date, then?' one of the young men called out. 'Didn't think you'd be able to get one at such short notice.'

Effie pulled Hugo to one side as they lined up to buy their tickets. 'I thought we were going dancing on our own?'

'What difference does it make?' He stroked her chin with the tip of his finger. 'Don't look so cross, pet. It will be fun. You know what they say – the more the merrier!'

Effie glanced at the frosty faces of the student nurses. They didn't seem very merry to her. 'I suppose so,' she sighed. Although it was hardly the romantic evening she had been expecting.

The dance hall was lively, much busier than the village dances she'd been to in Killarney. The band was more sophisticated, too, with their evening jackets and slicked-back hair. The low-lit floor was already filled with couples swaying to the music. Effie watched them, wondering if she would ever be able to follow all their steps. She didn't want Hugo to have to drag her round the floor like a sack of potatoes.

She wasn't sure whether she was relieved or disappointed when he ushered her over to sit at a corner table with his friends.

'Aren't we going to dance?' she asked.

'Plenty of time for that later, angel.' Hugo winked at her. 'What can I get you to drink? I'm afraid it may have to be port and lemon and not champagne since I'm rather low on funds.'

But the promised dance never came. Effie sat beside Hugo, listening to him laughing with his student friends. On her other side the nurses were talking among themselves. Effie cradled her drink and thought about the fun she and Jess could have been having.

She had a sudden image of her friend standing there at the hospital gates, all forlorn in her best pink coat.

'Everything all right, my love?' Hugo reached out and squeezed Effie's hand. She smiled back. She didn't want to complain and ruin everyone's evening. Hugo would think she was a bore, and she didn't want that.

Besides, she thought, it should be enough that she was here, in a dance hall, with the most handsome man in the room. It was the kind of thing she'd always dreamed of in Killarney, and now her dreams had come true. The least she could do was try to enjoy them.

She decided to make more of an effort and turned to talk to the girl next to her. 'How do you do?' she said. 'I'm Effie.'

'Frances Bates,' the other girl replied in a chilly voice.

It wasn't the warmest introduction she'd ever had, but

Effie was determined not to be put off. 'I've seen you in the students' home, haven't I? Which ward have you been assigned to?'

'Parry.'

'I'm on Parry, too!' Effie smiled. 'I'm so nervous about it. It will be nice to have a friendly face there.'

Frances gave her a look that was anything but friendly. 'I don't know about that,' she said. 'I'm senior to you, you can't just chatter away to me.'

'Oh, for heaven's sake!' Effie laughed. 'You're only in the set above mine. That doesn't make you a senior!'

'Yes, it does,' Frances snapped. 'Senior to you, anyway.'

Fortunately, one of the students claimed her for a dance then.

'You'll have to forgive Bates,' said another of the girls, leaning across the table towards Effie. 'She's just spent three months scrubbing bedpans in the sluice. She's looking forward to having someone junior to her that she can pass the dirtiest jobs on to.' She smiled. 'I'm Hilda Ross, by the way. I'm in the same set as Bates, and I'm going to be on Parry too.'

'Pleased to meet you. Although I don't know if we're allowed to speak, after what your friend said.'

'Take no notice of her.' Hilda waved her comment aside. She was a big girl, as tall as Effie but more solidly built. She might have looked mannish but for her artfully teased brown curls. 'Between you and me, she's in a sour mood because she used to be sweet on Hugo herself.'

'Oh!' Effie looked towards the dance floor, where Frances Bates was twirling in the arms of a lanky, fair-haired student. 'I didn't know.'

'How could you?' Hilda shrugged. 'Anyway, it didn't last long. And now she's with Andrew, so it doesn't matter. But I'm afraid you may have to get used to the other girls resenting you, now you're with Hugo,' she said. 'He's quite a catch.'

Effie stared at her, not sure how to reply. She hadn't imagined anyone being jealous of her.

The song ended, Frances and her partner returned to the table and Hilda started gossiping with the girl on her other side. Effie turned her attention back to Hugo. He was guffawing with his friends over the latest prank they'd pulled, when they'd telephoned one of the student nurses on night duty to tell her there was an emergency admission on the way.

'We only did it to wake her up a bit,' he said. 'How were we to know she would go into a complete panic and summon the Night Sister?'

'Or that Miss Tanner would wake up the Senior Registrar?' put in his friend Andrew.

'By the time we telephoned back to let her know it was a joke, the whole place was in uproar!' Hugo laughed.

'What happened then?' Effie asked.

He shrugged. 'Miss Tanner was completely furious, of course. The poor little night nurse was sent to Matron, who tore a huge strip off her for wasting everyone's time.'

'What about you? Didn't you get punished for it too?'

Hugo and his friends exchanged knowing looks. 'The nurse was a good sport. She didn't give the game away.'

'So you got away with it?'

'We lived to fight another day!' Hugo and his friends clashed glasses in mutual salute. Effie watched them, frowning. That poor girl must have been frightened out of her wits. And she'd got into trouble on their account. It all seemed rather cruel to Effie.

Hugo glanced at her. 'Cheer up, angel.' He nudged her. 'It was only a harmless prank. You'll have to get used to them if you're with me.'

'Hugo's the joker of the pack!' another of the young men announced, and they all laughed.

Hugo squeezed her hand, and this time Effie made herself laugh with them.

Chapter Twenty-Eight

The brand new pros arrived on the ward promptly at seven o'clock, the pair of them huddled together in the doorway as if for protection.

Dora recognised Katie's sister Effie straight away. She had the same dark curls and blue eyes as her sister, but while Katie was all plump curves, Effie was as slender and leggy as a young gazelle.

She looked as terrified as one, too, her wide eyes gazing about apprehensively. Her pale skin had a distinctly greenish tinge.

'Look at those two. Little do they know what's in store for them!' Dora heard one of the new juniors, Hilda Ross, commenting to her friend.

'I bet they think they know it all, just because they've got through PTS,' the other junior, Frances Bates, agreed. 'Let's see how they feel when they've spent three hours scrubbing toilets to Sister's satisfaction!'

'Have a heart, you two,' Dora said. 'You were in their position yourselves once.'

'Not any more, thank God!' Frances Bates muttered with feeling.

Dora approached the pros, who shrank back towards the doors. 'Sister doesn't come on duty for another half an hour, so you might as well make yourselves useful and get the bedpans ready,' she said. 'And make sure that cap is on straight,' she added to Effie. 'Sister Parry inspects everyone first thing.'

They rushed off to the sluice, giggling nervously together. Dora smiled as she watched them go. Frances Bates had a point, she thought. She wondered how long it would take for the novelty of the bedpan round to wear off.

Sister Parry came on duty at precisely seven-thirty, and took the night report. Lucy Lane was at her side as usual. Then Sister summoned the nurses around the table in the centre of the ward and handed out the worklists.

'You have arrived on a most auspicious day,' she told the pros. 'It's ward-cleaning day today. It will be a chance to put all those cleaning skills you've learned in PTS to good use. I hope you will make Sister Parker very proud.'

But it wasn't just the pros who had to help. Everyone was involved in ward-cleaning. Once a week, the beds were pulled into the middle of the ward, and the floors behind were thoroughly swept, mopped and polished. The lampshades were taken down and washed, and the bedframes cleaned and dusted. The children took it all in their stride. In fact, they seemed to enjoy the novelty of having the nurses bustling around them with mops and brooms.

'Please, Nurse, Sister has told me to use a pad when I'm scrubbing the floors,' Dora heard Effie approach Lucy, her voice barely above a whisper.

Lucy frowned. 'Yes? And what do you expect me to do about it?'

'I – I don't know where they are. I can't find any pads in the cleaning cupboard.'

'Oh, for heaven's sake!' Lucy rolled her eyes. 'Use your common sense, girl. Or are you completely stupid?'

Effie flinched. 'I – I—'

'It's all right, O'Hara, I'll help you.' Dora stepped in. 'You have to make a pad for yourself. Come with me, I'll show you.'

As they walked away, Effie whispered, 'I'm sorry I'm being dense, Nurse.'

'You're not being dense at all. You're here to learn, and we're supposed to help you.' Dora shot a sideways look at Lucy. 'Here, you fetch a towel from the linen cupboard and put it in a pillowcase. Use that as a pad when you scrub.'

'Thank you, Nurse.'

'And if you need to know anything else, you'd best come to me,' Dora added.

'Oh, I will,' Effie replied with feeling.

For once Dora was excused ward-cleaning. Daphne Anderson was off duty until twelve, so Dora had to look after Ernest.

She was surprised to find he wasn't alone in his room. Archie was sitting at Ernest's bedside. He looked up when Dora walked in.

"S'all right, it's only old Doily,' he said with relief.

'What have I told you about calling me that?' Dora scolded. 'And what are you doing in here, Archie Duggins? You know you're not supposed to be out of bed.'

'I got bored,' he said. 'And I thought Ernest might like to play with his train.'

'It's your train now,' Ernest reminded him.

'We can share it,' Archie said magnanimously. He turned to Dora. 'We weren't doing any harm, honest.'

'All the same, I don't think Sister would like it.'

'Sister doesn't have to sit in bed until her bum gets numb, does she?' Archie said. 'Go on, Doily – I mean, Nurse Doyle,' he amended. 'Just another five minutes, please? Me and Ernie are mates.'

'So I see.'

Dora looked at Ernest, his plump face turned to her in silent appeal. He had almost recovered from his rheumatic fever, he would be going home in a couple of weeks. And Archie was making a good recovery from his bout of pleurisy, too. What harm could it possibly do to let them have some fun together?

'Five minutes,' she said firmly. 'But by the time ward-cleaning is over I want you back in your beds. Promise?'

'Scout's honour, Doily!'

Dora sighed. Archie was far too naughty ever to be a boy scout. 'I have to check Ernest's temperature first, then I'll leave you to your game.'

Archie sat beside Ernest, making faces as Dora did his TPRs. Ernest was trying so hard not to laugh that he could barely keep the thermometer between his clenched lips.

'You're really not helping, you know!' Dora scolded Archie. But deep down she knew he was. Ernest had lost his pale, miserable appearance. She had never seen him looking so healthy, or so happy.

She came out of the side room later to hear the sound of girls giggling. Frances Bates and Hilda Ross were hanging around the sluice-room door, laughing together.

'What's so funny?' asked Dora.

Hilda fell guiltily silent, but Frances smirked. 'Look what the new pro's doing!'

Dora peered around the corner. Effie was on her hands and knees, kneeling on the pad in the middle of the ward, scrubbing for all she was worth.

'Oh, dear.' Dora looked around. Lucy was at the far end of the ward, but thankfully there was no sign of Sister. 'You could have told her,' she said.

'And spoil our fun?' Frances muttered.

Dora tiptoed up the ward to stand behind Effie. 'Nurse O'Hara?'

Effie jumped so suddenly at the sound of her name, she nearly sent the bucket of soapy water flying. She caught it just in time and scrambled to her feet, tucking her stray dark curls inside her cap. 'Yes, Nurse?'

'That pad isn't to save your knees, Nurse. You're supposed to put it under the bucket to stop it making rings on the clean floor.'

Effie looked down at the pad, then at the bucket. Colour swept up from her starched collar, engulfing her whole face in burning scarlet. 'Oh! I – I thought Sister was being kind, Nurse.'

Dora smiled. 'Sister isn't that kind, I'm afraid. Not to us nurses anyway.' She caught sight of Effie's helpless expression. The poor child looked as if she might cry. 'Don't get upset about it. It's only your first day, you can't be expected to get everything right,' Dora said kindly.

'But I'm not getting anything right!'

'You're doing better than I did on my first day, I assure you.'

Effie gave her a trembling smile. 'Thanks, Nurse.'

After ward-cleaning was over and everything had been put away, it was time to serve lunch to the patients. The porters brought the food up to the ward on trolleys, and Sister Parry served it out for the nurses to take to the patients.

Dora was given the job of feeding Emily. As the child was refusing solid food, Sister instructed Dora to prepare some bread and sugar soaked in warm milk for her instead. Dora sat beside the bed, one arm under Emily's pillow to prop her up, and encouraged her to take the mixture from the spoon she held to her lips.

'Come on, love,' she coaxed. 'Just try a little bit. It'll do you good.'

Emily didn't resist Dora's efforts, but she didn't welcome them either. She lay in Dora's arms like a doll, looking up at her with those great wide eyes. The vacant expression in them frightened Dora. Being sent back to the orphanage must have been hugely upsetting for her, Dora thought. It had sent her into some kind of deep shock, as if her spirit had somehow abandoned her body, leaving behind an empty shell.

'I wish you could tell us what was wrong with you, love,' Dora whispered. 'Then we could make you better.' But Emily didn't respond.

After a great deal of encouragement, Dora finally managed to spoon half the bowl of bread and milk into the little girl's unresisting mouth. She had expected Sister Parry to complain about her taking so much time, but she merely inspected the bowl, nodded and said, 'That's more than she managed yesterday. Very good, Doyle.'

'Thank you, Sister.' But just as Dora was glowing from the unexpected compliment, Sister added, 'Now perhaps you'd like to explain what Archie Duggins is doing in a private patient's room?'

Lucy was sent off duty at one, and told to return at five. She was changing out of her uniform at the nurses' home when the maid knocked on the door and announced there was a telephone message for her, and could she call Mr Bird at her father's office urgently?

Lucy's heart jumped in her chest. It was all she could do to stay composed as she told the maid, 'Thank you. I'll be down in a moment.'

She forced herself to finish changing, but all the time her thoughts were racing. It had to be news at last. And surely it had to be good news, too? If it were very bad, Gordon would have come to the nurses' home himself.

She risked a smile at her reflection as she smoothed her chestnut hair, carefully arranging the waves over her shoulders. It was good news, she knew it. Her father had returned, and he had managed to sort out all their problems, just as she had known he would. Now everything would be back to normal, and she wouldn't have to worry herself to sleep any more.

Gordon Bird took a long time to come to the telephone. Lucy stood in the empty hall, tugging at her thumbnail between her teeth, listening to the echoing silence.

Finally, she heard his voice at the other end of the line. 'Lucy?'

'Uncle Gordon?' Anxiety got the better of her. 'Is it my father? Has he come home?'

'I'm afraid not, my dear.' Gordon's voice sounded weary. 'I'm sorry.'

Lucy swallowed down her disappointment. She had got used to the constant nagging feeling of anxiety ever since her father disappeared. But to have her hopes raised and dashed again was almost too much for her.

'But I'm afraid something else has happened,' Gordon went on. 'Something very unfortunate, that I felt I should warn you about.'

Every muscle in her body tensed in instant terror. He was going to say her father's body had been found, she knew it. It was the news she had been expecting ever since he went missing.

'Yes?' She could barely manage the word.

'It's about Leo Alderson. He knows your father has disappeared, and about the problem with the bank. He has the whole story, and he intends to print it.'

Lucy's mouth went dry, remembering that night outside the nurses' home. She might have known Leo wouldn't stop digging until he'd uncovered everything. 'Where did he get it from?'

There was a long silence. 'He invited your mother out to tea,' Gordon said heavily. 'She told him everything. It wasn't her fault,' he added hastily. 'Alderson caught her unawares. Clarissa thought it was an interview for the society pages. You know what your mother is like, she doesn't always grasp the seriousness of a situation.'

'Oh, I know what she's like,' Lucy said. She could just imagine Leo Alderson plying her mother with champagne, flattering her, making her feel as if she could confide her troubles in him.

Clarissa was already overcome with self-pity; all it would take were a few drinks and some sympathetic flattery from a handsome stranger, and she would be only too willing to pour out all her bitterness and resentment about her husband.

Oh, Mother, how could you be so stupid? Lucy thought.

'What can we do?' she asked her godfather.

'There is nothing we can do, at the moment. I will instruct your father's lawyers, prepare them for the worst. They may be able to issue a few veiled threats to the newspaper's proprietors. But I'm afraid we must sit and wait, see what happens next.' Her godfather sighed heavily. 'I'm so sorry to be the bearer of bad news, my dear. But I thought you should know, just in case . . .'

'Just in case our name is splashed all over the newspapers in the morning,' Lucy finished for him.

Her mind was racing as she put the receiver down. Just when she thought the situation couldn't get any worse, it did.

She didn't blame her mother, not really. Lady Clarissa was simply no match for someone as clever and charming as Leo Alderson.

Lucy suddenly remembered the card Leo had given her. She had meant to throw it out, but for some reason she had kept it in her drawer. Now she was glad she had.

Sit and wait and see what happens, Gordon Bird had advised.

'I'm sorry, Uncle Gordon,' Lucy murmured to herself. 'I was never very good at waiting.'

Chapter Twenty-Nine

Lucy met Leo in a pub in Fleet Street, the kind of ancient place where men in powdered wigs had once gathered to gossip. Today it was crowded with journalists in shabby suits and lawyers in pinstripes, clustered together around battered tables. Rows of dusty bottles lined the walls, and the air was filled with the sound of guffawing laughter and cigarette smoke.

It took her a moment to pick Leo out in the crowd. But he must have been watching out for her because he stood up and waved.

Lucy picked her way through the crowd towards the corner table where he stood waiting for her.

'Well,' he grinned. 'This is an unexpected surprise, Miss Lane.'

'You gave me your telephone number.'

'Yes, but I didn't expect you'd have the nerve to use it.'

He held out his hand in greeting. Lucy ignored it.

'You're the one with the nerve, Mr Alderson. What do you mean by harrassing my mother?'

He looked so pleased with himself, Lucy wanted to slap him. 'No harassment, I assure you. I merely extended an invitation to tea at the Ritz, which your mother graciously accepted.'

I'll bet she did, Lucy thought. She could imagine how willing her mother would be to accept such an invitation. Such treats had been rare lately.

'Lady Clarissa is a charming lady,' Leo went on. 'Very – forthcoming.'

'And I'm sure you're more than capable of winning women round!' Lucy spat at him.

He gave her a maddening smile. 'I don't seem to have managed with you. Perhaps we could start again? Can I offer you a drink?'

'No, thank you.'

'At least sit down.' He pulled out a chair for her. 'Unless you want to draw attention to yourself in a public house full of journalists?'

Lucy plonked herself down reluctantly opposite him. 'I won't allow you to print that story,' she said.

There it was again, that maddening smile of his. 'I fail to see how you can stop me. Or do you plan to get your father to make it go away? I guess that's what you usually do in times of crisis, isn't it? Turn to Daddy. Except in this case you can't get him to ride to your rescue because you don't know where he is.'

It was the truth, but it still made her angry. 'You know nothing about me or my family!'

'Excuse me, but I think I do. As I said, your mother was most forthcoming.'

Lucy took a deep breath and launched into the speech she'd prepared. 'Look, I don't know what my mother told you, but she's got it wrong,' she said. 'My mother is easily confused. She doesn't understand my father's business.'

'She seemed to have a pretty fair grasp of the situation from what I could gather,' Leo replied. 'Unless you have some other information for me, Miss Lane? If you could tell me where I might find your father, for instance, I would happily not run the story and admit my mistake. Can you do that?'

She stared down at the worn wooden surface of the table. 'No,' she muttered.

'I thought not. Now, are you sure I can't get you that drink? You look as if you need one.'

As she watched him at the bar, his fair head towering above everyone else's, Lucy wondered if she had started off on the wrong track. Leo was a man, after all. Perhaps she should have appealed to his sense of chivalry, rather than storming in and making demands?

She forced herself to smile charmingly at him when he returned with her drink.

He eyed her uneasily. 'What's that for?' he asked, setting her glass of brandy down in front of her.

'What?'

'That smile.' He tilted his head consideringly. 'Oh, I get it. You're turning on the charm, now.' He smiled. 'Novel though it might be to find out what you're like when you're trying to be nice, I have to warn you you're not going to change my mind. I'm still running that story.'

Lucy glared at him. 'You're despicable.'

'I'm just doing my job.' He spread his hands.

'You're going to ruin our lives, purely so you can see your own name in print?'

'Unless you can give me a good reason why I shouldn't?'

Lucy gulped down her drink. The brandy burned a fiery trail down her throat but she hardly noticed. 'If word gets out that my father is missing, we lose everything,' she said simply.

Leo frowned. 'I don't understand?'

'He borrowed heavily to fund this German deal. If the banks find he's disappeared, they'll foreclose. We'll lose our home, all our money, probably the clothes we stand up in. My mother and I will be destitute.' She looked at him. 'I suppose my mother didn't mention that part?'

It gave her a small sense of satisfaction to see Leo

263

Alderson lost for words. He sank back in his seat, his blue eyes fixed on hers.

'Are you serious?'

'I'm hardly going to lie about it, am I?' It was strangely liberating to tell the truth for once. Lucy felt a weight lift from her shoulders.

'How could your father do something like that? I mean, risking his business is one thing, but gambling your home . . .'

'I suppose he thought it would pay off.' Lucy shrugged. 'It always has in the past. He didn't know the German government would step in and nationalise the factories, did he?'

Leo stared at her. 'And still you defend him,' he marvelled. 'Even after he did this to you.'

'He's my father,' Lucy said. 'He's given my mother and me everything we could ever want. He made a mistake, but he's still a good man.'

'So where is he now?' Leo leaned forward, his hands flat on the table. 'Why isn't he here, taking care of you when you need him? I'm sorry, Lucy, but where I come from a good man would stay and protect his family, not put them in danger and then run off and abandon them to their fate.'

'Shut up!' She cut him off abruptly, her nerves strained to snapping point. 'You don't know what's happened to him. None of us does. He might even be . . .' She broke off. Even now, she couldn't allow herself to say the word.

Leo was silent for a moment. 'You think something might have happened to him?' he said softly.

'I can't think of any other explanation.' Lucy traced a sticky ring on the table with one finger. 'My father would never abandon us. Truly, he's not that kind of man.' He was her hero, and she couldn't allow herself to think badly of him, no matter what. 'But he's not used to losing either. I worry that perhaps his pride just couldn't take it, and he – he decided to end it all instead.'

She drew in a deep, steadying breath. She wouldn't allow herself to cry in front of Leo. That really would be too humiliating.

'Hey, come on. You just said yourself, your father's no quitter. He wouldn't do something like that.' Leo reached across and covered her hand with his. 'He'll show up, you'll see.'

'If he does, it will be too late.' Lucy slid her hand out from under his. Leo Alderson was the last person she should be seeking comfort from.

She set her glass down on the table and stood up. 'I should go,' she said. 'Thank you for seeing me, Mr Alderson. I'm sorry I took up so much of your time. I daresay you have a story to write.'

As she started to walk away, he suddenly said, 'I won't run it.'

Lucy stopped. 'I beg your pardon?'

'I'm not going to write the story. I can't see you and your mother out on the street, no matter what a scoop it might be.'

Lucy stared at him warily. She couldn't allow herself to feel relieved or grateful. Life had dealt her too many blows lately for her to let her guard down. 'What changed your mind?' she asked.

His eyes met hers. 'I reckon you deserve a break, don't you?' he said. 'Just promise me one thing. When your father comes home, I want to be the first to know about it.'

Lucy smiled. 'It's a deal.'

Chapter Thirty

Pass. With Merit.

Jess stared down at the School Certificate in her hands. People milled around her in the main hall of the Institute, jostling her this way and that. But she stayed rooted to the spot, gazing at the words.

'Top of the class, Jess. I expected nothing less from you,' Mr Haddaway her tutor had congratulated her warmly. 'Now I hope you'll use your education wisely?'

'Oh, I will. Don't you worry about that.'

She came out of the Institute into the bright July sunshine, still in a daze. It was her day off, and the whole day stretched in front of her to do as she pleased.

But first she had a promise to keep.

Sam was behind his dad's bookstall as usual. He was waiting for her, Jess could tell. He chatted to the customers, but every now and then he would look up, scanning the crowded market.

Jess lifted her hand and waved to him. He waved back enthusiastically.

'There you are.' He grinned as she threaded her way through the crowd towards him. 'I've been looking out for you. Well?'

She had been practising how she would say it all the way to Columbia Road. But now she was standing in front of Sam all she could manage was a shy, 'I passed.'

'I knew you could do it!' Sam gave a whoop of delight.

The next moment he'd come round to the other side of the bookstall and gathered her up in his arms.

'Put me down, you fool!' Jess laughed as he swung her round in the air. 'Everyone's looking at us.'

'I don't care. We're celebrating.' He set her down on the ground. 'I've got you a present, too.'

He reached under the counter and pulled out a carefully wrapped package.

'For me?' Jess stared at him.

'No, for that woman on the fish stall. Of course it's for you, you daft ha'porth.'

Jess took it from him. 'How did you know I was going to pass?'

'Of course I knew. You're the cleverest girl I know.' He nodded towards the package. 'Go on, then. Open it.'

She tore off the wrapping. Inside was a book, bound in black with gold lettering.

Great Expectations.

'It's a brand new one, too, not that scruffy old copy,' Sam said proudly. 'I reckon you deserve the best.'

'It's beautiful,' Jess murmured, running her hand over the grainy leather cover. 'I don't think I've ever owned a brand new book before.'

'You've earned it,' Sam said. 'Your mum would have been proud of you, Jess.' He nodded towards the book. 'That's what I've got for you, see? Great expectations.'

Jess looked up and met his gaze. For once he wasn't larking about. His eyes were serious, full of intent and affection.

A lump rose in her throat. 'I dunno what to say,' she murmured.

'You could say you'll go out with me? Properly, I mean, not just a cup of tea after the night class.'

For once she felt no hesitation. But just as she opened

her mouth to accept, a commotion from the other end of the market made her swing round.

'Oi! Come back here, you thieving little sod!' one of the costermongers roared.

The next moment Jess was spun off her feet by a figure shooting past, dodging through the crowd with lightning speed.

'Stop him!' the coster yelled, coming panting up behind. 'Little bugger's nicked my takings!'

Jess heard an insolent laugh, and looked round. The boy had broken free from the crowd and was sprinting towards the main road, leaving a jingling trail of coins behind him. As he flashed past, Jess caught a tell-tale glimpse of mud brown hair under his scruffy cap.

'Cyril!' she yelled.

The boy stopped, distracted for a second, just as a delivery van rumbled round the corner.

Everything happened quickly after that. There was an ugly squeal of brakes, then the sound of screaming, and footsteps running.

'Jess, don't!' she heard Sam's warning voice but she was already running with them, pushing her way through the crowd to the lifeless figure lying in the road. His body looked strangely twisted, like a broken doll's.

'It wasn't my fault!' the driver of the van was saying. 'He ran straight out in front of me – there was nothing I could do . . .'

'Call an ambulance!' someone shouted.

'I reckon it's too late for that,' someone else said. 'Look at all that blood.'

Jess felt Sam's hand on her arm, trying to hold her back. But she shook herself free and moved towards her stepbrother.

The sight of all the blood stopped her in her tracks. The

gutter ran red with it, so much it was impossible to see where it was coming from.

'Jess!' Sam's voice implored her. But she moved forward on legs that didn't seem to belong to her, dropping to her knees at the boy's side.

'Cyril?' she whispered, her heartbeat pounding in her ears. 'Cyril, it's me, Jess.'

He groaned faintly in response. 'My leg—'

'He's alive!' someone in the crowd shouted. 'Thank God. Where's that ambulance?'

Jess steeled herself to look down. Cyril's left trouser leg glistened crimson, soaked in blood. It pumped from a wound just above his knee.

Without thinking, she tore off her cardigan and wrapped it around his upper thigh, tying it as tight as she could. She had never done this before, and wasn't even sure she was doing it right. Blood still pumped from the wound. She pulled the cardigan tighter, but the wool was too bulky.

'Here, try this.' Sam was suddenly beside her, pulling off his tie. 'It should be better.' He handed it to her and Jess wrapped it around her brother's leg, pulling it tight with every last bit of strength she had.

'The bleeding's slowing down,' Sam said. They looked at each other, shocked by what they'd done. 'It's worked, Jess!'

The jangling bell of the ambulance woke her, as if from a trance. Jess looked up, suddenly aware of the circle of faces around her, watching her. She looked down at her hands, glistening and sticky with blood. The last thing she heard was Sam's voice calling out her name, before the world started to spin around her, and everything turned black.

*

A fractured thigh, torn muscles and severe concussion was the Casualty doctor's pronouncement on Cyril.

'But it could have been a lot worse, if he'd gone on bleeding from that wound,' he said. 'I reckon you saved your brother's life with your quick thinking, young lady. Where did you learn to apply a tourniquet?'

'I must have read about it somewhere.' Jess kept her gaze fixed on the floor of the waiting room. She was too embarrassed to admit she'd read it in a medical textbook. Once she'd finished reading Sister Sutton's anatomy book, she'd taken to borrowing other medical books from the Institute library.

'Well, it's a lucky thing you did. This young man owes you a great debt. Wouldn't you say so?' He turned to Gladys, who sat with her mouth pursed, clutching her handbag on her lap. Even now, her stepmother couldn't bring herself to say a kind word to Jess.

But as they left the Casualty department together after Cyril had been transferred to the Children's ward, Gladys muttered through tight lips,

'The doctor's right. I suppose I should thank you.' Then, just as Jess thought she was witnessing a miracle, she added, 'although from what I hear, it was you who nearly got him killed in the first place,' she added.

Jess stared at her. 'How do you work that out?'

'If you hadn't shouted out to him, he wouldn't have stopped in the middle of the road, would he? And he wouldn't be in trouble with the police neither.'

'If he hadn't nicked the takings off that stall, he wouldn't have had to run away in the first place,' Jess shot back.

But there was no point in arguing with her stepmother. Gladys would never see the good in her, whatever Jess did.

'I want you to go and visit Cyril,' Gladys said. 'Make sure you keep an eye on him for me.'

'What, in case he starts pinching off the other patients?'

'I'm worried about him.' Gladys' scarlet-painted mouth trembled. 'He's my son, ain't he? I'm not allowed to visit him often, but I bet you could sneak in?'

Jess looked at her. She was surprised to find that underneath that hard, painted mask, Gladys had some kind of maternal feelings. It was a shame Jess had never seen them before.

'I'll see what I can do,' she promised.

She left Gladys at the gate and went back to the nurses' home. All she wanted to do was sink into a hot bath. She had managed to clean herself up in the Casualty department, but the hem of her dress was still spattered with blood, and her whole body ached.

But at least it was lunchtime, which meant she would have the place to herself, apart from the few students who were sent off duty from one until five. With any luck they would stay in their rooms studying, and Jess could have some peace and quiet.

Or so she thought. As she made her way down the passageway towards her room, she heard the creak of footsteps on the stairs above her and Anna Padgett's voice rang out.

'I say. You there!'

Jess stopped. 'It's my day off,' she called over her shoulder. 'If you want anything done, it'll have to wait till tomorrow.'

'I don't care what day it is. I want to talk to you.' Anna reached the bottom stair. 'Where is it?' she asked.

'What?'

'You know very well what. My perfume.'

Jess turned slowly to face her. 'I don't know what you're talking about.'

'My mother bought me a bottle of perfume for my birthday. Midnight In Paris. I kept it in my drawer, but now it's gone.' Anna took a step towards her. 'I want to know what you've done with it.'

'I haven't seen it.'

'Don't lie to me! You're always snooping about in our rooms, going through our things. You must have taken it.'

'Are you calling me a thief?' Jess looked up into the other girl's plain, pugnacious face, and fought the urge to slap it.

Anna Padgett must have read the anger in her eyes, because she stepped back. 'I can't think who else would have taken it,' she said.

'Me neither,' Jess snapped. 'I can't imagine why anyone would want a cheap bottle of scent that smells like old tom cat! But I certainly ain't taken it, I can tell you that!'

She left Anna standing open-mouthed and let herself into her room, slamming the door in the other girl's face.

Jess sank down on her bed and fought to calm herself. Take no notice of her, she told herself. You're not a thief, you know you're not.

And to think that the day had started out with so much hope and promise. It seemed so long ago that she had been in the market with Sam, being caught up in his arms, her School Cert in her hand . . .

Her School Cert! She'd forgotten all about it in the chaos of Cyril's accident. She must have left it lying in the road, with the book Sam had given her.

The pent-up tension of the day crashed over Jess like a huge wave, and she buried her face in her hands to shut it out. All she had to show for her big success was the lingering smell of blood on her fingers.

Chapter Thirty-One

Effie propped herself up against the sluice sink and allowed her eyelids to droop closed. She had only been on duty for an hour, and she had never felt so tired in all her life.

She had been on the ward for two weeks, and each day had been worse than the last. Every muscle in her body seemed to be crying out in agony from her head to her feet, which were swollen and blistered inside her stout black shoes. She'd even borrowed Katie's shoes, which were a size larger, but after twelve hours' standing could barely hobble down the ward.

Every night Effie would collapse into bed and fall asleep before her head touched the pillow. And every night in her dreams she would hear Sister Parry's voice ringing out.

'Are those damp tea leaves you're scattering, Nurse O'Hara? They look positively wet to me . . . What do you think you're doing, sweeping while the dressings are being changed? . . . Have you rinsed those nappies properly?. . . Don't shake those sheets, do you want to spread disease all over my ward?'

Effie's head spun from trying to remember everything she had been told. But no matter how hard she tried, she always seemed to get something wrong.

Her latest crime had been the most humiliating. She could still see the look of incredulity on Sister Parry's face when she'd presented her with a pile of the children's slippers that she'd collected from their lockers.

'What are these, O'Hara?' she'd demanded.

'You – um – told me to collect the slippers, Sister,' Effie reminded her, wondering if the ward sister was losing her marbles.

Sister Parry went white to her lips. 'Are you trying to be funny, girl?' she'd snapped.

'No, Sister.'

Effie was genuinely puzzled, until Hilda Ross had explained that slippers was another name for bedpans.

The other students found it hilarious, needless to say. Frances Bates was still smirking about it when Effie helped her make the beds later.

'Fancy you not knowing that!' she said, as they tucked in the corners of a patient's drawsheet.

'I can't be expected to know everything, can I?' Effie defended herself.

'Nurses! Please don't chatter over the patient, it's most unprofessional,' Sister Parry said as she swept past. 'And I hope you're supporting that limb with both hands, O'Hara?'

'Yes, Sister.' Effie quickly slipped her other hand under the boy's splinted leg. He had been admitted two days before with a fractured femur, the result of a road accident.

Sister Parry stopped at the foot of the bed and regarded them with narrowed eyes. 'Is that your idea of a well-made bed?'

Frances and Effie exchanged looks of dismay. Neither of them spoke.

Sister Parry tutted. 'I'll show you what a well-made bed looks like, shall I?' She pulled a penny out of her pocket. 'If the sheet is drawn sufficiently tight, this coin should bounce. We'll try it, shall we?'

Effie watched her spin the coin in the air. It landed with a dull thump in the middle of the sheet, where it lay unmoving.

'You see? Just as I thought.' Sister Parry shook her head. 'Take the whole lot off and start again.'

'That was your fault,' Frances hissed as they stripped the bed again. 'I was the fastest bed-maker in my set, but you're just hopeless!'

Effie ignored her. She knew Frances was just jealous because Effie was courting Hugo Morgan. She claimed to be happy with her new boyfriend Andrew, but Effie had caught the longing looks Frances cast Hugo's way when she didn't think anyone was watching.

They remade the bed quickly, not speaking. 'There,' Effie said, when they'd finished. 'That should be more comfortable for you.'

'Ta, Nurse.' The boy gave her a smile, but Effie couldn't smile back. There was something about him that unsettled her, though she didn't know why.

'Don't you think there's something strange about him?' she asked Frances as they gathered up the dirty bedlinen.

'The fractured femur?' Frances shrugged carelessly. 'Not that I'd noticed.'

'He seems rather sly to me.' Effie glanced back at the boy. He was watching her. When he caught her eye he gave her an insolent grin. 'I feel like I know him from somewhere, but I can't think where.'

'You wouldn't forget a face like that, would you? Not with that whopping great birthmark on his cheek.'

'I suppose not.'

As they loaded the linen into the basket ready for collection, Frances said, 'So . . . has Hugo asked you to go to the ball with him yet?'

Effie sighed. She had been wondering when Frances might ask that. Not a day went by without her mentioning it. 'Not yet.'

'Really? He's taking his time, don't you think?' Frances smirked.

'I daresay he'll get round to it,' Effie shrugged, but deep

down she was troubled. The Founder's Day Ball was only a couple of weeks away, and most of the girls in her set had already found themselves partners. Effie had thought she might be among the first to be asked, but despite her hints Hugo didn't seem inclined to suggest it.

If she wasn't careful, she would be joining the lonely ranks of the wallflowers, and wouldn't Frances Bates love that?

'Here he is now,' she said. 'Perhaps you should ask *him* instead?'

Effie looked up. Hugo was approaching them, looking every inch the doctor in his smart white coat, bearing a sheaf of notes for Sister Parry. He barely had time to give Effie a smile and a wink before the ward sister intercepted him.

'Can I help you, Mr Morgan?' she asked, shooting Effie a warning look over her shoulder.

'Perhaps he's asking Sister to the ball instead?' Frances suggested unkindly.

After they'd served lunch to the children, Effie was given the task of putting away the clean linen delivery.

'I want everything counted and put away in the linen room before the consultant does his round,' Sister Parry warned her. 'Don't be too long about it, but don't be slapdash either. If there is so much as a pillowcase out of place, I will know about it.'

Effie was relieved to escape to the safety of the linen room. It was little more than a cupboard lined with shelves, but to her it was a warm, starch-scented haven out of reach of Sister Parry.

Effie closed the door and set about taking the linen out of the hamper the porter had brought up to the ward, smoothing out the sheets, pillowcases, towels and nappies, and setting them all on the correct shelves. She carefully counted each pile, then counted them again, and made a note on the laundry sheet that came with the linen.

When she was satisfied it was all done correctly, she signed her initials at the bottom of the sheet and then went to take it to Sister Parry.

That was when she found the door was locked.

She turned the brass knob again, but it was stuck fast. Her heart racing, Effie leaned her shoulder against it and gave it a shove. Still it didn't budge.

She stood for a moment, trying to collect her thoughts. Calm down, she told herself. It's just jammed, that's all. It can't be locked. Who would lock the door, knowing she was inside counting the linen?

She tried once more, heaving her weight against the door again and again until her shoulder was numb and her arm ached. On the other side of it she could hear the nurses moving around, preparing for the consultant's visit. She knocked on it and called out, but no one heard her.

Effie sat down on the edge of the wicker basket to get her breath back. Outside, the ward had gone silent. She looked at her watch. Five minutes until the consultant's ward round was due to start. She was supposed to be making his cup of tea for when he arrived. Sister Parry would be furious if the kettle wasn't boiling and ready for him.

She stood up and threw herself at the door one final time. It burst open, and Effie flew out into the middle of the ward and fell at the feet of the consultant, Mr Hobbs.

Her fearful gaze travelled up from his highly polished shoes and pinstripe trousers to his bearded face. He was surrounded by a ring of white-coated medical students, the other nurses – and Sister Parry.

'What are you doing, Nurse?' she hissed. 'Get up immediately!'

As Effie struggled to her feet she caught sight of Hugo, standing at the end of the line. He had his head down, and she could see he was struggling to keep a smile off his face.

The consultant gave her a withering look and moved on without a word, the rest of his firm trailing behind him. Effie quickly went to join the line of nurses bringing up the rear, but Sister Parry stopped her.

'Where do you think you're going? Tidy yourself up, Nurse, before you even think about showing your face. And you can be sure I'll be mentioning this disgraceful behaviour in my ward report!' she added.

Effie fled to the bathroom. When she looked at herself in the mirror, she could see why Sister had dismissed her. A collar stud was missing, and her cap sat rakishly on the black curls.

She pulled out the pins and had started to rearrange her hair when Hilda Ross came in.

'Poor you,' she said. 'Are you all right?'

'I'm mortified,' Effie replied through a mouth full of pins. 'I might never be able to look that poor consultant in the eye again. I could have sworn that door was locked.'

'It was,' Hilda said. 'Your boyfriend locked you in.'

'What?' Effie swung round to face her. 'Not Hugo? Why would he do such a thing?'

'You know what he's like. He loves his silly pranks.' Hilda rolled her eyes. 'And Bates was egging him on, of course. If you ask me, she's every bit as much to blame as he is.'

'Little cat.' Effie glared at her reflection in the mirror and jabbed another pin into her cap. But underneath her anger, she was also hurt. Why would Hugo do something like that, knowing it would humiliate her in front of everyone?

Hilda must have got it wrong, she decided.

Effie got her chance to ask him later that afternoon. She was in the kitchen, making up some egg custard for Emily, the little girl who wouldn't eat, when someone crept up behind her and put their hands over her eyes.

'Guess who?' Hugo whispered.

'Go away!' Effie shook him off. 'Haven't you got me in enough trouble for one day?'

She expected him to try to deny it, but he just laughed. 'That was priceless, wasn't it? The look on your face as you came flying through that door. Cheered up a dull old ward round no end, it did.'

'Sister wasn't very cheered,' Effie said. 'That's another black mark in my ward report, thanks to you.'

'Oh, come on, darling! I thought you'd see the funny side. I know you enjoy a good joke.'

'Not when it's on me!'

Hugo frowned. 'You really are cross, aren't you?'

'Of course I'm cross! You made a fool of me in front of everyone. And you promised you wouldn't play any more stupid pranks on me.'

'Did I?'

'Don't you remember? That first evening you took me to dinner.'

'So I did.' Hugo grinned at the memory, then quickly sobered when he saw Effie's expression. 'I'm sorry, my sweet. *Mea culpa*, and all that. How can I make it up to you?'

Effie considered this as she strained her custard. As usual, it seemed to be more lumps than liquid, but she didn't care for once because a smashing idea had occurred to her.

'You could invite me to the Founder's Day Ball?' she suggested.

'Oh!' She caught Hugo's look of surprise out of the corner of her eye. 'Well, I wasn't planning on taking anyone with me, but I suppose – why not?' He shrugged. 'Yes, my angel, if it will stop you being cross with me, then I would be delighted to invite you.'

'And I would be delighted to accept,' Effie replied.

And wouldn't Frances be surprised when she found out? Effie thought.

Chapter Thirty-Two

It was the first time Kathleen Fox had ever summoned Lucy Lane to her office.

The young nurse stood before her desk first thing in the morning, hands behind her back, face composed. But Kathleen could see her legs quivering under her perfectly starched uniform.

For the first time in her career as Matron, Kathleen felt almost as nervous as the girl standing before her. She wasn't looking forward to what she had to say.

'Don't worry, Nurse Lane, you're not in any trouble,' she began kindly. 'It's just that something has occurred and I feel you should be made aware of it.'

'Yes, Matron.' The girl's expression didn't change. She went on staring straight ahead, past Kathleen's shoulder and out of the window.

Kathleen reached into her drawer and took out the newspaper that Mr Hopkins had delivered to her office that morning. He was the first: since then there had been a parade of ward sisters, the Home Sister and Sister Tutor, the Assistant Matron and various junior housemen, all lining up outside her office to deliver the same news.

The only one who didn't seem aware of it was Lucy Lane herself.

Kathleen laid the newspaper on the desk in front of her, folded open at the story. 'Perhaps you would like to read it for yourself?' she said.

Lucy's eyes flickered down to the newspaper, then back

up again. 'Thank you, Matron, but I don't need to read it. I think I know what it says,' she replied in a flat tone.

'Very well.' Kathleen slid the newspaper back into her drawer and closed it. 'I understand this must be a very difficult time for you, Nurse Lane.'

'Yes, Matron.'

'Perhaps, under the circumstances, it might be best if you went home? I daresay you would like to spend some time with your mother.'

A look of dismay flashed across Lucy Lane's face, but was quickly masked.

'Yes, Matron,' she said.

'Go back to your room and pack. I will inform the Home Sister that you will be leaving for a few days.'

The look of dismay was back in place. 'If it's acceptable to you, Matron, I would like to return this evening?' Lucy ventured.

Kathleen frowned. 'That really isn't necessary, Lane. I know Parry is short-staffed, but I'm sure we can come to some arrangement . . .' She saw the girl's expression and reconsidered. 'Very well. You may decide how long you need to be away. But you must stay overnight at least,' Kathleen added. 'I'm sure your mother will need you.'

'Yes, Matron.' Lucy lowered her eyes.

Poor girl, Kathleen thought as she dismissed her. She didn't seem to grasp that home was the best place for her at the moment. By the end of the day, the whole hospital would be gossiping about her. With everything else that lay ahead of her, at least Kathleen could try to spare her that.

Lucy had never seen Jameson looking so shell-shocked as when he opened the door to her.

'Miss Lucy.' He greeted her with his usual gravity, but there was a tremor in his voice.

'Is my mother—' Before she could even ask the question, Gordon Bird appeared from the library.

'Hello, Lucy,' he said. 'I thought I might come round, just to see if I could be of any use.'

'I'm glad you're here, Uncle Gordon.' She hadn't been looking forward to facing her mother alone. 'How is Mother?'

'She's gone back to her room to rest. I'm afraid she's finding all this rather upsetting.'

'*She's* upset?' Lucy said scornfully. She glanced at Jameson to make sure he wasn't listening, then lowered her voice. 'She was the one who got us into this mess. If she hadn't talked to that wretched Leo Alderson—'

'Now, Lucy, let's not point the finger of blame at anyone,' Gordon said mildly. 'It won't help the situation at all. We should all be pulling together.'

'You're right,' Lucy sighed. Although she knew it would be very difficult to show her mother any sympathy.

But if anyone was to blame, it was Leo Alderson. And after he'd promised her he wouldn't write the story. The feeling of betrayal was like a punch in the stomach. Lucy didn't know who to trust any more.

She pulled herself together, and faced her godfather. 'Is there anything that can be done, Uncle Gordon?'

'I've been called to a meeting with the bank this morning. They're not best pleased, as you can imagine. I'm hoping I can convince them that it has all been a dreadful misunderstanding, and that we didn't set out to pull the wool over their eyes regarding your father's – absence.'

Lucy could see from Gordon's expression that he didn't hold out much hope of succeeding. 'And what if they don't believe you?'

He shook his head. 'Let's hope it doesn't come to that,' he said. 'We'll see what they have to say for themselves before we start thinking the worst, shall we?'

They had some tea, and discussed the situation further. Gordon kept telling her not to worry, that there was every reason to be optimistic, to believe there was a way out of their problems. He was doing his best to cheer her, Lucy could tell. But she could also tell he didn't believe what he was saying, any more than she did.

When he'd left for his meeting with the bank, Lucy went upstairs to see her mother. The bedroom blinds were drawn, and in the half-light she could see Clarissa reclining on her chaise-longue, one hand over her eyes as if even the shade was too much for her.

When she saw Lucy she sat up and reached out both arms to her.

'Oh, Lucy! My darling girl!' A sob caught in her throat. 'What's to be done?'

Lucy forced herself to go to her. Her mother's hands felt fragile in hers, tiny bones under papery skin.

'Uncle Gordon has gone to see the bank. I'm sure he'll be able to sort something out.'

'Oh, he won't be able to do anything,' Clarissa dismissed impatiently. 'They won't listen to him.'

At least he's trying, Lucy thought. At least he hasn't just retreated to his bedroom, pulled down the blinds and given up. 'We don't know that yet, Mother.'

'It's no use,' Clarissa declared dramatically. 'Why did your father have to be so foolish and greedy? Look at the mess he's caused.'

You haven't helped, Lucy thought. But then she remembered Gordon's advice. They had to pull together.

'Uncle Gordon will do all he can, but you're right. We have to be realistic,' she said. 'Whatever happens, it's likely we'll lose this house, so we'll need to find somewhere else to live.'

'Lose this house?' Her mother looked aghast. 'But I've

worked so hard on it. It's taken me years to finish the alterations. I've designed every room myself, decorated it so beautifully . . .'

'I know, Mother, but it belongs to the bank now,' Lucy pointed out patiently. 'As I said, we will have to find somewhere else.'

Her mother sighed. 'You're right, my dear, of course. Perhaps we could rent somewhere? There are some wonderful apartments close to Kensington Gardens. Or we could go abroad? Paris, or Switzerland—'

Lucy stared at her mother. She obviously still didn't understand. 'I don't think we'll have the money to go abroad, Mother,' she told her gently.

Before her mother could reply, there was a knock on the door.

'There is a visitor downstairs, your ladyship,' Jameson announced. 'A Mr Alderson.'

'That evil man!' Clarissa jumped to her feet. 'How dare he set foot in this house after what he's done? I'll have words with him . . .'

'Please, Mother, try to calm down.' Lucy held on to her mother's hand, guiding her back on to her chaise. 'Let me talk to him. You stay here and rest.'

Leo was waiting in the library. Lucy was pleased to see he looked ill at ease, but it still took all her control not to fly at him and claw at his self-satisfied face.

'What are you doing here?' she asked coldly. 'Have you come to gloat? Or did you just want to see for yourself the devastation you've caused?'

'I didn't write that story,' he blurted out.

Lucy laughed. 'Are you suggesting it wrote itself?'

'I know you won't believe me, but it's true.' He looked downcast. 'I swear, I didn't write it.'

'Then who did?'

'I don't know.' Leo shrugged his broad shoulders. 'I guess someone must have overheard us talking in the pub. It was pretty crowded . . .'

'Oh, please! You're going to have to do better than that.' Lucy shook her head. 'I trusted you,' she said. 'I opened my heart to you—'

'I know,' he said. 'I'm sorry.'

'Looks like I was right, wasn't I? You do have a way of winning women round. You certainly played me for a fool!'

'Miss Lane. Lucy—'

'I'd like you to leave now.' Lucy reached for the bell pull.

'But I want to help you. I came here to help—'

'I think you've done enough, don't you?' Jameson appeared in the doorway. 'Will you show Mr Alderson out, please, Jameson?'

'Certainly, Miss Lucy.'

For a moment it seemed as if Leo Alderson wasn't going to budge from his place by the fireplace. Lucy wondered how they were going to shift him if he decided not to leave.

But then he gave up. 'Fine,' he said. 'If that's what you want. But I meant what I said, Lucy. I want to help you, if I can.' His blue eyes met hers, without flinching. 'You know where to find me if you need me.'

Chapter Thirty-Three

'Have you heard the news about Lane?' Katie could barely contain her excitement as she plonked herself down at the dining table opposite Dora.

Dora cast a sideways glance at Millie. 'Not you, too?' she sighed.

Everyone was talking about it. Even on the Children's ward, the gossip had spread like wildfire that Lucy Lane's wealthy father had disappeared owing millions.

'One of my patients lent me his newspaper. Look!' Katie thrust it under Dora's nose. There, under the headline, was a photograph of Lucy with her parents at some society function or other, all dressed up and looking pleased with themselves. 'How the mighty are fallen, eh?'

'It says he's been missing for some time, but his disappearance has only just come to light,' Millie said, reading over Dora's shoulder. 'Poor Lane, I wonder how long she's known?'

'Poor Lane?' Katie looked incredulous. 'I don't feel sorry for her at all. It serves her right for putting on all those airs and graces, making out her family is so grand and the rest of us are just peasants.' She smiled. 'Well, they're not so grand now, are they?'

Millie looked shocked. 'That's a horrible thing to say.'

'What if it is? She's said some horrible things about us,' Katie replied through a mouth full of mince. 'Isn't that right, Doyle?' She looked at Dora expectantly.

Dora glanced up from the photograph of Lucy and her

parents. Looking closer, she could see their smiles weren't self-satisfied at all. They were brittle, as if they might shatter at any moment.

'That's no reason why we should make more trouble for her,' she said.

Katie stared at her. 'I can't believe you of all people would say that. Not after the way she's treated you over the past three years.' She leaned forward. 'Imagine it, Doyle. She's been caught out at last. How can you say you don't want to see her suffer?'

Dora looked at the photograph again. Katie was right, she should have been the first one cheering at Lucy's fall from grace. But she couldn't help thinking how she would feel if it were her family's dark secrets displayed in the newspaper for all to see.

'I reckon she's suffering enough, without us adding to it.'

'Doyle's right,' Millie said. 'Lane's probably feeling wretched, poor girl. She's in our set. We should all look after each other.'

'She never looks after me. Or you, either.' Katie fixed her gaze on Dora.

Katie refused to walk back to the ward block with them, she was so bitterly disappointed.

'You do realise she won't keep it to herself, no matter what we say?' Millie said.

'It doesn't matter. It's all over the hospital anyway.'

Millie glanced sideways at Dora. 'I suppose O'Hara has a point. Lane has been rather mean to everyone, particularly you. I don't blame her for wanting to see her taken down a peg or two.'

'There's a difference between being taken down a peg and being shamed,' Dora said. 'Besides, she can't help what her father's done, can she?'

'I know, but she does rather show off about them. She's always talking about how wonderful her parents are.'

And now we know why, Dora thought. Poor Lucy probably made up all those stories to hide the truth from herself as well as everyone else.

Back on the ward, Sister Parry had been reshuffling her nurses again.

'Since we don't know for sure when Lane will return, Anderson will have to take over the Staff Nurse's duties,' she announced to the students gathered around her desk. 'Doyle, you can special Ernest Pennington.'

Only because he's practically recovered and doesn't need nursing, Dora thought. She wondered how desperately short-staffed Sister Parry would have to be before she assigned Dora to the stand-in Staff Nurse's post. Sister would probably give the job to Effie O'Hara before me, Dora decided.

But when she went to check on Ernest, she found he'd taken a turn for the worse. He lay sullenly against his pillows, staring out of the window.

'Oh, Nurse, I don't feel very well today,' he said. 'I've got a terrible headache, and I ache all over.' He shivered dramatically. 'And I'm hot. Boiling hot.'

'Let me see.' Dora put her hand on his forehead. 'You don't look flushed, and you're not perspiring.' She consulted his chart. 'And your temperature was normal when Nurse Anderson checked it an hour ago.'

'Perhaps I'm cold, then. Yes, that's it. I'm freezing cold.'

'In that case, I'll fetch you a hot water bottle.'

Ernest pulled the covers up to his chin and eyed her over the top of them. 'Do you think the rheumatic fever is coming back?'

'I doubt it. You seem a lot better to me.' She smiled at him. 'Don't worry, Ernest. You're not going to get ill again.

There'll be nothing to stop you going home at the weekend.'

'But how do you know I'm not going to get ill again?' he insisted. 'I told you, I have a headache. I should stay here, just to be on the safe side.'

She sent him a long look, then suddenly it dawned on her. 'You don't want to go home, do you?'

Ernest was silent for a moment. 'I like it here,' he admitted finally in a small voice, then added, 'You won't tell my mother, will you?'

'Of course not.' Dora shook her head. 'But why don't you want to go home? Most of the children here can't wait to get back to see their family and friends.'

'Yes, well, I haven't got any friends, have I? I'm not allowed to play when I'm at home. My only friend is Archie, and he's in here. That's why I want to stay.' He looked up at her with imploring eyes. 'Can't I stay, Nurse? Just for a few more weeks? You could write it on my chart, couldn't you? Say I have a temperature?'

'I think Sister would soon find out, then we'd both be in trouble,' Dora said. 'Besides, your parents will be looking forward to seeing you.'

'No, they won't.' Ernest's face was stubborn. 'They're still in Europe. There's only Mrs Philpott and the rest of the staff at home. No one will even notice if I'm there or not.'

Dora regarded him with pity. She had never met a child who loved hospital before. No matter how humble their home, usually they still preferred to be with their loved ones than surrounded by strangers.

But poor Ernest didn't have any loved ones.

'I'm sorry, Ernest,' she said. Then, to cheer him up, she added, 'Tell you what, why don't we play cards? You can show me that game Archie taught you the other day.'

Ernest's plump face brightened. 'Can Archie play too?'

Dora thought about it for a moment. 'Perhaps if Sister takes a break he can sneak in for a minute or two,' she said.

With Lucy Lane and Staff Nurse Ryan absent, the ward was a busy place, and it was a relief when Dora finally went off duty at nine o'clock.

She was so weary she could barely put one foot in front of the other on her way back to the nurses' home. But as she passed the Porters' Lodge, Mr Hopkins called out to her.

'One minute, if you please, Nurse Doyle. I've got something for you.'

Dora stopped, her heart lifting. Had Nick written at last?

She'd almost given up on hearing from him. A week after he'd left she'd received a postcard from somewhere outside Southend, scrawled with a few lines to say he was doing all right, that life at the fair wasn't as bad as he'd thought, and that she wasn't to worry about him.

And after that – nothing.

Dora had read those few scrawled lines so many times they were imprinted on her memory. She knew Nick wouldn't be one for writing long, flowery love letters, but she wished she could have heard more from him. She missed him terribly. Whenever a porter was summoned to the ward, she always looked up expecting Nick to come through those double doors.

Now she had no idea where he was, or how he was faring, and she could scarcely bear it.

In spite of her aching feet, she ran back to the Porters' Lodge. Mr Hopkins eyed her with disapproval through his glass hatch. 'You know you're not supposed to run, don't you? Only in case of fire or haemorrhage, isn't that what you're told?'

Dora ignored him. 'You said there was a letter?'

'Not a letter. A message. Now where is it . . . ?'

He shuffled off to search through the cubby holes. Dora watched him, disappointment crashing over her. If it was a message, it wouldn't be from Nick.

'Ah, yes. Here it is.'

Mr Hopkins retrieved the note and handed it over. 'Young girl brought it round. Said she was your sister. Mind, I could have told that straight away, what with her having the same red hair. Dead spit of you, she was.'

'Bea?' Dora frowned.

'She didn't give her name and I didn't ask for it.' Mr Hopkins squinted at the note, trying to read his writing. 'Now, what does it say? I really need my glasses to read this . . .'

'Shall I read it for you?' Dora offered.

'Certainly not!' Mr Hopkins' moustache bristled with offence. He held the note at arms' length and peered at it. 'She says she needs to see you urgently. She'll wait for you by the park gates at nine o'clock.' He looked up at her. 'Well, I don't hold with young girls hanging around parks at this time of night. That's hardly what you'd call respectable, is it? Anything could happen—'

But Dora was already hurrying away, heading towards the hospital gates. As she went, she heard Mr Hopkins' voice drifting on the air behind her.

'Nurse Doyle! Come back at once. You know you're not supposed to go out in your uniform. I shall tell Matron . . .'

Tell whoever you like, Dora thought, quickening her steps. If her younger sister had come all this way to ask to see her, then it must mean trouble. Dora's mind was already racing, wondering what had happened. Had her grandmother been taken ill, or her mother? Had Lily gone into labour early?

By the time Dora saw her sister waiting for her beside the stone lions outside the park, her stomach was already churning, fearing the worst.

'Dora!' Bea ran across the road towards her.

'Bea, what is it? What's happened?' Dora grabbed hold of her. 'Has there been an accident? Is someone hurt?'

'No!' Her sister gave a puzzled smile. 'Everyone's fine. Nanna's moaning about her lumbago as usual, but that's all.'

'Oh, thank God!' Dora put her hand to her chest, feeling the flutter of her heart. 'You really had me worried there. When your message said it was urgent—'

'It *is* urgent,' Bea said. 'But it's not bad news.' She grinned. 'It's good news, Dor. Really good news.'

Dora sighed. 'Go on, then. What's this good news that you can't wait to share?'

Bea lowered her eyes. 'I've got a secret,' she said.

'You?' Dora laughed. 'You couldn't keep a secret if you tried!'

'That's where you're wrong, see?' Bea snapped. 'I've been keeping this secret for months now. I wanted to tell everyone the minute I found out, but he said it would be better to keep quiet. Make it more of a surprise, see? But he reckoned I could tell you, because he knows you can keep a secret too.'

Dora went very still. 'He?' she said. 'Who's he, Bea?'

'That's it,' Bea replied. She was grinning from ear to ear now, fit to burst. 'That's my surprise.' She looked over her shoulder. 'You can come out now,' she called.

Dora looked up and saw a familiar figure emerging from around the corner.

'Hello, Dora love,' said Alf Doyle.

Chapter Thirty-Four

'Bet you're surprised, ain't you?' Bea grinned. 'You lot are always saying I can't keep a secret, but I can – see?'

Dora was hardly aware of her sister. All her attention was focused on her stepfather.

He had hardly changed in three years. His greasy black hair was threaded with more grey, but that hulking body and fleshy face were the same as she saw in her nightmares.

She felt bile rising in her throat and it was all she could do not to be sick.

'What's he doing here?' she heard herself say.

'Dad met me from school a few months ago, said he wanted to see me.' Bea beamed up at her stepfather. 'You missed me, didn't you, Dad?'

'I missed all my girls.' Alf took a step towards Dora, his arms held out. 'Ain't you got a kiss for your old dad, then?'

Dora backed away. 'Don't touch me!' she hissed. 'Don't you dare come near me!'

'Dora!' Bea's voice was hurt. 'Don't be like that. Dad's back – ain't you pleased?'

'It's all right, Bea,' Alf said. 'I don't blame your sister for being angry. I know I've made a lot of mistakes. But that's why I'm back, see? I want to make up for what I've done. I want a second chance.'

I'm going mad, Dora thought. I must be. This is all a terrible dream, and any minute now I'm going to wake up.

'And you honestly think you can just crawl back as if nothing's happened?' she said.

'Oh, no, love.' Alf did a good job of looking contrite. 'I know I hurt your mum too much for that. I don't expect nothing from her, honest. That's why I asked to meet Bea in secret. I was too ashamed to face my Rosie, after what I've done to her.'

He lowered his gaze. Anyone else might have been fooled, but not Dora. She knew from bitter experience how low and conniving Alf could be.

He'd certainly managed to fool Bea.

'He's being daft, ain't he, Dor?' she said, putting her arm through his. 'I've tried to tell him Mum would take him back if he wanted. We could be a family again. Wouldn't that be smashing?'

Alf smiled shakily. 'It's all I've ever wanted, love.'

Dora looked at him, his hand resting on her innocent young sister's, and felt sick. 'Over my dead body,' she said.

'Dora!' Bea turned on her.

'Shhh, love. I've told you, I don't blame your sister for being angry. She's only doing it to protect your mum. Ain't that right, Dora? Anyway, she's probably right,' Alf added mournfully. 'Your mum would never have me back. Not after I abandoned her.'

'Yes, she would! Take no notice of Dora. She don't even live with us. She ain't in charge. I don't even know why we had to tell her,' said Bea, shooting her sister a sour look. 'All she ever does is spoil everything.'

Alf's gaze fixed on Dora, pinning her. 'Your sister likes a secret,' he said softly.

Dora's legs buckled, but she forced herself to face him. He was never going to see her cowering and scared ever again. She was more angry than frightened, angry that he still had so much power over her.

'Go,' she said. 'Go back to wherever it is you came from. I don't want you anywhere near my family, do you understand?'

Alf sighed. 'If that's what you really want—'

He turned to go, but Bea ran after him. 'No!' she cried. 'Don't go, Dad! You belong with us. We need you. Mum needs you. Please stay. I'll talk to Mum, I promise.'

'Let him go,' Dora said, holding on to Bea's sleeve as Alf shuffled down the street.

Bea wriggled free of her grasp, shooting her a filthy look. 'I hope you're happy now?' she spat. 'You're the one keeping this family apart, Dora. We'd all be happy if it wasn't for you!'

'Bea!'

'Get lost!'

Dora watched her sister running down the street after Alf. He wouldn't go far, Dora thought. He'd get to the next corner, and then he'd let the girl persuade him to stay.

She fought the urge to run after her sister. Bea would never understand because she didn't have the same fear of him that Dora did. Alf had never laid a hand on her youngest sister. Bea had never known what it was like to lie awake at night, dry-mouthed with fear, dreading the sound of his footsteps outside her door.

And Dora could never explain. Because to do so would mean betraying a secret she couldn't bring herself to say out loud.

She was still very shaken when she returned to her room at the student nurses' home. Millie was there, sitting up in bed, poring over her textbooks. She looked up at Dora in surprise.

'Are you all right, Doyle? You look as if you've seen a ghost.'

'I'm fine.'

'Are you sure? You're trembling.'

'I said, I'm all right!' Dora snapped. She saw her friend's hurt look, and regretted it instantly. 'I'm sorry. I've just got a bit of a headache, that's all.'

'You should see Sister Sutton for an aspirin.'

'I'll be right as rain when I've had a good night's sleep.'

But she knew that would never happen. Dora lay awake most of the night, staring up at the ceiling in the darkness, too terrified to go to sleep in case the nightmare came back. Why had she ever imagined she had overcome her fear? It was still there, lurking in the shadows, just waiting to pounce.

Everything would be all right, she tried to tell herself. Her mother would never take Alf Doyle back in a million years.

Dora desperately wished Nick was there. She knew she could never bring herself to tell him about Alf, but she felt safer when he was around.

'I hate to ask, but you and Mother have worked on so many charity committees together, and I know she considers you a great friend. It wouldn't be for long, but she really needs somewhere to stay, just until we're back on our feet . . . I see. No, I appreciate that . . . Thank you, anyway . . .'

Lucy put the telephone receiver down, just as her godfather entered the library.

'Another rejection?' he said.

Lucy nodded. 'They would love to help, but with things being as they are . . .' she sighed. 'It's strange how people who couldn't wait to come to our parties and spend the summer with us in Antibes have suddenly become unavailable now we're broke.'

'There's nothing like a scandal to help you find out who your real friends are,' Gordon agreed.

'We don't seem to have any friends, real or otherwise.' Lucy stared at the telephone, willing it to ring. She had been calling her parents' friends all morning, begging them for help. 'It's not as if I'm asking for charity. I only want to find Mother somewhere temporary to live, until our business affairs are sorted out.'

Gordon patted her shoulder. 'I'm so sorry all this has fallen to you, my dear.'

'It's all right. I can't see Mother doing it anyway.' It was nearly noon and Clarissa was still in her room, asleep with a silk mask over her eyes.

'I just wish the bank had been more amenable.'

'I know,' Lucy agreed. 'I realised they would want their money, but I didn't think they would spring into action quite so quickly.' She gazed past Gordon towards the hall, where a pair of removal men in brown overalls were shifting the Chippendale cabinet out of the door. 'I daresay the neighbours are having a field day, aren't they?'

'I'm sure they're very sympathetic.'

Lucy laughed. 'Sympathetic? I doubt it, Uncle Gordon. Be honest, how many of them are watching and thinking it's about time the upstart Lanes got their comeuppance?'

Jameson appeared in the doorway. It was strange to see him in his everyday suit and not the black tailcoat he usually wore.

'I'll be off now, Miss Lucy,' he said gruffly.

She rose and went over to him. 'Are you the last to leave?'

'Yes, Miss. There's only Higgins left, and she and I are sharing a taxi to the station.'

Lucy nodded, not trusting herself to speak. Jameson had been the family butler since she was a small child.

She couldn't imagine not seeing his face at the front door, or hearing his footsteps in the hall.

She took a deep breath. Her mother would be most disappointed in her if she lost control now. Lucy went to the library desk and picked up an envelope. 'I've written you a cheque in lieu of notice.'

'Oh, no, Miss Lucy.' Jameson shook his head. 'I couldn't take it. Not with things being as they are.'

'Nonsense, Jameson, we owe it to you.' She tried to press the envelope into his hand but he wouldn't take it.

'No, Miss Lucy, it wouldn't be right.' He straightened his shoulders, and Lucy saw tears glistening at the corners of his eyes. 'I don't want any money. I'm just sorry I have to leave in these circumstances.'

'I'm sorry too, Jameson. But we couldn't ask you to go on working for nothing, could we?' Lucy forced a bright smile.

'I suppose not, Miss Lucy.' He cleared his throat. 'Will you say goodbye to your mother for me? Please convey my best wishes, and tell her I hope it's not long before your – situation improves.'

'Thank you, Jameson.' Lucy held herself rigid, listening to his footsteps crossing the hall for the last time. And then the front door closed and he was gone.

Lucy let out the breath she'd been holding. 'Well, I don't think our situation can get much worse!' she said. 'It's too bad of Mother not to come down and say goodbye. Jameson is practically part of the family.'

'You mustn't be too hard on Clarissa,' Gordon said. 'She's finding it all very difficult.'

'*She's* finding it difficult? She hasn't been on the telephone all morning, begging for a roof over her head.' There was a crash in the hall as one of the removal men dropped a tea chest full of porcelain. 'Speaking of which,

I suppose I'd better make some more calls before those men take the telephone away too!'

Her mother came downstairs just before lunch. At least she had managed to dress and make herself look present-able, Lucy was relieved to see.

'Have you had a nice rest, Mother?' she asked.

'As if anyone could rest with such a racket going on!' Clarissa shuddered delicately. She looked around at the half-empty room. 'How depressingly bare it all looks, now the bank has finished taking its pound of flesh.' She turned to Lucy, her smile brittle. 'Never mind, I'm sure we shall get used to it. Shall we have some lunch?'

She went to ring the bell then stopped, her face falling. 'Of course,' she faltered. 'They've gone too, haven't they? Just like everything else.'

Lucy got to her feet. 'I'll make us a sandwich, shall I?'

'I don't think I want anything after all.'

'You have to eat, Mother. Let's go and see what's in the kitchen.'

'Oh, do stop it, Lucy! I feel like I'm on some kind of ghastly camping trip.'

She watched her mother sink gracefully into a chair, fingers pressed to her temples. Perhaps Uncle Gordon was right, and Lucy was being too hard on her. She had forgotten how helpless her mother was, after being waited on hand and foot for so many years.

'I have some good news,' Lucy said brightly. 'I've found us somewhere to live.'

Her mother looked up. 'Where?'

'Your cousin Antonia has offered us a very nice flat in town.'

Lady Clarissa pulled a face. 'I do hope you haven't been going around cap in hand to all my friends and relatives? I really don't think I could bear that.'

'Of course not,' Lucy lied. 'But Cousin Antonia was kind enough to ring up and offer us a place, and I thought it would be rude to refuse.'

'I suppose so,' her mother sighed. 'Where is this flat?'

'Kentish Town.'

Her mother stared at her in horror. 'Kentish – you mean, North London?' She shook her head. 'Oh, no, we couldn't consider living in such a place. How would we entertain? Who would come and visit?'

Why does that matter, when all our friends have abandoned us? Lucy wanted to reply. But she could see her mother was already trembling on the verge of one of her rages.

Clarissa got up and poured herself a large gin. 'I know why Antonia is doing this,' she muttered. 'She's always been jealous of me, and this is her way of putting me down. She's doing it to show how superior she is.'

Lucy stared down at her hands. 'Superior or not, at least it's a place to stay,' she said. 'Let's start to pack, shall we?'

Lucy stayed overnight with her mother and returned to the Nightingale early the following morning.

She felt guilty at how relieved she was to see the wrought-iron gates of the hospital ahead of her. Her mother's depression and despair weighed heavily on her.

But she wasn't looking forward to going back on the ward either. It was the first time Lucy had shown her face in the hospital since the scandal of her father's disappearance broke, and she was worried that everyone would be talking about her. She couldn't bear the idea that they might be laughing at her, or worse, pitying her.

Fortunately Dora and Millie had already left when Lucy reached their room. She changed quickly into her uniform and reported to Parry. As she passed down the passageways, she could feel heads turning in her direction and a tide of whispers following her. But Lucy kept her head up high and her eyes fixed straight ahead. She wouldn't give anyone the satisfaction of seeing her looking shaken.

Appearances were everything, as her mother would say.

Sister Parry treated Lucy as if she had never been away, and sent her straight off to prepare a linseed poultice for a small girl with pleurisy. Lucy was grateful for the ward sister's lack of emotion. If Sister Parry had gushed or asked her how she was feeling, she might have crumbled. As it was, she was proud of her composure as she stirred the linseed and boiling water in the bowl. She was doing very well, keeping herself together.

And no one here had said anything either. There had been no whispers, no curious sideways looks.

As she spread the linen out on the board, Lucy started to wonder if she'd been worrying over nothing. Perhaps no one on Parry knew or even cared about her father?

But then, as she was spooning the linseed mixture on to the linen, she heard two pros whispering on the other side of the door.

'Did you see her?' Hilda Ross was saying. 'Like butter wouldn't melt. I don't know if I could be that hard-faced if my father had done something so shameful.'

Lucy tensed, gripping the spatula.

'And she gives herself so many airs and graces too, doesn't she?' Hilda went on. 'Acting as if she's better than the rest of us. I don't know how she has the nerve.'

'I know! That's what's so shocking, don't you think?' Effie O'Hara's lilting Irish voice joined in. 'My sister Katie said she was always too big for her boots, even when they were pros.'

'Well, I reckon this will bring her down a peg or two,'

Hilda said. 'She won't be able to lord it over the rest of us now.'

'She'd better not try!'

Lucy froze. Part of her wanted to throw open the door and confront them; the other wanted to run away and hide, and never come out.

'What are you two laughing about?' She heard Dora's voice then, and her heart sank even further.

There was an uncomfortable silence. Then O'Hara ventured, 'We were talking about Nurse Lane.'

'Gossiping, you mean?'

'We were just discussing what was in the newspaper,' O'Hara insisted stubbornly.

'I don't care if it was up in lights in Piccadilly Circus,' Dora said. 'You've still got no business talking about a senior like that. And if you've got time to stand there gossiping like a pair of fishwives, you obviously don't have enough to do. O'Hara, you can go and clean the bathrooms. Ross, you can help with the nappy round. That should keep you nice and busy.'

'But . . .'

'And if I hear either of you say another word about this, I will tell Sister,' Dora went on. 'Remember, Lane is a senior, and should be treated with respect.'

'Yes, Nurse,' O'Hara mumbled.

Their footsteps faded down the ward and Lucy finished making the poultice, her mind still grappling with what she had just heard.

Uncle Gordon had said there was nothing like a scandal to let you find out who your friends were. And it looked as if he had been right.

Chapter Thirty-Five

Anna Padgett was complaining about Jess again.

'I know she's taken it,' she said, as they queued for the bathroom on Monday morning. 'She denies it, but I can see it in her face.'

Effie sighed. 'We're not talking about that bottle of scent again, are we?'

'It's not just any scent, it's Midnight In Paris. But, no, that's not what we're talking about,' Anna replied huffily. 'Now my brooch has gone missing.'

'You mean that ugly one shaped like a cat? Why would anyone want to steal that?'

'I don't know, do I? Out of spite, I expect. Or because she's a thief and can't help herself. And it isn't ugly, by the way,' Anna told her.

'Jess isn't a thief either,' Effie said.

'Oh, well, you would say that, wouldn't you? What with her being a particular friend of yours.'

The queue shuffled forward, and Effie finally reached a basin. Jess might be her friend, but Effie hadn't seen much of her since she'd passed PTS. She had been too busy finding her feet on the ward, and spending time with Hugo. She was guiltily aware she still owed Jess a night out after abandoning her at the last minute.

'Friend or not, I know Jess isn't a thief,' she insisted.

But there was no convincing Anna Padgett. 'I'm going to be watching her,' she said. 'I'll catch her out sooner or later, you'll see.'

It was always a tearing rush to get washed, dressed, finish breakfast and report for duty before seven o'clock. Effie screeched through the double doors with seconds to spare, her shoes skidding on the linoleum.

'You're late,' Lucy Lane snapped. 'There's a pile of bedpans waiting for you in the sluice. And make sure you clean inside the handles this time. I'll be checking,' she warned.

I bet you will, Effie thought as she stomped off to the sluice. Far from being humbled by her fall from grace, Lucy had become even more short-tempered and unbearable.

Effie was up to her elbows in hot soapy water when she heard Hugo's voice outside the sluice-room door. She perked up immediately. Abandoning the bedpans, she wiped her hands on her apron and went to the door to see him. She knew she would be in trouble if she was caught, but Sister Parry wasn't on duty for another twenty minutes and Effie was sure she could risk a quick hello. It had been nearly a week since she'd seen him.

By the time she stuck her head out of the door Hugo was at the far end of the ward, talking to Frances.

'Make way!' Hilda came towards her, arms full of precariously balanced bedpans. 'Quick, before I drop this lot.'

Effie stepped aside automatically to let her pass, her gaze still fixed on Hugo and Frances.

'What's Hugo doing here at this hour?' she asked. He wasn't known as an early riser; he'd often boasted to Effie about missing lectures because he'd stayed up all night playing cards.

'God knows. Maybe he wants to impress Mr Hobbs by being an eager beaver for once?' Hilda put the bedpans down with a clatter.

Frances made a comment, and Hugo laughed. Jealousy

shot through Effie as she watched them both, their dark heads tilted close together.

'They seem very pally?' she commented.

Hilda came to stand beside her. 'They're probably just planning their next prank. You know what they're like, always having fun at someone else's expense.'

Usually mine, Effie thought. She had forgiven Hugo for locking her in the linen cupboard, but couldn't forget Frances' part in it.

'Anyway, I wouldn't take much notice if I were you.' Hilda shrugged. 'Frances may be his partner in crime, but you're the one he's taking to the ball, aren't you?'

Only because I forced him into it, Effie thought miserably.

'You there!' She flinched as Lucy Lane appeared out of nowhere, her face like thunder. 'Why are you standing around gossiping when there are bedpans to wash? And have you done those handles yet? I'm going to inspect them, and if I find they're dirty . . .'

She bustled past Effie, who trailed miserably after her into the sluice. Why was it always Effie who ended up in trouble? Hugo and Frances could be locked in a passionate embrace at the other end of the ward, and Lucy would still only notice the dirty bedpan handles.

Sister Parry arrived on the ward at half-past seven, took the report from the night nurse and then handed out the worklists.

Effie was delighted when she was told to set the trolley for the dressings round. At last, some proper nursing! It made a change from endless cleaning and scrubbing.

But just her luck, she had to assist Nurse Lane. And even worse luck, their first patient was the boy with the fractured femur.

'I don't like him,' Effie confided as she followed Lucy down the ward with the trolley.

'It doesn't matter whether you like the patient or not, as long as you're pleasant and courteous at all times,' Lucy replied shortly.

Effie scowled at her back. I'd like to see *you* being pleasant and courteous to anyone, she thought.

Lucy seemed to be taking her job as stand-in Staff Nurse very seriously. Instead of getting on with the task as quickly as possible, she insisted on quizzing Effie on fractures.

'What are the unfavourable symptoms to look out for in these cases?' she asked.

Effie stood still, hands knotted behind her back, and racked her brain for an answer. 'Er . . . blue fingers or toes?' she ventured.

'And?'

Effie glanced sidelong at the boy. He was watching them, arms crossed, enjoying the show. 'Cold and numbness?'

'Anything else?' Lucy tutted impatiently. 'You've forgotten swelling, persistent pain and a temperature.'

'Sorry, Nurse.'

'You don't have to apologise to me, O'Hara. It's you who'll fail your State Final if you don't know this.'

Give me a chance, I've only just got PTS out of the way! Effie thought. She had three years until she had to worry about her State Final and anything could happen before then. She might even marry Hugo and give up nursing altogether.

Lucy was called away by Sister Parry halfway through the dressings round, and left Effie to finish attending to the boy, Cyril. She could feel him watching her as she struggled, all fingers and thumbs, to fit the new dressing.

'Not very good at this nursing lark, are you?' he observed.

Effie opened her mouth to make a stinging reply, then remembered Lucy's warning. Be courteous and pleasant at all times.

So she gritted her teeth and tried to do just that.

'How did you hurt your leg?' she asked. 'Were you playing football?'

'Hardly!' Cyril snorted. 'If you must know, I was running away.'

'Who from?'

'Someone who wanted to catch me, of course! Except that bloody van got in the way.'

But Effie wasn't listening. Somewhere in her brain, a penny dropped. 'It's you!' she exclaimed. 'I remember you now. *You* were the one who stole my bag.'

He blushed to the roots of his hair. 'No, I didn't.'

'Yes, you did! You offered to carry my bag for me, then ran off and left me stranded. I thought I recognised you, but I couldn't work it out until just now.'

He looked shifty. 'Sorry, Nurse, I reckon you must have the wrong lad. As if I'd do something like that. That's wrong, that is. That's thieving.'

'You are a thief! And I've a good mind to call the police and have you arrested.'

'You wouldn't do that.'

'Wouldn't I? Just watch me.'

'Oh, keep your hair on. You got your bag back, didn't you?'

'Well, yes I did, but—' she broke off. 'Hang on a minute. How did you know I got my bag back?'

He grinned. 'You mean you ain't worked that out yet?'

Lucy's mother was right. Kentish Town wasn't the most salubrious address in the world. Lucy hadn't been expecting a mansion, but as she trailed around the flat Cousin Antonia had offered, from one cramped room to another, she could feel her spirits sinking. The whole place would have fitted easily into the servants' quarters at Eaton Place.

Her mother was even less impressed. She walked around, listing the faults.

'It's so small,' Clarissa said. 'And dark. I wonder when the windows were last cleaned?'

She rubbed at a grubby pane with the finger of her glove and peered through the patch.

'Oh, well, I can see why they haven't bothered,' she said. 'The view, if you can call it that, is absolutely shocking. Nothing but dismal grey rooftops as far as the eye can see, with a couple of factory chimneys in the distance to break the monotony.'

'At least Cousin Antonia is letting us have it for next to nothing,' Lucy said.

'I'm not surprised. No one in their right mind would think of paying money to live in a hovel like this.' Clarissa sniffed the air, her nose wrinkling. 'Can you smell damp?'

Lucy searched her mind desperately for something encouraging to say. 'Well, we won't have to get rid of any of our furniture. It should all fit in here nicely.'

Her mother smiled thinly. 'The amount of furniture we have left would fit in a doll's house.'

Lucy gritted her teeth. She'd had to organise the removal from Eaton Place because her mother had done nothing about it, except complain about the inconvenience.

And she'd had to beg for time off to be there. Sister Parry had been very annoyed about it, and Lucy was sure it would mean a bad ward report, which in turn could affect her chance of getting a permanent place at the Nightingale.

She rubbed her eyes, which were gritty from lack of sleep. If she wasn't lying awake worrying about her exams, she was worrying about her mother, or her father, or what everyone was saying about them.

Lucy took a deep breath to steady herself. She had to make this work. It was their only option.

She tried flattery. 'You know what marvellous taste you have, Mother. I expect you'll soon have this place looking wonderful.'

Lady Clarissa scowled. 'Even I can't make a silk purse out of a sow's ear.'

'Yes, but surely once we've put some pictures up, and had the curtains altered to fit, and given the walls a lick of paint . . .'

'A lick of paint?' Her mother's mouth curled in contempt. 'It will take more than a coat of paint or a roll of wallpaper to make this place attractive. The only thing that could improve it is to flatten it all and start again!'

'Yes, well, we can't do that, can we?' Lucy's last shred of patience finally snapped. 'Beggars can't be choosers.'

'And whose fault is it that we're beggars?' her mother flared back. 'Don't take this out on me, Lucy. You're treating me as if I'm being difficult, when it's your father's fecklessness that's got us in this mess.'

Lucy saw her mother's martyred expression, and something inside her exploded.

'Do you ever stop to think why he was so feckless, as you put it?'

Clarissa's chin lifted. 'Because he was selfish, I suppose.'

'No, Mother, *you're* the selfish one. Do you ever think about the pressure Father must have been under, trying to keep us in the luxury we expected? He must have been worried sick about this business deal, but he had no one to turn to. How do you think he must have felt, knowing it was all collapsing around him? Aren't you ashamed that he couldn't confide in his own wife?'

Her mother turned pale. 'How dare you speak to me like that?'

'Why? What are you going to do? Drink yourself into a stupor, as usual? We can't afford a bottle of gin, in case you hadn't noticed. Or are you going to flounce off to your room for a few hours? It's about time someone told you the truth, Mother. Perhaps if Father had felt able to do that, we wouldn't be in this mess now.'

Her mother turned her back and stood staring out of the window. Lucy could see her thin shoulders trembling as she went to stand behind her.

'The truth is, you've been far too cosseted for far too long. You were never interested in Father's business. All you were ever interested in was how much money he was making, and how fast you could spend it.'

'And you weren't, of course?'

'Yes, I was. And, believe me, I'm bitterly ashamed of it now,' Lucy admitted quietly. 'We've both been spoiled, and let Father carry all the burden. I had no idea how hard it was for him. No wonder he ran away.'

'He let us down,' her mother insisted stubbornly. 'He promised to take care of me . . .'

'No, we let him down,' Lucy cut her off. 'And it's about time you started taking care of yourself. Look at you. You're a grown woman, and you have no idea how to make yourself a sandwich or even a cup of tea. You should be ashamed!'

'Get out.' Her mother's voice was a low growl.

'Oh, I'm going,' Lucy said. 'I'm sick of listening to you complaining all the time, and I'm sick of trying to protect you. You're by yourself now, Mother. It's about time you started standing on your own two feet!'

Chapter Thirty-Six

It was strange to see Alf Doyle sitting at the kitchen table in Griffin Street again. Strange – and unnerving.

The atmosphere was strained. Nanna Winnie sat in hatchet-faced silence, the only sound the squeak of her chair as she rocked furiously back and forth.

But Bea and Little Alfie were all smiles. After a moment's shy hesitation, Little Alfie was soon firmly ensconced on his father's knee while Bea draped herself around his chair, never leaving his side.

'Look at him,' Nanna muttered to Dora. 'He acts like he's never been away.'

Dora glanced at her sister Josie. She sat on the opposite side of the fireplace, staring into the empty grate. She was smiling, but the way she picked at her fingernails betrayed her tension.

It was much harder to tell what was going on in their mother's mind. Rose treated their guest with detached civility, fetching tea and making polite conversation as she would with any stranger visiting her home. But Dora noticed that she didn't sit down or keep still once. She constantly found an excuse to be up and moving about the room, restlessly going from the scullery to the kitchen and back again. She seemed to be busy, but Dora guessed she didn't want to sit down and look her husband in the eye.

Alf seemed oblivious to the atmosphere he'd caused as he played with Little Alfie's toy cars, running them backwards and forwards on the table.

'I can't get over how much he's grown,' he said.

Rose smiled fondly at her son. 'He's a proper little bruiser.'

'Like his dad, eh?'

'Except he's got a brain in his head,' Nanna muttered.

'Dad's been telling us about his travels,' Bea piped up. 'He's been all over the world, ain't that right, Dad?'

'So he says.' Nanna addressed the empty grate.

'Well, I dunno about the world.' Alf shrugged. 'But I've been to France.'

'Can you speak French?' Little Alfie asked.

Alf twirled an imaginary moustache. '*Mais oui*,' he said in an exaggerated French accent that made Little Alfie and Bea fall about laughing.

'Say some more!' Little Alfie shouted, bouncing up and down on his knee.

'I reckon he's said enough.' Nanna Winnie looked over at their visitor. 'Ain't you got somewhere else to go?' she asked.

'Mum!' Rose turned on her. 'Alf's come for his tea, remember?'

'Oh, I remember, all right. Though Gawd knows why you invited him, after what he did to this family. Have you forgotten what he did to you, Rose? How he humiliated you?'

'Stop it, Mum.'

'No, she's right,' Alf sighed. 'I was a fool, Rosie.'

'A fool! You were more than a fool, Alf Doyle. I can't forget what you did, even if my daughter can.' Nanna's hands trembled in her lap, and Dora could tell it was all she could do to stop herself taking a swing at him. 'You carried on with that young girl behind my Rose's back. A girl young enough to be your daughter, I might add!' Dora flinched at her grandmother's words. 'You got her

313

pregnant and then ran off and abandoned us all. The poor girl nearly died getting rid of your kid. And my daughter ended up taking her in!'

Alf looked at Dora's mother. 'I never knew that, Rose. I'm sorry.'

'Too late to be sorry now!' Nanna's toothless mouth trembled. 'She cared for that girl for months, until she could get back on her feet. Even though it made us a laughing stock, Rose didn't turn her back on her. And where were you when all this was going on? Gallivanting round France, I suppose, learning all your fancy French words.'

'Nanna, don't!' Bea snapped. 'Leave Dad alone.'

'I'll leave him alone, all right! Just like he left your mother on her own, with all you kids to bring up and hardly a penny coming in. You can sit there making faces, Beatrice Doyle, but do you remember when we nearly froze to death 'cos we didn't have enough coal for the fire? Do you remember when we had the Means Test man knocking on the door, taking away all our furniture? I didn't see your precious father showing his face then, did you?'

Alf put his son off his lap and stumbled to his feet. 'I should go—'

'No, Alf. You stay where you are.' Rose Doyle's voice was firm and calm. 'You've come for your tea, and that's what you'll get. And you can be quiet, Mum.' She raised her hand to silence Nanna Winnie. 'Alf is still my husband, and he's a guest in this house. So I'll thank you to say no more about it.'

She turned on her heel and walked into the scullery, letting the curtain drop behind her. They all looked at each other in shocked silence. Alf stared at his boots, looking awkward.

'That's told you, Nanna,' Bea muttered.

Dora got up and followed her mother into the kitchen. Rose stood at the sink, her head in her hands.

'Are you all right, Mum?' Dora asked.

Her mother looked up at her, her expression despairing. 'Oh, Dora, I dunno what to do for the best,' she confessed. 'It's been such a shock, seeing Alf here. And there's your nanna having a go at him on one hand, and the kids so pleased to see him on the other . . . I dunno whether I'm coming or going, I really don't.'

'I know, Mum.' Dora put a comforting arm around her mother's shoulders. 'But Nanna's right, you know. He doesn't deserve to be here, not after the way he treated you.'

'But did you see the kids' faces? I haven't seen them so happy in a long time. Bea's been such a mare lately, this might be just what she needs. And as for Little Alfie—'

And what about Josie? Dora wanted to ask. Surely her mother had seen the shocked, vacant look on her middle daughter's face when Alf had walked in? Josie hadn't spoken a word since.

But then, hadn't Rose gone for years without noticing the pain either of her elder daughters was in? Dora subdued the unworthy thought. It wasn't her mother's fault. No one would ever suspect something so dreadful was going on under their own roof, in their own family.

'What about you?' Dora asked. 'Are you pleased to see him?'

Her mother sighed. 'I don't know, love,' she said. 'I don't know if I could ever forgive him, after what he did. I'm not sure if I could trust him either. But I suppose everyone makes mistakes, don't they? Everyone deserves a second chance.' She put her hand up to her face. Seeing Alf again seemed to have put years on her. 'And he has changed, I'm sure of that. You can see he's been through some hard times.'

Her mother actually felt sorry for him, Dora realised. Alf had been very clever, winning her over with a sob story or two. He knew as well as anyone that Rose Doyle couldn't resist looking after any waif or stray who came her way.

'Anyway, it's not about what I want, is it?' Rose went on briskly, pulling herself together. 'It's about what's best for everyone else. The kids need a father, when all's said and done.'

'I don't know if him coming back is best for . . .' Dora started to say, but they were interrupted by Alf sticking his face around the curtain.

'Can I give you a hand, love?' he offered. 'I could mash the potatoes for you, or fry the sausages?'

Rose smiled thinly. 'That's the first time I've ever heard you offer to lend a hand in the kitchen!'

'I told you, I'm a changed man!'

'And you're also a guest in this house. So you go and sit down.'

'Typical Rosie. You always did spoil me.'

Dora saw the look they gave each other, and felt sick. He was going to win her mother over, she was sure of it. Much as Rose disliked Alf at the moment, she had loved him once. And Dora knew her mother missed having a man in the house to fuss over. Little by little, Alf Doyle was going to reclaim his place in the house again, she was certain.

The thought made her feel so ill she could barely eat. She noticed Josie was the same, pushing the food around on her plate with no enthusiasm.

Dora left as soon as she could after tea. 'I'll walk with you to the end of the alley,' Josie offered straight away, jumping up to fetch her coat.

'I was going next door to see Danny . . .' Dora started to say, then she noticed the desperate look on her sister's face. 'Why don't I see if he fancies a quick stroll in the park with us?' she suggested.

Danny was delighted at the chance to get out of the house. His face lit up as Dora helped him into his coat, watched by his mother. June Riley puffed on a cigarette as usual, watching her son through narrowed eyes.

'I'm glad you came round. Little bugger was starting to get on my nerves, always under my feet,' she said.

Dora said nothing. She understood why Nick had so little time for his mother. June Riley had never paid either of her boys much attention.

'Nick promised he'd look after us, and now he's cleared off too,' June went on, her voice an insistent whine. 'God only knows why he had to give up his job and go off with a travelling fair, of all things. I suppose it's the last we've seen of him,' she said. 'You know what they say – like father, like son.'

Nick's nothing like his poor excuse for a father and you know it, Dora wanted to snap. And he will be coming back. He loves me.

But she had to admit to herself, she was worried. Nick still hadn't written to her. And even thought she kept telling herself that Nick was not the type to put pen to paper, she was beginning to fear that he'd forgotten her.

June puffed viciously on her cigarette. 'Knowing that little sod, I expect there's a girl involved. That's why he's gone, to get away from someone. He's always been one for running away from his responsibilities, my son.'

'That's not true!' Dora couldn't help snapping back, then wished she hadn't when she saw the surprised look on June's face. She had no idea about Dora and Nick. If she did, it would be all over Griffin Street in no time.

'Nick's never run away from anything,' she defended him stoutly.

'He walked out on his missus, didn't he? And he's walked out on us, too.'

'H-he's gone to America,' Danny said. 'To f-fight Max Baer.'

June gave a harsh laugh. 'Listen to him! Still reckons his brother's a bleeding hero. I've tried telling him Nick's done a runner and ain't coming back but he won't believe me.' She shook her head pityingly.

Dora caught Danny's look of wide-eyed distress. The boy doted on his brother, as much as Nick did on him. 'He'll be back, Dan,' she whispered.

'Don't you go filling his head with ideas, Dora Doyle,' June snapped. 'The sooner he gets used to the fact that his brother's gone for good, the better.' She took another puff on her cigarette. 'Talking of coming back – did I see Alf Doyle turning up a while ago? What's he doing round here? Don't tell me he's come back?' She blew a thin stream of smoke out of the corner of her mouth, towards the ceiling. 'You wait, next thing my old man will come crawling out of the woodwork, too. Wouldn't that be a sight to see?' She laughed so much she brought on a coughing fit.

Dora left her wheezing for breath and ushered Danny outside to where Josie was waiting for them in the back yard, scuffing the toe of her shoe mindlessly against a chipped paving slab.

It was early evening and the park gates were still open. It wasn't the best day for a stroll – the sun had been cowering behind a heavy veil of dirty grey cloud all day, threatening rain. But Dora and Josie barely noticed the spitting drops as they sat on a bench overlooking the boating lake. Danny stood at the water's edge, watching the ducks.

'Alf's staying, isn't he?' Josie said in a flat voice.

'Not if I can help it.'

'But you can't, can you? There's nothing you can do. There's nothing any of us can do.' Josie aimed a pebble at the water. 'I can see it in Mum's eyes. She wants him back.'

'I don't think she does,' Dora said. 'But she's confused. She just wants to do what's best for the children.'

'He'll win her round in the end.'

'Nothing's been decided yet,' Dora insisted. 'Try not to worry.'

Josie was silent for a long time, aiming pebbles into the water. 'It was here,' she said, finally. 'Right here that we first talked about it. Do you remember?'

'I do.' Up until that point, Dora had thought she was the only one to suffer Alf's vile abuse. Until the day she realised it was happening to her younger sister too. It was then that Dora had made up her mind to stop their stepfather.

She looked at her sister. Josie was now seventeen and a young woman. But at that moment she looked just like the frightened little girl who'd plucked up the courage one day to whisper her tale of abuse.

Josie let out a long, shuddering sigh. 'Oh, Dor, I don't know if I can live under the same roof as him. Not again. What if he tries to – you know . . .'

Dora read the panic in her sister's face. 'He won't,' she said. 'I won't let him. Not this time.'

'What can you do about it?'

I'll kill him, Dora thought. She'd threatened him once before, but this time she would have no hesitation.

She paused for a moment, already knowing what Josie's reaction would be to her next words. 'We could tell Mum the truth,' she said

'No!' Josie cried.

'But if she knew what Alf was really like, there's no chance she would ever let him back.'

'Dora, we couldn't. I couldn't stand for her to know. I'd be so ashamed . . .'

'You've got no reason to be ashamed, Josie. It wasn't your fault what that monster did to you – to both of us.' Dora put out her hand to calm her agitated sister. 'He's the one in the wrong, not us.'

'You promised.' Josie's voice was choked. 'You swore to me she wouldn't ever have to know.'

'That was before he came back, wasn't it? When I thought we were safe.'

Once Alf was out of their lives, they had agreed their mother shouldn't have to know what he had done to them. There was no point in dragging it up, they'd reasoned, especially when they both knew Rose would only blame herself for not protecting them.

Josie put her hands up to her face. 'I couldn't bear it, Dor,' she whispered. 'I couldn't bear the thought of her knowing. It would change everything.'

Dora understood. It was the same reason she herself had stayed silent for so many years. Whatever she said to Josie about it not being their fault, it didn't take away the deep sense of shame Dora still felt.

Her mother would try to understand, she knew that. She would go on loving them no matter what. But something between them would change, Dora was certain of it. Once Rose knew, she wouldn't be able to look at them again without thinking of what Alf had done to them. They would be somehow tainted in her eyes. They wouldn't be her girls any more.

'Perhaps Mum's right,' Josie said in a small voice. 'Maybe he is a changed man. We should give him a chance . . .'

Dora looked at her sharply. 'You don't really believe that, do you?'

'No.' Josie sighed. She aimed another pebble and it landed with a plop in the still water. 'I suppose I could move out, go to live with Auntie Brenda in Haggerston?'

'But Griffin Street is your home. And besides, what if he starts on Bea?'

'Don't!' Josie cut her off sharply.

'That's why we've got to tell Mum.'

'I can't, Dora.' Josie's eyes filled with tears.

'I'll do it, then. I won't tell her about you. I'll tell her he just did it to me.'

'No! I can't let you do that, it's not fair.'

'Josie, we've got to do something.'

'I know, but not that. Anything but that, Dora. Please, promise me you won't tell her?'

Dora looked at her sister. She had that haunted, vacant expression in her eyes again, the same expression Dora used to see when she looked at herself in the mirror.

'I promise,' she said.

Chapter Thirty-Seven

It was lunchtime, and Sister Sutton was in one of her manic spring-cleaning moods. All morning Jess had been up a ladder, bucket of soapy water balanced in one hand, scrubbing at the ornate plasterwork on the ceilings with the other. Sister Sutton stood at the bottom with Sparky, offering encouragement.

'Make sure you get into all the nooks and crannies,' she called up. 'That's where the dirt hides. Are you sure you've cleaned round those grapes properly? They don't look very clean to me. I'm sure I can see . . .'

She fell silent suddenly. Jess glanced down at her. The Home Sister had one hand to her abdomen and had gone very pale.

'Are you all right, Sister?' Jess called down to her.

'Yes, yes. Just a silly pain, that's all. It's nothing serious.'

'Are you sure?' Jess dropped her brush into the bucket and started down the ladder. 'Would you like me to fetch you something? A glass of water?'

'Really, there's no need to fuss!' Sister Sutton shook off Jess' hand. 'It was just a twinge, that's all. It's gone now.' She drew herself upright and glared at the girl. 'Well? What are you doing? Get back up that ladder at once.'

Jess put her hands on her hips. 'At least go and have a sit down while I finish.'

'So that you have an excuse to shirk?'

'You know me, I never shirk.'

Sister Sutton pursed her lips. 'I suppose that's true.'

'Then, please, go and sit down. I'll bring you a cup of tea when I've finished.'

'I suppose that would be acceptable,' Sister Sutton agreed reluctantly.

Jess waited until Sister had bustled off to her sitting room and then headed back up the ladder. No sooner had she reached the top than the front door opened and Effie came in, dressed in her uniform.

She stopped dead when she saw Jess. Even from her lofty perch, Jess could tell she had something on her mind.

'Hello,' Jess greeted her. 'You off duty?'

'Until five.' Effie nodded, her face pensive.

Jess turned back to her cleaning, but Effie stood at the foot of the ladder, watching her.

'You'll never guess,' she said at last. 'I found the boy who stole my bag.'

The brush slipped from Jess' fingers but she managed to grab it before it fell. 'Oh, yes? How did you manage that?' she said.

'He's been admitted to the ward with a fractured femur. Running away with something else he'd stolen, apparently.'

'Well, I never.' Jess soaked her brush and went on cleaning.

'Do you think I should go to the police?'

Jess feigned a careless shrug. 'It's up to you.'

'I suppose I couldn't prove anything,' Effie mused. 'I got my bag back, after all.' She paused for a moment. 'How did you know where to find it, by the way?'

Jess didn't dare turn round. She kept scrubbing, her shoulder aching in protest. 'I told you, it was under a bush in the park.'

'So it was. What a lucky coincidence, you stumbling across it like that. I mean, can you imagine the chances?'

Jess felt perspiration breaking out on her brow. 'You know, don't you?' she said flatly.

'That Cyril is your brother? Yes, he told me. He was quite gleeful about it, actually.'

I'll bet he was, Jess thought. Any chance to cause more mischief. Her knees were wobbling so much she could barely hold herself upright on the ladder.

'I didn't put two and two together at first,' Effie went on. 'Stupid of me, really. I didn't know Jago wasn't a common name. You don't even look alike.'

'He's my stepbrother,' Jess mumbled.

'Why didn't you tell me?' Effie asked.

Jess paused briefly, then went on scrubbing. 'I didn't tell you because I knew what you'd think,' she replied at last.

'And what's that?'

'That if Cyril's a thief then I must be one too.'

She heard Effie gasp. 'I wouldn't think that! You're my friend.'

Jess risked a glance in Effie's direction. The sight of her hurt expression nearly weakened Jess. 'We're not friends,' she said.

'How can you say that? You helped me pass my PTS exams . . .'

'I helped you out because you asked me to, that's all. But we ain't friends, Effie. I told you, we can't be. You've got your set and I've got—'

And I've got no one. The words were on the tip of her tongue for a moment, but Jess ignored them. 'At any rate, we're not friends,' she said firmly.

Out of the corner of her eye Jess caught sight of Effie's trembling lower lip. 'I'm sorry,' she murmured. 'I didn't realise that was what you thought.'

She walked off towards the stairs. Jess fought the urge to call after her, tell her she was sorry, that she didn't mean it.

But what was the point? Effie had said she wouldn't judge her. But sooner or later something would happen and she wouldn't be able to help herself. And Jess couldn't bear that. Far better to make the break herself now than to risk rejection later on.

She'd been so foolish to think anything would be different for her here. She had come to the Nightingale looking for a new start, to escape everyone judging her because of who she was and where she'd come from.

But her old life followed her, clawing at her, dragging her back like a clanking ball and chain, no matter where she tried to go.

She finished scrubbing, then came down the ladder and carried the bucket of dirty water outside. She sloshed it down the drain then turned round to find Sparky watching her from the doorstep.

'Blimey, where did you come from?' she asked, bending down to ruffle his velvety ears.

She looked up, expecting to see Sister Sutton bustling into the kitchen, but there was no sign of her.

Jess looked back at Sparky. 'I dunno what you're doing, wandering about on your own, but Sister ain't going to be too pleased about it. Come on, let's get you back to her before you're missed.'

She scooped Sparky up into her arms and carried him through the kitchen and up the passageway. The door to Sister Sutton's sitting room stood half-open.

'So that's how you escaped,' Jess muttered. 'Proper little Harry Houdini, ain't you?' She tapped on the Home Sister's door. 'Sister? Guess who I found wandering around outside?'

There was no reply.

'Sister?' Still holding Sparky under her arm, Jess pushed gently at the door. It swung open. 'Sister Sutton? Sorry to disturb you, but—'

Then she saw the bulky form sprawled on the mat in front of the fire, and didn't finish the rest of her sentence.

Effie returned to the ward at five o'clock, still feeling hurt at what Jess had said to her. Why would she come out with something so spiteful? It was almost as if she wanted to drive her away.

Unless Jess was speaking the truth, and they had never been friends after all? It was all desperately confusing.

She walked through the double doors and straight into Hugo and Frances, having what seemed like a very cosy chat in the sluice. They jumped apart when she came in.

'Oh, it's only you!' Frances laughed with relief. 'I thought it was Sister!'

Effie looked from one to the other. 'What's going on?'

'I was looking for you, darling,' Hugo said smoothly. 'I just wanted to know what time you wanted me to pick you up for the ball tomorrow? Would about seven be all right? Outside the nurses' home?'

'If you like,' Effie replied, still staring at Frances.

'Jolly good. I can't tell you how much I'm looking forward to it. I expect you'll look utterly ravishing, as usual.'

'I'll do my best.' Effie made a big point of kissing him on the cheek before he left, and was pleased to see Frances looking positively green with jealousy.

'You shouldn't do that, you know,' she said sourly. 'You'd get the sack for sure if Sister caught you.'

'So would you, if she caught you alone with him,' Effie pointed out. 'You shouldn't be talking to him anyway. He's my boyfriend, not yours.'

Frances gave her a patronising smile. 'Oh, do grow up, O'Hara. He was my friend before you came along. We've known each other for ages. Honestly, you sound like a silly schoolgirl sometimes.'

Effie ignored her and went to the sink. 'What were you laughing about anyway?' she asked, trying to sound casual.

Frances shrugged. 'Hugo was just telling me about the great joke he and the other students are planning to play at the ball.'

Effie glanced over her shoulder at her. 'What is it?'

'You'll find out.' Frances looked maddeningly mysterious.

'I don't know why he can't let me in on the joke,' Effie said, watching the hot water run into the big steel sink.

'I expect he thought you wouldn't want to know,' Frances dismissed. 'Let's face it, you're not much of a sport, are you? You seem to get cross about his pranks.'

'Only when they're hurtful.'

Frances smiled. 'They're only really funny when they're a bit hurtful.' She gave Effie a pitying look. 'Really, O'Hara, if you don't understand that then you don't have a hope of keeping up with Hugo Morgan.'

'I keep telling you, I'm quite well. It was just a dizzy spell, that's all!'

Sister Sutton glared over the doctor's shoulder at Jess. 'You see what you've done? You've caused a lot of silly fuss over nothing.'

'You collapsed,' Jess pointed out.

'Collapsed, my eye! You're being over-dramatic.'

'Over-dramatic or not, she was quite right to call me,' Dr McKay said, putting away his stethoscope. 'Well, you'll be pleased to know your heart sounds very strong.'

Sister Sutton regarded Jess triumphantly. 'You see? I told you there was nothing wrong with me.'

'Nevertheless, I would like you to spend a couple of days in the sick bay, so I can do some further tests.'

'Certainly not!' Sister Sutton replied tartly. 'I told you, I'm . . .'

'As fit as a fiddle – yes, I know.' Dr McKay looked weary. 'But I would like to make sure. Your maid tells me you've had some abdominal pain?'

'She had no business telling you anything!' Sister Sutton shook her head. 'I'm sorry, Doctor, but it's quite impossible. I have my duties here to think about.'

'I'll look after everything,' Jess offered.

'You?' The Home Sister sent her a withering look.

'Or surely one of the other sisters could help?' Dr McKay suggested.

Sister Sutton sighed. 'I suppose I could ask Miss Hanley to look after the office,' she agreed reluctantly.

'And I'll look after Sparky for you until you come back,' Jess offered.

'That's settled, then.' Dr McKay smiled. 'I'll summon a porter to bring a wheelchair.'

'A wheelchair?' Sister Sutton looked affronted. 'Oh, no, Doctor. If I must submit to the sick bay, then I fully intend to go there under my own steam, thank you very much. Now if you'll excuse me, I need to pack.'

She bustled off, quivering with bruised dignity. Dr McKay turned to Jess.

'I know you, don't I?'

Jess blushed. 'I don't think so, Doctor.'

'Yes, I do. I never forget a face. Now let me think . . . ah, yes. I have it now. You're the quick thinking young lady who saved your brother's life. Fractured femur, wasn't it?'

'Yes,' Jess replied, frowning at the mention of her brother. After the way Cyril had betrayed her to Effie, she would have pushed him under the wretched van herself, given another chance.

'I thought so. I told you, I never forget a face. And now you've come to Sister Sutton's rescue.' He smiled approvingly at her. He was a youngish man, with a kind face and a nice smile. 'You're quite the Florence Nightingale, aren't you?'

'I dunno about that, Doctor.'

'Well, I'm most impressed with you.' He leaned forward, lowering his voice. 'Now, I should make the most of the peace and quiet, if I were you,' he advised. 'Because no doubt Sister Sutton will drive everyone so mad in the sick bay, they'll send her straight back as soon as possible!'

Chapter Thirty-Eight

The Founder's Day Ball was held in Bethnal Green Town Hall.

'Of course, it's not really a ball at all. More of a glorified tea dance really,' Hugo said to Effie as they climbed the broad marble staircase to the ballroom. 'But hopefully we can liven things up a bit.'

There it was again, that maddening smile. He'd been grinning like the Cheshire Cat ever since he'd come to collect her at the nurses' home.

'I know you're up to something,' Effie accused him. 'What is it?'

Hugo tapped the side of his nose. 'All in good time, my angel. All in good time,' he said.

Everyone else seemed to be in on the joke. Hugo's medical student friends couldn't stop grinning, and even Hilda and Frances were looking pleased with themselves. Effie's only consolation was that Frances' dress looked as if she'd butchered it from an old curtain.

Effie, on the other hand, was pleased with the dress she'd chosen, a simple pale blue column her mammy had made, finished off with some pearls she'd borrowed from Katie. It matched her eyes, and for once made Effie glad that she didn't have her sister's curves.

'You look like an angel, darling,' Hugo had said when he first saw her. 'I hope you're not too virtuous for me?'

Hugo may have been rather dismissive about it, but the ballroom seemed very grand to Effie. The room was filled with people, voices, laughter, and the rich sound of the orchestra. Enormous chandeliers overhead showered diamonds of light over the marble and mirrored walls. Effie looked around, barely recognising the nurses and ward sisters in all their finery.

'Let's dance!' She grabbed at Hugo's hand, pulling him towards the floor. She knew once he got chatting to his cronies wild horses wouldn't drag him away, and was determined to have at least one dance with him before the evening was over.

Hugo smiled indulgently. 'Anything to make you happy, my sweet,' he said, following her on to the floor. The band started playing 'Cheek to Cheek', and Hugo pulled her into his arms.

It was blissful, whirling around the floor, knowing she was dancing with the most handsome man in the room. Even if his eyes did seem to keep wandering elsewhere. Effie could feel him looking over her shoulder, his gaze moving around the ballroom, resting everywhere but on her.

'Are you looking for someone?' she asked finally.

Hugo gave her another mysterious smile. 'Just making plans.'

'What kind of plans?'

'You'll see.'

They whirled past Anna Padgett and the rest of her set, sitting in a glum-faced line, sipping punch under the frosty eye of Miss Hanley. She was standing in for the Home Sister since Sister Sutton had been taken to the sick bay.

'They look happy, don't they?' Hugo commented. 'She's a bit of a battleaxe, isn't she, your Assistant Matron?'

'I'll say! She told me off yesterday because my skirt was an inch higher than it should be.'

'She needs to loosen up and have a bit of fun.' Hugo

raised his eyebrows. 'Maybe someone should get her a glass of punch?' he suggested.

'I don't think she drinks,' Effie replied. 'Besides, I don't suppose the punch is even alcoholic, knowing Matron.'

Hugo smiled. 'You never know!'

Effie sent him a quizzical look. 'Is that what you're doing? Have you spiked the punch?'

'We might have.'

She giggled, pleased to be in on the joke at last. 'In that case, I hope Miss Hanley does have a glass!' she said.

The music stopped, and Hugo released her immediately.

'Where are you going?' Effie asked, disappointed.

'I just need a word with someone,' Hugo called back over his shoulder. 'I'll be back in a minute, sweetheart.'

Effie met her sister Katie as she was helping herself to a glass of Hugo's alcoholic punch. Katie was with her boyfriend Tom, clinging to his arm as if she daren't let him out of her sight.

'Don't touch that,' Katie warned. 'You don't know what's in it.'

Effie stared at her. 'How did you know it was spiked?'

'Because it always is,' Katie said. 'The medical students do it every year.'

'One glass won't hurt.' Effie went to fill her glass, but Katie took it away from her.

'I mean it, Effie. Stick to lemonade.'

'I have tried alcohol before, as you well know,' Effie replied loftily. 'Remember Da's poteen?'

'It's not the alcohol I'm worried about,' Katie said. 'Last year they laced it with cascara. I can't tell you the trouble that caused.'

'Well, I know what they're putting in it this year, because Hugo told me,' Effie said, very pleased to know better than her sister for once.

'I might have known he'd be involved.' Katie looked around. 'Where is he, anyway? Why isn't he with you?'

'We don't have to stick to each other like glue,' Effie muttered. 'Not like some people,' she added, shooting a look at her sister's arm, tightly threaded through Tom's.

'Hugo Morgan is a troublemaker,' Katie said. 'I know all medical students are bad, but from what I hear he's the worst. You should steer well clear of him.'

Effie rolled her eyes. 'One minute you're complaining that he's not with me, the next you're saying I should keep away from him. I wish you'd make up your mind!'

'You know what I mean.' Katie leaned closer, peering at Effie's throat. 'Are they my pearls you're wearing?'

Lucy was on duty until nine on the night of the ball.

'I'm sorry if that spoils your plans, Lane, but someone has to stay and look after the patients while everyone else is at that wretched ball,' Sister Parry had said.

'I don't mind, Sister.' It was a relief to have an excuse not to go. It was bad enough getting through each day knowing that everyone was whispering about her, without spending the evening being talked about too. At the end of her shift, all Lucy ever wanted to do was to slink off to her room and take refuge alone with her books.

But she wasn't alone this evening. Dora was sitting on her bed, her flannel nightgown tucked around her, lost in study.

'Oh!' Lucy stopped in the doorway. 'I'm sorry, I thought you'd be at the ball?'

'Benedict has gone, but I didn't feel like dancing,' Dora said. 'I thought I might as well catch up on some revision.'

'Me too. But I can study in the sitting room since everyone is out. I'll just fetch my books.'

333

She started to cross the room but Dora said, 'You might as well stay here. We could keep each other company.'

Lucy paused, unsure what to do. She and Dora had never been in the room together for long without Millie there to keep the peace between them.

Dora gave her a wry smile. 'It's all right,' she said. 'I promise I won't bite. Besides, it's your room, too. You've got as much right to be in here as I have.'

Lucy changed out of her uniform and sat cross-legged on her bed, then opened up her physiology textbook. They both read for a while, the silence stretching uncomfortably between them. Lucy shot a sidelong look at Dora. Her head was bent over her book, red curls falling around her face.

Lucy cleared her throat nervously. 'We could help each other, if you like?'

Dora looked up. 'What, you and me? Work together?' The look she gave Lucy made her wither inside.

'Why not?' she said. 'We could test each other. And you know what they say, two heads are better than one.'

'Depends whose heads they are, doesn't it?' Dora muttered. But just as Lucy was bracing herself for a crushing rejection, she added, 'I suppose we could give it a try.'

'Is there anything you're particularly stuck on?' Lucy asked.

Dora bristled. 'What makes you think I'm stuck on anything?'

She looked so defensive, Lucy was taken aback. 'I just thought there might be something you found difficult, that's all?'

'Because I'm not as clever as you, is that it?'

Lucy sighed. 'Perhaps it's not such a good idea if we help each other after all.'

She went back to her book, flicking over the pages. She

had tried to be friendly, and Dora had bitten her head off. That was just typical of her.

Perhaps you asked for it, a voice inside Lucy's head whispered. How many times had she sneered at the other girl in class when she couldn't remember something? And how often had she taken pleasure in pointing out her mistakes on the ward?

'Fevers,' Dora said.

Lucy looked up. 'I beg your pardon?'

'I'm not very good on fevers.' Dora sent her a wary glance from under her mop of curls. 'You could test me on those, if you like?'

Lucy smiled. 'Right you are.'

They went through them all, from Diphtheria to Rubella, Scarlet Fever to Enteric Fever. It was awkward at first, but gradually they forgot their reserve as they swapped symptoms, throwing questions at each other back and forth across the room.

'You see?' Lucy said, when Dora had successfully listed all the complications of Measles. 'You remember it better than you think.'

'It helped to go through it with someone.' Dora glanced shyly at her room mate. 'Who'd ever have thought we'd be studying together one day? Benedict would have a fit if she saw us!'

Lucy smiled. 'We've managed to go nearly half an hour without a single argument. That must be a record!'

'I think we deserve a break, don't you?' Dora put down her book and fumbled under her mattress. She drew out a packet of cigarettes and offered it to Lucy.

She glanced towards the door. 'Are we allowed? You know Sister Sutton doesn't like it.'

'Sister Sutton's not here, is she? And everyone else is at the ball, so I don't suppose they'll notice.'

'That's true.' Lucy took a cigarette from the packet and Dora lit it for her.

'Benedict and I usually stand on the bed and blow the smoke through the skylight. Look, I'll show you.'

Lucy held Dora's cigarette while she climbed up on the bed and opened the window. Then she put out her hand and helped Lucy up. Together, they balanced precariously, blowing curls of smoke into the night sky.

'Hard to believe we've nearly finished our training, ain't it?' Dora mused. 'It feels like only yesterday I was unpacking my case in this room, wondering if I'd last a week. I was so nervous.'

'Me too,' Lucy said.

Dora shot her a sideways look. 'You?' she laughed. 'You were always so sure of yourself. I remember you in the dining room that first evening, showing off to everyone.'

Lucy remembered it too. 'I was just as terrified as everyone else,' she admitted. 'But my parents always taught me to put on a good face, whatever I might be feeling. Appearances are everything, they've always . . .'

She stopped, realising what she was saying. She wished she'd never mentioned her parents, but now it was there between them, hanging in the air like one of Dora's smoke rings.

Lucy felt the weight of Dora's silence, knew what she was going to ask before she said it. She would want to pry, to know all the nasty little details. She would probably want to gloat, too. God knows, Lucy wouldn't blame her for it, after the way she'd treated her.

She steeled herself, ready to retaliate, to tell Dora it was none of her business. But her question, when it finally came, caught Lucy unawares.

'How are you?' Dora asked quietly.

'Shell-shocked.' Lucy's hand was shaking as she lifted

the cigarette to her mouth. 'It's all happened so fast, I can't really take it in.' She blew a stream of smoke high into the air.

'Have you heard anything from your father?'

She shook her head. 'We've no idea where he is, or even if he's—' Lucy pressed her lips together, not trusting herself to speak. She wouldn't let herself show weakness, no matter how much Dora's concern touched her. 'It gets harder every day to believe that he's still alive,' she managed to say finally.

Dora was silent for a moment. Lucy was grateful that she didn't ask too much.

'And how's your mum taking it?' she asked finally.

Lucy sighed. 'I'm not sure. I'm afraid we've had rather a falling out.'

She hadn't been to see her mother since their argument. Lucy pretended it was because she was busy on the ward, but the truth was she didn't want to see Clarissa.

Dora looked sideways at her. 'What about?'

Lucy wasn't going to tell her, she had no intention of sharing her personal business with anyone, least of all her worst enemy. But there was something about the way Dora said it, the kind concern in her eyes, that made Lucy weaken.

And so she told her. She spilled out everything: about how selfish her mother had been, how she had leaned on her husband too heavily, and now she was leaning on Lucy too.

'It's as if she doesn't want to stand on her own two feet,' Lucy complained.

'I daresay she doesn't know how, after all these years,' Dora said.

'I suppose so.' Lucy sighed. 'But all she does is whine and complain about how bad everything is. As if I didn't know that! I'm doing my best to make everything less difficult for her, but she doesn't help herself.'

Dora considered it for a moment. 'Even so, you shouldn't fall out,' she said. 'You've got to stick together, now more than ever. You've only got each other.'

'So Uncle Gordon – my godfather – keeps telling me, but we're not used to sticking together.' Lucy smiled sadly. Up until now, she hadn't realised how far apart her family had stayed. They'd been more like three people living under the same roof.

For some reason an image of Ernest Pennington came into her mind. His parents were like hers, showering him with expensive gifts when all he really wanted was their time and attention. The only way he could earn their approval was through excelling at music.

Lucy was just the same, striving to be the best at everything. She'd always thought she liked to win, but all she had really wanted to win was her parents' love.

'You don't know how lucky you are,' she told Dora.

She stared back in surprise. 'Me?'

'I've always envied you your family, being so close to each other.'

'Like rats in a sewer?' Dora's brows rose ironically.

Lucy felt the heat rising in her face, meeting the cool of the evening air through the skylight window. 'I'm sorry,' she said. 'I shouldn't have said that. It was very unkind.'

'You've said worse.'

'I know.'

They were silent for a while. Dora smoked her cigarette and contemplated the stars.

'Anyway,' she said finally, 'not all families get on all the time. Not even mine.'

Lucy shot her a glance. There was something on Dora's mind, she could tell. She wondered if she dared to ask. But the harsh set of Dora's mouth stopped her.

They finished their cigarettes, stubbed them out and threw them out of the skylight.

'I suppose we'd better get back to our books,' Lucy said reluctantly. The truth was, she was enjoying her chat with Dora.

'Or we could go downstairs and play cards instead?' Dora suggested.

Lucy smiled. 'Why not? I reckon we deserve a treat, what with everyone else being at the ball.'

'Proper little pair of Cinderellas, ain't we?' Dora grinned. Her face seemed softer, almost pretty, with her curls hanging loose around it.

Lucy smiled back at her. 'I don't think we're missing anything, do you?'

The first Effie knew something was wrong was when Anna Padgett was violently sick into a Grecian urn.

'Looks like someone can't hold their drink!' Hugo remarked. He took a hip flask out of his pocket and offered it to Effie.

'No, thanks.' She watched as two of the other girls helped poor Anna off to the cloakroom. Her face was a strange greyish-green colour. 'How much did you put in that punch?' she asked.

'Not how much, darling,' Hugo replied. He and his student friends grinned at each other. They were all swigging from hip flasks, she noticed with a feeling of unease.

'I don't understand,' she said. 'What's going on?'

'Putting alcohol in the punch is a bit old hat,' Hugo explained.

'Everyone expects it,' his friend Andrew joined in.

'So we thought we'd do something different to liven things up,' Hugo finished.

Effie's mouth fell open. 'Not cascara again?'

'Oh no,' Hugo shook his head. 'Although I must admit, that was rather amusing last year.' His mouth twitched.

Sister Wren pushed past them, heading for the doors. She had the same greyish tinge as poor Anna Padgett.

'Ever heard of antimony?' Hugo asked. 'Antimony potassium tartrate, to be precise.'

Effie shook her head. 'What is it?'

'One of the most powerful emetics known to man,' Andrew said.

'Or medical student!' Frances laughed.

Effie stared around her. The band had stopped playing as people rushed from the dance floor, hands clamped over their mouths. Even the trumpeter was looking queasy, doubled up where he sat.

She turned back to Hugo. 'You didn't?'

He looked pleased with himself. 'I did! Rather a lot, actually.'

'But why?'

'Because it's fun!' Frances said. 'Look around you. Have you ever seen the ward sisters in such a state? What a chance to get our own back for all those awful things they make us do every day.'

Effie looked over to where Matron stood, watching the mayhem around her with narrowed eyes.

'We should tell someone,' she said.

'I think they'll work it out for themselves soon enough, don't you?' Hugo smirked.

'Oh, for heaven's sake, O'Hara, don't be such a spoilsport!' Frances snapped.

'*You're* the spoilsport. Everyone was really looking forward to this evening, and now you've ruined it.'

Effie thought about the girls in her set, rushing round to get ready, agonising over their dresses and borrowing each other's lipstick. They had all been so excited about having a night off, the chance to dress up and be glamorous for once. And now they'd been humiliated.

'It's just a prank, darling,' Hugo said soothingly. 'A harmless prank, that's all. Everyone will have a good laugh about it in the morning.'

'Or the morning after that,' Andrew suggested.

Effie stared at them both with loathing. 'And who is supposed to run the wards and look after the patients if half the staff are in the sick bay?' she snapped. 'It's all right for you medical students, you just hang around the place and no one would notice if you were there or not. But some of us have work to do!'

Before Andrew could reply, a cry went up from the far side of the room.

'Quick! Mulhearn's collapsed!'

Effie rushed over, following the surge of people. But Miss Hanley was already there, clearing a circle.

'Stand back! Give the girl some air!' she ordered.

Effie glimpsed over a porter's shoulder. Poor little Prudence was on the floor, twitching and jerking like a puppet on the end of invisible strings.

'She's having a seizure,' Miss Hanley said. 'Someone call for an ambulance.'

Effie watched as the Assistant Matron moved swiftly into action, loosening Prudence's clothing and putting her into a safer position. One of the waiters produced a wine cork and Miss Hanley set it between the girl's teeth.

Effie sensed someone at her side and looked round. Frances was standing there, her face pale with shock.

'Not so funny now, is it?' Effie muttered.

Frances shot her a dark look and pushed her way back through the crowd towards the doors.

The ambulance arrived shortly afterwards, and Prudence was taken away. Matron went with her. But the party had already started to disperse. Those guests who weren't still locked in the cloakrooms groaning in agony were fetching their coats to leave.

Effie looked for Hugo, but there was no sign of him or his friends. They had all cleared off and left her.

She searched for her sister, but her friend Millie Benedict said Katie had already left with Tom, before all the fuss started.

'Are you all right?' she asked Effie. 'You look a bit grey. You didn't drink any of that filthy punch, did you?'

'No . . . no, I didn't.'

'Good thing, too,' Millie said. 'Anyone with any sense brings their own supply. That poor pro,' she sighed. 'I do hope she's all right. It looked rather serious, don't you think?' She frowned at Effie. 'Are you sure you're all right? I would offer to share a taxi back to the hospital with you, but I have a sleeping-out pass so my fiancé and I are going to the Café de Paris. Will you be able to get back by yourself?'

Effie reassured her she would be fine. But privately she wasn't so sure she had the money for a taxi. She'd left in such a hurry, all she'd stuffed into her evening bag was a lipstick and a few coins.

She stood outside the cloakroom and delved into her coat pocket, hoping that a miracle had happened and her taxi fare might have magically appeared, stuck in the lining.

And then she found it.

She pulled out the test tube, and stared at it. How did that get into her pocket? She peered closer. It was empty, but there were traces of a buff coloured powder clinging to the bottom of the tube.

Effie was peering at the label, trying to make out the words on it, when the test tube was snatched out of her hands.

'Let me see that!'

She looked up in dismay. Miss Hanley towered over her, the test tube held aloft in her manly hand.

'Where did this come from?' she demanded.

Effie stared at it helplessly. 'I don't know,' she whispered. 'I've never seen it before in my life.'

'I don't believe you.' Miss Hanley's eyes narrowed. 'I think we'd better show this to Matron, don't you?'

Chapter Thirty-Nine

'Have you ever heard of Adams-Stokes Syndrome?' Kathleen Fox asked.

Effie O'Hara looked blank. 'No, Matron,' she whispered.

'It's a sudden, transient episode of fainting and seizures, caused by temporary heart failure. And do you know what causes the heart to fail, O'Hara?'

'No, Matron.' The girl's eyes were already straying towards the floor.

Kathleen held up the empty test tube. 'Antimony poisoning,' she said. 'Little did you know before you played your stupid prank that you could have killed poor Prudence Mulhearn.'

Effie looked up at her sharply. 'It wasn't my prank, Matron.'

'This tube was found in your pocket.'

'Yes, but I don't know how it got there.'

'Well, if you didn't put it there someone else must have.' Kathleen regarded her calmly. 'Who was it, O'Hara?'

She leaned forward, willing the girl to speak. Effie opened her mouth, then closed it again. 'I don't know, Matron,' she mumbled.

'I think you do. Was it one of your friends? Another nurse in your set perhaps? Or was it one of the medical students?'

Say it, she urged silently. Just say his name, for God's sake.

Kathleen knew exactly who had poisoned the punch.

Hugo Morgan had a reputation as a joker. He didn't seem to care how far he went, or who suffered in the process, as long as he amused himself and his foolish friends. It wasn't the first time Kathleen had been made aware of his little pranks, but so far there had been nothing she could do about him. His father Roderick Morgan was an eminent cardiac surgeon at the Nightingale, and it had been made clear to Matron by the Board of Trustees that she should do nothing to offend him or his family. As far as Roderick was concerned, his son could do no wrong.

If Kathleen had had her way, Hugo would have been out on his ear a long time ago. As it was, he and his friends were allowed to swagger around the wards as if they owned the place.

But if she could prove that Hugo had endangered some-one's life, it would be a different story. Even his father couldn't protect him then.

All she had to do was to persuade Effie O'Hara to give up his name. But she was either too frightened, too loyal or too lovesick to do it.

'If you know who it is, you owe it to Prudence to speak up,' Kathleen said.

'I don't know who put the tube in my pocket, Matron.'

'But you do know who poisoned the punch?'

Effie bit her lip to stop it trembling. Silly girl, Kathleen thought. She was clearly besotted by Hugo. And she wasn't the first either. The little snake was always getting nurses to take the fall for him.

Effie was glancing towards the door now, as if she expected him to come in and rescue her at any minute. She would wait a long time, Kathleen thought. Hugo Morgan was as cowardly as he was cruel.

Impatience made her snap, 'If you don't tell me I shall have to assume it was you who did it, and the consequences will be very serious for you. Do you want that, O'Hara? Do you think it's fair that you should be punished for something you didn't do?'

Effie's blue eyes swam with tears. 'I don't know . . . but I didn't do it, Matron.'

Kathleen sighed. 'In which case someone has planted the evidence on you, haven't they?' she said. 'Someone has done this dreadful thing and then arranged matters so that you take the blame for it. Tell me, does that sound to you like the action of someone who cares for you?'

'No, Matron.' Her voice was barely above a whisper.

'No, indeed. So why would you defend someone like that?'

'I—'

There was a knock on the door. Kathleen saw Effie O'Hara's shoulders sag with relief.

'Come in,' she said.

She would have been surprised to see Hugo Morgan. But she was even more surprised to see Effie's sister Katie standing before her.

'Please, Matron, you can't punish my sister for the antimony,' she blurted out. 'It was me who put the tube in her pocket.'

Effie whipped round to stare at her sister. 'Katie!'

'Quiet!' Kathleen silenced her with a wave of her hand, her eyes still fixed on Katie. 'What are you talking about, girl? Explain yourself.'

'I did it,' Katie whispered, her gaze fixed on the inkstand on the desk. 'I – I thought it would be a lark to put it in the punch. And then I had nowhere to put the empty tube, so I – I stuck it in my sister's pocket in the cloakroom.'

'I see.' Kathleen regarded her coolly. The poor girl was trembling so much she could barely get a sentence out.

'It wasn't her!' Effie said.

'Shhh!' her sister hissed.

'But it wasn't!' Effie turned to Kathleen. 'It was me,' she said. 'I did it. She's just trying to cover up for me.' She stood up straight. 'You can punish me, but Katie had nothing to do with it.'

'Be quiet, Effie!'

'Be quiet, both of you!' Kathleen's voice rose, silencing the bickering sisters. They both shut up at once and turned guiltily to face her.

'Sorry, Matron,' Katie said. She nudged her sister, who mumbled an apology.

Kathleen took a deep breath. 'I don't believe it was either of you,' she said. 'It's quite clear to me that you –' she pointed at Effie '– know perfectly well who the culprit is, but from reasons of misguided loyalty you have decided not to give up their name. And you –' she pointed at Katie '– from reasons of equally misguided loyalty, have decided to place yourself in the firing line to protect your sister. Meanwhile, the real villain of the piece is allowed to go Scot free.'

She eyed them both severely. 'I cannot waste any more of my time on this matter,' she said. 'I can't punish either of you since I know you're both innocent of poisoning the people at the ball. But please understand that I am deeply disappointed in your behaviour.' She addressed herself to Effie in particular. 'I gave you a chance to stay here against my better judgement, and it seems that was a mistake. The next time I see you before me, it will be to dismiss you. Do I make myself clear?'

'Yes, Matron.'

Kathleen watched them both shuffle out of her office, then sat back with a sigh.

Hugo Morgan lived to fight another day. But not for much longer, she hoped.

*

Effie couldn't speak to her sister as they made their way in silence down the corridor from Matron's office. It wasn't until they had emerged into the sunshine of the courtyard that she finally found her voice.

'Why did you do it?' she asked. 'Why did you try to take the blame?'

Katie didn't look at her. 'Because you're my sister,' she said.

'But you could have been sacked.'

Katie shrugged. 'I promised Mammy I'd look after you and not let you come to any harm.'

Effie felt a lump of suppressed emotion in her throat. 'Thank you,' she whispered.

Katie turned to her. 'If you really want to thank me, you'll stop behaving like such an eejit,' she said. 'You'll forget all about falling in love and finding a boyfriend, and especially about that fool Hugo Morgan, and you'll settle down to some hard work.' She jerked her head back in the direction of Matron's office. 'You heard what Matron said. The next time she sees you, you'll be dismissed.'

'I know.' Effie's heart was only just beginning to slow down to a regular beat after skipping all over the place. She hadn't slept a wink since last night. 'I will work hard, Katie, I swear. I'll be a changed person. I'll never get into trouble again, I promise.'

Katie gave her a sideways smile. 'Trouble will always find you, Effie O'Hara,' she sighed. 'But at least you can stop trying so hard to look for it.'

As Effie approached the double doors to Parry ward, she could see Frances Bates on the other side. She was lurking in the doorway to one of the bathrooms, pretending to fold towels. But from the anxious way she looked at the doors, it was obvious she was looking out for Effie.

Sure enough, Frances pounced on her as soon as she walked in.

'Have you seen Matron? What did she say?' she hissed.

'Don't worry, I didn't tell her who it was who spiked the punch.' Effie shouldered past her. 'You and your friends are quite safe.'

She went to walk away, but Frances followed her down the ward towards Sister Parry's desk. 'I couldn't believe it when Hugo told me he'd put that test tube in your coat pocket,' she said, stumbling over her words. 'I thought that was going a bit too far, actually.'

Effie glanced over her shoulder at her. 'Is that supposed to be an apology?'

Frances blushed. 'I suppose so. But Hugo didn't know you were going to whip it out in front of Miss Hanley, did he?'

'No, and I don't suppose he really cared either.'

Frances hung back as Effie reached Sister's desk to receive her orders for the morning. Cleaning and more cleaning, just for a change.

Frances fell back into step beside her as Effie headed to the bathrooms. 'Why didn't you tell Matron it was us?' she asked.

'I thought you might do the decent thing and come and own up yourselves.' But Effie was beginning to realise how naïve that was. She'd defended Hugo out of loyalty, but he felt no loyalty towards her at all.

Frances blushed. 'I'm sure Hugo would have, if he'd known you were going to get into so much trouble . . .' she started to say, but Effie cut her off.

'If you believe that then you're even dafter than I am,' she said.

*

Ernest was going home. Mrs Philpott came to collect him with the family chauffeur.

Lucy had never seen anyone so upset to leave hospital. Ernest was in tears as the housekeeper fussed around, packing up his belongings.

'Are you sure I shouldn't stay longer?' he pleaded. 'I still feel unwell, you know.'

The only one more upset than him was Archie. Sister Parry had grudgingly allowed him to get out of bed to see his friend go. He watched from the doorway, skinny shoulders squared, jaw clenched. But he couldn't hide the desolation in his eyes.

'You will write to me, won't you?' Ernest asked him.

"Course I will,' Archie promised. 'And you could come and visit, if you like? We can play tin can copper with my mates, and I'll show you the place by the canal where me and my brothers made a den.'

Lucy caught the housekeeper's look of shuddering disapproval. Not long ago she would have disapproved too. But so much had changed for her in the past few months, she barely recognised the snobbish girl she used to be.

'I'd like that,' Ernest was saying. 'But I don't know if my mother would allow it.'

'Then I'll come and see you,' Archie said. 'And you can teach me how to play that fiddle of yours.'

Ernest grinned. 'I don't know what my mother will say about that, either.'

They looked like two little old men, shaking hands in the doorway, both very formal, both struggling not to show their feelings. Archie managed it better than Ernest: a tear rolled down his fat cheek.

'Look at you, crying like a girl!' Archie teased.

Ernest gave him a watery smile. 'Promise we'll stay friends for ever?'

Archie held up his hand. 'Scout's honour!'

Mrs Philpott rolled her eyes at Lucy. 'We'll see about that,' she said. 'Can you imagine these two being friends?'

Lucy looked up and caught Dora's eye as she pulled off the bedclothes. Stranger things have happened, she thought.

Sister Parry sent her off duty at one, and Lucy decided to go and visit her mother in Kentish Town. Ever since her talk with Dora the previous night, it had been playing on her mind that she needed to go and make the peace. It had been a couple of weeks since she'd seen her, and Dora was right; family should stick together.

But Lucy wasn't looking forward to it. She approached the tall, Edwardian building with a sense of trepidation. What kind of mood would her mother be in? she wondered. Drunk, probably. And consumed by self-pity, as usual. Lucy wasn't sure if she could cope with any more tears or recriminations.

Or what if it was worse than that? What if her mother had felt truly abandoned and had done something to herself? Lucy ran up the narrow flight of stairs to the top floor, already feeling sick with terror and anticipation.

And then she heard it, drifting down from above her. The unmistakable sound of laughter.

Lucy stopped dead. It had been so long since she'd heard her mother laughing, it took her a moment to realise what she was hearing. In fact, she couldn't remember Lady Clarissa Lane mustering more than a cynical little smile in years.

Yet here she was, roaring with laughter.

The door to the flat stood half-open. Lucy crept inside. A smell of fresh paint greeted her.

'Mother?'

There was no reply. Lucy pushed open the door to the sitting room, then stepped back in astonishment.

She hardly recognised the place. What had been a dingy, cramped space had been transformed into a light, inviting room. The paintwork had been brightened up, the windows cleaned and hung with fresh curtains. Mirrors reflected light around the room, and the worn floorboards were covered with an Indian rug.

And in the middle of it her mother sat on the floor, a scarf tied round her head, polishing silverware. There was another woman with her, hemming curtains. They were so deep in conversation they didn't notice Lucy standing in the doorway.

'Mother?'

Clarissa looked up. 'Lucy!' She put down her duster and got to her feet. 'What a delightful surprise. I wasn't expecting you.'

'I'm sorry I haven't called sooner.' Lucy stared around her in a daze. 'I see you've been busy.'

'Well, I thought I should make the effort, rather than stare at those nasty brown walls for ever.' Clarissa smiled. 'What do you think?'

'It looks – wonderful.'

'Such a transformation, isn't it? Your mother has a wonderful eye,' the other woman put in.

'Have you met Lavinia?' her mother introduced them. 'Turns out she's a distant cousin of mine. She and her husband live downstairs. They're in straitened circumstances, too,' she laughed gaily.

'We're absolute paupers!' Lavinia grinned. 'I ran off and married a disgraceful musician, and my stuffy brother cut me off without a penny. Like your mother, we are living on Cousin Antonia's charity.'

'How she must love it!' Clarissa cackled. 'I expect she's

told all her friends about it, bragging about the hordes of impoverished relations she's rescued.'

'Makes a change from cats, I suppose!' Lavinia said, and they both snorted with laughter. Lucy watched them, open-mouthed with astonishment.

'Would you like something to drink?' her mother said. 'Lavinia has taught me how to make the most marvellous Turkish coffee. Come with me.'

She led the way into the kitchen. This also was transformed, with bright wallpaper and framed prints hanging on the walls.

Lucy watched her mother boiling water and mixing up the coffee in a silver pot. If Lucy hadn't seen it for herself, she wouldn't have believed it. Clarissa looked ten years younger then the last time she'd seen her. And much, much happier.

For some reason, the sight of her made Lucy want to cry.

Clarissa looked over her shoulder at her. 'Lucy, what is it? Whatever's wrong?'

'Nothing. I just can't quite believe what I'm seeing, that's all.' She fumbled for a handkerchief. 'I've been so worried about you. Last time I saw you, you seemed so utterly defeated . . . I wasn't sure what to expect when I arrived,' she confessed.

'You thought I might be a drunken, sobbing mess on the carpet?' Clarissa said. 'Or that I'd starved because I didn't know how to butter a slice of bread? I'm not quite that helpless, darling. Although I admit I have allowed myself to get a little – feeble since I married your father.' She paused, holding a cup in her hand. 'Bernard was always so strong, you see. He liked looking after us so much, I quite forgot what I was capable of.'

'You've certainly remembered now,' Lucy said, looking around the kitchen.

Her mother smiled. 'I just needed a little kick to get me started.'

She carried the tray back into the sitting room, and the three of them chatted together. Lucy found out that, far from being a pauper, Lavinia's husband was a respected band leader, and Lavinia herself was a talented singer. She made them laugh with outrageous stories about some of the places they'd played, and the people they'd met. Lucy was glad her mother had made a friend; she needed someone lively and vivacious to keep her spirits up.

'I've been talking to your mother about going into business, decorating other people's houses,' Lavinia said.

Clarissa waved her hand. 'Oh, no, I couldn't possibly.'

'Why on earth not? You have such a flair for design. And, to be blunt, London is absolutely awash with wealthy Americans since dear old Wallis seduced our former king, all with lots of money and absolutely no taste at all. They're desperate for someone like you to come along and give their new country homes some English refinement.'

'Lavinia is right, Mother,' Lucy agreed. 'You could do that. You're so good at design, and putting things together.'

Her mother blushed. 'And how would I find these wealthy Americans?'

'You won't have to find them, darling. Once they know about your talents, they'll be beating a path to your door,' Lavinia assured her.

'What do you suggest I do, place an advertisement in *Tatler*?'

Lucy put down her cup, her expression thoughtful. 'I think I know a better way than that of spreading the word,' she said.

*

'Does this mean I'm forgiven?' Leo asked.

'Absolutely not,' Lucy replied tartly. 'But you said you wanted to help, and now I'm taking up your offer. Unless you've changed your mind?'

'Not at all.' He shook his head. 'I'd be happy to help. But what exactly do you want me to do?'

He listened attentively as Lucy explained her plan.

'What do you think?' she said finally.

'That's very – enterprising,' he said. Lucy's heart sank.

'You don't think it will work?'

'Oh, I'm sure I'll be able to find some willing clients,' Leo said. 'I'm just not sure your mother is up to the job, that's all. I get the impression Lady Clarissa isn't used to getting her hands dirty.'

Lucy thought about her mother sitting on the floor with the silverware, and smiled to herself.

'I think you'll find my mother's attitude has changed somewhat since my father left,' she said.

'And what about you?' Leo asked. 'How are you coping since he's been gone?'

Lucy reflected on the question. She would never have believed it, but her father's leaving had forced her to grow up, just like her mother. She had had to stop seeing the world from up on her cloud of wealth and privilege, and it had taught her a great deal.

'My attitude has changed too,' she admitted.

'And yet you still can't find it in your heart to forgive me?' asked Leo.

Lucy looked at him. It was very hard not to. As well as those blond, blue-eyed good looks, he had an irresistible boyish charm.

But he also had a cold, conniving heart, she reminded herself.

'You ruined my father and destroyed my family,' she said. 'That's somewhat hard to forgive.'

'I told you, I didn't write that story. I promised you I wouldn't, and I kept my word.'

There was no reason for her to believe him. And yet there was something about the way he looked at her, the frank appeal in those aquamarine eyes, that made her wonder.

'Then why are you so keen to help me, if you don't have a guilty conscience?' she asked.

'Maybe because I like you.'

Lucy snorted dismissively. 'I find that very hard to believe!'

'That someone could like you? You don't think much of yourself, do you?'

She opened her mouth and closed it again. He was right, she thought. Everyone always imagined she was big-headed because she bragged about herself and everything she had. But really she was trying to convince herself as much as everyone else that she was worth knowing.

'I hope you're not after my money?' she said, to cover her confusion. 'You're forgetting, Mr Alderson, I'm no longer a wealthy heiress.'

'So? You think the only interesting thing about you is your money?' He leaned closer. 'You're bright, clever, pretty – and you've got a hell of a lot of courage,' he said. 'How could anyone not like you, Miss Lane?'

Chapter Forty

'Well, this is a nice, ain't it?' said Alf. 'Afternoon tea with my daughter. What could be better than that?'

Dora sat rigid at the table, staring down at the cloth, unable to meet his eye. She wished she'd never asked to meet him. Just having him close to her, even in a public place like a café, made her feel sick.

But she couldn't stop thinking about Katie O'Hara, and the way she'd tried to take the blame for what went on at the ball, to save her sister.

Everyone thought she was daft, but Katie was adamant it had been the right thing to do.

'Effie's my sister,' she'd said simply. 'You have to do what you can for your family, don't you? Whatever it costs.'

Her words had struck a chord with Dora, which was why she'd forced herself to meet Alf. She couldn't allow Josie to go through all that heartache again. Whatever it cost.

'How are you, love? Your mum and I were just saying the other day, we haven't seen much of you lately.'

The word 'we' made Dora wince. 'You've been making yourself at home, then?' she muttered.

'Oh, yes, we've been getting on like a house on fire.' Alf's smile was bland, but Dora could see the glint in his eyes. 'Your mum's a very warm-hearted and forgiving woman, Dora. I don't deserve the kindness she's shown me, I really don't.'

'No,' Dora said. 'You don't. Anyway, Mum would never take you back.'

'I wouldn't be too sure of that. Like I say, Rose is a very forgiving lady. And she appreciates that Bea and Little Alfie need their dad.' Alf smiled up at the waitress who came to take their order. 'I'll have a cup of tea and a toasted teacake, please, love.' He turned to Dora. 'What are you having?'

'Nothing.'

'Go on, I'll treat you.'

'I don't want anything from you!' she snapped.

The waitress looked taken aback, and Alf grinned appealingly at her. 'Looks like someone's lost their appetite,' he said.

'And their manners,' the waitress murmured.

Dora fumed quietly. How did Alf manage to do that? she wondered. How did he manage to fool and charm people so much they were blind to his true nature? Or was she the only one who could see it?

'Why did you come back?' she hissed at him. 'We were doing all right without you.'

He shrugged. 'I got tired of travelling, I suppose. I missed my family. And I missed you, my girl.' He put his hand across the table towards her. Dora stared down at his thick, coarse fingers and a shudder of revulsion went through her.

She clutched the edge of the tablecloth, not wanting him to see how much she was shaking.

'I want you to go,' she said. 'Go, and never come back.'

Alf looked hurt. 'But I want to be with my family.'

'We don't need you.'

'That's not what your mum reckons.' He smiled at Dora across the table. 'Between you and me, I reckon it won't be long before she asks me to move back in. Won't that be nice?'

The waitress returned with his order, and Dora fought to compose herself. She watched as Alf spooned sugar into his tea.

358

'Look,' he said. 'I know you've got no reason to trust me, after what happened in the past. But I've told you, I'm a changed man. I've got my family back, and now I want to make a new start. Ain't there any chance we can start again, too?'

Dora stared across the table at him. His gaze was fixed on her, full of appeal.

But she could see in his eyes he hadn't changed. Alf Doyle was trying to charm her, just like he charmed everyone else.

'I don't care if you have changed,' she said in a low voice. 'I'll never, ever forgive you for what you did. That's why I want you away from here. Away from me, and away from Josie.'

'That's charming, that is. So you'd see me back on the streets, would you? Your own dad.'

Her mouth curled with contempt. 'You're not my dad. You're nothing to me.'

'But you mean the world to me, love. You and the other kids. I love my family. Being with them again has made me realise how much I've missed them all this time.' His expression grew wistful. 'It would take a lot for me to leave them again . . .'

Dora saw the calculation in his eyes and suddenly realised the meaning behind his words. 'How much?' she said.

'What, love?'

'How much would it cost for you to leave us and never come back?'

He didn't even pretend to be shocked. 'Well, let's see.' Alf considered it for a moment. 'It's going to break my heart to go, and it's going to break the kids' hearts, too. I dunno if I should really . . . but I suppose I could make a new start for twenty quid?'

'Twenty? I ain't got that sort of money, and you know it!'

'Well, then, looks like you're stuck with me, doesn't it?' Alf shrugged. 'You and your sister,' he added meaningfully.

Dora stared at him, hatred and revulsion building up inside her. He no longer scared her, but she couldn't stand to think of him under the same roof as Josie, and the terror her sister would have to go through every day.

Katie O'Hara's words came back to her. *You have to do what you can for your family, don't you? Whatever it costs.*

'You'll get your money,' she said.

For someone who had spent their whole life caring for others, Sister Sutton was not a very good patient.

'Are they ever going to allow me to go home?' she snapped, when Jess came to visit her. 'I'm getting rather tired of all the prodding and poking.'

'Perhaps they think you just need a nice rest?' Jess said.

'A rest?' Sister Sutton's tiny eyes glittered feverishly. 'Why should I need a rest? Does Matron think I'm not up to the job any more? Is that it?'

'No, I don't think . . .'

'Because no one is putting me out to grass until I'm ready. Rest, indeed! I don't need a rest. I need to be up and sorting out those lazy students. I daresay they're causing mayhem in my absence.'

'As a matter of fact—' Jess was about to tell her that she and Miss Hanley were managing to run the home very well between them, but she had a feeling that wasn't what Sister Sutton wanted to hear. 'We do need you back,' she said.

'Just as I thought.' Sister Sutton looked grimly satisfied. 'I expect I'll have a great deal to do when I return.'

She lay back against the pillows, exhausted by her outburst. Her face was flushed, and perspiration gleamed on her brow. She might not believe she was ill, but Jess could see it a mile off.

Dr McKay could see it, too. Whatever he'd diagnosed from the tests had worried him enough to demand that Sister should stay in bed for a few more days.

'Well, if I'm to stay in here then I suppose I might as well make myself comfortable.' Sister Sutton gave a martyred sigh. 'Perhaps you could bring me a clean night-gown next time you come. And my spectacles. I can't read my book without them.'

'I'll bring them tonight,' Jess promised.

'There's no need to put yourself out and make a special journey.'

'It's no trouble,' she said cheerfully. The fact was, she missed the Home Sister's presence in the house. Even though she generally lived in dread of her heavy tread down the hall or her voice rapping out instructions, Jess still felt better when Sister Sutton was there.

Sparky missed her, too. He had taken to sleeping on the end of Jess' bed, cuddling close to her for comfort in his mistress' absence.

Jess went back to the nurses' home and let herself straight into Sister Sutton's flat to pick up the things she'd asked for. It felt strange, being in the Home Sister's private quarters on her own. Sparky trotted around proprietorially, inspecting the furniture and sniffing at all the ornaments and knick-knacks to make sure everything was present and correct.

She went into Sister Sutton's bedroom. Jess came in here every morning to bring the Home Sister's breakfast in bed, but it still seemed odd to see it empty, the pillows perfectly plumped, sheet turned down neatly and the pink satin eiderdown spread out so it draped exactly the same amount on each side. Jess smiled to herself. Old habits must die hard when you were a nurse, she thought.

The last of the summer's roses were blooming outside

the bedroom window. Jess decided to pick some later to take to cheer up Sister Sutton's sick room. They were her pride and joy, and she would be furious to miss a single day of their blooming period.

She found the spectacles in their case on the bedside table, and then opened the chest of drawers to find the nightgown. A smell of lily-of-the-valley talcum powder and dried lavender drifted up to greet her as she rifled through Sister Sutton's nightgowns, all neatly folded in rows.

Jess took out the top one, and was just about to close the drawer when a glint caught her eye. Curious, she opened it again and looked inside. There was something at the bottom of the drawer, half hidden under the pile of nightgowns. Something small, shiny – and cat-shaped.

Jess recognised it immediately as the brooch Anna Padgett had complained of losing. And there were other things, too, lurking between the nightgowns. A string of pearls, a letter addressed to one of the second-year students, a single earring, a half-empty perfume bottle . . .

Jess sniffed it. Midnight In Paris.

Guiltily, she stuffed the things back into the drawer and closed it. Sister Sutton must have a very good reason for keeping them here, she told herself. Even if she couldn't quite imagine what it was.

Sister Sutton was looking much better when Jess arrived to see her that evening.

'I've seen Matron,' she announced. 'She's said I can go back to my own room as long as I have sufficient rest. She quite rightly thinks I will be far more comfortable in familiar surroundings.' She gave Jess a superior smile. 'So I'll be able to keep an eye on you again, young lady!'

Jess smiled back, but her mind was racing. She wanted

to ask Sister Sutton about the missing items, but couldn't bring herself to do it.

As usual, Sister Sutton didn't miss a thing. 'What?' she demanded impatiently. 'You're positively twitching, child. Either you have a bad case of worms or you have something you want to say. Well? Spit it out.'

Jess hesitated. 'It's about Nurse Padgett's brooch,' she began uncertainly.

Sister Sutton looked blank. 'What brooch?'

'The one that went missing a few weeks ago. Do you remember, she searched high and low for it, but she never found it?'

'Yes, well, the careless girl probably lost it in the street.' Sister Sutton shrugged. 'Either that or it disappeared up that wretched vacuum cleaner, never to be seen again. Things often go missing, it's the way of the world.'

'That's just it,' Jess started to say. 'Don't you think it's odd that so many things have gone missing recently? Bottles of perfume, pearls, letters, that sort of thing?'

'Have they gone missing? I don't recall.' Sister Sutton frowned. 'No one's told me about anything going missing. And I'm sure they would have come to me first, as I'm the Home Sister.'

Jess stared into Sister Sutton's blank face. Either she was the best liar in the world or she genuinely had no recollection what Jess was talking about.

The porter arrived, pushing an empty wheelchair. 'Taxi for Sister Sutton!' he said cheerily.

She sent him a withering look. 'I beg your pardon?' she said. 'May I remind you, young man, I still carry the rank of Sister within this hospital, which entitles me to a suitable show of respect from the likes of you. Kindly address me properly, or not at all.'

'Sorry, Sister.' The young man hung his head. 'Begging

your pardon, I've been sent to take you back to the nurses' home.'

Sister Sutton eyed the wheelchair. 'And I don't suppose I have any choice in the matter,' she said with a martyred sigh.

'I'll go and get your room ready,' Jess said quickly, edging towards the door.

Sister Sutton eyed her suspiciously. 'Get it ready? What do you mean?'

'I'll light the fire. You need it nice and warm when you're poorly, don't you?'

She darted away before Sister Sutton could point out it was August and the sun was blazing outside.

Jess ran back to Sister Sutton's flat, tripping headlong over Sparky as she went. He seemed to sense her agitation, prancing at her feet and yapping his head off.

'Shhh!' Jess hissed. 'I'm trying to get your mistress out of trouble, not land myself in it!'

She stuffed the stolen items into her pocket and slammed the drawer shut, moments before the porter arrived with Sister Sutton sitting like a stately Britannia in the wheelchair.

'You're looking very shifty again,' she said to Jess. 'What are you up to now?'

'Nothing.' Jess couldn't meet her eye. 'I've just got to fetch something from my room.'

As she hurried away, she heard Sister Sutton mutter, 'Good gracious, Sparky, I don't know what's the matter with the girl today. I suspect she may have worms after all.'

Jess went into her own room and put the missing belongings under her mattress, then sat down on the bed.

At least they were safe there. Now all she had to do was work out what she was going to do with them.

Chapter Forty-One

It was almost a week before Hugo Morgan finally showed his face on the ward. Effie watched from the milk kitchen as he slunk in through the double doors, looking this way and that before he crept down the ward towards Sister's desk.

'Look at him,' Hilda Ross said. 'Doesn't look so cocky this morning, does he?'

'He's probably expecting me to pounce and crown him with a bedpan,' Effie said.

Hilda looked sideways at her. 'And will you?'

'I'm not even going to talk to him if I can help it.'

'None of us are,' Hilda said loyally. 'We don't think it's right, what he did to you and poor Mulhearn. Even Bates thinks he's behaved like a cad.'

Just at that moment Frances emerged from behind a screen. She saw Hugo and stalked past him with a dismissive toss of her head. He watched her go with a puzzled frown on his face.

'You see?' Hilda nudged her. 'We stick together, us nurses.'

'Better late than never, I suppose,' Effie muttered.

Hilda looked at the bottle Effie was making up. 'Is that for Teddy Potts? Be careful how quickly you give it to him. You know how he greedy he can be if you let him.'

'I know, all right!' Effie had been through more clean aprons feeding Teddy than any other baby. Sometimes he was as good as gold, other times he was like an unexploded bomb. The pros sometimes took bets on when he would go off.

Effie had meant to avoid Hugo if she could, but as luck would have it he had come to write up notes on some of the babies. Effie sat on the nursing chair, giving Teddy Potts his feed, while Hugo moved stiffly around her, avoiding her gaze. At least he didn't try to talk to her while Sister was watching.

But then Sister disappeared behind the screens with Nurse Lane to examine a bad burns case, leaving the ward unattended.

'Alone at last!' Hugo joked weakly. 'I was hoping I might have a moment to talk to you, darling.'

'Oh yes?' Effie feigned innocence. 'What about?'

Even from three cots away, she saw him gulp. 'I feel simply awful about what happened at the ball.' His words tumbled out in a rush.

'Not awful enough to own up,' Effie said.

He was silent for a moment. Then he tried again. 'You were a real brick, not telling on me to Matron.'

Effie looked up at him, meeting his eyes for the first time. 'I wanted to give you the chance to do it yourself.'

Hugo laughed, then quickly sobered when he saw her face. 'You're serious, aren't you? Good God, Euphemia, do you know what this could do to my future if it came out?'

'Do you know what it's done to mine that it hasn't?' she flared back. 'Why did you plant that test tube in my pocket anyway?'

'I didn't plant it, but I had to hide it somewhere,' he said. 'When that girl was taken ill I thought they might search us medical students. I couldn't throw it away so I stuffed it in the first place I could think of.'

'So you didn't care if they searched me?'

He looked guilty. 'I didn't think anyone would suspect you. And I thought you'd see the funny side,' he mumbled.

Effie stared at him. Even now, a smirk was tugging at the corners of his mouth. 'What happened to Mulhearn wasn't funny.'

'I didn't know that stupid girl was going to be taken ill, did I?'

'She could have died.'

Hugo rolled his eyes. 'Don't be over-dramatic. It was just a fit, that's all. She's perfectly recovered now.'

'Except she has been sent home for good,' Effie said. 'Matron says she's no longer fit to be a nurse.'

Hugo's mouth fell open. 'I didn't know,' he murmured.

'And you didn't care enough to find out.'

'Look, I said I'm sorry,' he snapped. 'What else do you expect me to do?'

Effie looked at him. How could she ever have thought he was handsome? she wondered. His face was far too petulant ever to be good-looking, with his mouth set in a sulky line and that arrogant look in his eyes.

'Go to Matron,' she said. 'Tell her it was you.'

Hugo flushed. 'I can't do that.'

'Why not?'

'Because it would look so bad, and my father would never let me hear the end of it. Look, darling, you've got to understand my position.' He was pleading for her understanding. 'My father's a big cheese in this place. We've already had a couple of run-ins since I've been here and he's made it very clear I'm not to embarrass him further. He could make my life very uncomfortable.'

'And what about my life?' Effie said. 'Thanks to you, I have a permanent black mark against my name. I daren't do one thing wrong in the next three years, or I'm out.

And even if I'm a model student, they probably won't let me stay on after my Finals.'

'That's different,' Hugo dismissed her objection.

'Why? Because I'm just a nurse and not an important doctor like you?'

'Be reasonable, darling. It's vital I get through medical school. My parents really won't be impressed if I don't. They're expecting great things from me. But you . . .' His mouth twisted. 'Well, you've already told me you're not that interested in nursing. You're only here so you can escape from Ireland. And it's not as if you're ever going to be as good as your sisters. What does it really matter if you're sent home?'

Effie looked down at the baby in her arms so Hugo wouldn't see the hurt and anger in her eyes. You're wrong, she thought. It does matter to me. It matters a lot.

She hadn't realised how much it mattered until she was standing in Matron's office, about to lose it all. It wasn't just that she was worried about being sent back to Ireland in disgrace. The two months she'd been on the ward so far had been the hardest of her life. She spent every day veering between fear and sheer exhaustion, wondering what the next minute would bring. But she had also learned a lot, far more than she'd ever imagined. Almost without realising it, she'd absorbed so many skills, done far more than she'd ever thought she could. And she desperately wanted to learn more.

Perhaps Hugo was right, and she might never be as good a nurse as her sisters were. She might even turn out to be the worst nurse in the world. But she still wanted the chance to try, to find out for herself.

She heard him sigh. 'Anyway, I hope there are no hard feelings over this? We had fun, didn't we?'

Effie glanced up at him. No, she thought. The only time

you have fun is at someone else's expense. All she'd ever been was the butt of his jokes, or else a willing audience. Being with Hugo had been like boarding one of those waltzer rides they'd started having at travelling fairs: thrilling at times but also terrifying. And now she wanted to get off.

Teddy finished sucking noisily. Effie took the bottle from his mouth and held it up to check how much he'd taken. The bottle was almost empty.

'Is that the Potts baby?' Hugo asked. 'I'm supposed to be making notes on him next.' He held out his arms. 'Give him to me.'

'Yes, but he's going to . . .'

'Just give him to me, Euphemia. For heaven's sake, I don't have all day!'

Effie looked into the baby's eyes. She could already feel the spasms of his distended belly under his shawl. It might have been wind, but she was sure Teddy was grinning at her.

She stood up. 'Whatever you say, Hugo.'

She dumped the baby in his arms and started to walk away. 'Wait!' Hugo called after her. 'Aren't you going to help—'

She had barely closed the door to the milk kitchen before the unexploded bomb that was Teddy Potts went off. She heard Hugo's yell of horror and disgust but didn't dare go out. She could only imagine what he looked like, his white coat dripping with baby vomit. With any luck that sour smell would linger on him all day.

Effie put her hand over her mouth to muffle her laughter. Looks like the joke is finally on you, Hugo Morgan, she thought.

'What have you been told about getting out of bed? Get back in at once!'

369

Sister Sutton glared at Jess. 'I was only fetching my button box from the sitting room.'

'I'll fetch it for you.' Jess put the cup of tea she had brought down on the bedside cupboard. 'And if you need anything else, just let me know.'

As Jess ushered her back, Sister Sutton huffed, 'I feel so useless, here in bed. I'm quite well, as you can see. I shall tell Matron when she calls to see me today.'

Jess frowned. 'But Matron came this morning.'

'Don't be silly, you must be getting confused,' Sister Sutton corrected her. 'She came yesterday morning, before church. But she hasn't visited yet today. Good gracious, child, don't you think I would have remembered?'

Would you? Jess thought. She was going to explain that Matron had come *this* morning on her way to church, but decided against it. Sister Sutton always became so agitated when Jess pointed out her forgetfulness.

And she had been forgetful quite a lot recently. Last night Jess had been woken up at midnight by the sound of the Home Sister crashing around outside in her nightgown, saying the roses needed pruning. Jess had managed to get her back to bed, but when she'd mentioned it that morning Sister Sutton had stared blankly at her and told her she must have had a nightmare.

Jess wondered if the old girl might have taken those trinkets in other bouts of forgetfulness. She might have picked them up without realising then stuffed them away in her drawer and forgotten all about it. If she'd found them again, she probably wouldn't even remember what they were or how they came to be there.

'Are you going to clean out those kitchen cupboards this morning?' The next moment Sister Sutton was back to her old self, her sharp eyes fixed on Jess. 'I asked you to do them last week and you haven't.'

'Yes, Sister.' No point in telling her that today was Jess' day off. She wanted to spend it looking after the Home Sister anyway. Matron had made it clear either Jess looked after her or she would have to go back to the sick bay. Sister Sutton was too poorly to be left on her own, Miss Fox said.

If only Matron knew how ill Sister Sutton really was, Jess thought. She wondered if she should tell her about the Home Sister's odd behaviour, but somehow she couldn't bring herself to do it. It felt too much like a betrayal.

'See that you do,' Sister Sutton said. 'I don't want anyone looking in those cupboards and saying I don't know how to keep a tidy house.'

Jess saw the panic in her eyes and felt for her. Poor Sister Sutton. She lived in fear of losing her place at the Nightingale and ending up like her friend Rosemary, packed away in a home for retired nurses, living out the last of her days among strangers.

Which was why Jess had decided to put the missing things back where they belonged. With any luck, their owners would find them and think they had simply misplaced them.

She had been keeping them in her apron pocket, and when she found the girls' rooms empty she put the items back, carefully selecting a safe place down the back of a drawer or under the bed where she knew the owners would find them eventually. She had already returned the letter and the pearls. Now all she had to do was return the brooch and perfume to Anna Padgett.

Luckily for her, as it was Sunday the students had all been taken off to church. They had set off over an hour ago in a shuffling crocodile, led briskly by Miss Hanley.

Jess crept into Anna's room. It was deadly quiet with

no students around, and Jess jumped at the squeak of her own footsteps as she crossed the room to Anna's dresser.

As usual it was in disarray, littered with make-up and odd bits of jewellery. Sister Sutton would have a fit if she saw it, Jess thought. The students were obviously making the most of the Home Sister's absence to fall into slovenly ways.

Jess smiled to herself. She was even beginning to sound like Sister Sutton now!

She took the scent bottle out of her pocket and put it carefully on its side underneath the dresser, so it looked as if it had rolled there. Then she took the brooch and placed it in the back of the top drawer, closing it gently, trying not to make a sound even though she knew there was no one in the house to hear her.

The front door suddenly banged open downstairs, startling her. Jess jumped, and sent a jewellery box flying. It skittered across the room, spilling its contents all over the floor.

The sound of girls' voices drifted up from downstairs, followed by Miss Hanley booming out, 'Quietly, girls, please!'

Jess scrabbled around desperately, gathering up the jewellery. Panic made her clumsy, her fingers slipping as she gathered up the trinkets, her heartbeat thundering in her ears, drowning out the flurry of footsteps up the stairs.

She had just emptied the last handful into the box when the door swung open and Anna Padgett walked in.

They both froze, looking at each other, Anna framed in the doorway, Jess crouched on the floor, the box in her hands.

'What are you doing?' Anna demanded coldly.

'It fell,' Jess mumbled. 'I was just picking it up.'

She straightened up. Anna crossed the room in a couple

of strides and snatched the box out of her hands. 'What were you doing in my room?' she demanded.

'I—' Jess glanced at the doorway where a few other girls had gathered, drawn by the commotion. Effie was among them. 'I was cleaning,' she finished lamely.

'I don't see a broom or any dusters.' Anna looked around, then her eyes flashed back to Jess. 'Turn out your pockets,' she demanded.

Effie gasped. 'Really, Padgett, I don't think—'

'Shut up, O'Hara! I caught this girl red-handed with my jewellery box. If that doesn't prove she's a thief, I don't know what does.' Anna faced Jess, hands on her hips. 'Come on, let's see your pockets. If you haven't stolen anything, you've got nothing to hide, have you?'

Jess reached into her pockets and turned them out. 'You see? Empty.'

'What about that other one? In your apron?'

'I told you, I ain't stolen . . .' As Jess plunged her hand in, her fingers found a small, hard object. The earring. She didn't know who it belonged to, and she'd forgotten all about it.

Her shock must have shown on her face, because Anna pounced. 'What is it?' she said. 'You've got something there, haven't you? Show me!'

She grabbed Jess' hand and prised her fingers open. There, in her palm, lay the tiny stud, carved in the shape of a rose.

'That's mine!' Anna clawed it out of her hand.

'I found it downstairs,' Jess gabbled the first thing that came into her head. 'I didn't know who it belonged to.'

'Liar! I haven't worn them since I came here, so it couldn't have been downstairs.' Anna turned to the others, holding up the earring like a trophy. 'You see?' she said triumphantly. 'I told you she was a thief, didn't I? And this proves it.'

The other girls mumbled in agreement. Jess looked up, meeting their hostile faces. And then she caught Effie's eye. The disappointment in her expression upset Jess far more than the other girls' anger.

'I ain't a thief,' she muttered.

Chapter Forty-Two

'I ain't a thief,' she repeated half an hour later, as she stood before Matron in her office.

The figure on the other side of the desk wasn't the same kindly woman who'd sat at Sister Sutton's bedside every day since she was taken ill. Even her calm manner was terrifying as she sat there, her steely eyes fixed on Jess.

'You were caught in the act of stealing jewellery from one of the students,' she said. 'And I'm told several items have gone missing since you started working at the nurses' home. I would say the evidence against you is compelling, wouldn't you?'

'I was putting the stuff back,' Jess said. 'Have a look if you don't believe me. It's all there, everything that went missing.'

She realised what she'd said as soon as she saw Matron's eyebrows rise. 'How do you know that, if you didn't take the items in the first place?' Her voice was mild, but there was an undertone of pure granite.

'I found them,' Jess said.

'That's very convenient, I must say. Where did you find this treasure trove?'

Jess hesitated, thinking of Sister Sutton. 'I can't say.'

Matron gave her a long look. 'Very well,' she said. 'If you insist on staying silent, I have no choice but to take your silence for a confession of guilt.' She regarded Jess gravely. 'You are dismissed.'

Jess gasped. 'But – that's not fair! I haven't done anything!'

'The evidence suggests otherwise. Unless you want to tell me what really happened?'

Their eyes met and held for a moment. Jess thought about Sister Sutton again. Even if she did speak up, she doubted if Matron would ever believe her word against that of the Home Sister.

'I can't say,' she repeated.

'Very well.' Matron sat back. 'I want you to pack your things and be gone by the end of the day. If you leave a forwarding address with the Head Porter, I will arrange to have any outstanding wages sent on to you. But I want you to leave this hospital immediately. Is that clear?'

Sister Sutton didn't take the news very well when Kathleen went to see her later.

'But I simply don't understand it,' she kept saying. 'Jess is such a good girl, a hard worker, and scrupulously honest.' She shook her head. 'I'm a very good judge of character, and I don't believe she would do such a thing.'

'I must confess, I was surprised too,' Kathleen admitted. She had seen Jess every day since she had started visiting Sister Sutton, and she had seemed like a very pleasant, conscientious girl. Loyal, too. She rarely left the Home Sister's bedside, attending to her every need with great patience. Matron couldn't imagine that was a rewarding task, given Sister Sutton's irascible character. 'But I can't deny the evidence against her. Nurse Padgett caught her red-handed, and with other witnesses present, too. One cannot argue with the facts, no matter how much one might wish to do so.'

'But did she say why she did it, Matron?'

'She didn't say a great deal, except to maintain that she was returning the stolen objects to their rightful place. A rather curious assertion, given the circumstances.' Kathleen frowned. If Jess Jago wasn't the thief, then she certainly knew who was. And she would rather go to the gallows herself than offer them up for punishment.

Sister Sutton's eyes glistened, and she dabbed at them with her handkerchief. 'Thief or not, Sparky and I shall miss her dearly,' she said.

'I know, Sister. Which, I'm afraid, brings me on to the real reason I'm here.' Kathleen smiled at her sympathetically. 'Since there is no one to nurse you . . .'

'You want me to return to the sick bay?' Sister Sutton finished for her. 'It's quite all right, Matron, I have been expecting you to ask me that. I shall be happy to oblige. I don't wish to be a nuisance. Although I'm sure I'm quite well enough to resume my duties.'

'Really, Sister Sutton, I wouldn't want you to return until you're fully recovered.'

'But you will want me to return?' The Home Sister's face was suddenly anxious.

'Of course.' Kathleen frowned. 'I can't imagine why you would think otherwise.' She leaned forward and patted the elderly woman's hand. 'You just concentrate on getting better, my dear.'

'Yes . . . yes, of course. Thank you, Matron.' A faraway look came into Sister Sutton's face then and she frowned, as if a troubling thought had just struck her. 'Matron, those items that were stolen . . . can you remember what they were?'

Kathleen considered it for a moment. 'Let's see. A couple of items of jewellery, I believe. And some perfume.'

'Midnight in Paris.' Sister Sutton's voice was faint.

'Yes, that's right.' Kathleen frowned. 'Why do you ask?'

'No reason. I just had a vague recollection . . . no, it's gone.' She smiled at Kathleen, her face clearing. 'I'm sorry, Matron, I don't know what I was thinking. I suppose this business with Jess Jago has unsettled me rather. I feel so terribly disappointed.'

Kathleen nodded. 'That girl has disappointed us all,' she agreed.

'You see?' Anna was telling anyone who would listen at the pros' table that evening. 'I told you, didn't I? I said she was a thief. I could see it the moment I looked at her. She's got a thief's eyes, hasn't she? Sly and shifty.'

'Oh, do shut up, Padgett,' Effie said wearily, picking at her food. 'We're all tired of hearing about it.'

'You just can't bear it that you were wrong and I was right,' Anna said. 'And to think you were her friend! You must be feeling rather foolish now, I imagine. All those hours she spent in your room, pretending to help you study. She was probably having a good look round, working out what to steal. You should have a look through *your* belongings, O'Hara. She's probably already pawned half of them!'

Effie opened her mouth to defend Jess, then realised she had nothing to say. Anna was right, there was too much evidence against her.

Effie thought about the day she'd arrived in London, when her bag was stolen. She still didn't believe that Jess had been involved, even if it was her stepbrother who had taken it.

But today, in Anna's room, Jess had stood there, with the stolen earring in her hand, and guilt written all over her face. Effie had been thinking about it all afternoon, but even she couldn't find an excuse for her friend.

Even so, she wished she had been allowed to say

378

goodbye to her before she left. But Jess had been whisked off to see Matron, and when Effie knocked on her door an hour later there was no answer.

'Let's face it, O'Hara, you're far too naïve,' Anna said, helping herself to more bread and ham. As it was Sunday the kitchen staff were off, so they made do with cold cuts in the dining room. 'You placed your trust in someone and they betrayed you. But we did try to warn you, didn't we, girls? None of this would have happened if you'd stuck to your own kind.'

And who are my own kind? Effie wanted to snap. She hadn't seen any of her own kind giving up their time to help her when she feared she might fail her exams. She hadn't seen any of her own kind risking the wrath of Sister Sutton to smuggle her in through the window when she'd stayed out late, either. Jess Jago might not have called herself a friend, but she had been more of a friend to Effie than any of the other girls.

After supper the rest of her set had planned a trip to the cinema, but for once Effie didn't feel like going out. One or two of the girls tried to persuade her to come, but Anna said, 'Oh, leave her alone if she just wants to mope about.'

'I don't want to mope about. I just don't want to listen to you telling us all how you were right all along,' Effie retaliated.

When they'd gone she tried to settle in her room and read a book. But reading always made her restless. Once again she thought about Jess. It had never ceased to amaze Effie how Jess could lose herself in a book for hours on end, to the point where she was oblivious to the rest of the world. Seeing all those words on the page just gave Effie a headache.

She wandered downstairs to the sitting room, looking

for a diversion. It felt odd to be able to walk around the nurses' home without fear of Sister Sutton descending at any moment. It was quiet too, without Sparky yapping about the place. He had gone off to stay at the Sisters' home, where he was under the dubious protection of Sister Parker. Effie didn't envy him, if she treated the dog the way she treated her students.

But even the sitting room seemed too quiet and empty. Effie flicked through the selection of gramophone records. Nothing caught her eye. What was the point of music anyway when there was no one to dance with? She found some playing cards and arranged them to play Patience. Jess had often watched her play, and they'd laughed at the idea of Effie having patience with anything.

Sure enough, she gave up halfway through the game. She could almost hear Jess' voice teasing her – 'There should be a game called No Patience for you!' – as she put the cards away.

It was no use, Effie thought. She was simply too miserable to be entertained. Perhaps she should have gone to the cinema with the others after all. At least there she could have been unhappy with other people rather than on her own.

As she headed for the stairs her eyes turned towards the door to Jess' room at the end of the passageway. Even though she knew there would be no one in there, Effie couldn't resist taking a look inside.

The room was empty, stripped bare, the pillows and quilt neatly folded. It felt strange not to see Jess' books on the shelves above her bed, or her brush and comb set out neatly side by side on the dresser.

But there was something. On the bedside table was an ancient-looking anatomy textbook together with a note reading: 'For Sister Sutton'.

Effie picked it up. This must be the book Sister had lent

Jess, she thought. But what kind of thief returned a book? Once again, she had the nagging feeling that none of this was right. Jess was far too honest to steal from anyone.

And yet . . . hadn't she as good as admitted it to Matron? Effie sighed. There was something staring her in the face, if only she was clever enough to work it out. She felt as if she was letting her friend down by not seeing it.

Effie took the book back to Sister Sutton's flat. She knew the Home Sister would not be there, but thought she might leave it somewhere for her to find. At least Sister Sutton would know Jess was an honest soul.

She had never been into Sister Sutton's flat before and was instantly overwhelmed by the knick-knacks and ornaments crowded on to every surface. She moved cautiously, being careful not to dislodge anything. She had never seen so many bits and pieces: little dolls from different countries, tiny vases, paperweights, pottery puppies and kittens, a leprechaun . . .

Effie stopped short, eyes flicking back to the little man in green, sitting cheekily on a pottery tree stump, nursing a crock of gold. She recognised the ornament immediately. She had given it to her sister Katie as a birthday present, just before she came to England. They'd joked about how she would find her own crock of gold in London.

What was it doing on Sister Sutton's mantelpiece? wondered Effie. Either she'd been on a trip to Ireland, or else Katie must have given it to her.

She picked it up and examined it. Surely it must be Katie's? She was still puzzling over it when she heard the front door opening. Guiltily, she shoved the ornament back on to the mantelpiece and slipped back into the hall, closing the door behind her.

Katie returned just after nine o'clock.

'I'm so tired.' She collapsed backwards on to her bed.

'Casualty never stopped. Three people got run over, a boy came off his motorbike, and a woman fell off a chair while putting up curtains. Honest to God, I didn't know whether I was coming or going.' She stuck out her foot. 'Pull my shoes off for me, there's a love. I don't think I've got the strength to do it myself.'

As Effie unlaced her sister's shoe, she said, 'Do you remember that leprechaun I bought you for your eighteenth birthday?'

'I think so. What about it?'

'Do you know what happened to it?'

'I think it's on the windowsill . . .'

'It isn't. I looked.'

Katie sat up, glancing around. 'Well, it's around here somewhere.' She frowned at Effie. 'Why? What do you want it for?'

Effie shook her head. 'No reason. I just wondered, that's all.'

Chapter Forty-Three

September blew in, and the weather changed from glorious summer to bleak autumn. Almost overnight the sky blackened, the wind pulled at the plane trees in the courtyard, and rain lashed at the windows.

Inside the wards the maids lit the fires and the babies' prams were covered with mackintoshes as they sat out on the verandah.

It was strange that little Emily Jarvis, a child who had drawn so little attention during her life, should choose such a dramatic day to die.

No one knew exactly when it happened. The night nurse had checked on her at four and she had been sleeping peacefully. But by the time they'd gone to wake her two hours later, Emily was gone.

It came as no surprise to anyone. Even though it had taken weeks for her body to waste away, everyone knew Emily had stopped living a long time before.

But Dora still struggled to contain her emotions when the Night Sister delivered the news at seven o'clock. There was something very special about Emily. She had never made a sound while she was on the ward, had never even looked at Dora or acknowledged her when she tried to feed her or hold her hand. And yet Dora felt a connection with her she found hard to explain.

Even when she and the other nurses went around the ward checking on the patients before Sister Parry arrived, Dora couldn't bring herself to look at the curtained-off corner where Emily's bed had stood. She had to look away when the pros stripped it and took away the mattress and pillows to be cleaned.

Luckily, Dora had managed to check her emotions by the time Sister Parry arrived on the ward at half-past. She received the news of Emily's death with her usual sang-froid, although she did surprise everyone when she announced that she would perform last offices herself.

'And Doyle will assist me,' she ordered.

Dora opened her mouth to argue, then closed it again when she saw Sister Parry's forbidding expression. 'Yes, Sister,' she muttered.

She was setting up the trolley in the sluice when Lucy came to find her. 'Are you all right about doing this?' she asked. 'If you really can't face it, I could tell Sister you've been taken ill?'

Once, Dora might have assumed Lucy was trying to get one over on her, or to curry favour with Sister. Now she understood that she was acting out of genuine concern for her, and she appreciated it.

'Thank you for the offer, but I'd best do it myself,' she said. 'You remember how Sister played merry hell with me when I did last offices instead of Elliott once? I'd hate it if she took you to task for the same reason.'

'I suppose you're right,' Lucy said. 'I just didn't want to see you upset, that's all. I know how fond you were of little Emily.'

'That's probably why Sister picked me, the horrible old boot,' Dora said gloomily. 'Anyway, it's the last thing I can do for Emily, so I'd like to do it.'

She wheeled the trolley to the room where the child had been laid to rest. Sister Parry was already there, standing at the foot of the bed, her hands folded in front of her.

'Close the door, Nurse Doyle, and we shall pray.'

Dora folded her hands and listened as Sister Parry prayed that God might take Emily's soul into His safe keeping, and deliver her from suffering. Dora steeled herself as Sister Parry ended her prayer and pulled back the top sheet. Emily looked even more like a doll in repose, her frail body so tiny in the vast whiteness of the bed.

Sister Parry was brisk and efficient as they worked together. Dora washed the girl while Sister cut her nails and brushed her hair.

'You were very attached to the child, weren't you?' Sister Parry said suddenly, breaking the silence.

Dora didn't look up. 'I had a soft spot for her, Sister,' she replied.

'Then I daresay you must think I'm being rather cruel, asking you to do this?'

'It's my job, Sister.'

Sister Parry nodded. 'At least I've taught you not to question orders during your time here, which is something,' she said.

Dora took a deep breath. 'Is that why you asked me to do this, Sister? So you could test me?'

It was an impertinent question, and she expected Sister to bite her head off for asking it. But she didn't.

'Yes, I suppose I am testing you, in a way.' She paused. 'You've always wanted to work with children, haven't you, Doyle?'

'I did,' Dora muttered.

Sister Parry smiled. 'But I've put you off the idea, is that it?'

Dora met her gaze. 'It's not quite what I expected, Sister.'

'No, I daresay it isn't. I suppose you thought you could play with the children all day long? That they would love and adore you, and you could bring joy to each other's lives?'

Dora winced at her mocking tone. 'I don't see what's wrong with caring for the children, Sister.'

'Neither do I, Doyle. And that's what we do for all the children on this ward. We care for them. But we don't love them. We certainly don't allow ourselves to go soft over them.'

She put down the scissors. 'I suppose you think I'm hard-hearted, don't you? I wonder what you'd say if I told you I was once very much like you are now.'

Dora looked up at her in surprise. 'Sister?'

'Oh, I expect it's hard for you to believe, isn't it? But I came from a big family myself and I loved children. I always wanted to work with them. And when I was a Staff Nurse at my first children's hospital, I would fuss over those patients as if they were my own brothers and sisters. I would play with them and make them laugh, cry with them when they were in pain. I adored them all.'

Dora stared at her blankly, trying to fathom what was coming next.

'But it hurt,' Sister Parry went on. 'Because children in hospital are in constant pain, I was in constant pain too. And when they died, I bled for them, just as you are bleeding now for this poor child, no matter how you try to hide it from me.' She stroked a lock of fair hair away from Emily's marble-pale face. 'In the end I couldn't bear it and considered giving up nursing completely, because I couldn't stand to break my heart every day.'

'So you hardened it instead.' The words were out before Dora had time to think about them. She blushed. 'I'm sorry, Sister, I didn't mean to criticise—'

'No, you're quite right. I did harden my heart, in a way. Not completely, you understand. Believe it or not, there are still children who manage to get under my tough skin.' She smiled sadly at Emily. 'We wouldn't be human if we didn't feel something for the patients in our care. But you mustn't bleed for them, Doyle, because then you are not doing your job. You have to build a wall between you and them, learn to stand back from it. Otherwise you will never be a good children's nurse.'

'I don't think I'm good enough anyway,' Dora sighed.

Sister Parry frowned at her. 'On the contrary, Doyle, I believe you have the makings of an excellent children's nurse. In fact, I was rather hoping you would consider returning to Parry after you qualify?'

'Me, Sister?' Dora stared at her in astonishment. 'But I thought . . .'

'You thought because I was hard on you it meant I considered you hopeless?' Sister Parry shook her head. 'No, Doyle, that is far from the case, I assure you. But I did think you were over-emotional and undisciplined. Hopefully that's something I will be able to train out of you. If, that is, you would consider coming to work for a horrible old boot like me? Those were your words to Lane earlier, I believe?'

A hot blush crept up Dora's neck, and she couldn't bring herself to look at Sister Parry as she hurried to finish washing Emily.

They dressed the girl in a clean nightgown and white stockings, and Sister Parry arranged a posy of flowers in her hands.

'Poor child,' she said. 'Another one with no one to mourn her.'

'Did the doctors ever find out what was wrong with her, Sister?' Dora asked.

Sister Parry shook her head. 'None of the tests proved conclusive. In medical terms, she was in perfect health.'

'It was strange that she went on wasting away, even when we fed her,' Dora said.

'It was,' Sister Parry agreed. 'But I have seen it happen before. A child just makes up their mind that they don't want to live any more, and their body slowly fades away. The mind is a very powerful thing, Doyle. It can make an enormous difference between whether someone chooses to live or to die.'

'And Emily chose to die,' Dora said. 'I wonder why?'

Sister Parry lifted her shoulders in a shrug. 'Sadly, we'll never know,' she said. 'But there was so much sadness in her, more than I've ever seen in a child. Those eyes of hers, so strange and detached . . . They say the eyes are the windows to the soul, don't they? But looking into hers, you almost felt as if her spirit had detached itself from her body a long time ago, leaving an empty shell behind.' Sister smiled tightly. 'We can but hope it's flying free now, wherever the poor child wants to be.'

But Dora was hardly listening. Her thoughts were racing, flying away like little Emily's freed spirit.

'Do they know why she was returned to the orphanage?' she asked, as they folded the sheet around her to make a shroud.

Sister Parry shook her head. 'All her mother would say was that she thought it was for the best. I must say, it seems rather an odd notion to me.'

Dora agreed silently. She couldn't imagine what would drive any mother to give up her child, even an adopted one. 'It seems so cruel,' she said.

'It isn't for us to judge,' Sister Parry said wisely. 'Perhaps Emily was traumatised by the adoption in some way, and couldn't settle with them? Or perhaps she and her husband realised they weren't cut out to be parents after all? That can happen, I suppose. A couple take on someone else's child thinking they can love it as their own, only to find they are not capable of such unselfishness.' She carefully folded the sheet over the child's sleeping face. 'At any rate, she is at peace now.'

An idea, dark and poisonous, began to uncurl in the back of Dora's mind.

'Did the doctor examine Emily thoroughly when she was first admitted?' Dora knew she shouldn't be asking, that she could be punished for daring to question her superiors, but she also knew she wouldn't be able to rest unless she did.

Sister Parry frowned. 'I don't think Mr Hobbs considered there to be any need. All the usual blood and urine tests were carried out, to rule out medical causes for her decline. What on earth is this about, Doyle? Why do you ask?'

'It's not important, Sister. I just had a thought, that's all.'

'Would you like to tell me what it is?'

Dora shook her head. 'I was just being silly.'

Emily should rest in peace, she decided. If Dora was right in her suspicions, the child didn't deserve anything else to happen to her, even in death.

As Sister Parry had talked, Dora had suddenly realised why she felt such a bond with Emily. It was those eyes of hers, with the strange, vacant stare of someone who had left their body behind, shut it off because it was easier to deal with the pain that way.

It was the same vacant stare Dora used to see every day in the mirror when Alf had been part of her life.

She thought about Emily's adoptive mother. What must it have taken for her to bring Emily back to the orphanage? It must have been something truly desperate to drive her to return a child she had wanted so badly for so long.

What if she did it to protect Emily? What if she discovered something was happening to the child, something that meant it was no longer safe for her to stay at home? Her father, an uncle, a grandfather, perhaps? And rather than expose the sordid secret, she had quietly returned the child to a place where she would be safe.

It was for the best, she had said. Little did she know the damage had already been done, and that poor Emily would be so traumatised that she would simply waste away.

Dora shuddered, thinking about the past. She had tried to push all thoughts of Alf Doyle from her mind, but now they refused to go away.

She had to find the money to get rid of him, Dora decided. Otherwise Josie or Bea might end up like little Emily one day.

Chapter Forty-Four

Effie watched the penny spinning high into the air. It twisted for a moment, catching the light from the tall window. Then it came down, landing and instantly bouncing off the drum-tight drawsheet.

Sister Parry nodded her satisfaction. 'That,' she said, 'is how you make a bed. Well done, O'Hara.'

Effie preened herself. It was only a bed, but it was practically the first thing she'd done right since she'd arrived on the ward. Her new leaf must be working, she thought.

Now if only she could sort out the whole business with Jess, everything would be perfect.

It had been two weeks since her departure. Sister Sutton had been discharged from the sick bay and was firmly back in charge at the nurses' home, having recovered from what turned out to be a severe kidney infection.

There was now a new maid sleeping in Jess' room, a surly girl called Pearl, who spent most of her time on the hall telephone and whose shelves contained nothing but old copies of *Picturegoer* and photos of her various boyfriends.

Everyone seemed to have forgotten about Jess Jago. But there was something about her absence that troubled Effie. And she knew she had to do something to put it right.

She had tried talking to her sister about it.

'Are you mad?' Katie had said. 'Effie, please tell me you're not serious?'

'Why shouldn't I speak up?'

'But you're doing so well. You haven't blotted your copy-book in ages. Don't start causing trouble again, please!'

'I'm sorry, Katie, but I can't just sit by and watch Jess be blamed for something she didn't do.'

'What difference does it make?' Katie reasoned. 'She's gone now, it won't affect her either way. But you . . . you're skating on thin ice as it is, Effie. I don't want you to get into any more trouble. You heard what Matron said. If you get another black mark against your name . . .'

'Do you remember why I got that black mark?' Effie interrupted her.

'Of course I do. You were accused of poisoning that wretched punch.' Katie shuddered. 'Don't remind me.'

'Exactly. I was accused of something I didn't do,' Effie said. 'And now the same thing is happening to Jess.'

'That's different.'

'How?'

'Because – oh, I don't know, it just is.' Katie pointed an accusing finger at her. 'I'm warning you, Euphemia O'Hara. If you do this, I won't be responsible for my actions!'

Which was why Effie decided not to tell her sister when she went to see Matron after her duty finished that evening.

By the time it dawned on her that Katie was right and it might not be a good idea, she was already standing in Matron's office. And just to make it even more terrifying, Miss Hanley was there too. She stood behind Matron's shoulder like a fire-breathing dragon, glaring at Effie as if she couldn't fathom who would have the sheer gall to request such an audience.

Matron, by contrast, was calm and kindly-looking.

'You wanted to see me, O'Hara? How odd, it's usually the other way round,' she said.

392

Effie smiled nervously. 'Yes, Matron. '

'Well?' Matron prompted her. 'What can I do for you?'

Effie took a steadying breath. 'It's about Jess Jago.'

Matron frowned. 'You mean the maid who was dismissed for theft?'

'That's just it, Matron,' Effie said. 'I don't believe she stole those things.'

Matron tilted her head, considering this. 'I see. So does this mean you know who the real culprit was, O'Hara?'

'I think I do, Matron.'

'Spit it out, girl!' Miss Hanley broke in impatiently. 'Matron doesn't have all day!'

Effie squared her shoulders. She was doing this for Jess, she told herself. 'I think it was Sister Sutton.'

A shocked silence filled the room. Matron sat quite still, her face giving nothing away. Miss Hanley, by contrast, was gasping like a stranded fish.

'Well!' she finally managed to roar. 'The impertinence! To accuse the Home Sister of such a thing! I can scarcely believe it—'

'Perhaps you'd like to explain how you came to this conclusion, O'Hara?' Matron's voice cut clearly across the Assistant Matron's blustering.

'It's the leprechaun, Matron.'

Matron's eyes widened. Effie saw the astonishment in them and realised she hadn't explained herself very well.

'Are you saying one of the little people told you?' Miss Hanley snorted with derision. 'Did it whisper in your ear? Really, Matron, I don't know why we're listening to this nonsense . . .'

'You don't understand,' Effie blurted out. 'My sister Katie has a china leprechaun. I gave it to her for her birthday. But it's sitting on Sister Sutton's mantelpiece now.'

'And you believe Sister Sutton stole this – ornament?'

393

'Preposterous!' Miss Hanley snapped.

'I don't think she meant to do it,' Effie went on, ignoring her. 'I think she took the leprechaun and the other things by mistake – without even realising.'

'Go on,' Matron said.

'She's been ill with a kidney infection,' Effie said. 'We had a lecture on infection during PTS, and I remember one of the doctors saying mental confusion is a symptom of kidney disease.'

'Mental confusion?' Miss Hanley echoed in disbelief. 'The very idea!'

'I just wonder if it's possible that Sister Sutton might have taken the things without knowing about it?'

Effie was aware of Miss Hanley, red-faced and hissing as if she was coming to the boil. But she fixed her gaze on Matron instead, willing her to believe her.

Miss Fox took a deep breath. 'I will consider what you have told me, O'Hara,' she said calmly.

'But do you think it's possible, Matron?'

'I said, I will consider it.' Her voice was firm, brooking no argument. Even Effie understood it was time to beat a hasty retreat.

She'd done her best. She only hoped she wouldn't be punished for it.

Kathleen waited for the door to close, then turned to her deputy. 'What do you think?'

The Assistant Matron stared at her. 'Surely you can't be taking her seriously? It's clear to see the girl is unhinged. I blame the Irish blood. Coming in here, spouting all kinds of nonsense about leprechauns and the like!'

'All the same, there was a modicum of sense to it,' Kathleen said. 'Mental confusion *is* one of the symptoms of kidney infection, and Dr McKay said Sister Sutton's case was quite severe. That it was likely she had been suffering a mild form for months before it became acute.'

'Yes, but Sister Sutton would never do such a thing!'

'Not in her right mind,' Kathleen said.

Miss Hanley looked quietly furious. 'So you're accepting the word of a silly student nurse over the Home Sister?'

Kathleen Fox was silent. For once, she truly didn't know what to think.

'What do you think?'

Lucy's mother opened the magazine and set it down on the coffee table in front of her. 'Inside the charming London home of Emerald Channing' the headline read, followed by several photographs of Mrs Channing, wealthy American hostess, draped across various chairs and sofas in her salon.

'It's beautiful,' Lucy said admiringly.

'I wish I could say the same about her.' Clarissa shuddered. 'Ghastly woman. But absolutely pots of money and no idea how to spend it. Do you know, she seriously considered having some kind of artwork done on her ceiling? I told her, it's South Kensington, not the Sistine Chapel. But at least they mentioned my name in the article.' She pointed it out. 'Hopefully it will lead to more commissions.'

Lucy smiled. She couldn't remember the last time she'd seen her mother so happy and animated.

'You sound as if you're quite busy already?' she said.

'Yes, I am. Things are really taking off, thanks to Mr Alderson. He's been an absolute wonder, introducing me all around the place. For someone who's only been in town for a year, he knows simply everyone.'

'Yes, he seems like the kind of man who'd ingratiate himself everywhere he goes,' Lucy said sourly.

Her mother sent her a reproachful look. 'Now, Lucy, don't be mean. Leo has been terribly helpful. I couldn't have launched my business without him.'

'I'm sure you could,' she said. 'Anyway, he owes it to us to help, since he was the one who got us into this trouble in the first place.'

'That's just it, you see. He didn't.' Clarissa closed the magazine and leaned back against the cushions of the sofa. 'It was one of Leo's colleagues who got hold of the story, through a former employee of your father's. Leo found out a few weeks ago, from his editor. I suppose it was bound to happen, with all those disgruntled people being put out of jobs. At any rate, it wasn't Leo's fault. If anything, *he* was the one who got into trouble. The poor man was fired when they found out he'd sat on the story to protect us.'

Lucy stared at her. 'I didn't know that!'

'Oh, yes, poor darling. But now he says he's going to write a novel about the British upper classes. I can't wait to read it. He's such an amusing man, it's bound to be absolutely scurrilous.' Then, as an afterthought, Clarissa added, 'I've invited him to supper tonight, by the way.'

'Oh, Mother! Why did you do that? I was looking forward to spending a pleasant evening.'

'It will be pleasant, darling. I told you, Leo's a charming man when you get to know him.'

'Well, I'm immune to his charms,' Lucy said crossly. She reached up and smoothed her hair. 'And I'm in the most dreadful state, too. I haven't been to the hairdresser in months.'

'Why should that worry you, if you're as immune to Leo's charms as you claim to be?' her mother teased. She leaned forward confidingly. 'Between you and me, I think the only reason he has been so helpful to me is so he can get into your good books.'

'Stop it, Mother!' Lucy snapped, but she couldn't help feeling rather pleased at the idea.

There was a knock on the door. 'There's your admirer now!' Clarissa smiled. 'Go and let him in, please, darling, while I finish supper.'

It was a wonderful, relaxed evening, full of laughter. Her mother's friend Lavinia and her husband came up from downstairs and entertained them all with outrageous stories. It was positively Bohemian, nothing like the stuffy dinner parties they'd had in Eaton Place.

Her mother had made sure Lucy was sitting next to Leo.

'I'm sorry you lost your job,' she said to him when she had the chance. 'Why didn't you tell me?'

'Would you have cared?'

'Probably not, at the time.'

'How about now?'

She glanced sideways at him. He was rather attractive, once she allowed herself to admit it.

'Mother also tells me you're writing a novel?' she said. 'Is it as racy as she thinks?'

'I don't know about racy.' He swirled his wine around in his glass. 'It's about a young American who comes to England and meets a very grand society girl.'

'That doesn't sound like much of a plot to me.'

'You're right,' Leo agreed. 'She's a real pain in the rear and it's kind of hate at first sight. But then she loses all her money and he realises she's not so bad after all.'

'A riches to rags story?'

'Cinderella in reverse.'

'And does it have a happy ending?' asked Lucy.

He leaned towards her, his blue eyes meeting hers. 'You tell me,' he said softly.

A sharp knock on the door broke the spell. Clarissa looked up, frowning. 'Who can that be?'

'I'll go,' Lucy said, folding up her napkin and laying it beside her plate.

It was Gordon Bird. He stood on the doorstep, clutching his hat in his hands, looking as lugubrious as usual.

'Uncle Gordon!' she greeted him happily.

'I hoped you'd be here, Lucy. I tried telephoning you at the nurses' home but they said you were out.' He glanced past her. 'You're entertaining. I'm sorry.'

'It's all right, please come in.' She stood aside to let him enter. 'Mother won't mind at all. It's very different from the old days, when she used to fuss for hours over table plans. But then, I suppose it's hard to fuss for hours when your table's the size of a postage stamp!'

She laughed, then saw her godfather's sombre expression and stopped abruptly. Uncle Gordon always looked grave, but this time something about the way he looked at her sent a warning shiver up her spine. 'What is it, Uncle Gordon? What's wrong?'

Please, she begged silently. No more bad news. I don't think I can stand it.

'It's your father,' he said. 'He's been found.'

Chapter Forty-Five

'I must say, I was surprised to hear from you at last,' Alf said. 'I thought you'd changed your mind?'

'Let's get this over with, shall we?' Dora shivered in the chill breeze that rose from the canal. It was past nine, and all she wanted was to be safe back at the nurses' home. The thought of being alone in the dark with Alf Doyle scared her, although she refused to let it show as she confronted him. She knew he had chosen the isolated meeting place deliberately to unnerve her.

'Suits me, love. Where's my money, then?' His eyes gleamed greedily.

Dora took the note out of her purse and handed it to him. Alf looked at it, his mouth curling in derision. 'A fiver? We said twenty.'

'I ain't got it.'

He thrust the money back at her. 'Then we ain't got a deal.'

'But that's all I have.'

He regarded her, a smile spreading across his broad face. 'You know what I reckon? You don't really want me to go. That's why you ain't come up with the money.'

He reached out for her, but Dora shrank away. 'Don't touch me!'

'Don't be like that. That's not what you say to that Riley boy when you're letting him paw you, is it?' He leered at her. 'Down here, wasn't it? By the canal? That's your favourite spot, as I recall.'

Sickness rose in her throat as she remembered the rustling in the bushes and the footsteps she'd put down to her imagination. And then there had been all the other times she'd imagined she was being followed. 'You've been watching me!'

'Had to keep an eye on you, didn't I? I must say, you put on a right show with that boy, kissing and cuddling. But I bet I could teach him a thing or two, eh?'

Dora pushed the money back at him. Her nerve gave way, flooding her chest with panic. 'Take it, please. I'll get the rest to you later.'

'And pigs might fly!' Alf shook his head. 'Besides, I've changed my mind. I don't think I want to go after all.'

'But you promised—'

'Yeah, well, I've got cosy here, ain't I? I reckon it won't be too much longer before your mum's begging me to move back in. And once I'm back under her roof, that'll be it for me. No one's going to warn me off again. Not you, nor your thug of a boyfriend.'

Dora frowned. 'What's Nick got to do with this?'

'Don't pretend you don't know!' Alf snarled. 'You're the one who put him up to it, ain't you? Collaring me in a dark alley like that.'

'Nick threatened you?'

'He did more than threaten me.' Alf put his hand up to his jaw. 'Made it plain what would happen if I showed my face round here again. As if I stood a chance against that vicious little sod!'

Dora hardly took in what he'd said, she was reeling with shock at the idea that Nick had confronted him. How had he known? And what did he know? Could it be that all this time he'd known her secret?

'Still, he ain't here any more, is he?' Alf continued with a sneer. 'I can come and go as I please.'

'He'll be back,' Dora said. 'The fair will be back in London soon, and then he'll come home.'

'Is that what you think?' Alf grinned at her. 'Well, I got news for you, my girl. The fair's already back. And I don't see any sign of your boyfriend, do you?'

All her blood rushed to her feet, leaving her light-headed. 'You're lying,' she said flatly.

'Go and see for yourself, if you don't believe me. The fair's in Wanstead now. Not a million miles away, is it?' Alf grinned nastily. 'You'd think Nick would find the time to come and visit his girl.' He shook his head. 'Poor Dora. Looks like you've been left in the lurch again, eh?'

He's lying, she told herself. He's only saying it to hurt me. But she couldn't stop a feeling of dread from creeping through her. Wasn't it just as she'd feared: Nick had grown tired of her and the whole idea of divorce, and just upped sticks and gone?

And if he knew what Alf had done to her, then surely that was even more reason why he would stay away. She suddenly remembered all the times he'd stopped himself from touching her. That night when she'd offered to spend the night with him, but he'd run away. At the time, she'd told herself it was because he cared for her, respected her. But now she wondered if the real reason was because he couldn't bring himself to touch her because she was damaged goods.

Alf seemed to read her thoughts. 'Go on, tell me you ain't been thinking the same thing,' he goaded softly. 'Let's face it, he ain't got much to rush home to, has he? You ain't exactly Jean Harlow.' He looked her up and down with contempt. 'And from what I remember, you just used to lay there like a sack of coal. Not much to look at either. Not like your sister . . .'

Dora moved to slap him but he grabbed her wrist, his

fingers biting into her flesh. She recoiled from his smell of stale beer and bad teeth. 'But I do remember you liked it rough,' he whispered, pushing his bristly face close to hers.

'Leave her alone!'

Alf dropped his hold on Dora and swung round. Rose Doyle stood above them on the path, looking down, her face a mask of fury in the moonlight.

'Mum!'

'Rosie, I can explain.' Alf backed away from Dora, holding up his hands. 'It wasn't me, I swear. It was all her. She asked me to meet her tonight. I – I didn't want to but she said she'd make trouble for me if I didn't.' His panicked gaze darted between Dora and Rose as she picked her way down the bank towards them. 'You've got to believe me, Rosie, I'm telling you the truth. She made me do it—'

'And what about my little Josie? Did *she* make you do it, too?' Rose's voice was raw with emotion.

'I—' Alf had barely opened his mouth before Rose flew at him, kicking and spitting and clawing at his face like a wild animal. Caught off balance, he stumbled to his knees but she threw herself on top of him, fists pounding.

'I'll kill you, Alf Doyle! So help me, I'll kill you for what you did to my girls!'

She would, too, Dora realised. Rose Doyle was a woman possessed, wild with white-hot fury. Even Alf, bigger and stronger than she was, didn't stand a chance. Dora heard his muffled cries for mercy as he lay there, arms thrown up to protect himself from the blows that rained down on him.

'Leave it, Mum.' Dora caught hold of her mother and dragged her off. Rose fought against her, wriggling and twisting in her grip, still kicking out at Alf's hunched body.

'Rose, please. You've got it all wrong,' he pleaded.

'You're right there! I was wrong about you all these years, wasn't I? Letting you live under my roof, when all the time . . .'

Fresh fury gave Rose a new burst of strength. She broke loose from Dora's grip and threw herself at Alf again. This time Dora managed to grab her mother's wrist, holding on to it with all her strength.

She saw the flash of fear in Alf's face as he lay there gasping for breath, arms wrapped protectively around his battered body.

'You'd better go,' Dora told him.

He staggered to his feet. Blood oozed from his shattered nose. 'Bloody bitch!' he growled, voice muffled by his cut and swollen lips. 'You want to know why I had to have your daughters? 'Cos you weren't woman enough for me!'

'And you ain't going to be man enough for anyone by the time I've finished with you!' Rose spat back, fighting against Dora's restraining hands.

'Go!' Dora told him, struggling to keep a grip on her mother. 'Go while you still can.'

'And don't come back this time!' Rose screamed at Alf as he staggered off, climbing the bank, still clutching his ribs. 'Because if I see you again, so help me you really will end up floating in the Thames with your throat cut!'

She struggled in Dora's arms as they watched him climb the bank and disappear towards the street. 'Let me go after him!' she screamed. 'Let me kill the bastard!'

'He ain't worth swinging for, Mum.'

'But what he did to you—'

Suddenly all the fight seemed to drain out of Rose. She collapsed against Dora like a rag doll, spent and exhausted. Dora could only cling to her.

'How did you find out?' she whispered.

'Josie told me.'

Dora stiffened. 'But she wouldn't – she didn't want to say anything.'

'You're right, she didn't. But she knew she had to, for your sake.'

'For me?'

'She thought you were going to tell me, take it all on yourself.' Rose pulled away and wiped the blood from her split lip. 'Why didn't you tell me, Dora? Why didn't you come to me?'

'Because I didn't want it to be true.' She couldn't look at her mother. She'd imagined having this conversation so many times, but had never thought it would happen. Especially not like this, standing on a deserted canal bank in the moonlight. 'I thought if I didn't say anything, I could just pretend it was a nightmare.' She swallowed, her mouth suddenly dry. 'And he made me feel as if it was my fault, as if I was the one to blame. He said you'd hate me if you found out.'

She finally found the courage to look into her mother's face. The moonlight caught the tears glistening in Rose's eyes.

'Oh, my poor love.' Her voice was choked. She reached for Dora, stroking her face. 'As if I could ever hate you.' Rose shuddered. 'To think what that – that monster did to you and Josie under my roof, and I had no idea.'

She broke down then, sinking to her knees and sobbing as if her heart was torn beyond repair. Dora had never seen her proud East End mother brought so low, and it made her hate Alf even more.

But she couldn't share her mother's grief and shock. Dora felt detached, as if it had happened to someone else. But it was all new and raw to Rose, this agony. It would hurt like a fresh wound, bleeding and exposed. Dora had been through that stage, she was beyond feeling pain any more. Her wounds had healed, and all that was left were scars that would never disappear.

'I didn't see it, I didn't know,' her mother repeated, over and over again. 'I feel so ashamed.'

'Mum, don't. You mustn't blame yourself. Alf was clever . . . cunning.'

'But I'm your mother, I should have known. I should have protected you both. Only I was so busy thinking about myself, about making a nice home for my family, I didn't see what was going on right under my nose. I let you both down so badly . . .'

'You didn't, Mum, I promise you.' Dora pressed her face against her mother's shoulder. 'That's why we couldn't tell you. We knew you'd only blame yourself. But it ain't your fault, Mum, any more than it was Josie's fault, or mine. He's the one to blame, not us.'

'And to think he had the nerve to show his face here again!' Rose's voice was filled with disgust. 'I can't stand to think I let him back in my house, had him sitting at my table . . .'

'You weren't to know.'

'I didn't trust him.' Rose dashed the tears from her cheek with her sleeve. 'When he came back, there was something about him. But I thought it was just me, not being able to forgive him after what he did to us before. And then Josie came to me . . .'

Her voice trailed off, and she looked at Dora. 'You offered him money to leave?'

'I had to get rid of him somehow. For Josie's sake.'

'You should have told me.'

'I couldn't. You seemed so happy he was back.'

'Happy?' Rose stared at her in astonishment. 'I wasn't happy, love. I could hardly stand to look at him, after the way he walked out on us. But I've always tried to do what was best for the family, and I knew the kids needed their dad, so I thought I'd have to try for their sakes.' She looked at Dora, her face desolate. 'Little did I know I was inviting a monster back into our home. If I'd known then what I know now . . .' She broke off, her voice shaking.

'It's all right, Mum,' Dora whispered. 'It's over. Let's just try to forget it, shall we?' she pleaded.

'I don't know if I ever can, love.'

This was what Dora had always feared, and she knew it was what Josie feared, too. It was what had kept them both silent for so many years.

'You must, Mum. For our sake.' Dora looked out across the canal, its dark, oily ribbon of water stretching towards the railway bridge.

She knew her mother was right; she should have spoken out about what was happening to her. But deep down she knew she'd never have been brave enough to say the words. In the end it was her sister, the little girl she'd always striven to protect, who had found the courage to speak up, for both their sakes. Dora was glad it was all out in the open at last. At least now she could face her family without feeling there was a barrier between them, a terrible unspoken secret she could never divulge.

But at the same time she was scared. She didn't want this to spoil things between them for ever. She couldn't bear the idea of her mother seeing Alf whenever she looked at Dora, remembering what he'd done to her child.

'Josie and I have lived with this for too long. We don't want to go through it any more. Please?' begged Dora.

Her mother turned to her with a face full of understanding. 'It's over, Dora.' She smiled tenderly at her daughter. 'We'll never have to see that man's face, or mention his name, ever again, I promise.'

*

The following day, Dora caught the bus to Wanstead. All the way there, she tried to tell herself that Alf Doyle had been lying. But no matter what she told herself, she couldn't silence her own fears.

She tried to tell herself the fair wouldn't be there. But as she got off the bus at the common, she could already see the glow of coloured lights in the sky and hear the faint, jolly strains of a fairground organ.

The fair was busy, crowded with sweethearts wandering hand in hand and families trying their luck on the various sideshows. Rich smells of toffee and frying onions filled the air.

Dora hardly noticed any of it as she pushed her way through the milling crowds, looking for the boxing booth. She circled the fairground three times before she realised it wasn't there.

'Lost someone, love?' a woman called out to her from the coconut shy. She was a small, dumpy creature, swaddled in various layers of clothing, her hair caught up in a scarf. 'That must be a dozen times you've walked past me.'

Dora stepped into the pool of light around the shy. 'I was looking for the boxing booth.'

'Oh, yeah? Fancy trying your luck, do you?' The woman cackled, showing a few brown stumps where her teeth should have been. 'Sorry, girl, you're going to have to find something else to punch. Boxing booth's closed down.'

Dora heard her heart pounding in her ears. 'What about Nick Riley?'

'Who? Oh, you mean the bloke who ran the stall? He's gone, too.'

'When?'

All the blood in Dora's head rushed to her feet, making her head spin. 'When?' she heard herself ask faintly.

'Let's see. . . . . .' The woman was distracted for a

moment as a customer approached. Dora waited, impatience gnawing away at her, as the woman took their money and handed over three wooden balls. 'Be lucky, love.' She grinned at them and then turned back to Dora. 'I reckon it must have been a good few weeks ago now.' She considered it for a moment. 'Yes, that's right. Just after we left Oxford.'

'Did he say where he was going?' Dora asked.

'Hah! Not to me, love. Surly little sod, he was. Getting him to say good morning was like getting blood out of a stone.' She kept her eyes fixed on the child aiming balls at the shy. Each one missed its target and landed with a soft thump against the thick canvas. 'Decided life on the road wasn't for him, I expect. Don't suit everyone.' She made a sympathetic face at the child. 'Oh, bad luck, son. Come back and have another go later.' She bent to gather up the wooden balls, groaning with the effort. 'No, if you ask me, he's headed off home. I expect that's where you'll find him.'

I wouldn't bet on it, Dora thought. She thanked the woman automatically and turned away.

'Friend of his, was you?' the woman called after her.

Dora smiled sadly. 'Once, maybe,' she said. 'But not any more.'

Chapter Forty-Six

Sister Sutton seemed rather flustered to see Kathleen Fox at the door to her flat.

'Matron! I wasn't expecting you.' She brushed down her uniform. 'Is anything the matter?'

'Not at all, Sister Sutton. I just thought I'd drop in and see how you're getting on after your illness?'

'Oh, I'm fully recovered, thank you, Matron,' Sister Sutton dismissed. 'It was really a lot of fuss over nothing.'

'Not according to Dr McKay. He says your kidney infection was very severe. He's surprised you didn't have any symptoms earlier?'

'Well, you know me, Matron. I'm as strong as an ox.'

Are you? Kathleen wondered. The Home Sister certainly looked strong enough, her bulky body filling the doorway to her flat. But there was something oddly vulnerable about her that Kathleen had never noticed before.

'That's a relief, at any rate.' She smiled. 'May I come in?'

Sister Sutton looked startled. 'Come in, Matron?'

'I thought we might have a cup of tea together. If you have time, that is?'

'Well, I do have to supervise that new maid –' Sister Sutton's hands twisted together, betraying her tension. 'But of course, Matron,' she said, remembering her manners. 'Please come in.'

She seemed even more agitated inside her flat, ordering tea from the maid and fussing around plumping up cushions, even though her sitting room was immaculate.

409

'Please don't stand on ceremony on my account,' Kathleen said. 'This is purely a social call.'

'Is it?' Sister Sutton's eyes were sharp.

'Of course. Why else would I be here?'

The maid arrived, bringing the tea tray. Kathleen smiled to herself as Sister Sutton inspected it: snapping at the girl for not remembering a tray cloth, and sending her to fetch a clean spoon.

'How is she settling in?' Kathleen asked, when the maid had gone.

Sister Sutton sighed. 'She tries hard, I suppose. But she's not terribly quick on the uptake. Not like . . .' She abruptly stopped speaking.

'Not like Jess Jago?' Kathleen finished for her. 'You miss her, then?'

Sister Sutton nodded. 'Very much. She seemed so bright and willing to me, I always thought some of the students could have learned something from her. But as it turned out, I was wrong.' She stared down at the dog at her feet. 'I still can't quite bring myself to believe it,' she said.

Neither can I, Kathleen thought. She had dismissed Effie O'Hara's pleas from her mind, too preoccupied with other hospital matters to give them much thought. But she couldn't forget what the student nurse had said. The idea that Jess Jago might have been unfairly accused played on her mind.

And since she had spoken to Dr McKay the previous evening, it had been weighing even more heavily on her.

Her gaze drifted up to the mantelpiece. 'You have a lot of treasures,' she remarked.

Sister Sutton smiled shyly. 'I do like my little keepsakes,' she said. 'I know it's a silly indulgence, but I'm rather fond of them. And I think they brighten the place up a bit.'

'They certainly do. May I?' Kathleen rose to her feet to inspect them. 'I suppose you remember them all?' she said.

'Yes, of course,' Sister Sutton replied. 'Each one was a gift from a friend or a grateful patient, or else a souvenir of a place I've visited. They're all memories, which is why I treasure them.'

Kathleen's eye moved along the crowded rows of figurines, coloured glass and miniature models of landmarks, until she found what she was looking for, nestling behind a pair of coy-looking china children holding hands.

'What about this one?' she asked, picking up the leprechaun. 'Was this a gift?'

Sister Sutton put down her cup and reached for her spectacles. 'I'm not sure,' she said. 'I suppose it must have been, since I've never visited Ireland . . . yes, I think it was a present.' She frowned at the figure in Kathleen's hand, her face troubled. 'How odd that I can't recall who it was from. I can remember all the others perfectly.'

'I don't wonder you can't recall it, since it was never given to you.'

The Home Sister's head went back. 'Whatever do you mean, Matron?'

'I mean this ornament was taken from Nurse O'Hara's room some time ago.'

Sister Sutton's tiny dark eyes filled with alarm. 'I hope you're not saying – you don't think I stole it?'

'No, Sister, I don't think that at all. But I do think you might have taken it without realising. And I think you might have taken other things, too.'

The Home Sister unhooked her spectacles and rubbed her eyes. Kathleen watched her carefully. She had expected her to react with outrage, but Sister Sutton seemed unsurprised, almost resigned.

'Do you think you might have taken it, Sister?' Kathleen prompted her gently.

'I – I don't know.' Sister Sutton's voice faltered. 'I might have, but I really have no memory of it. My thoughts have been all over the place lately. I've found myself saying and doing the most extraordinary things . . .' When she looked up at Kathleen, her broad face was creased in fear. 'You're right, Matron. I believe I did take those things. I have no recollection of it, but since Jess was accused, I have begun to wonder more and more whether she found the items and decided to return them to their owners.'

'So she was telling the truth when she said she was putting them back?' Kathleen spoke her thoughts aloud.

'I believe she did it to protect me. And that's why she didn't speak up to clear her own name.' Sister Sutton's mouth trembled. 'I've been so troubled by it, I wondered if I should say something myself. But having no recollection, I didn't know if I was mistaken.' She looked at the china leprechaun. 'But I suppose this proves it,' she sighed heavily. 'I am a thief, and Jess Jago was innocent all along.'

Kathleen watched as Sister Sutton lumbered to her feet, her movements slow and stiff. The Home Sister seemed to have aged twenty years in the last five minutes.

'I will hand in my resignation at once,' she said with dignity. 'I know I have no right to ask it of you, Matron, but I wonder if you would allow me some time to pack my belongings and find somewhere else to live? Although I will understand if, under the circumstances, you would prefer me to leave straight away.'

Kathleen stared at her in astonishment. 'Sister Sutton, what are you talking about?'

'Obviously I will have to leave now my – disgrace has come to light.' Sister Sutton stood before her, holding herself upright, every inch the proud nurse. 'You cannot have a thief in charge of the students. It would sully the respected name of the Nightingale Hospital.'

'Sister, please sit down. I know you're not a thief. You said yourself, you don't even remember taking those things.'

'And that makes it all the worse!' Sister Sutton's jowls wobbled. 'Even if I am not a thief, then I am certainly no longer competent to do this job.' There was a catch in her voice. 'You don't want an old woman like me here, blundering around, forgetting things and causing trouble. I have always said, the day I am more of a hindrance than a help is the day I hang up my uniform for the last time.' Her hands shook as she fumbled with the strings of her apron. 'I had hoped that wouldn't be for some while. I'd always thought I might be able to live out my days here, being useful. But I can see now I was mistaken.'

'Sister Sutton—'

'Please, Matron, I don't want any pity. I accept that this is the way things must be. You need a younger, more conscientious woman for this job. One whose mind isn't letting them down.'

'Sister Sutton! Will you please be quiet for a moment and listen to me?' Kathleen cut her off. The Home Sister shut up immediately and stared at her, startled.

Kathleen took a breath, calming herself. 'I don't want you to go anywhere,' she said. 'Not just because the Nightingale is your home, but because I simply can't imagine where I would find a woman who is more conscientious than you when it comes to looking after the students. And as for your mind letting you down, that was due to illness, not age. I had a word with Dr McKay last night, and he confirmed that it's highly likely the kidney infection caused your confusion. Now you're recovered, everything should return to normal.'

Sister Sutton looked perplexed. 'So I'm not losing my marbles?'

Kathleen smiled. 'I'm not sure Dr McKay would approve of that medical terminology, but no, you're not losing your marbles. In fact, I daresay you're sharper than the rest of us put together.'

The Home Sister was silent for a moment, considering this. 'I can stay here then? I won't have to leave?' Her expression was dazed. 'I was so worried about having to go to the home for retired nurses. I wasn't sure how I'd cope . . .'

'You won't have to go anywhere, Sister Sutton,' Kathleen reassured her. 'This is your home for as long as you want it to be. As I said, I can't imagine anyone who could keep order among the students better than you.'

'Thank you, Matron. That means a great deal to me.' Sister Sutton's voice was choked.

'I'm glad that's settled, then.'

As Kathleen turned to go, Sister Sutton said, 'What about Jess?'

Kathleen took a deep breath. 'Ah, yes. I think we still have some amends to make to Miss Jago, don't you?'

Chapter Forty-Seven

'There you are, love. I reckon you'll enjoy that one.'

'I will if it's anything like the last one you recommended.' The woman smiled as Jess handed over the book, wrapped in brown paper.

'And don't forget, if you bring it back you can have a penny off the next book you buy.'

Jess turned to give the coins to Sam, who was watching her admiringly.

'Do you have to do that?' he asked.

'What?'

'Make me look bad.' He grinned. 'You've already doubled our takings in three weeks. My dad will give me the sack if you carry on like that.'

'You'll be leaving anyway once you pass those engineering exams.'

Jess turned away from him to sort out the box of books Sam's father had dropped off that morning. It amazed her that neither he nor Sam had thought of grouping together books by the same author. How was anyone supposed to find their favourite if they were all muddled up together?

'I mean it,' Sam said. 'You're a natural.'

Jess pretended to study the spine of a book so he didn't see her blush. 'It was kind of you to offer me the job,' she said. 'There's not many round here would give a chance to a thief.'

'You ain't a thief,' he said. 'Anyway, I couldn't care less what other people say. I told you before, I make my own mind up about people. And I made my mind up about you a long time ago.'

Jess caught his admiring look, and smiled back at him. She still wasn't sure if they were courting, but he'd taken her to the pictures – 'just to cheer you up,' as he'd said. She sensed he was going slowly, not sure how to approach her.

'Are you all right?' he asked.

''Course I am. Why do you ask?'

He shrugged. 'You've always got a smile for the customers, but you seem so sad when you don't think anyone's watching.'

'I've just got a lot on my mind, that's all.'

'Is it your family giving you trouble? Because you know my mum thinks the world of you. She'd be happy for you to lodge with us . . .'

'What, live and work with you, you mean?' Jess teased. 'I dunno if I could stand it!'

'I ain't that bad!'

Jess shook her head. 'It ain't my family,' she said. 'I reckon I can put up with them by now.'

That had been the worst thing for her, having to go back to the hatcheries. Of course, Gladys had loved every minute of Jess' humiliation, and never stopped crowing about it.

'How the mighty are fallen, eh? What's the matter, did your posh mates turn their backs on you? I said they would, didn't I? I've a good mind not to take you in, after the way you've treated me.'

In the end she'd relented. Mainly because her aunts and uncles had pointed out that Jess was a Jago and belonged there, but also because Gladys knew she still owed Jess for saving her son's life.

But that didn't stop her humiliating her stepdaughter

at every turn. 'You're a dark horse, ain't you?' she kept saying. 'All those times you've made out you're better than the rest of us, when it turns out you're as light-fingered as our Cyril. You're a true Jago all right, girl – your dad would be proud of you!'

'So what's wrong?' Sam asked Jess. 'Don't tell me you're bored of my company?'

'Bored of standing here in the cold all day, listening to you flirting with the customers? Not likely!'

Jess stamped her feet and blew on her gloved hands to warm them up. September had brought a nasty chill to the air.

'Tell you what, why don't you go and have a cup of tea, warm yourself up?' Sam said. 'You might as well take a break before the rush starts.'

Jess looked up and down Columbia Road, near empty of shoppers on this grim, cold autumn afternoon. 'Ta, I will,' she said. 'Let me know if all those customers get too much for you, won't you?'

'I'll try not to be trampled in the rush,' he joked.

She made her way to the café at the end of the street. Inside, the tables were crowded with stallholders like her, all trying to get warm. The room was enveloped in a pleasant fug of steam, and the smell of coffee and fried bacon hung in the air. It felt blissfully warm after being out in the cold. Jess took off her gloves and wrapped her hands around the steaming cup of tea.

She enjoyed working with Sam, and knew she should be grateful to have a job at all. But she dearly missed the hospital. She missed the order and routine, and the chatter of the nurses going to and from duty. She missed Sister Sutton and Sparky, and her bedroom lined with books. Most of all she missed being part of the whole Nightingale world.

She shook herself. This won't do, Jess Jago, she thought. All that's in the past, you can't turn the clock back. It was only memories that made you sad.

There was a tall woman at the bookstall, browsing through the books. She didn't seem like their usual class of customer: smartly dressed in a rust-coloured coat, a stylish felt hat pulled down low over her eyes.

Sam turned to greet Jess as she approached. He looked very pleased with himself, she noticed.

'What are you smiling about?' she asked. 'Don't tell me you've sold a book while I was gone?'

Sam's grin widened. 'Better than that. You've got a visitor.'

He jerked his head in the woman's direction. As she turned, Jess found herself looking into a pair of calm grey eyes, and felt a shock of recognition.

'Matron?'

'Hello, Jess.' Kathleen Fox smiled at her. She looked younger and more approachable out of her starched black uniform.

'What are you doing here?' A terrible thought struck her. 'It's not Sister Sutton, is it? Don't tell me she's ill again?'

'Sister Sutton is quite well,' Miss Fox assured her with a smile. 'It's you I've come to see.'

'Me? Why?'

Before she could reply, Sam pulled off his leather money belt and handed it to Jess. 'I'm going to take my tea break now. Leave you two to have a chat.'

'Thank you, Sam.' Matron smiled at him.

Jess frowned. Sam, was it? He'd obviously been getting acquainted with their visitor. She hoped he hadn't tried flirting with her.

Jess watched him sauntering off up the street. And then she and the visitor were alone.

'I suppose it must be a shock for you, seeing me here?' Matron said.

'I wasn't expecting it, that's for sure.' Suddenly nervous, Jess rearranged the books in front of her, making sure their spines all faced the same way. Anything rather than stand still and look Matron in the eye again. 'What can I do for you?' she asked.

'I came to apologise.'

Jess looked up sharply. 'What for?'

'For the way you were treated. We misjudged you, and I'm very sorry for that.' She paused. 'We discovered it was Sister Sutton who took those items.'

'It wasn't her fault!' Panic made Jess gabble. 'She didn't mean to do it, I know she didn't. You mustn't get rid of her, the Nightingale is her whole life. I don't know what she'd do if you put her out to grass in some old folks' home . . .'

'Calm down, no one is sending anyone to an old folks' home, least of all Sister Sutton!' Matron regarded Jess consideringly. 'That's why you covered up for her, isn't it? You were worried she would lose her job.'

Jess lowered her gaze. 'I knew she wouldn't have stolen those things on purpose,' she said quietly. 'She just couldn't remember doing it.'

'I know,' Matron agreed. 'It was her illness that made her do it. Fortunately, she has made a complete recovery. But she feels terrible, as do I, about the dreadful miscarriage of justice that occurred. You should never have been dismissed, Jess.'

'It's done now,' she mumbled, embarrassed.

'Perhaps, but it was very wrong of us. We misjudged you, and we are deeply sorry. Sister Sutton is particularly remorseful, since she has always maintained you are a girl of excellent character.'

Jess glanced up at Matron, her expression uncertain. 'She said that – about me?'

'She is most impressed with you, as am I,' Matron said. 'That's why I hoped you might consider returning to the Nightingale?'

Jess' mouth fell open. 'You're offering me my old job back?'

'Not quite.' Jess saw Matron's grave expression and her heart sank. She might have known it was too good to be true. 'We have engaged another girl in your place. But I think I have another position you might be interested in?'

There was something about the glint in those grey eyes that Jess didn't quite understand.

'What did you have in mind?' she asked.

Lucy barely recognised her father.

Sir Bernard wasn't the dapper man he'd once been. He'd lost so much weight his suit jacket hung limply from his shoulders. His neatly trimmed beard was overgrown, and there were dark shadows under his eyes.

But it wasn't just his appearance that had changed. The confident, charismatic man who had once commanded every room he entered now sat at a corner table in a rundown café, shredding a bus ticket nervously between his fingers.

'Look at him,' Lucy's mother whispered as they watched him from the doorway. 'I suppose we're meant to feel sorry for him.'

I do, Lucy thought. But one look at her mother's hard expression and she realised Clarissa didn't feel the same.

'Oh, what's the use?' his wife muttered. 'I knew I shouldn't have agreed to this, it's a complete waste of time.'

She turned towards the door, but Lucy grabbed her arm. 'Please, Mother, let's just listen to what he has to say?'

'I don't want to hear any more of that man's lies.'

'Look, he's seen us. We have to go and speak to him.'

He rose from his seat as they approached. 'Clarissa!' He opened his arms to her but his wife recoiled.

'Please don't touch me,' she hissed. 'It's bad enough that I have to speak to you.'

She took the seat farthest away from him and sat there, her hands tightly clasped, feet turned towards the door, as if poised to run at any moment. Lucy noticed her face had the pinched, hostile expression she'd always worn when Sir Bernard was around.

'Hello, Father,' Lucy said shyly.

'Lucy, my dearest.' He embraced her. He smelled of soap and water, and not the expensive hand-blended French cologne she was expecting.

They sat down. 'I've ordered us some tea,' Sir Bernard said.

'I hope you can pay for it,' Lucy's mother snapped. 'Or will you be running away and expecting us to foot the bill, as usual?'

'Mother!'

Sir Bernard winced. 'It's all right, Lucy, I suppose I deserve your mother's spite.' His smile was strained. 'How are you both?'

'Very well, thank—' Lucy started to say, but her mother cut her off.

'As if you care!' she said. 'Why are you here anyway, Bernard?'

'Because I wanted to see you. I missed you.'

'Well, we certainly missed you, didn't we, Lucy? Especially when the bailiffs were banging our doors down and marching off with our furniture.' His wife sent him a quick, hostile glance. 'We thought you were dead.'

'I didn't plan to leave, I swear. But when the deal collapsed and I realised how much trouble I was in, my first instinct was to go into hiding. And the longer I stayed away, the easier it became to simply stay hidden.'

'It wasn't easy for us!'

'I know, I'm sorry.'

The waitress arrived with their tea. They sat in strained silence until she'd walked away. Then Clarissa said, 'Where did you go, anyway? Timbuctoo?'

'Nearly.' His expression was rueful. 'I got as far as Europe, then I boarded a steamer bound for the Far East. I didn't know what I was doing, I just wanted time to think, to plan my next move. I desperately wanted to make things right, to come up with a way to get us out of this awful mess.'

'But instead you landed us in an even worse one.'

Bernard nodded. 'You must understand, I never wanted this to happen,' he said. 'When I borrowed the money for that deal, I truly expected it to pay off. I've taken many such gambles before, and they've always worked out.'

Clarissa said nothing as she picked up the teapot. She poured a cup for her husband first, Lucy noticed. Perhaps that was a good sign?

'Why didn't you tell us what was happening, Father?' she asked.

'I didn't want to worry you at first,' he admitted, looking down at the tablecloth. 'And then, when it all went wrong, I felt so ashamed. I knew you both looked up to me, expected me to be the strong one, and I couldn't do it.'

Lucy turned to her mother. Clarissa was staring at the door.

'I'm surprised you bothered to come back,' she said

stiffly. 'After all, the business is gone, there's nothing for you here.'

'I came back for you.'

It was such a simple, honest admission, but Lucy had never seen her father so sincere. And it worked on her mother far better than any of the expensive gifts he'd ever bought her.

Clarissa looked startled. 'I – I don't understand,' she faltered.

'I came back because I missed you, Clarissa. You and Lucy. Being away from you made me realise I don't care about the business, or how much money I've lost. I don't even care if I spend the rest of my life in a debtor's prison, so long as I have the love of my wife and daughter.'

Lucy looked at her mother. Clarissa eyed him warily. 'I wish I could believe you mean that,' she said.

'Then I'll just have to try to prove it to you, won't I? If you'll let me, that is.'

He put out his hand towards his wife, and this time she didn't turn away.

Chapter Forty-Eight

A month later, at half-past ten on a wet October morning Lucy lined up with the rest of her set to collect her hospital badge from Matron. As everyone had predicted, she was also awarded the Nightingale Medal for the most outstanding student in her set.

Her parents were there to see her collect her award. It gave her a jolt to see them talking animatedly, heads close together. She had never known them be more than civil to each other the whole time she'd been growing up.

They were waiting for her in the courtyard after the ceremony, when the rest of the students had dispersed. Matron had generously allowed them all the rest of the day off to celebrate their success.

'Lucy, darling!' Clarissa greeted her, enveloping her in a perfumed embrace. 'You were simply marvellous. We're so proud of you.'

'Very proud,' her father agreed quietly. 'You've worked very hard, my dear.'

'Thank you, Father.' Lucy touched the tiny Nightingale crest nestling just beneath her starched collar. Once upon a time she'd longed for nothing more than her father's approval. But the last few months had taught her how wrong she'd been to place him on a pedestal. How could he help but topple down from such a dizzy height?

Now she no longer needed his attention or his approval. It was enough that she was proud of herself and the person she had become.

But although she didn't live in awe of her father since his spectacular fall from grace, she loved him even more. Now he had revealed himself to be an ordinary man with failings and weaknesses like any other, she was no longer afraid of him.

'Now, I thought we might go to the Ritz to celebrate your . . .' He caught sight of his wife's disapproving frown, and sighed. 'I'm sorry. Old habits die hard.'

'You'll get used to it, dear.' Clarissa gave his arm a comforting pat.

'But not for long, I hope.' With Gordon's help, her father was slowly rebuilding his business, using the contacts he'd made in the Far East to import new goods. Lucy knew it was difficult for him, especially as he had to work very hard to regain the trust and goodwill of the banks. But this time her mother was at his side. Far from stepping back and allowing him to run everything, Clarissa was taking part. She showed a new interest in her husband's business, advising him on the most fashionable lines to import from the East, and helping to secure contracts with some of the smartest shops in the West End. She'd also firmly squashed Bernard's plan to rent a larger, more showy home in Belgravia.

'I don't care what everyone thinks, we must live within our means,' she'd insisted. 'Besides, I find I rather like Kentish Town.'

And as it turned out Bernard rather liked it too. He also liked the idea that his wife had become something of a celebrity among the smart set, and that no home was complete without the artistic flair of Clarissa Lane. Lucy could see the quiet pride in his face as he looked at his wife.

'And see who else is here.' Clarissa nodded past Lucy's shoulder. She turned round to see Leo Alderson, looking sickeningly tanned and athletic in a tweed sports jacket, a trilby set rakishly on his fair hair. He looked like he'd stepped straight from an advertisement for a gentlemen's outfitters.

But for some reason the sight of him didn't irritate Lucy quite so much as it might once have done.

'Hello there,' he said. 'I hope you don't mind me turning up like this? Only your mother was kind enough to invite me.'

Of course she did, Lucy thought, trying not to smile. Her mother was utterly determined to throw Leo in Lucy's path at every opportunity. And much as she hated to admit it, Lucy didn't mind at all.

'How's the novel coming along?' she asked him.

'Fine,' he said. 'But y'know, I'm still struggling with that ending. I just can't make up my mind whether the fellow gets the girl in the end or not.' He tilted his head enquiringly. 'Maybe you could decide for me?'

'I'd be glad to help,' she said.

'I have an idea,' Clarissa jumped in. 'Why don't you two take that table at the Ritz? It would be such a shame to waste it, wouldn't it?'

Sir Bernard looked puzzled. 'But I thought you said we couldn't afford . . .'

'Some investments are worthwhile, darling.' His wife threaded her arm through his. 'Come along, we'll catch the bus back to Kentish Town.'

Dora left the other students celebrating and walked back towards the nurses' home. Millie, Katie, Daphne and a few of the others were going off to the local café for a treat, but she didn't feel like following them.

Six weeks after the fair had returned to London, and Nick still hadn't come home. Dora was angry with herself for thinking he would, but even so couldn't stop herself from scanning the audience as she went up to collect her badge from Matron.

He's gone, she told herself firmly. If he was going to come home he would have been here today. Or perhaps he'd forgotten that this was the day she officially qualified. Perhaps he'd never given her a second thought since leaving her behind.

The attic room seemed sad and empty as she packed her things, ready to move to the staff nurses' home. Looking around, she thought about the day she'd arrived, almost three years ago, so nervous about what to expect. She remembered her first bruising encounter with Sister Sutton, and how kind Helen had been to her, helping her with her collar and pinning on her cap for her. She remembered how she had sat in the dining room, her stomach too tied up in knots for her to eat, looking around at the other students and wondering how she would ever survive.

But survive she had. And, in spite of her worst fears, the last three years had been the happiest Dora had ever known. She had made real friends, including some she could never have imagined making. She'd met some extraordinary people and learned a great deal, and not just about nursing.

And she had fallen in love. Dora pushed the thought from her mind as she stuffed her shoes into the corner of her suitcase. She had to stop thinking about Nick, otherwise she would send herself mad.

Think about the future instead, she told herself. Now Nick Riley was out of her life, she could stay on as a nurse. She had already made up her mind to apply for the Children's ward when she had her interview with Matron the following day.

Three months ago she would never have believed she could contemplate working for Sister Parry. But they'd reached an understanding over the past few weeks. They'd stopped clashing heads since Dora began to realise that the ward sister wasn't the heartless dragon she'd imagined her to be.

A lot had changed in three months, Dora realised.

She looked up as there was a knock on the door. It was Pearl, the maid.

'Sister Sutton says to let you know there's a message for you at the Porters' Lodge.'

Dora's heart skipped in her chest. 'A message? Who's it from?' she asked.

The poor maid looked blank. 'Dunno, miss. Sister just told me to tell you,' she whispered.

Dora abandoned her packing and hurried down to the Lodge. Mr Hopkins saw her coming, and a broad grin spread over his face.

'I've got some good news for you, Nurse,' he said.

Dora shoved her hands into the folds of her skirt to stop them from trembling. He was here. He'd come back for her after all.

But before she could say Nick's name, Mr Hopkins went on, 'Your brother's wife had a baby boy this morning.'

It took her a moment to register what he was saying. 'Oh,' was all Dora could reply.

'I've sent Peter home to be with his wife,' Mr Hopkins said, looking pleased with himself. 'But he asked me to pass on the good news. He thought you'd want to know?'

'Yes – thank you, Mr Hopkins,' Dora managed to say politely.

'I daresay you'll be wanting to go over and see them yourself, since you've got the day off?' he went on. 'Now you've got two things to celebrate, haven't you?'

'Yes, Mr Hopkins.' Dora kept a smile fixed on her face until she was alone in her room again. Only when she'd closed the door behind her did she allow herself to cry.

But after a while she realised Mr Hopkins was right. She had so much to be thankful for, she had to stop moping and get on with it. And a visit to Griffin Street to see her new nephew might be just what she needed.

The baby was beautiful, born that morning at home. There was never any question of Lily going into hospital, even though the Nightingale had a brand new maternity department. Most of the East End women Dora knew preferred to rely on the services of Granny Hatton, who turned up whenever a birth or a death was imminent.

The baby boy was as sturdy as his father, but he'd inherited his mother's dark colouring rather than the Doyles' ginger curls.

Lily settled back against the pillows, her baby in her arms, while the rest of the family cooed and fussed over him.

Nanna, of course, had to have her say about the new arrival.

'Simon?' She grimaced to Dora. 'What kind of name is that for a baby? We ain't never had a Simon in this family.'

'About time we did then, ain't it?' Peter said. 'Anyway, my missus likes it, and that's good enough for me.'

Dora grinned at her big brother. He looked dazed with happiness.

Downstairs Rose dismissed the tea Nanna had made and sent Bea down to the Rose and Crown with a tin jug for filling.

'We need to wet the baby's head properly,' she announced. 'And we mustn't forget our Dora's good news either. Who'd ever have thought we'd have a nurse in the family?'

Rose smiled warmly at her daughter. Dora looked away, feeling suddenly shy. The Doyles didn't go in for fussing over each other much, and all the attention embarrassed her.

'Where's Bea with that beer?' Nanna interrupted gruffly, bringing them all back down to earth. 'I wouldn't put it past her to go off and spend that money you gave her.'

'Leave her alone, Mum,' Rose said. 'She ain't that bad.'

'Not that bad? She brought that bugger Alf Doyle back to our doorstep, didn't she?'

The mention of his name caused a ripple of tension in the room. Dora saw her mother's face stiffen, her dark eyes growing cold. She glanced across at Josie, who was busy stoking the fire. She had her back turned to them, but her shoulders were rigid.

'Still, at least he didn't stay long,' Nanna went on. 'Dunno why he bothered to show his face in the first place.'

'Nor do I,' Rose muttered.

Ten minutes later, Bea returned with the jug of beer and the party carried on late into the evening. Dora sat in the midst of it, her troubles forgotten as she laughed and joked with the rest of the family. Even Bea seemed to forget to be surly as she ran up and down the stairs, checking on the baby and not giving poor Lily a minute's peace. Dora was pleased for her sister. Whatever anyone else might have thought about Alf Doyle, Dora knew Bea had loved him. Hopefully becoming an auntie to baby Simon would stop her fretting too much about Alf leaving again.

'It's just like old times, ain't it?' Nanna said with satisfaction, looking around her.

'It's better than old times,' Josie said. Dora caught her sister's eye across the room. She understood what Josie meant. For as long as she could remember, the shadow of Alf had hung over all their happy family occasions. Even when everyone else was having fun together the two eldest girls would be tense and watchful, dreading what might follow. They would watch Alf larking around with the rest of them, a knot of fear gathering in their stomachs, knowing that later on one of them would hear his heavy tread outside the door.

Dora had been worried about her sister since she had plucked up the courage to confess everything to their mother. But seeing the way Rose put her arms around Josie tonight and hugged her fiercely, Dora could tell that it had changed things between them – for the better.

At half-past nine Dora finished her drink and said her goodbyes.

'Do you have to go, love?' Rose looked disappointed.

'Sorry, Mum, I'm back on duty at seven tomorrow. And I don't think the Home Sister will be too pleased if I'm caught coming back late on my last night in the students' home!'

It was a dark, cold night, and Dora turned the collar of her coat up against the lashing rain as she set off down the back alley that led from Griffin Street to the main road. She cursed the fact that she'd left her umbrella behind; by the time she reached the Nightingale her carefully tamed hair would be a wild mass of frizzy curls again.

She was so busy worrying about her hair she barely noticed the footsteps behind her, getting louder as they drew close.

Her heart leaped into her mouth. Alf!

Not daring to turn round, Dora kept her head down and charged on against the lashing rain, speeding up her steps. The soles of her shoes slithered on the rain-slicked cobbles but she kept going, not daring to turn round. Her heartbeat was crashing in her ears so loudly she could barely hear the footsteps behind her, but she knew they were speeding up too.

She kept looking ahead, focusing on the greenish-white of the streetlamp at the far end of the alleyway. If she could reach that, everything would be all right . . .

'Dora?'

The sound of the man's voice stopped her in her tracks. Slowly she allowed herself to turn around. There, standing just a few feet behind her, shrouded in shadow, was a tall, familiar figure.

'Nick?' she whispered.

'Did I frighten you?' he said. 'I was going to knock on your door but it sounded like you were having a party so I went next door to see Danny first. I called to you as you came out, but I don't think you heard me for the rain.' He grimaced into the sky. 'Blimey, you didn't half put a sprint on up that alley. Who did you think was chasing you?'

Dora couldn't speak. She could only stare at him as he stood before her, rain dripping off his dark curls. He was dressed in a black overcoat, and the darkness of the alleyway cast sinister shadows over the sharp contours of his face. She didn't know whether to throw herself into his arms or beat him with her fists.

She kept her distance, still wary. 'I thought you weren't coming back,' she said.

He looked puzzled. 'I made you a promise, didn't I?'

'But you left the fair. No one has seen you since.'

His face darkened. 'It didn't work out at the fair,' he said. 'Lew Smith was happy enough with my work, but he didn't want to pay me for it. We parted ways just after we left Oxford.'

'Why didn't you come home then?'

'I told you, I made a promise. I didn't want to come home without the money I need for the divorce.'

'I wouldn't have cared.'

'No, but I would. Anyway, it turned out I could make

a decent living as a labourer, so I decided to travel around the farms offering my services. What with that and everything else . . .'

'Everything else?' Dora echoed.

Nick looked down. 'I did a bit of fighting,' he muttered.

Dora grabbed his hands and looked at them. Even in the weak light from the streetlamp, she could see they were scarred and swollen. 'Bare-knuckle fighting,' she said.

'It makes good money,' Nick said defensively. 'Better than Lew Smith was offering anyway.'

A picture came into her mind then of Nick in a village square, slick with sweat and blood, taking on all comers like a cornered dog. She shuddered. 'You could have been killed.'

'Not likely! Not when I had you to come home to.'

He smiled that rare smile of his, and Dora felt her insides melting.

'I – I didn't think I'd see you again,' she said. Suddenly she was trembling, whether from cold or pent-up emotion she didn't know.

'I'd always come back to you, you should know that. I love you, Dora.'

'Oh, Nick.' The next moment she was in his arms, pressed against the dampness of his coat, his strong arms crushing her to him as he kissed her. Her hands went up to trace the harsh planes of his face, his firm jaw, the thick springiness of his hair . . . touching, exploring with desperate urgency, breathing in the male scent of him, as if five senses alone would never be enough to it all.

Finally he broke away, taking in a gulp of air. 'Well, I reckon that was worth waiting three months for!' He grinned, his inky blue eyes twinkling in the darkness.

'I've missed you so much.' Dora held on to the lapels of his coat. Rain streamed down his face. 'You're never going away again, Nick Riley, do you understand? I don't care what anyone thinks, all I want is to be with you. I don't even care about getting married.'

He frowned. 'I told you, I want to do this properly.'

'Yes, but I don't think I can wait.'

'You won't have to.'

She looked at him in disbelief. 'Do you mean – you've got the money?'

'I told you I would, didn't I?' He patted his pocket. 'I've got an appointment to see the solicitor first thing in the morning. And I saw Ruby when I went to visit Danny. She's still as keen to get this sorted out. Reckons her fellow wants to name the date.' He smiled at Dora. 'I'm practically a free man. Which means now I can do this . . .'

'Nick!' Dora laughed as he sank to one knee in front of her. 'For Gawd's sake, stand up. You'll get all wet.'

But he ignored her, his expression deadly serious. 'Shhh,' he warned. 'Be quiet, woman, I'm trying to do this properly.'

'Properly?' Dora looked up at the darkened sky. 'We're in a dirty back alley in the pouring rain. It ain't exactly proper, is it?'

'Dora!' he growled. 'Do you want to marry me or don't you?'

She smiled down at him. 'If you put it like that, how can I say no?'

Chapter Forty-Nine

The day after the third years collected their badges, a new set of probationers moved into the student nurses' home.

Effie O'Hara was moving too. With her sister Katie moving over to the staff nurses' home, Effie had been assigned to another room, up in the attic, to make way for the new students. It was dark and a bit draughty, with the autumn wind whistling through the single ill-fitting skylight window, but at least up here she would be able to hear Sister Sutton stomping up the narrow staircase. And Katie had told her how she and her friends used to stand on the bed and smoke cigarettes through the skylight.

'But I don't want you to get any ideas,' she'd warned her sister. 'I might be in the nurses' home, but I'll still be keeping an eye on you!'

'And Bridget will be keeping an eye on you!' Effie laughed. How funny to think that their stern elder sister Bridget would now be watching over Katie's every move. There would be no more sneaking up the drainpipe after lights out for her!

Effie threw open her case and unpacked her uniform, selecting the top drawer of the dresser and leaving the other two drawers empty for her room mates when they arrived.

As she put away her neatly folded aprons, collars and cuffs, she spotted something in a corner of the drawer. She took it out and dangled it in front of her eyes in the

435

dim lamplight. It was a silver charm on the end of a fine chain. Looking closely, Effie could see it was shaped like a tiny hand.

'What the—'

'It's a *hamsa*,' a voice behind her said. Effie turned around. A solemn, dark-haired girl stood in the doorway. 'It's a Jewish symbol of good luck.'

Effie gazed at it, dangling on the end of its chain. 'Someone must have left it here, I suppose.'

'Perhaps it's an omen?' the girl said. She dragged her case into the room and placed it at the foot of the middle bed. 'I'm Devora, by the way. Devora Kowalski.'

'Euphemia O'Hara. But you can call me Effie.' She regarded the girl with interest. 'Where is that name from?'

'My parents are Polish.' Devora looked around her. 'Is it your first day, too?'

'Oh, no, I've been here six months. I've finished PTS and I've already had three months on the wards.'

'Really?'

Effie was gratified that the other girl looked so impressed. She began to understand what her sister must have felt like, knowing the ropes.

'Any sign of our other room mate yet?' Devora asked, eyeing the empty bed in the corner.

Effie shook her head. Please God, don't let it be Anna Padgett, she prayed.

'I hope it's someone nice,' Devora said.

'It would be good if we could all be friends,' Effie agreed.

Meanwhile, downstairs, the newest Nightingale probationer was hauling her battered suitcase up the front steps of the students' home. The Home Sister was there to greet her, arms folded across her formidable shelf of a bosom, face like thunder.

436

'You're late,' she snapped. 'I do hope you're not going to make a habit of this, Nurse?'

'No, Sister.'

'We have rules here, you know. And I expect them to be obeyed to the letter. Do you understand?'

'Yes, Sister.'

'And I hope you won't expect any special treatment?'

'Definitely not, Sister.'

'Because I intend to treat you just the same as all the other students here.'

The girl allowed herself a smile. That was what she wanted, too. It was all she'd ever wanted.

Sister Sutton looked her up and down. 'I don't know,' she sighed. 'I suppose you'll do.' For a brief moment her expression softened and a hint of warmth flickered in her tiny dark eyes. 'Welcome home, Nurse Jago,' she said, giving Jess a brief nod. 'I hope you'll be happy here.'

Jess grinned and bent to stroke the little dog capering excitedly around her feet. 'Thank you, Sister. I'm sure I will be,' she said.

On New Year's Eve 1937, Lady Amelia Benedict, daughter of the Earl of Rettingham, married Sebastian, youngest son of the Duke and Duchess of Claremont, in a glittering society wedding at St Margaret's, Westminster. Her bridesmaids were her best friends, Helen Dawson and Dora Doyle.

Three months later Dora wore the same pale blue silk bridesmaid's dress when she married Nick Riley at Bethnal Green Register Office. Her bridesmaids, Bea and Josie, wore flowery dresses their mother had made for them.

It wasn't nearly as grand as Millie's wedding, but Dora couldn't have been a happier bride as she finally exchanged vows with Nick. She trembled as he slid the ring on to her finger, still scarcely able to believe that it was finally happening. It was only when the registrar announced that they were man and wife and she looked up into his eyes that she allowed herself to breathe.

Her friends were waiting for her as they walked arm in arm out of the register office into the early spring sunshine.

Millie Benedict, or Lady Rushton, as she was now, was looking very grown-up and already every inch the married woman in an elegant apricot silk dress and coat. Hard to believe this was the same girl who'd regularly slithered in through the skylight window when they were students.

Helen and Katie were there too, as was Lucy Lane. She and Dora exchanged wary smiles through the shower of fluttering confetti. Dora wasn't sure which of them was more surprised by their friendship, but she was glad it had happened.

She glanced at Nick, but he'd already read her thoughts. 'Go on, then.' He smiled, leaning in to plant a kiss on her forehead. 'I've got you for the rest of my life, I reckon I can spare you for a couple of minutes.'

Dora squeezed his hand and hurried off to talk to her friends. There were lots of delighted squeals as they greeted each other and admired each other's dresses.

'You look beautiful,' Helen said.

Dora looked down at her dress, embarrassed by the compliment. 'It's so lovely, it seemed a shame not to wear it again.' Besides, she thought, she could never have afforded a wedding gown half as beautiful.

'You look radiant,' Millie said.

'So do you.' Dora looked closely at her friend. There was something about Millie that seemed different. 'Married life suits you.'

'She's right,' Helen agreed. 'You're quite glowing.'

A blush rose in Millie's cheeks. 'I don't know if that's married life or something else entirely.'

They looked at each other, then it dawned on Dora. 'You're not . . . ?'

Millie nodded. 'I'm not sure, but I think so,' she said.

Dora laughed. 'Blimey, you haven't wasted any time, have you? I bet your grandmother is pleased!'

'She doesn't know yet, but I daresay she'll be delighted.' Millie pulled a face. 'Gosh, can you imagine me as a mother? I'll probably leave the baby somewhere and forget about it completely.'

Helen and Dora exchanged knowing looks. Millie had calmed down a lot towards the end of their training, but she had always been a bit of a scatterbrain.

'So what's happening at the Nightingale?' Millie said. 'Go on, I want to hear all the gossip!'

They looked at each other. 'Well,' Katie said, 'I'm a staff nurse on Blake now.'

'With your sister?' Millie laughed. 'How delightful for you.'

'Don't!' Katie grimaced. 'Bridget lives to make my life a misery. Still, I expect Tom will propose soon, then I can leave like you two,' she added brightly.

Dora and Lucy exchanged knowing looks. Poor Katie seemed to be the only one who didn't know her boyfriend wasn't the marrying kind.

'And what about you?' Millie asked Lucy. 'I'm surprised you aren't chasing Matron for her job yet!'

Lucy shrugged. 'I'm happy enough in Theatre, thank you. I've still got a lot to learn there.'

Dora caught Millie's look of surprise. She'd probably been expecting Lucy to bite back, or at least to brag about how well she was doing. But her experiences over the past year seemed to have humbled her. And Dora liked her a great deal more for it.

'So that's it, I suppose,' Millie sighed. 'The end of an era, as they say. You know, I adore married life, but I do miss the Nightingale,' she said wistfully.

Katie laughed. 'You miss getting up at six in the morning and queuing to wash in cold water? You must be mad!'

'Or being shouted at for fourteen hours a day by a ward sister?' Lucy suggested.

'Or going back to the home and being shouted at by the Home Sister?' Helen added.

'All right, perhaps I don't miss it that much!' Millie agreed with a grin. 'But I do miss chatting to the patients, and seeing them get better. And I miss seeing my friends every day, too.' She turned to Dora. 'I expect you'll be the same, now you're married.'

'I expect I will,' she agreed. Much as she'd longed to be married to Nick, she also knew what a wrench it would be to hang up her uniform and walk away from the Nightingale for the last time.

'Don't get upset about it,' Lucy urged. 'We can stay in touch can't we?'

'Of course we can,' Millie said bracingly. 'We'll write to each other all the time, and you can come and visit me.' She smiled. 'We'll always be Nightingale girls, won't we?'

'Always,' Dora said. 'And, you know, I've got a funny feeling we might all be back there one day.'

Millie laughed. 'What on earth makes you think that?'

'I dunno,' she shrugged. 'Just something makes me think we haven't seen the last of the Nightingale. And it definitely hasn't seen the last of us!'